I0637060

The Rebel Christian Publishing

Copyright © 2023 Valicity Elaine

ISBN: 978-1-957290-50-8 (eBook)
Print: 978-1-957290-51-5

This is a work of fiction. Any references to historical events, real people, or real places are used fictitiously. Names, characters, and places are products of the author's imagination. Inclusion of or reference to any Christian elements or themes are used in a fictitious manner and are not meant to be perceived or interpreted as an act of disrespect against such a wonderful and beautiful belief system.

Cover designed by Valicity Elaine

The Rebel Christian Publishing LLC
350 Northern Blvd STE 324 - 1390
Albany, NY 12204-1000

Visit us: http://www.therebelchristian.com/
Email us: rebel@therebelchristian.com

Content

Trilogy Order:

Decipis

Exodus

Eternus

Decipis

Book I in the Treachery Trilogy

By Valicity Elaine

A Rebel Christian Publishing Book

Prologue

A wise man once said, *No one is so brave that he is not disturbed by something unexpected.* Do you know whose quote that is? Extra points on the next pop quiz. Not that anyone needs those points. A few weeks ago, I did. A few weeks ago, I would've been excited to show off and let everyone know I could freely quote Julius Caesar. Now, none of that matters.

I used to think I was brave. Used to believe that even I would not be disturbed by the unexpected. But I was wrong. It's not entirely my fault—like—I'm not upset about not being brave. Who could call themselves brave after watching their own friends die? Who could be brave when faced with starvation and death?

None of us are brave.

I stand in the middle of the Field of Death, one hand holding a knife, the other dangling at my side. Limp. Unusable. I think my thumb is dislocated. My knife is coated in blood, it's thick and visceral, coagulating already. The blood isn't mine, and that's what scares me. It scares me to think that just a few weeks ago the Field of Death was just my university's soccer field. That I had run this field with the track team and had rested in the grass on my break after orientation.

It scares me to think that weeks ago my friends were just guys I went to frat parties with, now they're staring at me like they want to kill me. Some of them *do* want to kill me. Not because I've done something wrong. Not because I've betrayed them.

It's because I've threatened them. Because I made the decision to share our supplies with the other dorms. Supplies we need. Supplies that could make the difference between life and death.

At the beginning of the semester, these bloody, half-starved men before me were my best friends. Now, they could slit my throat in my sleep for a glass of water. That's what happens when chaos breaks out. When terror rules over peace, hunger is the driving force in all your decisions.

What was the great unexpected that happened here? What turned these men into monsters?

The end of the world. At least that's what it feels like. A global apocalypse.

It happened so fast; a flicker of light and it was all over. *A power outage*—that's what we kept saying as we emptied our fridges and opened canned goods. *The grid is down, it'll be back.* That's what we told ourselves when the water stopped running. *Someone will send help; they won't leave an entire college campus to starve and die.*

But they did.

It took four weeks for Cross North University to go from an excited, thrilling campus to a battleground. I won't wait another week. I don't think I'll *live* another week.

I tuck my knife into the makeshift sheath at my hip, sighing loudly as I dry my bloody hand on my pants. There is a dead man at my feet. His head is tilted back, eyes wide and unblinking, mouth open in a silent scream.

I didn't kill him, I swear. But I wish I had. I wish I weren't such a coward. I wish I could make the decisions my friends need me to make. The decisions that will keep us alive, fed, healthy. But I'm not that guy. The problem is, I realized that about myself a long time ago. My friends? They still haven't gotten the memo.

I can see it in the way they stare at me, gazes flicking between me and the corpse on the ground. They're waiting, trying to see if I'll declare war or tuck my tail and run. This would be the perfect reason to run. The excuse we need to get out of here and find our own way. But we're divided on that point.

Half of us still believe help is coming. The National Guard is just around the corner with a truckful of food and water and medical supplies. The other half knows the truth. That we're on our own. That we will die if we stay here.

Yet, we've remained.

Because we don't know what's out there. Cross North is a secluded campus, miles away from the nearest city. I can't imagine the time it would take to walk, especially not in a group this large. This hungry. This desperate.

We have few options if we want to live but leaving just might be the death of us. Not because we could miss the National Guard if we go, it could be the death of us because the city might be in worse shape.

Our seclusion prevented looters and enemies from finding

us just as much as it stopped help from coming. Now, we want to walk right into the lion's den. But we may not have a choice.

Whether we like it or not, the world is falling apart. All around us. The end has begun. Or maybe it hasn't. There has been no contact, no news, no radio connection. We could walk into the nearest city and realize the world is just fine. Maybe it's just us. Our own little bubble of misery. We can only find out by leaving.

1

Adrian

Rap music blasts in my ears as I run. I'm not running to the beat, instead, my feet follow the pace set by my heart. I'm sprinting through the city, trying to concentrate on my breathing. The deep bass of my music is thumping in my head, so loud I swear I can feel my chest vibrating.

My legs are getting tight, muscles pulling together as I push myself to my limits. My back feels stiff, my shoulders are rigid. I should stop soon. But I don't want to. In an odd way, I like the pain that tears through me. Knowing I'm breaking myself down just to be rebuilt as something better. Something new.

Without even meaning to, I pick up my pace. My feet hit the ground like someone's chasing me. Sweat pours down my face, my shirt sticks to my back, making me cold in the fresh morning breeze. The music blaring through my headphones bleeds into my body, into my *soul*, filling every part of me with energy—*power*—and I sprint even faster.

I run past buildings and stores, Ma and Pop shops with

little old couples shuffling at the doors with their keys. It's just past sunrise, the city is still asleep save for the early bunch. The ones who serve coffee and doughnuts to the morning shift.

There is something sacred, something *special*, about morning runs. I get to see things no one else sees in the orange light of the sun as it peels away from the clouds.

A thick morning breeze slams into my chest as I round the corner, a trail of sweat dripping behind me. At the end of the street is a bakery my mother used to love. I can smell cinnamon and honey and vanilla in the air as I draw near. Outside the front doors is a cloud of powdered sugar, I'm tempted to open my mouth and taste its sweetness as I sprint by but I'm more distracted by the sign out front.

In the window is a chalkboard that doesn't advertise sweet treats or baked goods—it's got large writing in neon chalk that says, **Batteries, Plugs, Matches Here!**

Every shop I pass is the same. Each store owner, each little business, has stockpiled survival gear like it's going out of style. It isn't an emerging sales trend, right now it's the difference between power and darkness. Life and death.

The city's been suffering rolling blackouts for weeks. Each one lasts longer than the previous, making everyone paranoid and anxious, wondering if the next one will be *The* One. The blackout that ushers in the long night. Total darkness.

It would plunge the nation into the Middle Ages; no electricity, no running water, no way to take pics of your campfire and post it on some worthless social media platform. The doomsday preppers are going nuts. Social media has been flooded with conspiracy theories. Political nutjobs are pointing fingers at every country they can think of. Religious quacks are once again claiming the end is near.

I like to think of myself as a social recluse. I don't give a crap about the world ending—biblically or otherwise. If I could, I'd wave a flag and show the apocalypse the best spots to hit first. But I've got people depending on me. A family that doesn't love me but needs me. And I suppose that's a good enough reason to care. To hope that things get better.

I don't even realize when I've come around to the start of my usual trail. The sight of my dark little house shocks me into a jog as I check my stopwatch. Three miles in just under twenty minutes. I was going faster than I thought. I'm tempted to take off on one more lap, but I can hear clanking and yelling as I stand outside the house. It's best I go in. Though I don't want to.

I let out a sigh as I climb the cracked stone steps of my home. Each step takes me closer to the screaming inside, it makes the hairs on the back of my neck rise.

I cannot stand my home. But it's the only one I've got.

When I open the front door, I find my mother shouting frantically in the living room while her husband throws something against the wall. I realize it's the landline when it crashes to the floor in a million pieces. This does not faze my mother. She might be 5'4, 110 pounds, but she is the most insane woman in all of Arizona. Maybe all of North America. Her response to my stepfather's outburst is to throw her head back and laugh, a shrill cackle that makes my ears hurt.

"You idiot. Now you have to buy a new phone!"

Her husband lets out a string of incoherent cuss words. He's drunk. At 7 in the morning. I shouldn't be surprised, there are beer bottles all over the floor, empty shot glasses, and half-eaten plates of food lining the hallway. If I didn't know any better, I'd wonder if my folks threw a party last night, but I do know better. The house always looks this way. Every part of it is covered in filth. Urine, spilled drinks, broken things my stepfather destroyed, burned things my bitter mother scorched in vengeance.

I hate this home.

Which is why I spend most of my time running or locked away in my room. I make a beeline for my personal haven while my mother screams out a list of all the things her husband has broken just this morning. The sound hushes when I step inside my room and close the door behind me.

I sigh and sag against it, but I don't get to relax because two little monsters attack my legs as soon as I'm inside.

"You're home!" the twins say in unison.

I smile as I pet their fluffy blonde heads. "Danya, Dinara, what are you doing up so early?"

Danya gives me a look that makes me feel stupid. Somehow, he's mastered this look at age eight. "Mom and Dad are going nuts."

Dinara agrees, tugging on my pants leg. She blinks up at me with quivering lips. "They've been fighting for an hour now."

"We came in here looking for you, but you were gone."

I took eight laps this morning, intrigued by the ominous signs hanging outside all the shops. Wondering if the sunrise would be our only source of light today. As I glance at the flashing clock on my bedside table, I realize the power is still here. Thank God.

"Sorry, I should've come back sooner," I mumble, scooping them both up and setting them on my bed. They're both small for their age, and I'm a giant compared to them so holding them both is easy but Danya squirms and complains

4

until I drop him on my blankets.

"I'm too big to be carried!" he shouts, jumping up on my covers.

The sight of him messing up my bed sends a flare of anger shooting through me, but I smother it with a breath. I hate when things are messed up. I hate things being out of order. Every other part of this miserable house is torn to pieces, my room is the only sense of order I have. The only slice of cleanliness in my life.

Still, Danya's just a kid. And he's only in my room because he's hiding from his horrible parents. My stepdad is a jerk whom I shamelessly hate, but he's the biological father of the twins. So I stopped planning to have him *accidentally* fall down and stay down in one of his drunken stupors a long time ago. I hate the guy, but my brother and sister deserve to have a father in their life. And he also keeps the lights on. Whenever he hasn't ripped the lamps from the walls, that is.

It doesn't matter, I remind myself, peeling my shirt from my body. I toss it into the hamper while Dinara runs over and sniffs like I've just brought freshly baked cookies into the room.

"You're so smelly, Adrian," she says with a frown.

Well, I ran like fire this morning. What does she expect?

Nothing, 'cause she's just a kid.

I roll my eyes, searching my drawers for a clean change of clothes. Almost everything has been packed away for college. I was supposed to move into my dorm three weeks ago when track training started, but I kind of got ticked off when my coach announced the captain title. I'm a senior, the best on the team, been the best since I joined my freshman year. Set two records and helped us qualify for the state tourney last year.

5

I did not make captain.

A junior I can't stand stole my title. He has no right to be chosen as captain—I don't care how fast he is. I promise I'm faster. I promise I'm better. But our coaches disagreed. So I packed up my gear and went back home.

They clearly don't need me for training, they've got their precious new captain. So I stayed home until now, spending my days running the neighborhood, watching everyone panic over the blackouts.

Classes start on Monday, so I've got to head out tomorrow. I'm all ready to go, except something tugs at my chest as I watch Danya and Dinara laugh at how smelly my sweat-soaked shirt is. I don't know what I'm worried about more; the blackouts or my stupid parents not doing their job while I'm gone.

The twins aren't small because our mother is short. They're little because they're hungry. Arms thinner than normal, bordering dangerously on bony, hair too fine to be healthy— Danya has a bald patch over his right ear, but it's not worse than the rash on Dinara's hands. They shake as she holds up my shirt, I'm not sure if it's from fatigue or anxiety as something crashes in the hallway.

She jumps at the sound. Rage crackles through my chest. I have to sit down or else I'll end up storming out of the room and strangling my mom and stepdad.

"You okay, Adri?" Dinara touches my hand; it's balled into a fist.

I nod, squatting in front of her. "You know Mrs. Carson? The bakery owner?" When I've got the money, I buy cookies from her. She knows about my parents and usually gives me sympathy treats for the twins. An extra free cookie, some leftover bagels from the morning rush. *For the children*, she would always say with a solemn nod. Like they're slowly dying at home. Sometimes I feel like they are.

Dinara nods, along with Danya who's paying attention now.

"If the power goes out, go to Mrs. Carson's bakery, okay? She'll help you out."

Danya makes that stupid face again. "We're ready for the next blackout, Adrian. Pop bought some ramen noodles and bottled water last night."

I doubt that'll be enough, considering they'll have to use their bottled water to make the ramen. And find heat to cook it. I want to go wring my stepdad's neck, but I stay focused on Danya instead.

"So, Ryan's bought food?" I ask. I always call my stepfather by his name.

Dinara nods. "That's what they're fighting over. Dad wants to use the rent money to buy Go Bags."

"Go Bags?"

"Bags ready to go!" She laughs like I'm dumb, looking just like her twin brother as she cocks her head to the side. "They're bags with all kinds of cool stuff inside so we can survive in the dark."

"Granola bars and flashlights," Danya says beside his sister.

Huh. Sounds decidedly responsible and totally unlike my stepfather at all. But I'm not complaining. At least *someone's* thinking ahead. I won't be here to make all the grownup decisions once I head out for campus tomorrow. I don't feel entirely confident in the parenting skills of my folks but knowing that my stepdad is at least *trying* to do something makes me feel somewhat better.

"Why is Mom so angry, then?" I ask.

Dinara tucks a blonde lock behind her little ear. "She wants to use the rent money for rent."

Duh.

"But Dad says there won't be any rent after the next blackout."

He might be right. Either way, I think the Go Bags are a good investment, that's why I turn to my dresser and dig out my savings box. In the bottom is a roll of money I keep stashed away, a wad of fives and tens I take off the top of my parttime job. It isn't much, but after saving all summer, it's enough for a couple Go Bags, I'm sure.

I pass half the roll to Dinara. "If the lights go out again, go to Mrs. Carson and ask for supplies."

I know better than to give the money to either of my parents. It's best to trust an eight-year-old and a stranger with it. I'll use the other half to buy some Go Bags before I leave for campus tomorrow in case the twins somehow aren't able to make it to the bakery if/when the lights go out again.

Dinara smiles, shoving the money into her pocket while Danya scowls. He's the older twin, but also the most rambunctious. I need Dinara in charge of this. I know I can trust her.

I ruffle Danya's hair. "You remember Ryan's code?" I remind him.

His eyes go wide as he nods. He knows exactly what I'm talking about. The safe inside our parents' room; it's locked by a six-digit code which I figured out three years ago. Inside the safe is more money and a weapon. I know it isn't wise to trust two kids with a gun, but I'm hoping they won't need it.

Chances are, Ryan will unlock the safe himself and get the money and pistol when they need it. But if that useless fart happens to be passed out drunk when the next blackout hits, I want to make sure Danya and Dinara will have a way to get supplies and protect themselves.

Dinara is the responsible twin. She won't forget or waste the money. But Danya is the brave twin. He won't be afraid to grab the gun if he needs it.

I feel sick just thinking about this. My younger siblings are only eight and I'm making sure they have access to a weapon. Despite their age, they aren't kids. They grew up a long time ago, when they found Ryan passed out on the sofa and drowning in his own vomit. They grew up when they had to take him and our mother to the hospital because he'd shattered her jaw and then nearly drank himself to death with guilt.

I'd been away at college when this happened. I couldn't return by the time I got the call; I was out of town with the track team. Mrs. Carson had taken care of the twins until our parents were both released from the hospital.

Ryan had alcohol poisoning. Mom couldn't speak for a month.

Anger pours into my heart at the dark memory. It is a familiar feeling, one that I know so well, I'm almost lost without it. I dance between rage and hope so much, I'm sure I give myself whiplash on a weekly basis. Rage toward my degenerate parents. Hope that my younger siblings will somehow turn out okay, despite the chaos they're growing up in.

I know the anger isn't healthy, I know the rage isn't good, but it's the only thing I can get myself to feel these days. There is no room for anything else. I need the anger. I need it to give me fuel, give me a drive to keep going. My parents will never change. Which means the day I'm not angry at them, at all the crap they do, is the day I've gotten complacent. The day I've decided I no longer care.

I cannot afford not to care.

So I trudge on in a bitter rage. Using my negative emotions to push me into each day, to remind me that this will all change someday. That's when the hope breaks through. The little voice that whispers there is more to live for than rage.

If only I could find it.

Some days I think I've found joy in the twins. The hope they give me is enough to keep me going. Enough to send me to my parttime job six days a week, working doubles whenever I can so I can give them the money they need for food when my stepfather drinks his paychecks away and my mother sells her food stamps for God knows what. The twins are the hope that keeps me here, living with my parents at age 22—because I know if I leave then no one will be here for them.

But there are days when the rage is too strong. Days when I just can't take my parents anymore.

The hope is strong enough to keep me here for as long as I need to be. But the anger is powerful enough to send me packing and heading out for college. I promise I'll come back during my breaks. I'll even visit on long weekends. But I just can't stay here. I'll crack if I do.

I push from my bed and stand on shaky legs. The twins blink up at me. They are the only people in the world I care about. And I'm about to leave them for the next few months in the middle of a possible citywide meltdown.

Something crashes outside my door, making us all jump. Despite the worry I feel for my brother and sister, I am desperately ready to get out of here.

2

Mya

Cross North University is just a 30-minute drive from the city of Wakedon, Arizona, but it feels more like 3 hours as I ride with my father. He points out every building while we're still in the city, surrounded by local restaurants, small museums, and plazas stuffed with businesses that reach toward the sky. We're just two hours away from Phoenix, but the cozy life of Wakedon might as well be across the country.

As we progress to the outskirts of the city, my father makes sure to drive by the new mega mall that was built last summer, and then goes past the clusters of vibrant suburbs.

"All these homes had no power last weekend." He shakes his head, his grey beard brushes back and forth against his chest with the movement.

"You're talking about the blackouts," I say.

He nods. "They're getting closer and closer to our neighborhood, that's the only reason I'm happy you're staying on campus."

I smile, *at least he's happy about something.* My father's the most overprotective man in the world. Part of it is in his nature, since I'm an only child and he's been a single father for the last two years. My mother's passing brought us closer together, coping and mourning, helping each other through the pain. But it also made him clingy. And paranoid. Like he thinks I'll drift away and never return if I'm gone for too long.

Part of his worry is justified. This will be my first time away from home, and it couldn't have come at the worst point in our lives. We've only just begun to get our lives back in order after losing Mama, and then the rolling blackouts started.

The first one happened a few weeks ago, as soon as I started packing little things away in preparation for the big move. It was all very dramatic with my father taking the darkness as some sort of omen.

"It's a sign!" he'd shriek each time the news reported another outage.

I do believe in signs, but my father's hysterics only made the blackouts seem more like electric companies trying to save money than any sort of divine judgment from God.

We live in Arizona; thunderstorms are normal all year round. Sometimes they're severe enough to knock the power out, even for an entire city.

"But every few days?" my father would challenge me, and I would sigh, throwing my hands into the air.

"I don't know, Dad."

"And they've been lasting longer and longer," he's saying now, shaking his head again and gripping the steering wheel.

Sadly, that's a fact I must admit is quite odd—if not disturbing. The blackouts started in smaller neighborhoods, once a week maybe. But they seem to have expanded somehow, and each time they hit, they last longer and longer.

The last one was over the weekend, lasted 52 hours before the power came back. The entire west side of Wakedon was dark, only a few blocks from my own neighborhood.

I shiver, not wanting to think about when the next one will hit or how long it will last. I'm just glad I'm getting out of town. Even if the blackouts roll through Wakedon, Cross North has backup generators that'll keep our lights on. One of the perks of going to one of the best universities on this side of the state.

"You don't have to worry about me," I tell my father. "I doubt I'll be without power if the blackouts continue."

Dad reaches over and pats my hand. "And you don't have to worry about me. I know how to handle myself."

That he does.

My father is a bit of a kook with his conspiracy theories and his quirky fashion—perfectly circular glasses, a finely knotted bowtie matching with his checkered dress shirt, and his shock of wild grey hair that makes him look like a brown-skinned Albert Einstein, except with his long beard. Now he looks like Gandalf, plus fifty pounds.

His belly jumps as he laughs, patting my hand again. "I can take care of myself."

My father's a nerdy guy, but I have never underestimated him. Not for a second. Because Dr. Joshua Brown isn't just *full* of conspiracy theories, he's the sort of crazy that acts on them.

Our basement is stashed with canned goods, we've got cases of water stacked to the ceiling, and a generator to power the house—he takes pride in the fact that he built the thing himself. Good old Dad was a physicist back in the day, got his second PhD in engineering, because he was bored, as he always tells me.

14

He's been weird all his life, even amongst friends, being the only Christian scientist in his field. But things got worse when Mom got sick. That's when the stockpiling started, when he built the generator, and insisted I always buy a pack of toilet paper whenever I go to the store. I have a pack for every day of the year, and he insists it still isn't enough.

He made me stuff a pack into my suitcase to take to campus with me.

I chuckle as I watch him drive, pointing out the small burst of forestry just outside of Wakedon. Beyond that is the trail that leads to Cross North University. My future home.

I haven't even declared a major yet, but I somehow feel excited, like I belong there. Probably because I'm going for more than just the education, more than the idea of striking out on my own, growing up. I'm going because there's someone at Cross North whom I haven't seen in far too long. We've been separated for two years, thanks to him being older than me, but I'm finally eighteen. Finally out of high school.

Now our lives can go back to the normalcy we had before my mother got sick and I moved away. I'm nearly bouncing in my seat at the thought of seeing him again.

My father notices and raises a bushy eyebrow at me. "Nervous?"

"Yeah." I sigh. "I don't really know what to expect."

He launches into a story about his first year of college, but I'm not listening. I'm busy staring at the sand kicking up outside my window, watching cacti go by as my dad drives at least 20 miles under the speed limit. I'm looking at anything and everything to keep me from thinking of *him*.

When we finally arrive on campus, there is a buzz of

15

excitement that penetrates the doors of our rusty jeep. I feel electrified as we check in with the dorm manager. I feel like I'm gliding across the campus when we receive instructions on where to go. And as my father drives through the block of dorms where I'll be staying, I feel like I really could drift away if it weren't for the seatbelt keeping me in place.

And then the car jerks to a sudden stop and I fly forward, almost whacking my nose on the dash.

"Dad!" I cry, snapping my head toward him.

He's holding the steering wheel so tightly, his knuckles are red on the tops—no small feat with his dark skin tone.

"Dad?"

I trace his gaze to the house across the street, it's a frat house—a giant white mansion with a group of guys scattered on the lawn. They're busy moving furniture and suitcases into the house, every last one of them shirtless and sweaty. The smaller, shier looking guys are obviously freshmen, uncomfortable without their clothes but likely left without a choice. They look pale and skinny compared to the upperclassmen who stroll around with toothy, arrogant smiles, humored by all the stares they're getting.

There's a sofa on the front lawn with a pair of shirtless guys lazily lounging in the hot Arizona sun. The garage door is open behind them with a pickup truck halfway inside and halfway in the driveway, the hood is popped and a lean figure is bent over the engine. The rest of the guys move around the house slowly, almost in an uncaring manner. There are smiles on their faces, laughs bursting from their mouths as they drag their bags inside. They are the image of summer, and they don't have a care in the world. I don't blame them for being totally unaware of my father's strangely growing wrath.

I can feel his anger coming off him in waves, like he hates the sight of happy young men.

"You alright?" I ask cautiously.

"Disgusting," he growls.

I blink. "Um…"

Dad releases his death grip on the steering wheel to point at the house. When I glance back, I see the sign at the edge of the lawn, a pillar of stone with an engraved plaque that reads, **Kappa Pi House of Brothers**. Right beside that is another sign, a handwritten one—sloppy, childish writing in bold permanent marker, that says, **Thank you for your daughters**.

I stifle a laugh.

It shouldn't be funny. A bunch of shirtless beefcakes casually collecting innocent college girls for their liking. It's obviously a bit of crude humor—a joke that isn't so funny to Dr. Brown.

"Dad—"

Before I can stop him, my father hits the gas and jerks the car to the curb, whipping it in park and hopping out in a quickness that shouldn't be possible for a man his size. I sink lower into my seat as he storms the front lawn, demanding to speak to the 'young man in charge.'

"Oh no," I groan.

The altercation that unfolds is both entertaining and humiliating. An insufferable mix of shame and pride stirs in my gut as I watch my father yell at the 'young men,' reminding them that they are 'better than this.' That this humor isn't funny, only 'foolish.' The guys all turn to stare at him, matching grins crawling over their handsome faces. Even some of the students moving into the house next door stop to watch.

To the credit of the frat boys, they don't get angry at my

father's outburst. They don't even laugh at him. One of the guys, the one that'd been bent over the engine of the pickup truck, simply strides over and takes the sign down. I can hear him apologize to my father and promise the sign will be destroyed. He does all this while wearing a perfect smile, it's so genuine and clean, I'm unsure if he's mocking my father or just being nice.

As my father finishes his rant, the guy looks up—right through the windshield of the car, right at *me*. My heart stops as he stares at me. Suddenly, his perfect smile looks more like a sly smirk, and I can't stop my cheeks from burning red when he lifts a hand and waves, wiggling his fingers. That's when it hits me. He isn't mocking my dad at all; he's making fun of *me*.

Great.

Dad climbs back into the car and buckles his seatbelt. "Young men these days," he grumbles.

I just sigh.

"Where are you staying?" he asks. "I hope nowhere nearby."

"I'll be in Hope House. It's a few blocks away," I tell him. "It's part of the campus ministry."

My father's simmering anger seems to cool down at the reminder that I'll be staying in a dorm filled with other Christian students. That doesn't make us angels, but I doubt it'll be anything like Kappa Pi.

3

Caesar

I'm leaning against the wall, staring out the living room window, when Noble walks into the room. There's a scowl on his face but I can see the way the corner of his mouth eases upward the slightest bit, threatening to smile. He's shirtless and cocky like the rest of us but he's also the assistant coach of the track team, which makes him the Big Brother of Kappa Pi. That means he's supposed to be responsible and adult-like, so I guess this is the part where he tells us we're in trouble.

"Alright," he says, holding up the handwritten sign. "Whose idea was it?"

His eyes land on me.

"Why are you looking at me?" I raise my hands, only *slightly* offended by the immediate accusation.

"Caesar, this has you all over it."

I might be captain of the track team, but I'm not an idiot. I would never encourage my boys to do something so stupid.

I lay a hand over my heart and hope I sound sincere.

19

"Coach Noble, I would never—"

"Sneakers on," he interrupts me, raising his voice so the other guys can hear him. We all start to groan because we know what's coming before he even says it. "Two miles, all of you. That's your punishment for this stunt."

"Oh, come on!" The complaint comes from the underclassmen crowded in the archway between the kitchen and dining room. They're in the middle of bringing in cans of gas for the generator in the basement. Everyone's prepping for the big scary blackouts.

I can see Maxwell Lions right in front, a sophomore with a southern accent so strong, he goes by the nickname *Memphis*. We refuse to call him anything else. Beside him is Connor O'Reilly, a senior who sucks at track and shouldn't be on the team. There's a nameless freshman I don't know or care about. And then a small sophomore we call Bunny, somehow, a nickname for Benson. He's small and blonde and even I can admit he's cute as a button. I guess the name fits.

All the guys look at me, as if I have a say in this. I do. But I don't want Coach Noble to realize the track team is more loyal to me than him—more loyal to me than the sacred rules of Kappa Pi, etched in stone 113 years ago. The laws of Kappa Pi are regarded with the same respect Hope House regards the Ten Commandments. They are divine, not to be questioned, and have kept peace and order amongst the brotherhood for over a century.

Seriously, there's a plaque outside the frat house with the rules on it and everything. I've never read them, but I assume they're important. 'Cause no one buys a big plaque and puts *un*important stuff on it.

The boys will follow me before they even look at Kappa Pi

20

Law.

Maybe it's because I'm the captain of the team, and their most awesome *best friend ever*. Or maybe it's because of my name. Since I was a kid, people have made the mistake of thinking that because I was named after an historic leader that must mean *I'm* an awesome leader too.

I'm not. But if someone's handing me power, I'm not going to pass it up. So I stuff my hands into the pockets of my baggy basketball shorts and nod at the guys who are still blinking dumbly at me.

"You heard Coach Noble. Two miles," I tell them.

"Three for you and Bunny," Coach says sternly.

Both of us frown.

"Why us?" I ask.

Noble turns to me, his face no longer hiding the smirk I saw earlier. He's all scowls and hard lines now, his black hair shining in the morning sun, his white teeth flashing as he speaks.

"Because I know the sign was your idea. But Bunny is the one who wrote it."

Bunny snorts. "How'd you figure that?"

Noble rolls his eyes. "No one else but you has chicken scratch for handwriting."

I laugh because it's absolutely true, but my laughter is cut short when a shadow darkens the kitchen doorway. I don't even have to look to know it's Adrian Nikols. I can feel the absolute hatred coming off him so powerfully I'm sure the devil himself would've flinched when he walked into the room.

I went to high school with Adrian. We weren't friends, but I played sports with him for years. He's a year older, a lot more muscular, and a lot more intimidating. Yet, I'm the one who got elected captain of the track team as a junior, forever ruining his dreams of being captain during his senior season.

The team made the decision during training camp before the semester even started. I won the team vote, taking just 53 percent of the tags. And I won the coach vote two to one—Coach Noble was probably the one who voted for Adrian.

Still, the whole thing was fair and square. I didn't steal Adrian's spotlight; it was handed to me by his own friends and his own coaches.

He's wanted to choke me ever since.

I can feel his grey eyes on me from his stance in the doorway; he hasn't moved since he walked in, like he saw me and was suddenly welded in place. I honestly hate encounters with Adrian, but I know he won't leave until I acknowledge his presence, so I turn and give him my friendliest smile.

"You're just in time. We're going on a run."

"I just got back from a run." His voice is raspy and strangled, like he's barely holding back a scream. Or a fart. I cunno.

Adri's covered in sweat so his white-blonde hair sticks to his skin. Unlike the rest of the shirtless boys hanging around the frat house, he's wearing a shirt with his gym shorts. No matter how hot it is, no matter how long he runs, Adrian always keeps his shirt on. Long-sleeves tugged down to his wrists with the hem tucked into his pants, so it never slips up to reveal his pale skin. I don't know if it's because he's albino that he doesn't want to go in the sun, or if he just hates everything brighter than his shadow, but I don't tell him to remove his shirt.

The rest of us are running in just our shorts, it's a Kappa Pi tradition, even in the winter. But not Adrian. Not even when he was a freshman and had been given a direct order to remove his shirt by his Big Brother and coach. I heard he crossed his arms and told them he would take it off if they could make him.

At 6'3 and too many pounds to mention, no one challenged him then. And I'm not going to challenge him now.

If there is a guy in Kappa Pi who *isn't* loyal to me. It's Adrian Nikols. He's been waiting for the day he could punch me in the throat and get away with it.

Today's not going to be that day.

"It's just two miles, you can do that," I tell him.

He grunts something—I'm not even sure if it's in English or not—and then walks back out the front door. The rest of the guys are already outside waiting, so I turn and walk out behind him. We fall in line without a word while Memphis picks up a cadence for us to keep in step with. It's some southern song I'm sure he made up himself, but I jog to the beat anyway, ignoring the wide-eyed stares of nervous freshmen moving into their dorms as we pass by.

We're halfway through our jog, running in two lines of twelve with me holding the rear on my own, when we round the corner and I see Hope House at the end of the street. That's where Mya is staying. My very best friend since childhood. She's been the center of my world since I could spell her three-letter name. Her mother was good friends with my foster mom, so we spent almost every day together until Mya's mom got sick, and her family moved two hours away, so she'd be more comfortable in the country.

That was a little over two years ago. The hardest point in my entire life. I lost my best friend and my best friend's mother at the same time. Mya had lived in Phoenix just two blocks from my house since my foster mom brought me home, and suddenly she was two hours away in Wakedon. A stranger.

During the summer before my first year of college, I rode my bike two hours to see her almost every day. Then I started at Cross North and Mya couldn't even catch a thirty-minute bus ride to come see me.

In her defense, Dr. Brown is a nut who probably wouldn't let her out of his sight, but still. We were separated for two years. The two most important years of my life. I'm bitter that she missed them, angry that I had to experience all this on my own. But she's here now, finally a freshman in college, and I can't wait to see her.

I slow to a walk as we near the house, studying all the students milling about the lawn and driveway. Hope House is actually two houses since it's a ministry dorm. The male students have House A and the females take House B. My eyes dart through the pretty girls outside House B, searching for the dark figure I saw hiding in the car as I gazed through the living room window at Kappa Pi.

I recognized Dr. Brown's beat up old Jeep as soon as he pulled to the curb. If there was any parent that would have a problem with the stupid sign, I knew it would be him. I don't know if it's a kooky parent thing or a Christian parent thing, but he's been smothering Mya since she was a kid.

A smile works its way over my face as I see the lady I've been looking for. She should've been easier to spot, dressed like a freak as she is. Mya's always been a little weird—all black clothing with ripped up stockings and dramatic eyeliner. She's got her afro hair all puffed out and as big as a Jackson Five wig. Her shoes are platform boots that make her at least five inches taller, which is saying something because she's laughably short. There are chains and silver buckles going down her shoes, making so much noise I *hear* her coming before I see her walking toward me.

Mya's gotta be the one and only Christian goth in all of Arizona. She's a certified rebel if I've ever met one. One of the few things her overprotective father has shockingly never tried to control about her.

"God looks at our hearts, not our wardrobe," is what he'd always say whenever one of his kindly church friends tried to give him lip about Mya's clothes.

To be fair, she *is* fully covered. No short skirts or cleavage showing, only the boring parts of her body are exposed. I think that qualifies as modest, right?

Mya spots me at the edge of Hope House's front lawn and a smile erupts onto her face. She jogs over and I hug her so hard she actually yelps from me squeezing too tightly.

"You made it," I say, pulling away.

"I can't believe it! You're really here."

"In the flesh."

"Julie," she slaps my arm, and even though her hand is cold, there's a distinct warmth that fills me at her touch. She's the only one who calls me by that nickname. Thanks to years of sports, everyone else calls me by my last name. Except one human being on this entire planet. *He* makes it a point to use my first name, which I hear growled at me by the wild animal that is Adrian Nikols.

"Julius," he says, jogging over to me. The rest of the team is at the end of the block now, going on without me.

Yes ... my first name is Julius and my last name is Caesar. My real parents thought it'd be funny to give me a crap name and then abandon me. I guess they thought it'd be easy to find me if they ever came looking.

25

They never did. But whatever.

I turn as Adrian walks over, expecting him to start yelling about how I should be leading the team, not slacking off. But as I glance up, I realize his attention isn't focused on me at all. He's looking at Mya. And she's looking back at him.

I shouldn't be surprised. Adrian's not just a big, handsome, Russian albino, he's also a former friend of Mya's. Maybe former *acquaintance*.

Well, we all went to school together. Mya and I were friends, Adrian was just there.

He developed a crush on Mya his senior year and asked her out. She told him no. He got angry and never spoke to us again. I was fine with that—he was a senior and she was a freshman, it never would've worked out with her crazy dad being all up in her business the way he was. But Adrian didn't see it that way.

Somehow, he convinced himself that *I* told Mya not to date him. Yet another reason he hates me. And then I followed him up here to Cross North and stole the captainship from him. And now Mya is here too, and he's probably thinking I'm going to get in the way again.

I'm not, but he wouldn't believe me even if I told him that. Mya's my best friend. Not my secret crush. She can date whoever she wants.

"Mya," he says, and it's the first time I've heard him speak that wasn't a growl or a bark. His voice is so soft, for a second, I glance around to see if someone else has spoken.

Mya stares at him. "I didn't know you attended Cross North."

"I do." It's such a blunt statement, all three of us blink at each other in a stupefied silence, waiting for Adrian to say

26

more.

He doesn't.

He just turns and jogs off.

"He hasn't changed," I say, smiling down at Mya. Like *way* down 'cause I'm 6'5 and she's like a foot and a half shorter. I'm probably the worst build for track in the history of the team. Everyone's always telling me I should've gone for basketball, but I love running, not shooting hoop. And I made captain, so I guess I'm doing something right.

Mya smiles up at me, her liner makes her eyes look catlike. Bold black lines swirling over her brown skin. "I'm guessing he's on the track team with you?"

I nod. "We're doing a two-mile run as punishment for the sign your dad went nuts over."

She gapes at me. "You saw that?"

"From inside."

"Tell me it wasn't your idea."

I smirk. "You know me well enough to know it was definitely my idea."

"Julie, you're horrible!"

We both laugh until I glance up and catch Adrian jogging ahead, he's looking back over his shoulder at me, that familiar murderous gleam is back in his eye. I sigh. "I should go. We'll catch up later, okay?"

Mya nods. "I've got to unpack, so I'll see you after."

As I jog away, I wonder if she's got survival gear and granola bars to unpack. Everyone has been freaking out about the blackouts, even though Cross North has a generator installed in each dorm and has even gone the extra mile by stashing canned goods in the basement of some of the houses. I hope the blackouts don't reach our campus, but I'm happy

27

Mya will be here if they do. We'll be trapped together. Which sounds creepy, but after two years apart, I'll have her presence any way I can get it.

A frown works its way over my face. If a blackout hits Cross North, Adrian will be trapped here too. That should be fun.

4

Mya

My roommate arrives just as I finish unpacking my things. I immediately offer my hand when I see her standing in my doorway. "Mya Brown. You must be my roommate."

The girl stares at my hand, at the black polish on my nails and the thorny silver ring on my middle finger. It's supposed to be the thorny crown worn by Jesus on the Cross, but with the way I'm dressed, most people think it's something creepy and demonic.

I sigh, steeling myself for the ridicule I know is coming. I've heard it hundreds of times—*Christians don't dress that way! You think Jesus wants to see you looking like a freak?*

But instead of criticizing me, my new roommate smiles and clasps my hand firmly. "Jupiter Star. I'm so excited you're my roomie!"

My eyes bulge. "You are?"

"Of course! I saw you carrying your bags in earlier, couldn't take my eyes off you." Jupiter pushes past me and walks into the room, dragging a huge suitcase behind her. She's got a duffle bag on her shoulder too, which she takes off and tosses onto the empty bed. She also reaches up and snatches off her wig to toss that onto the bed with it.

I gasp for two reasons.

First, I didn't know her hair was a wig. It's big and curly and thick, exactly what I'd expect from a girl with a face as pretty as Jupiter's. She's all eyes, large and round and rimmed in glittery liner. Her lips are tinted a subtle shade of pink, opposite of the neon pink of her real hair.

That's the second reason I gasp. Jupiter's hair beneath her wig is about half an inch of bright pink waves that she's smoothed into a 1920s style, like Betty Boop.

I can't believe what I'm seeing.

"Your hair is … very striking," I say with a laugh. Only God could've given me this roommate.

Jupiter grins. "So is yours. I love the afro."

"Thanks."

"And," she gestures up and down, "everything else too."

"Really?"

Jupiter points to her head. "I'm positive I've gotten the same number of complaints for my neon pink hair as you've gotten for your gloom and doom wardrobe."

I frown. Gloom and doom isn't how I would describe my attire. I suppose compared to Jupiter's bright hair and sparkly eyeliner; it *is* a little dark. But it isn't *gloomy*!

"So, have you toured the campus yet?" Jupiter asks, slipping a stick of gum into her mouth. She offers me the pack, but I wave her off. "I heard the tours are mandatory for freshmen," she goes on. "Apparently, they weren't mandatory last year, but with the blackouts going on, the campus directors want to make sure we know where to go in case of an emergency."

I chew my bottom lip. "Are they … Are they expecting a blackout?"

"Probably not. I mean, they started in Phoenix, right? We're, like, two hours away."

"But the blackouts keep expanding."

Jupiter is right, they'd started in Phoenix and Cross North is over two hours away, but at the rate of growth I've seen, I wouldn't be surprised if both Wakedon and the campus got caught up in the next outage. And there's no way to tell how long the next one would last. Could be days. Could be weeks.

What if the outage never ends?

Shame rushes through me as I shake my head. I sound like my father, getting all paranoid for no reason.

"I need some air," I say, interrupting Jupiter as she was complimenting the poster I'd hung over my bed.

"It's nice," she finishes.

I nod. "Thanks. My mother painted it."

The poster is a copy of one of her originals, a flourishing garden with outrageously sized fruits and vegetables. My mother called it *Serenity*, her personal take on the Garden of Eden.

She'd painted it with a bald head and a wheezing cough as she slowly died of cancer. I want to feel bitter about it. But when I look at that painting, all I feel is a deep sadness mixed with an odd sense of calm. I miss my mother, but I know she's in her own Eden now. She's at peace.

"Let's go for that tour now," I say.

To be honest, the tour isn't as boring as I thought it would be. Cross North campus is huge. Way too huge for us to walk through, so instead of marching through the grounds, we're divided into groups to take the tour on these speedy little golf carts.

My group is led by a senior named James who's tall and professional-looking but also handsome and good at his job. He drives us to each building, explaining which classes we'll be taking inside and even tells us the best spots for lounging.

"But the most important thing to remember," James says as he stops in front of the campus café, "is where to eat."

We all laugh.

"There are other things I want to go over with you guys." James passes us each a little map of the campus; I don't miss the way his eyes linger on me when he hands me mine. I'm not sure if he's flirting or just weirded out by my clothes. I don't look too deeply into it.

"Every building you see marked with a star has a backup generator in it," James announces.

We all stare down at the map, counting the buildings. The culinary clubhouse, aptly nicknamed Hot House, has a generator, probably because there's a hydroponic garden attached—it needs to be powered by electricity to keep the water filters working. Each dorm has a generator and so does the campus café, considering they wouldn't want all the food to spoil in the fridge.

None of the main buildings have generators which strikes me as odd but before I can ask about it, James explains, "If the power goes out for an extended period of time, we won't be having class anyway. It's better to preserve our food and make sure we've still got hot water to shower." He looks at us. "Good planning, right?"

"Yeah. Sure." Jupiter shrugs.

"Try to memorize all the powered buildings. An outage can happen at any moment, if it does, you'll want to hunker down in case panic spreads. People can get a little crazy during stressful situations. An entire campus of students without power could easily become a desperate battleground."

"How?" one freshman asks. "If the power goes out, I'll just sleep in my dorm until it's back on."

James folds his arms. "What if it doesn't turn back on? What if we're stuck in the dark for days? Our food begins to dwindle. Our water gets dirty and undrinkable without filters. Then what?"

An uncomfortable silence settles over us. No one wants to think about the *then what*. Because that's when people lose their humanity, when they value themselves above others and start behaving more like animals trying to survive than people trying to work together.

I shiver, thinking of my dad all alone in Wakedon. If an outage happened, he'd be by himself in an entire city full of panicking people. I'd be here on a campus full of uneasy young adults.

I don't know which is worse.

"Are there any stashes of supplies?" I ask suddenly. When everyone's eyes slide over to me, I gulp and add, "The school prepared for the blackouts by installing generators. But what about extra food and water? In case the outage lasts long enough for us to run out."

James nods slowly and holds up his map. "The buildings with a cross beside it have stashes in their basement."

I quickly scan my map, shocked to find Hope House with a cross beside it. "We have a stash?" I say aloud.

33

James answers, "Yes, ma'am. Hope House does a food drive each semester, usually dorm parents start collecting during the summer, so we have a short supply before classes even begin. With our stash of canned goods for the drive, it was natural we were pegged as a supply drop for the campus."

I frown. "But those canned goods are for the drive, not for the campus to use."

"If the power goes out, we'll need the food before anyone else does," James says.

I nod slowly. I guess that makes sense.

He starts up the golf cart again. "But if anyone is still a little anxious, don't worry. Hope House will be having a service tomorrow night; it's supposed to be for us to start the semester with some motivation. But I think we're going to take some time to pray for the campus, maybe inspire some hope that the blackouts will stop, and Cross North will be safe. It isn't mandatory, but there'll be free pizza." He glances back at us, but his eyes find mine immediately and he winks. "Don't miss it."

I glance away. Yeah… he's definitely flirting.

"You going to the service?" Jupiter nudges me.

I hesitate. "Uh…" It's not that I don't want to go, but I'm not sure if Julie has plans tomorrow night. I kind of wanted to spend some time with him. But I'm not sure that'll happen whether I go to the service or not.

From the flyers hung around campus, it seems like tomorrow night will have a lot of parties going on. The sorority house will be throwing their own tiki themed party, Kappa Pi is hosting a toga party while Hot House provides food and refreshments—not to mention two other dorms are hosting some sort of welcoming event. It seems like everyone else will be dancing while we eat pizza and pray.

I sigh, trying not to feel upset. I didn't come to Cross North to party anyway. And I doubt my father would be happy about me dancing with anyone from Kappa Pi.

I smile at Jupiter, still patiently waiting for an answer. "Maybe I'll go to the service. It might be fun."

5

Caesar

I stumble into the frat house after my morning run. Bunny happens to be standing *right there* and jumps back so the door doesn't hit him.

"Whoa! Caesar, you good?"

I nod, resting my headphones around my neck. "Might have pushed too hard on my run."

"How fast this time?"

I show him my watch and his blonde eyebrows hit the roof. Bunny's the opposite of me in every way, wavy blonde hair that he keeps tied back—oddly reminiscent of a rabbit's tail—with long lashes and a boyish smile. He's short, our pixie-sized marathoner, while I'm tall enough to hit my head on the sun when I wake up in the morning. My hair is raven and trimmed into an undercut, and while I'm fast enough to run the sprint, my height usually puts me on relays and middle-distance events. I don't mind. As long as I'm running, I'll complete whatever my coach assigns me.

"Keep it up and you'll almost be as fast as me," Bunny teases.

I take a swing at him, but he's so stinkin' fast, and I'm so stinkin' stiff already, he just steps to the side and laughs at me. "Go grab breakfast," he says with a wink. "You clearly need to refuel, Cap."

I sigh. He's right.

"What's to eat?" I ask, walking into the kitchen. I smell bacon and eggs and toast, but the chill I feel in the room keeps me from moving toward the food.

I know where the sudden ice is coming from before I even glance around.

Adrian Nikols is sitting in the far corner of the room, glaring. His eyes are so focused on me, I feel like he's been waiting for me to walk through the door just to give his pupils a purpose.

Adrian hates me. I've known that for a while, but today he seems more outraged than normal. Absently, I wonder if his extra dose of devilment has anything to do with Mya. He's well aware she's here on campus. And he's well aware he still has no chance with her.

Or maybe he's solely angry at me. Because I exist.

This is Adrian Nikols, after all. He's always scowling and glowering. When he speaks, it's either a growl or a bark. When he walks, it's more like a stomp.

I've never seen him smile.

He could be angry the sun is up, and the sky is blue. Every part of Adrian exudes rage. Even the way he eats—shoveling his breakfast into his mouth like he hates it.

I take this moment of hungry distraction to slip away and find my own plate.

"Ready for t'night?" Memphis asks in his slow drawl. He's stirring grits on the stove, determined to enjoy a southern breakfast no matter what.

"Of course." I wink.

With everyone moved in, Kappa Pi is throwing a party to welcome the freshmen. We do it every year, go all out with speakers and music and too much food to eat. This year's theme is ancient Rome, which means I *have* to show up in a toga.

"'Cause you're Julius Caesar!!!" Bunny had exclaimed when he first told me the theme.

I'd only laughed. But now that it's almost toga time, I'm a little anxious. Not that I care to be seen in the stupid costume, I'm nervous because I'd wanted to invite Mya to the party.

We didn't get to see each other again after unpacking and whatnot, so I sent her a text when I first woke up this morning, asking if she had plans today. She'd told me she wanted to go to some 'night of worship' at Hope House—she'd even invited me along.

I hadn't replied.

I know Mya's Christian and all that, but I can't help but feel annoyed. This is her first year of college, we're supposed to be going to parties and actually enjoying ourselves. Not going to *Bible study*. But I know if I dare say that to Mya, she'd force me to my knees and make me repent on the spot.

It's just…

Mya's my *best friend*. We should be experiencing this together.

After breakfast, I finally reply to her invitation.

Me: I'm running the frat party. Maybe I'll stop by after?

38

Mya: I'd love that, Julie XD

My heart does a little dance.

Me: How long is your service?

Mya: Dunno, but it won't be all night, so come before 10.

10? Sheesh. I'm sure Kappa Pi won't rest until sunrise. Last fall semester the party lasted so long, I didn't even go to sleep, just chugged a Red Bull and went straight to my first class— still too buzzed to even stand up straight.

Me: You sure you wanna spend the night in a church service? Kappa Pi is known for its parties.

Mya: Umm… I dunno. I promised my friends I'd go to the service.

Me: You made friends already?

Mya: James and my roommate Jupiter.

My eyes only register the name *James*. Don't know who he is, but I do know he's probably the reason Mya's skipping a frat party to go to a night of 'worship.'

I scowl at my phone. *Fine.* Mya and James can go pray while I put on a stupid toga and get blasted out of my mind.

I won't miss her.

Except I know I will… I'm clingy when it comes to Mya. My parents abandoned me, my foster mom was good to me, but she never adopted me. She took me in at age 4, raised me as her own, but never took that last step. Never made things permanent.

In my entire life, Mya's been the only constant figure. The only one who was always there. Until she wasn't.

I mute my phone and toss it onto my bed before I call her and say something stupid. Mya's finally back in my life, the last thing I need is to get an attitude and push her away. So I leave

39

my phone in my room while I hop into the shower.

I need to cool off.

The cold shower is a good idea, it chills me the heck out, so I'm calm enough to help the guys with the final touches for tonight's party. It takes us all afternoon to finish the decorations, plus another hour to set up the snack table and make outlandish promises to Noble about being responsible tonight. By the time the sun sets, I'm dressed in a toga and Roman style sandals. Bunny ordered them online, along with a golden laurel wreath, just like the actual emperors of Rome.

It sucks that the guy I'm named after was stabbed by his own buddies and all that, but I've always thought Caesar's accomplishments were admirable, despite what my history teachers always said. You don't invade Germania, defeat over 50 Gallic Tribes, and conquer land in Britannia while being a *bad* leader. But having the same name doesn't automatically make me as awesome as the real Julius Caesar.

Fortunately, I don't have to be a good leader to host a frat party.

The golden laurel wreath feels heavy on my head as I descend the stairs into the main foyer. There's music thumping throughout the house, some rap song I don't recognize, but it's good enough to have almost everyone dancing already.

Bunny greets me with a smile and a drink which he thrusts into my hand as the crowd cheers. He makes some sort of announcement that I don't listen to, then he slaps my back and I realize everyone's waiting for me to do something.

"Oh," I mumble. "Let's party?"

They cheer like I just gave the speech of my life and for a brief moment, I wonder if this is what my namesake felt like as he walked through a crowd of screaming Romans. Delighted

40

because it's a party, but uneasy because none of the people around you truly care about you.

He probably didn't feel uneasy at all. When Julius Caesar was stabbed in the back, he never saw it coming.

That's one mistake I'll never make, which is why I make it my business to find Adrian in the crowd as I walk through the house. I don't plan on starting any drama or even making friends with him, I just know he's been angrier than usual lately, so I don't want him out of my sights.

I don't trust him.

Adrian's in the back of the house, leaning against the wall like an angry ghost. I've never seen him drink, so I'm not surprised to find his hands folded over his chest instead of clutching a red cup. He's watching the beer pong tournament going on, but he looks like he's ready to flip the table over and murder the players. Everyone else seems to be enjoying themselves.

I chug down the bitter drink Bunny gave me and go for a refill. Memphis is serving the punch, some ungodly mixture he calls *Lizard Lemonade*. It tastes like vodka and lemons and more sugar than a bag of lollipops, but I guzzle it and ask for another before I feel good enough to go out and mingle with the crowd.

I find Bunny by the pool, surrounded by a group of girls who are all taller than him, but he doesn't seem to mind. He looks absolutely delighted by the company.

Connor O'Reilly is dancing in the clubroom, as soon as he sees me, he waves me over and I join him and the girls he's with. I wiggle my hips and entertain a redheaded bombshell I don't even know, but none of this *feels* fun. None of this feels right.

I know why, I'm just too much of a punk to say it aloud.

Or even acknowledge it internally.

I sigh as I pull away from the redhead when the song ends.

Connor grabs me as I pass into the hall. "Caesar, what's wrong?"

I shrug. "Nothing. I need a break."

He turns me back toward the clubroom. "We've got all the prettiest girls on campus here and you want to leave?" He burps in my ear. It smells like Lizard Lemonade. "You could spend the night with any one you want."

I've spent plenty of nights with pretty girls. But I don't want to tonight.

I shrug off Connor's meaty hand as I turn away again. "I just need some air."

I stalk off to my room with Connor staring dumbly after me. I don't care and I don't look back except to catch a glimpse of the time as I pass the ancient grandfather clock in the hallway. It's just after 11, which makes my heart pump.

Crap. Mya.

My feet slap against the stairs as I take them three at a time, rushing back to my room. I tear off the stupid toga and slip into a pair of jeans and a t-shirt, grabbing my phone from my bed as I run back into the hall.

My phone is still muted, but the screen is glowing with all the missed texts and calls from Mya. She was looking for me. Expecting me. And I'd blown her off to attend a party I'm not even enjoying.

I send her a desperate text as I push through the house, hoping against everything that it's not too late.

Me: Still up? I can head over now.

She replies right away. **Heading to sleep. 'Night.**

My stomach twists. It doesn't take a genius to know she's

42

angry at me. All I can do is try to make it up to her.

Me: How about breakfast tomorrow? My first class is at 9, I can meet you by the campus shuttle at 8.

Mya: Sure.

It's not much, but I'll take it.

A goofy grin spreads over my face as I stare at my phone, but it's wiped away when Adrian bumps my shoulder as he walks by. The gesture is so sudden and so hard that I stumble to the side and almost drop my phone. "Watch it," he grunts, marching past me.

I grab his arm. "What's your problem?"

He whirls around. "You're the one blocking the front door."

I smirk. "Sorry, I was distracted making plans with Mya. Something you'll never do."

Very slowly, Adrian takes a step forward so he's right in my face. "What'd you just say, pretty boy?"

Pretty boy?

Hold up.

Adrian might be angry and broody, but he's the prettiest guy I've ever seen. White lashes and eyes so fiercely grey, they look like the silvery undersides of rainclouds. It's the strangest thing that he would call *me* pretty, as if he hasn't looked in a mirror. He probably has … and then broke it when he realized he didn't look like the devil. I wonder if he hates being so pretty. It must be confusing. Like staring at a scowling angel.

Good looks aside, I know the pretty boy comment is meant to be an insult, so I step closer to Adrian and say, "I said I was—"

He shoves me back a step. "Save it. I don't care about your freaky girlfriend anymore."

43

I don't swing at him because I'm angry. I do it because he just shoved me in front of the crowd of students who've gathered around us. I can't let that pass.

Before I even realize it, my fist shoots forward. Adrian dodges—he's so much faster than I thought—the punch glances off his ear instead of cracking his jaw like I wanted.

I haven't missed that badly in my life.

Before I can react, Adrian counters with a left hook that absolutely *rocks* me. I stumble back two steps. There isn't much time to regain my footing. I'm still off-balance when I take another swing, but this time I'm expecting his speed, so I'm not surprised when he dodges again, but *he's* surprised when I swing with my left and catch him right in the face.

One of the perks of being so tall—I've got excellent reach.

Adrian's easily 6'3, big by anyone's standards, but I'm two inches taller and my arms are longer than his. Everyone says I missed my calling in basketball. I've always said I belong on the track. Maybe I should've been a boxer.

Adrian trips backwards and comically lands on his butt.

I step closer. "It's over," I tell him, though I do steel myself in case he swings again, but he doesn't get the chance. The next second, the lights go out and the entire house is plunged into darkness.

There's a mixture of cheers and shrieks as we realize we've been hit by a blackout. Half of us were expecting it, the other half has clearly been caught off guard.

Instinctively, I turn back to the door and stumble out to the porch. There are cars in the driveway and even parked on one half of the lawn, but my attention is focused on the dorms around me. Every house on the block is pitch black. The only light on our street comes from the Roman style torches decorating the lawn. If I squint, I can just make out the glow of the sorority tiki-shaped torches outside their house. They're a few blocks down, but with everything so dark, it's easy to catch the faint glow of fire.

I step down the porch, blinking into the night. This is probably the worst time to have a blackout. Half the kids on campus are too drunk to realize what's going on. The frat house is still packed with people, trying to keep the party going even though there's no music and no way to heat the leftover pizzas that've gone cold.

Wait...

Each dorm had a generator installed since the blackouts started. They should've kicked in by now. The lights should be on, and the music should be blaring. But it's not.

Kappa Pi is dark. The entire campus is still dark.

I turn around, about to run back inside to get Coach Noble so we can check the generator, but as soon as I pivot, I collide with Adrian's fist. He's still angry. He still wants to fight, even though the power just went out and we might be in trouble.

The hit rocks me backwards, and the next thing I see is stars bursting into my vision before darkness takes over.

6

Caesar

I wake to the sound of Mya's voice, but not the voice she uses when she's smiling and happy and being all girly. Nah, right now she's hissing like a baby viper and calling me lazy.

The curtains are suddenly drawn back, letting in a violent wave of sunlight that threatens to blind me. I groan as I lift my hand for cover.

"Mya, what…?"

"Get up," she huffs. "You were supposed to meet me for breakfast."

As my vision clears, I can just make out Mya standing in front of me, but she's not near my bed.

Huh.

I sit up, realizing I'd fallen asleep on my floor still wearing the same clothes as last night. The room tilts with the motion and I clutch the side of my head. All my hair is swooped to one side, the waves sticking up straight and matted together. There's a crust of drool on my chin, my eyelashes stick together from a layer of solid boogies, I blink them away as I rub at my eyes.

I can see Mya shaking her head at me, probably thinking I came home drunk and passed out. Little does she know, I got whacked over the head by a walking block of meatloaf. The guys probably carried me home and dropped me on the floor. It's a miracle they bothered to get me to my room.

Mya huffs again. "You look awful."

"Last night was awful," I mutter, standing up. It feels like I'm climbing a ladder, growing taller instead of rising to my feet. The room still sways, but Mya reaches out to stable me.

"Thanks," I grumble, stumbling toward the bathroom. I switch the lights, but nothing happens which makes me groan in frustration.

"Power's still out," Mya calls from outside the door.

I start the water at the sink, realizing my day is going to suck more than I planned. It doesn't get hot—not even tepid.

"Water's cold," I say.

"Our dorm is the same." Mya's voice sounds worried.

I brush my teeth, splash my face with icy water, and run my wet hands through my wrecked hair. When I step out the bathroom, I see just how troubled Mya is. She's chewing her lips and blinking at me like she might cry.

Sheesh.

Mya's standing there in platform boots with chains wrapped around the ankles, her stockings are artfully torn with holes over her shins and thighs, her black pleated skirt has gaudy zips up both sides and her black shirt is oversized and hanging over her shoulders. Her eyes are rimmed with thick liner, eyelashes long and black and bold. Even her lips are painted a shade of red so deep it almost looks like blood.

47

Despite her size, Mya's the toughest looking girl I know. All creepy goth and depressing emo—she didn't bat an eye walking through a frat house by herself. But right now, she looks afraid, clutching the silver crucifix around her neck, the only reminder that there's a sweet girl beneath all the chains and black nail polish.

"We'll ask around campus," I say in as confident a voice I can muster. "I'm sure they'll have the power back on by the afternoon."

"What if they don't?"

"Someone's got answers. We'll find out what's going on."

She nods. "I was worried something happened when you didn't show up this morning. Then I heard you got into a fight last night."

I laugh it off. "The other guy looks worse."

Mya doesn't laugh.

I sigh, peeling my shirt from my back. I'm covered in sweat since the A/C went out, but I'm not smelly enough to shower in that ice water.

I toss my shirt aside and unzip my pants, making Mya gasp and quickly turn around so her back's facing me. The sight makes me chuckle and I say in a low voice, "You've seen me naked before."

She doesn't respond.

"And I've seen you naked before," I remind her.

I can see the way her shoulders tense up, but Mya's voice comes out coolly, "That was a long time ago."

She's right. It was back when we were kids; we'd ride our bikes out of the city to the lake and go for a swim. Then we'd leave our clothes out to dry while we hiked naked through the woods. I couldn't have been older than seven or eight, Mya

48

trailing two years behind. Both of us were too young to be ashamed of our nudity. Too naïve to understand the differences between little boys and little girls. I remember thinking Mya was just a boy without a weenie, telling her she'd grow one when she got older.

I chuckle at the memory, scanning my floor for a reasonably clean pair of pants. Once I'm dressed, I step into my shoes and exhale a sigh.

"You can turn around."

Mya slowly faces me. To anyone else, she'd look fine, but I can tell she's blushing. Her skin is a creamy shade of brown, so her cheeks don't flush pink the way mine would. But I know Mya well enough to see when she's flustered. She can't even look me in the eye. I'm not exactly surprised. I'm comfortable around her, she's my best friend. But she was right when she said all that running around naked happened a long time ago. A lot has changed since then.

We're not kids anymore.

I reach for her hand. "Let's go."

The moment we step outside, I realize just how bad things are. I had expected all the cars parked out front to be gone by morning, considering the party got shut down a bit early, but they're all still here. Every single one.

I see Noble at his pickup with the hood popped, muttering curses as he tries to get it to start. The engine doesn't even rev.

"Why didn't anyone leave?" I say aloud.

Mya squeezes my hand. "You don't know? Everyone's cars are fried. Can't get any vehicles running."

"What? That means the shuttle to campus will be down."

She nods. "We'll have to walk."

"That's half a mile."

"We've got time."

I pull out my phone to check the time, frowning when I realize it's totally black. "Phones are dead?" I ask Mya.

She nods. "No phones. No working cars. No generators."

This is not how things were supposed to work out.

Cross North had the perfect setup; backup power, and caches of supplies stored throughout campus. But without the generators, our supplies could go bad. If our supplies go bad, panic will tear through the school. Once panic sets in, we'll be torn apart.

This campus will slowly fall into madness.

Mya tugs on my sleeve, making me realize I've been staring at my phone for longer than normal. "What do you want to do?" she asks.

Power is down for the entire campus. Generators haven't kicked in. All vehicles have been halted.

I blow a sigh through my lips and then wince. I'm aching all over from overdoing it on my run and then getting beaten like an egg by Adrian. My face is a mess. A black eye and blue bruises on my jaw and nose.

"Let's stay here," I tell Mya. "Power is down everywhere. No point in trying to make it to the main campus."

She nods.

"How are things at Hope House?" I ask. "You guys hit the sack at ten, right?"

She snorts as we turn back toward Kappa Pi. "We didn't go to sleep, the service ended."

"Then what did you do?" Because she definitely could've come to the party afterward, but I know as soon as I glance down at her that she never would've showed up. Mya's a good girl. Too good to be best friends with a frat boy like me.

She blushes. "I spent some time with James and Jupiter."

My stomach knots up. "Oh. Hope you had fun."

We walk back to Kappa Pi in an awkward silence. I'm honestly thankful for the blackout because it gives me something else to focus on besides the fact that Mya's *still* blushing over her night with stupid James.

When we walk inside, Coach Noble is there—having abandoned his useless vehicle in the garage. The entire track team has gathered in the living room, plus the rest of the Kappa Pi members. It looks like some sort of meeting is going on. Everyone's face is grim and lifeless, a dewy sheen of sweat making their foreheads shine. I'm suddenly aware of how hot it is; without power, we can't run the A/C.

"What's up?" I ask slowly.

"We were just discussing what we should do about the power," Bunny says.

"There's nothing we can do." Noble folds his arms. "Campus protocol instructs us to hunker down and wait for administration to send help if needed. That means staying in our dorms."

"How will administration *send help*?" Connor O'Reilly asks in an annoyed tone. "Our phones aren't working. They don't know we need help."

Bunny frowns. "The outage happened at night while administration wasn't on campus. They may not even know power is down."

"They'll know something's up once they realize their cars won't start and their phones have no signal," Noble says.

"We should walk back to town," Memphis suggests which earns a nod from Connor, but Coach Noble shoots him down.

"No one is leaving campus."

"Why not?" Connor demands.

"Because the nearest town is Wakedon, that's a thirty-minute ride in a car going sixty miles an hour. It'll take you hours to walk all the way. And if the outage hit the city, it could be dangerous."

Connor doesn't agree. "Something's up. The only way to find out *what* is to get out there and see for ourselves."

"It's just a power outage," Noble insists. "There's no reason for us to panic and leave."

"There's also no reason for you to keep us here," Connor says. He steps toward Coach. "We're all adults. You can't make us stay."

Noble pinches the bridge of his nose. "Listen, I've got procedures to follow, okay? When the power comes back and my bosses find out I let students go off on their own, I could get in trouble." He turns around in the circle of guys, making eye contact with each one of us, even Mya. "I can't just let you guys run around campus doing whatever you want. University staff was briefed on how to handle a blackout. Our first order is to settle in. Our second order is to wait. So that's what I'm going to do. That's what we're *all* going to do."

The room falls silent, all of us blinking at each other, wondering if trusting Noble is the right thing to do. He's our coach and our Big Brother. One of few staff members on campus since the professors and other employees likely couldn't start their cars to get here this morning. Coach Noble lives in the house with us so he's one of the handful of adults here right now. That gives him a lot more authority than even me, the team captain.

At thirty-four, Noble's the oldest of all of us, and the only one to be briefed on what to do during a campus-wide outage.

We should listen to him. We should follow his instruction. But I can't help but wonder if he's wrong.

None of us can deny there's something weird going on. We've experienced outages before, and they've never halted cars and blocked phone services. But I don't know how to explain this. I don't know if a dead car means all hope is lost.

"So what do we do now?" I ask, ignoring the stares I get as I speak up. I'm not sure if they're all shocked by my battered face or just paying close attention. Every eye is glued to me.

Speaking of my battered face, as I glance around, I realize Adrian's not here. But I can't focus on his absence. Making a plan is more important than settling things with him.

Coach Noble sets his hands on his hips, and sighs. "We've checked the generator downstairs, it's not working."

"Generators are gas powered," Bunny says. "Why isn't it working?"

"Because there are some electronic components to a generator," Noble explains. "Startup is electrically powered, plus voltage regulation. If the circuits are fried, the generator is useless."

"Can't we fix it?" I ask, immediately feeling dumb. I know good and well that no one here is capable of fixing that thing.

"I'm not a mechanic or an engineer," Noble replies. "And even if I was, there's nothing I can do about fried circuits."

I nod. "Well, there are still caches of canned goods in some of the dorms. We have food to eat while we wait for help to restore power."

"Not every dorm has a cache," Connor reminds us grimly. "Kappa Pi doesn't."

Memphis sucks his teeth. "What are we supposed to eat today? Leftover pizza from the party?"

"There's still food in the fridge," Noble reminds us.

"Power is out. Which means the food is getting warmer by the second," Connor says.

We all nod agreement which makes Noble roll his eyes. "Let's make a nice breakfast then. Cook the eggs and drink up the milk; we'll make whatever will spoil the fastest."

"How will we cook?" Bunny asks. "The stove doesn't work."

"I thought it was gas?" Memphis says.

"It is. But it's a newer model built with an interlock."

Everyone groans. I may not be a mechanic but even I know what this means. Most gas stoves will still be usable on the cooktop as long as you've got something to light it with, but newer models built with an interlock are designed to prevent gas from entering the stove unless there's electricity to power it. This means we have no way to cook our food.

Noble scratches his black beard. "There's a grill out back by the pool. We can cook on that."

I'm not looking forward to grilled eggs, but food is food and we've got no other choice. Still, I do have a question…

"What about the other dorms?" I ask. "There are others without supplies too." And if they're panicking like we are, they might get brazen enough to start demanding supplies from the houses that've got them. Like Hope House…

As if she's just realized this too, Mya shifts closer to me, and I take her hand without thinking. Coach Noble glances between us before he says, "All the dorm parents need to have a meeting. We can decide what to do about supplies together. But with any hope, power may be back by the afternoon."

I nod, though I'm not entirely convinced that's going to happen.

"Why don't you head back to your dorm?" Noble says to Mya. "Let them know I'd like to meet with whoever's in charge over there."

Mya takes a nervous breath, squeezing my hand. "Okay. Where do you want to meet?"

"You know where the soccer field is?" he asks.

She nods. "What time do you want to meet?"

Noble looks over his shoulder at the ancient grandfather clock resting against the wall. It's as old as Kappa Pi itself, a relic from the fraternity's early days. I'm not surprised it's still working, it's one of the few things in the house that doesn't require electricity to run. I can hear it ticking away, a calming noise that's been constant throughout my time at Kappa Pi.

"Noon," Noble says. "That's in three hours. Can you keep track of the time?"

Mya tugs at one of the chains hooked to her skirt and I realize there's a pocket watch attached to the other end.

Of course, the self-proclaimed goth carries a pocket watch instead of wearing an iWatch like the rest of us Gen Z kids. The saddest part is, I have no idea if the watch is a fashion statement or a quirky gift from her insane father. Probably both.

Either way, I'm thankful for the silver little thing. It doesn't require batteries or electricity of any sort to function. Other than our grandfather clock, that's probably the only thing on campus that has the time. And it's portable. So yay.

"I've got the time," Mya says with a smile, clutching the pocket watch.

Noble looks at her like he's proud. "Good."

"Do you want me to walk you back?" I ask as Mya turns toward the door. I haven't let go of her hand, but my grip isn't

55

tight. She could pull away from me if she wants.

She shakes her head. "Stay and eat breakfast. I'll see you at noon."

7

Mya

I know where the soccer field is located, but on my way to Hope House, I double back through the park to make sure I haven't misplaced it on the map in my head. From my two days on campus, I've managed to memorize a bit of the map James handed out the day before. I know the West Wing is nothing but dorms, a lounge, two gyms, and a small park with an open field for sports and a track that encircles the entire thing. The neighborhood is huge, large enough for over 1200 students to comfortably reside.

I cut through the park, heading past the student lounge nestled between a three-story dorm and the student garden. Beside the garden is the dorm responsible for taking care of it—it's suitably named the Green House.

I'm out of breath when I finally step onto the soccer field. I guess it'll be big enough to hold a meeting for the dorm parents of West Wing. There's only one or two per dorm, but I'm sure the students will want to spectate. Everyone wants to know when the power will be back.

It's only been one night in the dark and already I feel like the campus is slipping. Panic has taken root deep inside, it's growing faster in some than in others, but I know it's there. The only thing we can do to weed it out is gain control of the situation. Come up with a plan.

I don't know much about Coach Noble, but Julie seems to believe in him. I've only been here for two days; all I can do is trust my best friend's judgment on this. I pray that's not a mistake.

Once I catch my breath, I cut across the open field and head into the cluster of trees off the side of the track so I can get back to my dorm as quickly as possible. I'm not exactly in a rush, but some part of me feels wary. Like I shouldn't be outside alone.

It's broad daylight. Early afternoon in the middle of a college campus. Normally, I would feel perfectly fine, if not excited to be here. But the truth is that I don't feel safe at all. I feel the icy chill of fear biting into my chest, sending ripples of anxiety through my entire being. Every part of me is on edge. My legs begin to shake as I jog through the little burst of trees. I stop and rest against one to get myself together—that's when I see him.

A tall figure leaning against one of the trees, his head tilted upwards, his eyes closed. He's breathing deeply and I don't have to guess why. His shirt is soaked through with what I can only guess is sweat because he's dressed in gym shorts and sneakers.

The soft white material clings to him, revealing skin almost as white as the long-sleeved tee he's wearing. But it's not the curve of his abs or his chest that I'm focused on, my attention is stolen by the man's face.

It's Adrian Nikols.

It dawns on me just then that I hadn't seen Adrian in Kappa Pi. I'm not surprised to find him out here running, but on a morning like this, I would at least expect him to show a little more concern. To at least care that there's a campus-wide blackout. But he seems to be moving on with his life like this is no big deal, like he's still got a routine to keep and the rest of the world needs to get on board.

I stare at him a few moments more, wondering what on earth I should do. But just as I decide to turn and quietly leave, Adrian opens his eyes and looks right at me. His eyes are like chips of freshwater ice in his face, a shade of blue so pale they almost look grey. The coldness in them has nothing to do with the color, however. Adrian looks at me like he hates me.

In a sad way, I understand why. I was his secret crush back in high school, and he'd taken a chance and had asked me out in front of all his friends. My rejection burned him. I didn't think it burned him enough for the resentment to have lasted all these years, but I can see the disdain in his expression clear as day. It fills his icy gaze with an intense heat that ripples over the planes of his face, shifting his features into a hardened expression that sends a shiver down my sweaty spine.

I take a short breath, shift my weight from one foot to the other. "There's going to be a meeting about the power outage," I say casually, like we're old friends. "Coach Noble has more information."

He nods and pushes off the tree, stalking past me without another word. I stand there and watch him go, stunned into silence not by his demeanor but by the horror I see on his backside as he passes me.

Adrian's shirt sticks to him from the buckets of sweat he earned on his run. It clings to his skin like a film, folding over every curve and jagged line of his back. Scars. Dozens of gashes and zigzagging patterns cover him like a child took a crayon to a sheet of paper. Pink puckered skin, raised into hard ridges of flesh from years old wounds.

It looks so painful; I gasp as Adrian walks by and immediately regret it. But if he noticed or heard me, he doesn't react. Adrian keeps walking and after a few heavy steps, he starts into a jog like I'm not even there.

In the silence, I turn and walk back to Hope House on stiff legs. When I get to the house, I walk in on a meeting that looks exactly like the one I witnessed at Kappa Pi. All the boys have come over to the ladies' dorm—since it's twice as big—everyone is sitting in the lounge area while our dorm parents stand in the middle of the room and explain what's going on.

Kassandra Hanover, the leader of the ladies' dorm, is reading off a list of the supplies we have on hand while James stands with his arms folded over his chest, a concentrated look on his face. At the night of worship, he'd been kind to me, even charming. He'd poured me punch and introduced me to some of his friends. I was swooning the entire time, overwhelmed that a senior would be interested in me, especially one as handsome as James.

Jupiter nor I could believe how much attention he'd given me. But now he merely glances up and offers a tight smile when he notices me. It's like we've reverted to strangers.

"We have plenty of water," Kassandra says, "and enough food to last us at least a month."

"But that's just *us*," one kid speaks up. "What about everyone else? How will they eat?"

"Shouldn't we look out for ourselves?" another guy suggests.

"That's not very Christlike, Johnson." Kassandra frowns. "We can't call ourselves Hope House if we don't offer any speck of hope at all."

Johnson rolls his eyes. "I'm just saying. All the other dorms got their own stash of supplies, didn't they?" He glances at James. "That's what you told us at orientation."

"Not everyone's supplies have arrived," James admits sheepishly. "We didn't expect to get hit with a blackout before classes began. We're still waiting on a few boxes."

"Which means we've got to share," Kassandra adds.

Johnson rolls his eyes again.

"Besides, these supplies aren't even ours," Kass says. "The only reason we have so much is because of the food drive we've been preparing for."

James takes a step forward. "There's enough to last us a month. I doubt the blackout will go on for that long. We can definitely share."

Jupiter raises a hand, her pink hair looks a bit frazzled, like she woke up and went straight downstairs for this meeting. Now that I'm looking around at everyone, I think that's the case for each student here. Everyone's clothes are slightly disheveled, hardly any of the ladies are wearing makeup and the guys still look half asleep. Even Kassandra, who sported a skater dress and wedge heels to the party last night, is wearing baggy sweatpants and has her flat-ironed afro hair pulled into a messy bun atop her head.

It's clear just looking around... None of us saw this coming. Despite all our preparations.

"Yes, Jupe?" Kassandra nods at her.

"How do we know the blackout won't last a month?"

The room shifts uncomfortably.

"The power went out last night," James says. "We've had long blackouts before, but I'd say it should be back in a few hours."

"This doesn't feel like a blackout," Jupiter mutters.

Johnson frowns but nods. "She's right. The last few blackouts left us without power, but they didn't fry our generators, they didn't knock out our car batteries, and they didn't mute our phones. Something is going on."

I hold my breath as Johnson's words sink in. Some part of me had held on to hope that maybe Kapp Pi's generator was down. Maybe ours had started working while I was gone. Maybe someone somewhere on campus had managed to get things going, but that's clearly not the case.

Johnson and Jupiter are right. Something is going on.

That feeling of anxious dread begins to flood the room as murmurs fill the silence. I can see the moment when everyone else realizes what Jupiter and Johnson have been trying to say. Slowly, everyone's anxiety shifts into controlled desperation, but before any of these dangerous emotions can reach a boiling point, Kassandra raises her hands to diffuse the rising tension.

"Let's not start rumors and conspiracy theories. For now, all we can do is sort our supplies and wait for the power to come back."

"But what if it *doesn't* come back?" Jupiter presses.

Kassandra sighs. "Don't you trust God at all?"

Jupiter looks offended. "*Of course,* I do. I'm just asking if we have a plan for the long run. No need to start coming for my trust in Jesus."

"Or lack thereof," Johnson snickers.

Everyone scowls at him.

He huffs and looks away.

I figure this is probably the best possible time to interrupt, so I step forward and clear my throat. "If we're looking to sort supplies and make plans, I think we should get the other dorms involved. They've already arranged a meeting on the soccer field at noon. They want to discuss what's going to happen next."

"Noon?" James asks, then he glances at his wrist to check his dead iWatch and lets out a painful sigh. "I have no idea what time it is."

I hold up my pocket watch. "We've got about two hours."

8

Adrian

The meeting at the soccer field accomplishes literally nothing. At just past noon, groups of students and their respective dorm parents begin showing up. They appear like dots on the hazy Arizona horizon, shuffling through the heat to find relief in the shade. It's honestly cooler outside than in our houses without any power to run the A/C, but things heat up once the meeting begins.

Noble represents Kappa Pi, a pretty Black girl named Kassandra and a big Black guy named James represent Hope House, some chick called Delilah represents the Omega Zeta Chi Sorority, the Green House is led by a hefty man with a thick Irish accent—I can't tell you his name because I literally cannot understand a word he says.

There are other dorms that come along, but I don't listen as they introduce themselves, I'm too distracted by Mya who is almost hidden in the crowd of Hope House students. When Kassandra starts talking, she stands on her tiptoes and her head pops up over the shoulder of a guy who's blocking her way. She doesn't see me staring, but I glance off anyway.

I know she saw me earlier. I know she saw the reason I don't run without a shirt—not that it matters once I get all sweaty. The material sticks to me and becomes transparent, revealing my secret against my will. I know others have seen, but I don't really care what other people think of me. I've always cared what Mya thought. And I don't even know why.

I force myself to stay focused during this miserable meeting. We spend an hour establishing what Coach Noble told us within five minutes of waking up this morning. The power is out, the generators are down, we're all doomed.

Except, for some reason, no one thinks we're doomed other than a select few of us who are immediately silenced. One kid from Green House suggests we send a group of students to travel home, but that idea is shot down by every single dorm parent—all at once.

Coach Noble insists the staff has a protocol they've got to follow. They can't let anyone leave campus until help arrives. But no one knows when help is going to come.

Some idiot suggests the National Guard will drive up here to personally deliver supplies to us. The dorm parents don't even waste their time entertaining that idea. If the National Guard has been deployed, then things are worse off than we thought—things are *really* bad for us because a college campus three hours from the city will not be the Guard's priority. They will likely figure we are secluded and hunkered down with our supplies and our generators, like we're supposed to be. They will never know we've only got half the supplies we're supposed to have because our cache deliveries were late. They will never know our generators were fried when the power went out.

No one will know anything unless we go out and find help. But all the dorm parents are too afraid of losing their jobs to let us go.

I think of my little brother and sister as Coach Noble and the other dorm parents tally off a total list of supplies for the entire West Wing of campus. There is a North Wing as well, but we're nearly an hour away from them so our staff agrees to keep our worries limited to what's going on here. Once the supplies are sorted, we can consider making contact with North Wing—if the power isn't back by tomorrow.

When I think of tomorrow, I can't help but think of home again. In my mind's eye, the twins are smiling and happy. They have their Go Bags, and their bellies are full, and their clothes are clean. But I know the truth is likely much darker than that. The truth is written on my back, carved into my flesh.

The truth is that my stepfather is likely passed out drunk and my mother is probably gone with another man—making money the only way she knows how. The truth is that the twins are likely alone and afraid, wondering what they should do now.

I told them what to do. I left them money. I reminded them of the safe in my stepdad's room. I told them to get to the bakery. I told them who to ask for help if they needed it. I can only hope they listened.

I curse myself as I realize how stupid I am. It was dumb of me to trust my kid brother and sister to take care of themselves. It was dumb of me to value school and track and Mya over my family. Now I'm stuck here on campus without power; I have no way to contact them, and I'm not allowed to leave to go find them.

Not yet at least.

Coach Noble is talking again, but I'm not listening. I'm done with this discussion. Without waiting to be dismissed, I turn away and begin pushing through the crowd so I can leave. Something tugs on my arm, and I jerk back to find Julius holding my elbow.

His hand on my flesh makes me want to finish what we started last night, but then I glance up to see his battered face and all I can do is smirk at him. "What do you want?"

"You sure you don't want to stick around? This is information we all need to hear."

I am so sick of Julius always playing the good guy. I get that he's captain of the track team and all that, but he is not in charge here. He is not in charge of *me*. I don't need his permission or approval to leave, and I don't need his information. We're doomed. We established that this morning. Now we've established it again as a big dumb group.

"I'll stick around when you guys are ready to do something, not just talk about what-ifs."

He raises an eyebrow, though it only ticks upwards a fraction of an inch with his eye still swollen. Man ... I really did a number on him.

"We can't decide what to do if we don't talk first. Besides, we don't have to think about leaving until our supplies get low."

I tug my arm from his grasp. "We need to leave *before* the supplies get low."

Julius sighs. "You heard what Coach Noble said."

"Coach Noble is an idiot."

Bunny gasps beside Julius, which almost makes me spit at him. I hate Bunny.

"Don't you see?" I ask sincerely. "As our supplies dwindle, so will our peace. We have twelve-hundred students on campus, all anxious and worried. You throw in hunger and thirst, and we're a ticking time bomb." I jab my thumb into my chest. "I am *not* gonna be here when that bomb goes off."

"We're all friends here," Bunny says. "We're not going to turn on each other. We're sharing our supplies, remember?"

"Shut up, Bunny," I say flatly. "I wasn't talking to you."

He looks like he's about to cry and that just makes me angrier. I hate wimps like him. People like Bunny are nothing but deadweight. When all hell breaks loose, he will be the first to die in the flames. I'd bet a Go Bag on it.

Before this conversation can get any stupider, I turn and walk away. Julius is still talking behind me, but I ignore him and take off at a jog. I don't want to hear any more. I don't want to be told to calm down. I don't want to listen to them tell me that I'm overreacting.

Julius is an orphan. Nobody really likes Bunny. They don't understand what it's like to have people depending on you. They don't understand what it's like to be worried sick about people who need you for their very survival. I left my brother and sister and I have no way of knowing whether they're okay and no one around me seems to care.

Anger bursts through my chest and I pick up my pace, running like I can escape the blackout, like I can outrun every problem around me. If I could, I'd run home, but a small part of me knows that Noble and Julius are both right. The power *could* come back at any moment. If it comes back while I'm on the road, I'll have to trek all the way back to campus. I'll have risked Noble's job for no reason.

I'll give him a few days, I decide as I slow from a sprint and ease into a mild jog. *A few days for the power to come back and I'm out of here. No matter what.*

The Kappa Pi House is just ahead, I run up the steps and go straight up to my room. Every piece of clothing I own is folded perfectly and stashed in my drawers. I have my textbooks arranged on a shelf in alphabetical order. I have my shoes on a rack that is organized by style, then color. Every part of this room is in perfect order.

Nothing is out of place.

Nothing is beyond my control.

I gingerly slip out of my sticky clothing, fold them up, and set them in the bottom of my hamper. Then I walk naked to the bathroom and step into the shower. The water is still running but it's ice cold. Coach Noble says even that won't last long if the grid is down. At the meeting, we were advised to use the last of our running water to fill up bottles, but I'm not going to do that. I want to shower. I don't care what anyone says.

The showerhead spurts and blasts me with an icy spray. My back aches as the needles of water stab into my scars. It's so cold my teeth chatter, but I welcome the biting chill. In the middle of an Arizona summer with the A/C shot from the blackout, we're all trying to cool down. Yet, even under the spray of this arctic water, all I feel is pain so deep that it burns.

9

Caesar

Kappa Pi Fraternity Mansion stinks. It's been five days since the power went out. Five days since we lost access to hot water. Five days since any of these boys had a good shower. Green House was the last dorm to enjoy running water. It went out last night with a trickle. The rest of us had already said goodbye to showers and faucets. I'd been sponge-bathing from a bucket since Day One—thanks to Adrian Nikols.

He took a long shower the morning after the power went out, using the very last of the running water on himself. It wasn't just selfish, it was dangerous. That water could end up becoming the difference between life or death for us. Dehydration is not a pretty death. It's slow and painful, drives you mad before it finally takes you. I don't want to experience that, but this morning I feel like death is closer than we think.

Coach Noble calls us all into the living room on the first floor as soon as the sun goes up. We've been laying out our schedules by the sunlight since Day One. Without power, we have no electric clocks, and we have no lights. There's no modern way for us to tell time except for the grandfather clock in the hallway and Mya's pocket watch.

I think of Mya as I take up space in the far corner of the living room. I haven't seen much of her since the lights went out. She's been delivering boxes of canned goods to dorms without supplies. Hope House has been the driving force behind our survival thus far. A lot of kids on campus aren't interested in religion, but we've all been thanking God lately. If it weren't for Hope House, I wouldn't have eaten breakfast this morning.

A burp bubbles up my throat and I try to hold it in. It tastes like the corned beef hash I ate from a can today. Not the most appetizing meal in the world, but it's better than nothing.

"I have some bad news," Coach Noble says, and we all groan in response.

The power is out. The water isn't running anymore. It's hot and sticky and we all stink. It can't get much worse than this.

"You haven't heard from the National Guard yet," Memphis says, fanning himself.

Coach Noble releases a sigh. "No, we haven't heard anything from the National Guard."

More groans fill the air.

"Have you heard anything from *anyone?*" Connor O'Reilly asks in a desperate voice that cracks on each word. I wish we had an extra bottle of water just for him.

"No. I haven't."

"How is this possible?" Memphis groans.

Bunny starts shaking his head. Connor O'Reilly looks like he's going to faint or cry.

"Everybody, remember to stay calm. Okay?" Coach tells

us, but no one listens.

"How can you say that?" Memphis is nearly yelling which stirs up the rest of us.

I tuck myself further into the corner. If a fight breaks out, I don't want to be part of it. I've still got bruises from my tussle with Adrian—speaking of the guy...

My eyes scan the room to find him standing on the other side of the sofa, his arms folded over his chest, a serious look in his eye. He doesn't look hot or tired or thirsty like the rest of us. If it weren't for his white hair sticking to his forehead, I'd say he was just fine.

Coach Noble has his hands up, trying to calm everyone down. He manages to stop Memphis from yelling and seizes control of the conversation again.

"Look, we can talk about the National Guard later. Right now, there's more pressing news."

"What's more pressing than help showing up?" Memphis grumbles.

"Getting along is more pressing," Noble answers him. His gaze narrows as he lets that sink in. "Order is the key to survival. We cannot maintain order if we start panicking or freaking out."

"We haven't exactly reached that point yet," Connor O'Reilly says.

"But we might after you hear this." Noble takes a breath, his face going from serious to solemn. "A student from Green House got the last bit of water from their faucets last night. Apparently, there was only enough for half a bottle, which he stored in his room until this morning. When he woke up, he took a drink from that bottle. Moments later, he complained to his roommate about having an itchy throat. About ten

72

minutes after that, his itchy throat closed up."

The room falls silent as we all stare at Coach Noble. None of us want to believe this is true. We're all hoping there's more to this story. That, somehow, the kid from Green House was saved and he's doing all right. Lesson learned. But we know that's not the case.

"What happened next?" Bunny asks warily.

"You know what happened," Memphis growls across the room. "His throat closed. He suffocated."

Someone in the back gasps. The rest of the guys begin to murmur.

"This can't be happening." Connor O'Reilly steps forward. "I don't understand."

"Something is in the water," Coach Noble says.

"That isn't so bad, though, right?" I can't tell if Bunny sounds hopeful or desperate. "We're out of running water anyway, so it doesn't matter if something is in it."

Coach Noble shakes his head. "The point is, something is in the water because someone put it there." He swallows, then winces, probably feeling as thirsty as I suddenly feel. "I've spoken to the other dorm leaders and we're all in agreement... We could be facing something bigger than we thought. There's a chance this blackout isn't a coincidence."

"That's what I've been saying!" Memphis nearly screams. He's absolutely freaking out now, eyes bulging and spittle flying from his mouth. "We need to leave! The National Guard isn't coming, they're busy fighting a war!"

"That's not necessarily the case!" Coach Noble shouts, though his voice isn't raised in anger, he's simply trying to speak over the rising panic that's filling the room. "I said we might be facing something serious but that doesn't mean the nation is at war. It means this is bigger than we thought. The blackout could be statewide, not simply something that's impacted our city alone. If that's the case, then the National Guard is definitely coming. Due to the seriousness of the problem, I have no doubts the government is aware of what's going on." He takes a breath. "That means help is coming. It's just a matter of time."

In the silence that follows, Adrian steps forward, scowling mad and almost towering over Coach Noble. His voice comes out in a grated whisper, hoarse enough that I almost wince at the sound of it.

"How much time?" he asks.

All eyes are on Noble. "I-I don't know. Listen, the point is—"

"I've been wanting to leave from the start," Adrian cuts him off, "but you told me to stay at least for the sake of your job. So I've given you five days to convince me the power will be back or help will arrive. Neither has happened." He turns away, marching toward the staircase. "I'm leaving."

Coach Noble grabs his arm. "Hold on—I'm still the dorm leader, it's my job—"

"Screw your job!" Adrian shoves him off and we all gasp as Noble stumbles backwards.

"Adrian," he begins, but Memphis cuts in, walking over to stand by Adrian.

"You can't keep us anymore, Coach. Not if there's really a war going on out there."

"We don't know if there is truly a war happening," Noble says angrily.

"Why else would someone cut our power and then poison our water?" Memphis challenges. Then he raises his voice like the realization just hit him. "Someone *died*, Coach! This campus isn't safe anymore."

"Neither is the world out there," Noble argues. He holds his hands up like he's approaching a wild animal. With the deadly look in Adrian's eye and the panicked rage in Memphis's, he might as well be dealing with a feral creature. "If this poison has reached us out here, then I have no doubts it's probably in the city too."

"That's why I need to get home!" Memphis says hotly. "I've got family I need to check on!"

"If this is the state of our city, then you might not make it home! Don't you see?" Coach Noble shouts. His thunderous voice casts a net of silence over us that we can't find our way out of. Even Adrian just stands there with a stony look on his face, jaw clenched tightly, hands balled into fists. But he doesn't speak, and he doesn't move. He knows Coach Noble is right.

"Cars are not working anymore," Noble says. "That means if you want to get home, you've got to walk. That could be days of travel on foot. Days on the abandoned highways. Days in the Arizona desert. You could bump into wanderers who might not care that you're just a student trying to make it to your family. They could be just as hungry and desperate as you are. They could be plain old evil." He takes a short breath, and his voice comes out shakily. "They could be the people who've shut off the power and poisoned the water to begin with."

"So you really believe someone did this?" Bunny asks.

Noble nods slowly. "I do believe someone did this."

"Who?" Bunny begs.

"Terrorists," someone from the back blurts.

Connor O'Reilly's voice is an angry growl. "Probably

Russians." He openly glares at Adrian, but our lovely albino Russian doesn't even blink. I'm not sure how attached he is to his culture, but with all the political turmoil going on in the news lately, I doubt this is the first time Adrian's heard someone talk crap about his race. I also doubt he's ever cared.

"I can't let you guys leave," Coach Noble says seriously. "But not because of my job. It's for your own safety. Help is coming. I promise."

"You can't promise that," Memphis says. "You can't even promise we'll have water tomorrow."

Memphis is right. We're down to a single case of 24 bottles shared with as many guys. Hope House is probably done giving out supplies by now. This is all we've got. I can only wonder how the other campus is doing.

I gasp as an idea hits me.

"What if we can find more water?" I say without thinking.

Everyone turns to look at me, but I ignore their eyes as I stumble to the center of the room to stand beside Coach Noble. "The other student dorms... We can see if they've got supplies to spare," I suggest.

"That's not a bad idea," a freshman compliments me.

"They might be willing to help," someone else says. "They could have more supplies than us."

I can hear our spirits being lifted as the dark murmurs from before become lighthearted whispers. Someone even starts whistling in excitement—I guess the thought of food and water will do that to anyone.

But of course... Adrian speaks up and kills our joy.

"No," he says gruffly. "Our water supply is poisoned. No one in their right mind is going to share anything anymore."

My confidence deflates. Hope bursts like a bubble as a dark

cloud fills the room.

"What do we do then?" Bunny asks.

I startle when I realize everyone is looking at me again, like this has somehow become my problem to fix.

"Uh..." I say dumbly. "Maybe we can check the academic campus." It's a shot in the dark, but it lights up the room.

Coach Noble slaps me on the back. "The student café!" he nearly shouts. "We took supplies from the deli here in the West Wing, but there's an even bigger food court on the academic campus. The food in the refrigerators is spoiled by now, but I'm sure they had bottles of water and cans of things to eat."

Just like that, everyone thinks I'm a genius. Connor O'Reilly fist bumps me, and Bunny runs over and gives me a hug like I've just saved his life. Even Adrian nods in my direction, one downward jerk of his chin. It's almost imperceptible, but the two of us have been at war since high school. I've gotten pretty good at reading his dark emotions and interpreting his silent anger.

I think I've just bought us all a few more days of food, which means there's time for help to arrive. I don't want to think about what will happen in another five days if the water runs out again. I just want to enjoy this moment of happiness.

"I'll talk to the other dorm parents," Coach Noble says, and the suggestion sparks up another argument.

"Why would you do that?" Memphis asks. "We should keep whatever supplies are there to ourselves."

"They need food and water too," Noble insists.

"That's too bad." Memphis shakes his head.

"Hope House helped us when we needed it," I say angrily, thinking only of Mya. "We can't loot the café and keep everything for ourselves."

Memphis scoffs. "Watch me."

"Julius is right," Adrian says, shocking the room for multiple reasons. First of all, he just used my first name. Second of all, he just agreed with me. Third of all, it sounds like he wants to help someone else. This is not the Adrian I know… Then again, the Adrian I know has been madly in love with Mya Brown since he was a teenager. He's speaking up for the same reasons I am.

"If we raid the café, we do it as one with as many people as possible," Adrian says sternly.

"You're kidding, right?" Memphis looks at him like he's crazy, but the expression doesn't faze him.

"I'm not kidding," he says gruffly.

"Why on earth should we go with as many people as possible?"

Adrian gives Memphis his full attention, but his words fill the room, and everyone leans toward him to listen. "Because we don't know what state the other dorm wing is in. We assume they're better off than us. We assume they have more supplies than us. But what if the opposite is true? What if they're just as thirsty and hungry as we are? What if their plan is to raid the food court too?" He steps closer to Memphis, his voice coming out low and menacing. "What if they raid the café the same day we do?" He doesn't have to say anything else, but he finishes his thoughts anyway, hammering the point home. "It'll be all out war for supplies."

No one speaks for a long moment. Not even Coach Noble.

"Talk to the dorm parents," Adrian orders, catching Coach's attention. "Tell them we're raiding this afternoon. All hands on deck."

Coach Noble nods and we all watch Adrian turn to leave,

wondering if we're really up for this adventure.

10

Mya

The walk to the Academic Campus is long and hot but we get through it. We have no other choice.

Not everyone wanted to go, in fact the least number of volunteers came from Hope House, especially after Kassandra announced things could get ugly if other students showed up. I heard some guys from Kappa Pi wanted to leave campus altogether, but so far, they've been ordered to stay put. Initially, I thought staying put was the right thing to do as well, but now that someone has died, I can barely think straight. I need to check on my father. I need to know if he's got drinkable water and enough supplies to last. What if someone has tried to storm our house the way we're going to storm the Academic Campus?

My father can take care of himself. I have to remind myself of this every few hours because the worry keeps coming back, swinging through my mind on a pendulum of horrors. *God is with him*, I tell myself, *Jesus will protect him.* Just like He's

80

protected me so far.

No matter what condition my father is in, I can't leave campus without supplies. I'll need food and water and maybe even a weapon. I can find all of that at the Academic Campus.

Everyone who's decided to tag along has been broken into groups. I'm standing with three students from Hope House, two from Green House, and one from Hot House—that's the dorm dedicated to the culinary club, it's right next door to Green House. The other two groups are entirely made up of students from Kappa Pi and the Omega Zeta Chi Sorority. They look so different from the rest of us. The bulky athletes of Kappa Pi and the cutthroat beauties of Omega Zeta. As they stand in the parking lot outside the café, I feel like I'm looking at warriors and hunters versus the rest of us.

Green House is filled with botany enthusiasts who look like overly tanned nerds. Most of Hot House students are slightly out of shape, gorging themselves on the tasty food they cook each night. And Hope House has kids who are all confused and shaken by the sudden turn of events. A bunch of Christian kids grouping up to go loot a college campus? You're better off sending us out to sell Girl Scout cookies. I don't even know what *I'm* doing here. But I'm not going back to my dorm without something to show for myself.

God raised warriors too, I remind myself, thinking of King David and all the fierce soldiers who fought with him in the Bible. I am nothing like them. But I can pretend.

An Asian guy from Green House has taken lead of our group. He stands in front with his hands on his hips as he listens to an Omega Zeta girl issue instructions to everyone. Phil is the guy's name and he's got pit stains and red flaming cheeks; his jet-black bangs stick to his forehead, and he swipes

81

at them as he listens and nods. We're all sticky and sweaty.

I gave up the heavy goth makeup two days ago since we didn't have much water for me to wash it off every day. Right now, I'm bare faced with my thick hair braided back into a single plait that trails down to the middle of my back. I ditched all the chains and zippers in favor of a pair of black jean shorts and a black tee. I'm still wearing Doc Martens, but this pair isn't platformed. They're plain white combat boots I've had for years, creased from wear, and decorated with plenty of permanent marker doodles I made while I was bored in class. I'm sure I look awful and sweaty like everyone else but at least I'm comfortable. I can't imagine trying to fight or loot in my usual getup.

Once the instructions are done, Phil turns to face us. He looks nervous, licking his dry lips as he repeats everything the Omega Zeta girl just said. "We're heading in through the main entrance and spreading out so we can search as many places as possible in the allotted time."

"How long are we talking?" asks a girl behind me, her name is Tiana and she's the only person who came from Hot House.

"We've got twenty minutes," Phil answers. He pushes his glasses up the bridge of his nose. "I know that's not long, but we don't know if other students are here or not. We don't want to spend any more time here than necessary. So get in, grab whatever you can, and get out."

"Simple enough," says Tiana. "But how will we know when twenty minutes has passed?"

Phil glances at me. "Can you keep track of time?"

I open my mouth to answer but my voice gets caught in my throat. It's at this moment that I realize *everyone* is looking at me, not just my little group.

"Yes," I say, and I instinctively reach for the pocket watch tucked in my back pocket. I pull it out and look at the time. "I'll whistle once twenty minutes are up."

The leader of Omega Zeta steps forward; she's tall and pretty. Instead of looking flushed by the heat, she's got a permanent blush on both her cheeks that makes her look like a living Barbie doll—right down to the pink ribbon keeping her blonde hair tied back in a long ponytail. Her blue eyes sharpen on me as she crosses her arms over her very generous breasts. "Do not lose track of time, Freshy, got it?"

Freshy, I guess that's some sort of insult for freshmen students but I'm not the least bit offended. I just want to get this over with.

"Yeah. Got it," I say.

"Maybe she should wait by the door."

I recognize the voice right away, and before I can even search for him, I see Caesar shuffle to the front of the Kappa Pi boys. He looks right at me and then his gaze shifts to the Omega Zeta girl. Unsurprisingly, her sharp expression seems to melt once she sees him. He tends to have that effect on people.

"We've only got one timer, Delilah," Caesar says.

Delilah—the angry sorority chick—smiles when he says her name and I immediately know she's going to agree with whatever he suggests, though he explains himself anyway.

"We can't afford to let anything happen to her. Mya should wait by the entrance and track the time for us. The rest of us can handle the looting on our own."

Anger burns through me. I'm not stupid. I know why Caesar is really doing this—he thinks I can't handle this—but I don't speak up. If I say something, we'll get into an argument, and I don't want that to happen in front of everyone. I just feel so pathetic being told to wait by the door. Still, I can't ignore the genuine look of concern that flashes in Julie's eyes when he glances at me again.

I look away.

"Caesar is right," Delilah announces. "Stay by the door and whistle once time is up. That's your only job, Freshy, so do *not* screw it up."

"Yeah. Okay."

Everyone moves into the campus café in silence. There's a bell on the door that rings each time it opens and closes, with all of us walking in single file, it dings endlessly until I'm the last one standing outside. I catch the door and slip in with everyone else, leaning against it as a shiver runs down my spine.

The place has been trashed. The tables are overturned, chairs smashed or tossed aside with the legs removed. All the windows have been covered by what look like sheets or simply clothes tied together, not to mention the mess of trash all over the floor. The booths against the wall have been ripped out and piled up to block the entrance to the kitchen. The place looks like an abandoned warzone.

We'd already suspected the other campus might have come here to loot before us, but we didn't suspect they would tear the place to pieces. I can only hope there's something left in the kitchen. I actually hold my breath when one of the Kappa Pi guys climbs over the stacked booths and then hoots with joy. There must be food left inside.

I don't know why the other students trashed the lounge area but left plenty of food behind but there's no time to dwell on it. My friends immediately shove the booths aside and climb into the kitchen to collect whatever they can. I can see students scattered throughout the two-story cafeteria; a group of Kappa Pi guys wheels a cart of canned goods out of the kitchen with smiles on their faces. It looks like a bunch of cans of spaghetti sauce and massive cans of black beans. I'm not excited about whatever concoction we'll have to eat made from canned spaghetti sauce and beans but it's better than nothing.

There's also water. Some kids from my group are emptying the warm fridges together. I can see bottled water, iced tea, and other soft drinks. The warm sodas will taste awful, but it'll help ward off dehydration if/when the water runs out.

"Hey…"

I turn to find Julie jogging over. Even though he got me put on timer duty, I smile at him. "Hey yourself," I say back.

"I found this," he says, offering me something.

When I glance down, I can't stop myself from smiling. Julie found a Daisy Bar! It's a chocolate bar stuffed with raisins and walnuts, then topped with dried daisy petals. Yes … I said dried *daisy petals*. Some flowers are edible, and they actually go well with chocolate! It's not as bad as it sounds, I promise. In fact, the petals give the bar an amazing floral flavor that instantly makes the world a better place on the first bite.

Julie hates Daisy Bars, but he used to bring me one whenever he rode his bike to visit me after I moved. I can't believe he remembers how much I love these.

I take the bar and it squishes between my fingers, hot and melted from the Arizona heat. I don't mind. In fact, I'm sure the melted chocolate will taste delicious.

"Thank you," I beam, resisting the urge to open the bar right there.

Julie pokes me in the forehead and winks. "I gotta get back to scavenging. I just wanted you to have that since we missed our breakfast date before."

It wasn't a *date*, but I don't say that—not that it matters anyway; Julie's already jogging away by the time I've tucked the Daisy Bar into my back pocket. He joins a group of Kappa Pi guys who are raiding the cabinets for boxed dinners but that Omega Zeta girl from before calls him over to join her instead.

I watch as Delilah points to a cabinet too high for her to reach. Like the good guy that he is, Julie stretches his incredibly tall body out to grab the item for her. Delilah's eyes trespass every part of him as he moves, riding the curves of his muscular arms, roving over his toned chest, even glancing down at his lithe hips and tapered waist. It's amazing... Even covered in sweat and in desperate need of a shower, Caesar still manages to hold the attention of all the prettiest girls around.

I'm not surprised. Caesar has always been popular—how could he not be? He's sky-high tall with broad shoulders and a lean runner's body. Plus, he's always happy. I don't think there's ever been a time Julie wasn't smiling. He's smiling now as he hands Delilah a box of cereal. The smile is so wide it makes his cheeks bunch and his eyes crinkle. She plays with the pink ribbon in her hair as she grins back, stupidly convinced his smile is just for her.

He's like this with everyone. Kind, happy, like a burning ray of sunshine drawing in everyone around him, lighting them up. I don't blame Delilah for being attracted to him. Sometimes I wonder why we never tried anything romantic.

I've thought about it. But it's hard to think of Julie that way when I've seen him naked as a skinny kid swimming in a lake during summer break. Plus, Julie loves the attention he gets. He leans into that sorority girl and says something only she can hear—he's so close, I half expect him to kiss her. I wouldn't have been surprised if he had. Julie is popular and he knows it.

There's always been some party he got invited to, always some girl texting him, always someone or something between us. I can't imagine him with me any more than I can truly see him settling with the pretty blonde he's giggling with now. He doesn't belong to one person, with that sort of smile, it never seemed fair to try to hold on.

I pry my vision from Julie and glance around the room. Some guys have started approaching the main entrance with their supplies, so I have to step aside to let them out into the parking lot. That stupid bell dings and echoes through the cafeteria as I hold the door for a trail of students, one of those students happens to be Adrian Nikols.

I don't know what I expect from Adrian when he walks by, but I *don't* expect him to act like I don't exist. He is a stone statue passing by, carrying a case of bottled drinks as two other guys walk with armfuls of bagged potato chips and other unhealthy snacks from the checkout counter. The air between us does not electrify with Adrian's signature rage, instead, it feels cold as ice, and I cannot help but shiver.

Shaking my head, I quickly turn back around and force myself to focus on something else. As I hold the doors open, I look up to scan the second floor and I pause. There are students upstairs, but I don't recognize them.

There's at least a dozen of them, crouched and peering over the railing as my friends collect food and water. Some of them are squinting, others are ducking so only the tops of their heads are visible. That's when it hits me—*they're hiding.*

A whistle pierces the air, but it doesn't come from me. It comes from the second floor, and it's followed by a sudden shriek as the students upstairs hop over the railing and descend

87

the stairs. They're all screaming, running, charging toward the kitchen. Some of them are shirtless with paint covering their torsos. Others are wearing tattered-looking clothes and I immediately recognize them as students from the opposite campus.

Now it all makes sense. The broken chairs and overturned tables. The covered windows and the booths torn from the walls to block the entrance to the kitchen. These guys didn't trash the cafeteria and leave. They broke in and set up a base— a base that we've just been caught stealing from.

The crazy students rush our group all at once. It's immediately evident that we are not prepared. I watch in horror as Phil is charged by two guys; one of them is carrying a tennis racket, the other wields a saucepan—they attack him like he's a criminal. His screaming fills the cafeteria, but it's nothing compared to the frightened shrieks of the sorority girls. They scatter and run for cover as the enemy students descend the stairs and pour into the lounge and kitchen area. They carry makeshift weapons; baseball bats, the legs of chairs, and someone even starts throwing rocks. Meanwhile, the only thing my group can do is cower or run.

Panic burns inside my chest, it's hot and unbearable and almost bubbles from my mouth in a terrified scream. But I swallow my fears when I see Julie fighting back. He's only got his fists, but he's so big it doesn't matter. Two guys challenge him at once and he manages to hold his own. That's when I realize I've got to do something. He can't be the only one to put his foot down. But what can *I* do? I don't have a weapon and I'm not 6'5—I can't fight two crazy guys at once. But I can leave.

The thought blooms in the back of my head as I grip the

handle of the entrance doors. I'm not planning to abandon my friends—I plan to get help. Adrian and at least ten other guys are loading up supplies in the parking lot. I can run out and tell them what's going on. I can tell them to hurry and get the food back to our campus before we're all caught.

I quickly turn to dash out the door—but someone grabs me before I can even get it open. I scream, but a hand clamps over my mouth, and all I hear is ringing in my ears when something hits me hard in the back of the head. My eyelids flutter as I try to remain conscious, blinking away the blurriness in my vision. Eventually, I realize the ringing isn't in my head. It's the bell to the door, dinging madly because I'm still holding the door handle as my attacker tries to drag me away.

He jerks me backward one more step and my grip slips away. The bell chimes one last time and tears fill my eyes as I realize I'm not going anywhere anymore. Except wherever this man is taking me.

I can feel his breath on my neck as he pulls me away, it's hot and wet and makes my skin crawl. "Hold still…" he says in a rasp and that burning panic from before ignites in my chest again.

Except this time, it boils into rage.

I kick and throw my legs up, trying to knock us off balance, but the man is larger than me and his grip is ironclad. He's got one arm wrapped around my middle while his other hand is clamped tightly over my mouth. I can't even breathe from how hard he's holding me, but that just makes me fight even harder. Even wilder.

He curses as I kick and writhe in his grasp. "Get her legs!" he shouts to someone.

Another guy appears, he's shirtless and sweaty, wearing

nothing but a smirk as he reaches for my legs. I want to kick him—I even manage to get my foot in the air, but I'm so weak now. I still can't breathe. Little black dots swim in my vision. When I kick the man in front of me, he actually laughs as he catches my ankle and lifts.

Together, the two guys carry me backwards, away from the door. Away from any help I might have gotten. Instinctively, I scan the cafeteria as I'm dragged toward a back hall. My eyes are like a laser locking on to Julie. He's far away, busy fighting two guys with a bent piece of wood he's managed to grab. I can't scream for help. I can barely even breathe. But I don't give up. *God*, I pray inside... It's the last thing I hold on to as my vision clouds and the room fades away.

11

Adrian

It's so hot out I want to scream. It's always hot in Arizona but this feels like a punishment. I'm sweating from every single part of my body. It's awful. I know my shirt is sticking to me, but I'm not worried about anyone seeing my scars because this tee is navy blue. Even though it's soaked through, it hasn't turned transparent the way a white shirt would. My secret is still safe. For now.

"I'd give anything for some *cold* water," Memphis says as he opens a bottle from one of the packs we looted. He drinks half of it in three gulps and then passes the rest to Bunny who's waiting beside him.

"At least we found water," the midget says, desperately drinking the rest.

I don't respond. I hate Bunny.

Memphis opens a bag of Doritos and starts eating. "We got a good load of supplies. This should last us a little while."

I doubt it, especially not with these two eating through the food already. There are two other guys sharing a dry box of cereal and a sorority chick shoving trail mix into her mouth while her friend chugs down her second water. We're supposed to be loading up the supplies we looted, not enjoying them ourselves.

Yes, we've got two wagons full of food now, but at this rate, only half will make it back to campus.

I wipe sweat from my forehead as I turn to scold my dumb classmates, but the chime of that stupid bell at the door cuts me off. It's so loud and annoying, and it won't stop ringing. Like someone's yanking on the door. Irritated, I turn to see who's playing around at the cafeteria entrance, and my jaw goes slack.

It's Mya. But she isn't playing games—it looks like she needs help. Like she's holding on to the door for dear life, and when she yanks it open one more time, I hear more than the bell ringing. There's screaming coming from the café.

Memphis hears it too. He steps beside me and stares at the cafeteria. "What's going on in there?" he asks in his southern drawl.

I don't reply. I'm not even aware that I'm moving until I feel a heavy hand grip my shoulder and tug me to a halt. "Hold on!" Memphis says firmly.

I whirl around and shove him off. "She needs help!" I shout.

Memphis blinks at me. "Who needs help?"

I glance back at the door, but Mya's gone. For a second, I wonder if I just imagined that entire scene. I'm hot, tired, hungry, and dehydrated. I could be hallucinating. But something tells me that I'm not.

"There's something going on in the cafeteria," I tell

Memphis, walking back toward the door. "You heard the screaming too."

Before he can reply, I yank the door open. The bell chimes, but it's muffled by shrieks and wails and madness. Hell has descended upon the café. Everyone everywhere is fighting. I can't even tell who's winning, and I don't have time to figure it out. Mya was at the door moments ago. She needed help—

I suck in a little gasp as I turn and see two guys carrying her away. I have no idea who they are, but it doesn't take a genius to guess what they want. They move through the dark hallway, away from the fighting, and shove open a door before dragging Mya inside. I immediately run after them.

It takes a few strides to reach the door they went through. It's a men's bathroom—not one of those privacy, single stall rooms—that means there's no lock, so I have no trouble kicking the door in. It whacks the wall with a startling *thud!* gaining the attention of both the guys who are about to die.

They have Mya on the grimy floor; one guy holding her down while the other crouches between her legs. She isn't naked, but the second guy has his hands on her shorts. They're halfway down her thighs, like he was in the middle of yanking them down when I barged in.

Just in time.

Mya screams, it's weak and reedy, but there's a fire in her eyes that holds all the strength she doesn't have anymore. That fire burns through her, engulfing me, setting every part of my mind ablaze.

I don't attack them for Mya, I do it because they're disgusting pigs.

I think of my little sister as I grab the crouching guy by his stupid little ponytail and drag him backwards away from Mya.

93

I wonder what monsters like this would do to an innocent child in the city—and as I realize the ugly answer, I let out a growl of anger and ram my fist into Ponytail's face. He screams, but it's cut short by another punch. His skinny arms fly up to defend himself, but I've still got him by his hair. He isn't going anywhere.

One more punch silences him, but I feel like it's not enough. I want to break his neck, his hands, his knees. I want him to bleed for what he was about to do, but I don't get my vengeance just yet. The other guy has abandoned Mya, rushing over to help his friend. He slugs me hard across the jaw and I stumble to the side. Another hit rocks me, but I'm granted a moment of relief when Mya kicks the guy in the back of his knee. She's still on the floor, but she's conscious enough to fight. Fueled by a rage that matches my own.

The guy's knee buckles beneath him, and he yelps in pain and surprise. I don't hesitate to take advantage of this sweet moment. As he falls to the floor, I grab his head and shove his forehead down into my knee. There's an audible crack that makes Mya gasp. I'm shocked too, but I don't care. I hope he's dead.

Mya blinks up at me in silence. There are two guys lying on the floor around us, neither of us knows if they're dead or alive. I feel numb as I step over the guy in front of me.

"Are you okay?"

Mya's eyes are wide, they flicker down her body—at her jean shorts still yanked down to her thighs. She lets out a whimper as she reaches for them.

"Did they hurt you?" I ask, crouching beside her, and she snaps at me.

"Don't come closer!"

But it's too late. I'm right beside her now, and I can see the big wet stain on her pink cotton panties. Realization hits me the same time the smell does.

She wet herself.

I don't blame her. We both know what was about to go down in here. She has every right to be afraid—afraid enough to pee her pants. But that doesn't make this any less embarrassing.

I glance away as Mya tugs her shorts up and stands. We both ignore the puddle of urine on the floor between us. "T-Thank you," she says, looking everywhere but at me.

"You're welcome," I say back.

And then we stand there in an awkward silence because I have no idea what else to say.

"We should get out there. They need our help," Mya tells me.

Her words bring everything into focus. I'm suddenly aware of all the shouting still going on outside the bathroom. I'm aware of how hot it is in this room. I'm even aware of the footsteps in the hall, rushing right toward us.

The bathroom door flies open the next second, and Mya and I both whirl around to see who's barged in.

It's Julius.

My mood immediately blackens, but he barely notices me. His eyes are glued to Mya, then his gaze breaks when he notices the guys on the floor. That's when a wild, panicked look takes over his face, and he rushes to his childhood friend.

"Mya!" He pulls her into a hug, but it's awkward with the beam of wood he's holding in his hand. The plank is bent and has cracks splintered through it. I wonder if he got it that way or made the splinters himself from beating someone with it.

"I saw them grab you," Julius says to Mya, "but I couldn't get away—"

"It's fine," I interject. "I was here."

Julius glares at me, but the look doesn't last long. "Thank you," he says, and I can tell he means it.

"I didn't do it for you. Anyone would have helped."

"Are you guys still fighting out there?" Mya asks.

Julius closes his eyes for a second. "We're retreating. It's crazy, Mya. I have no idea how this happened. I have no idea *why* it happened—"

"People are hungry," I say, annoyed. "They're trying to hold on to the last of the supplies. They're trying to survive."

Mya scowls as she gestures to the guys on the floor. "Were they trying to *survive* when they grabbed me?"

She has a point.

"We've got to get out of here before things get worse," Julius wisely interjects. "There's an emergency exit not far from here."

"Lead the way," I say.

Outside, the chaos has died down somewhat, but I can still hear the grunts and groans of injured people. Someone is sobbing nearby, and further away there's a voice shrieking nonstop. I don't even want to guess what happened to him.

"This is awful," Mya whispers.

Julius glances back at her and extends his hand which she immediately takes. My stomach starts to hurt. They walk like that through the dark hallway, gingerly stepping around broken chairs and dismantled desks while I follow along in silence. The corridor is dark and creepy, but we move swiftly and quietly, ignoring the terrible wailing from the cafeteria.

After turning a corner, we find the exit Julius mentioned.

Sunlight spills into the hall as he opens the door, but no one moves for a moment. All three of us are frozen stiff, staring at the hallway around us. It was difficult to see in the dark with no lights or electricity, but with the afternoon sun falling onto the walls and floor, we have a good look at just how messed up the campus café is now.

The walls are stained red. There's red smeared on the floor, and other mysterious stains I can't name. It could be blood, but it could also be ketchup, tomato sauce, or even paint. There's no real way to tell but it's disturbing, nonetheless.

"What the heck…" Julius breathes, eyes growing wide as he turns in a circle, still gripping that wooden beam.

Mya holds his other hand; she squeezes it and gently pulls him toward the door. "Let's go. Please."

I couldn't agree more, so I step forward and shove past them both. The air outside is hot and sticky but it's so much fresher than the cafeteria. I actually close my eyes for a few seconds and just stand in the parking lot taking deep breaths.

"Is everyone okay?" Julius asks, shutting the emergency exit door behind him.

Mya nods and clasps her hands in front of herself, no doubt trying to hide the stain on the front of her shorts. I wonder if Julius knows what'd almost happened. I wonder if he can smell the urine on her clothes and legs. If he does, he makes no mention of it. Instead, he takes Mya's nod as confirmation that everything's dandy, and steps to the side to peer around the corner.

"Looks like the coast is clear. We should head back now."

"What about the supplies?" Mya asks. "What about the others? Has everyone made it out?"

"Delilah and a few others ran out as soon as they could,"

Julius explains. "Everyone is split up now. The best thing we can do is get out of here in one piece and hope the others make it back to our dorms."

"He's right." I nod. "We can't afford to wait around. It's safer to just get out of here while we can."

Mya looks hesitant but agrees with a forced smile. "Okay."

Julius says, "Let's stick together. It shouldn't take us long to get back."

He walks ahead of us without looking back, keeping watch left and right as he scans the parking lot around us. That wooden beam is gripped tightly in his hands, even from behind I can see the way his shoulders are tense, like he's a coiled snake ready to attack. I'm just as pensive. At this point, anything can happen. If it wasn't clear before, it's painfully obvious now. We're on our own. The laws no longer apply to Cross North campus. This could be the end of us.

"They're gone," Julius's voice breaks into my thoughts and I look up to find the wagons out front are missing. I'm not sure if that's good or bad, but we can't afford to stay here trying to figure it out.

"I left the wagons with Memphis and Bunny," I say. "They probably heard the fighting and got out of here while they could."

Or they were caught and beaten to a pulp.

"Let's hope that's the case," Julius grunts, then he turns to leave. "Let's go, guys."

We walk in silence, though our minds are anything but quiet. Beside me, Mya trips over a rock and stumbles. I reach out to help her and she sighs. "I'm sorry."

"You're good."

"I mean, I'm sorry for getting angry earlier." She glances

sideways at me. "What you said was true. They're trying to survive. Just like us."

"That doesn't give them the right to hurt you."

She nods. Chews her lip. "But they didn't hurt me. Because you were there."

I don't really know what to say now.

"Thank you again."

"You fought too," I remind her. "And you'll have to keep fighting, Mya. It's only going to get worse from here."

"I don't understand what's happening. One week ago, we were just college kids. Now we're fighting for our lives."

"That's what hunger does. That's what disaster does."

"It changes you," Mya mutters, but I shake my head.

"It reveals the person you've always been."

She looks over at me, a worried look in her eye. "What about us? Our campus is nothing like those students."

"Because we had enough supplies. We had you guys— Hope House."

She knows it's true. Without the Christian dorm and all their canned goods for the food drive they have every year; we'd be starving and mad just like those freaks in the cafeteria. The only real difference between us and them is another meal or two. Give it a few days, we'll be losing our minds as well.

"Do you think it's worse in the city?" Mya's question almost catches me off guard.

I grind my teeth together. I'd been trying to avoid thinking of the city since this whole mess began. I was supposed to leave days ago, but I put it off for Nobles's sake. Then I realized I couldn't leave without more supplies. But now I don't even know if we managed to get away with enough supplies to spare a trip back home.

99

I grunt as I walk, trying to control my anger. "I don't know what the city's like. But I plan to find out soon."

"You still want to leave?"

"Yes," I answer immediately. "And I'm not letting anyone stop me this time."

"I don't want to stop you," Mya says, shocking me enough that I snap my head to the side to stare at her. She looks me right in the eye. "I want to go with you."

12

Mya

The campus decides Hope House will hold the supplies. The guys' dorm has more storage space in their basement and their kitchen is set up like an actual soup kitchen, so they keep the food and water. The other supplies like lighters, kitchen tools, and even knives are passed around for anyone who wants to stay armed and ready. Most of the kids who went to the cafeteria grab the kitchen knives and meat cleavers. We're the only ones who know how bad things truly are.

Despite the trouble we faced earlier, we're still able to smile as James lights the Hope House grill and starts cooking for everyone. We got into an awful fight. Some kids were really hurt, someone even died. But the worst is behind us now.

James looks so comfortable on the grill, everyone else around us is relaxed too. No one's really talking, we're all just sitting, waiting for food. After a few minutes of silent grilling, Kassandra starts passing water bottles around. We have to share with someone, so everyone starts to buddy up.

I immediately scan the crowd for Julie. He's in the middle of a group of students, smiling and talking like this isn't the end of the world. I recognize some of the guys from the frat house but there are a ton of others I've never seen before. Despite the crowd, Julie's eyes find mine across the lawn and I hold up my bottle, silently asking if he wants to share. At the same time, Delilah pushes her way to the center of the crowd and practically shoves her bottle into his face. He laughs and takes it, glancing up to give me a sheepish grin before he enjoys a swig.

I sigh at his silent apology.

"I'll share with you."

I turn to find Jupiter smiling at me, both hands on her hips. "All the guys here haven't bathed in days. You don't wanna share with him anyway." She snorts as I pass her my bottle.

"*None* of us have showered in days."

"Yeah, but guys are extra gross. So it's worse for them."

I can't help but laugh. "I'm glad all the chaos hasn't changed you, Jupe."

Jupiter gives me a serious face and that's when I realize her smile is a front. She drops her gaze and swallows so hard I can hear her gulp. "What happened out there?" she asks, fidgeting with the water bottle cap. "I heard it was crazy."

"It was worse than crazy."

She blinks, waiting for more details. But I don't want to talk about this right now. I've barely swallowed the events myself. Images of those guys flash in my mind's eye and I rapidly blink away the tears I feel pricking the backs of my eyes. I can feel that guy's hand clamped over my mouth again. I can feel his breath on my neck. My skin begins to crawl.

"Just be thankful you didn't go," I say, shocked when my

102

voice comes out as a whisper.

Jupiter steps closer. "Was it that bad? Is it true someone really died? Do you know who it was?"

The only reaction I have is a frown, and I can't stop myself from turning and walking away. It happens without me thinking about it. One minute, I'm staring at my roommate as she asks me questions, and the next, my feet are moving and I'm leaving her there in stunned silence.

"Mya!" she calls, catching up to me. "I'm sorry. I didn't mean to—"

"I just need a moment," I cut her off and pick up my pace, thankful when the sound of her footsteps ceases. It isn't her fault, and I don't blame her for her curiosity, but I can't talk about this right now. It happened a few *hours* ago. I need time.

A heavy sigh blows between my lips as I walk through the thick grass of Hope House's backyard. Despite the darkness of the evening creeping in, I easily find my way to the stone bench in the back and take a seat.

I stare out at the night around me, listening to the crickets begin their songs, closing my eyes as a hot breeze blows over my bare arms. I'm still wearing the clothes I had on at the cafeteria. I've seen movies when women are assaulted, and they immediately go home and cry in the shower. I can't shower and I'm trying hard to preserve my last few clean pairs of underwear. This feels like a pile of awful events.

But I should be thankful. Nothing happened. Adrian saved me before it could get any worse. So then, why do I feel like crying?

I take a deep breath and wrap my arms around my middle as I feel the tears coming. "God..." I whisper, and that's all I get to say before I notice movement from the corner of my eye. My stomach knots up when I recognize the figure walking toward me.

It's Adrian Nikols.

He inclines his head, but the movement is hard and angry, like he jerks his head downward instead of nods. "I didn't mean to interrupt."

I blink. Then sniffle. "Um…"

"I saw you leave the crowd earlier."

"You followed me?"

He doesn't speak for a moment, then his voice comes out as gentle as the wind that dances between us. "I wanted to check on you."

Of course he did. He's the one who saved me earlier. He's the only one here who knows how I feel right now. Julie might have an idea—he saw me get dragged away and he barged into the bathroom afterward, but he's busy with Delilah and all of his friends who are staring at him with stars in their eyes.

"I'm fine," I say.

Adrian nods and turns to leave, but I call out to him for reasons I cannot explain.

"Wait…"

He turns back with his white-blonde eyebrows pinched together. "Yes?"

"Um… thank you. For earlier."

"You already thanked me, Mya."

I reach into my back pocket and pull out the Daisy Bar Julie gave me earlier. I have no idea if Adrian even likes chocolate, and I know Julie will probably be ticked that I gave away his gift to me, but this is all I've got to offer.

"Take this. As a gift."

Adrian stares at the bar before he reaches for it with a tiny little grin on his face—the left corner of his mouth tugged upward just enough to flash a dimple. The sight of it makes me smile too.

"I love these things," he says.

My heart soars. "You do?"

"I mean, it's weird to eat chocolate and flowers, but yeah. They taste good. My mom used to—" he cuts himself off suddenly, staring at the bar... Squeezing it.

"Adrian?"

He clears his throat and shoves the chocolate back toward me. "Take it."

"But I gave it to you."

"I don't want it."

When I don't make a move to take the Daisy Bar back, he steps forward and shoves it into my hands. "Hey!" I say, grabbing his hand. The gesture jerks him to a stop and we stand there staring at each other. Well, I'm staring at Adrian, but he's looking down at our hands clasped together.

I awkwardly pull away, but I notice that he holds on to the Daisy Bar.

"It's your gift," I say.

Adrian looks up at me. "You wanna give me a gift? Get me a bag of supplies so I can get out of here."

He's wanted to leave since the lights first went out.

"I can't," I say. "Hope House took in all the supplies, but James and Kassandra already have everything portioned out. They're assigning people to keep inventory and guard the food tomorrow."

"Volunteer for the job," he says urgently. "You can grab a couple things for me—"

"That would be stealing, Adrian."

"They're our supplies!" he snaps. "We fought for those. I deserve a few things."

"I know, but—"

"I thought you said you wanted to leave with me." He steps closer, towering over me with his great height. "I have a family that needs me. I've waited too long already. Don't you want to find your mom and dad?"

I wince at his words. "It's just my dad now."

The silence that hangs between us is nearly insufferable, until Adrian breaks it with a weak apology.

"I-I'm sorry. I remember your mother being sick—"

"It's fine," I cut him off. I couldn't blame him for not knowing. My mother got sick in the middle of my freshman year, but I didn't move away until my sophomore year. Adrian is three years older than me, by the time I moved away, he was already in college. He has no idea my mother passed when I was a junior.

"Don't you want to see your father?" Adrian asks me. His voice is gentle, prodding, like he isn't sure if this is safe territory to traverse.

It isn't.

"I want to see my father more than anything."

"Then why—"

"Because it's dangerous," I say angrily. "Don't you remember what happened just hours ago? If this is what's going on at a college university, then I can't imagine the city. Or the roads we'll have to travel to get there."

"Mya…" he blinks at me, "we have to try. We can't just abandon our families."

He's right. I know he is. But… I can't stop thinking of what happened earlier. I can't stop feeling his hot breath on the back

106

of my neck. I won't let that happen to me again. Not ever.

It's safe here on campus. It's safe near Hope House.

"Adrian—" I start to say but he cuts me off by stepping closer, right in my personal space. It's so sudden, I take a big step back, but I whack the back of my leg on the stone bench and suck in a painful gasp.

Adrian reaches for me, his large hand going to my waist to keep me upright. "I've got you," he says in a murmur, and I know he isn't just talking about this moment right now.

We blink at each other. In the ashen moonlight, I can just make out the cool grey of his eyes, the line of his square jaw.

"I'll protect you out there," Adrian says softly.

This is the kindest I've ever seen him, the gentlest I've ever heard him speak. Every other time I've encountered Adrian, he's been angry and sullen, on the verge of screaming or beating someone. Tonight, he's different. Tonight, he is a man I've never seen before—and I have no idea how to react. But before I can figure out how to handle what's happening, Adrian pulls away.

He wipes a hand through his hair and presses his lips together. "Sorry. Just think about it, okay?"

I nod dumbly, watching in silence as he turns and walks back toward the front of the house. I wait a few moments before I follow. I don't want to bump into him again, but I also don't want anyone to see us both leaving the backyard late at night. We're in the middle of a crisis, I'm positive everyone is more distracted with their food right now, but I don't want to take any chances. Besides, as I cross into the front yard, I realize this crisis has impacted some more than others.

Julie is still standing in the middle of his crowd of friends, but now his smile is wider, and his arm is draped over Delilah's shoulders. Even from my distance, I recognize the lazy look on his face immediately. It's a look I've seen a lot at house parties we snuck off to in high school, and the bottle in his hand is a dead giveaway too.

Julie is drunk.

We had to fight for our lives to get a couple cases of water. Where on earth did he find alcohol?

Just as the question pops into my head, Julie glances up and finds me. He raises the bottle and shouts, "Memphis had some vodka left! Come try, Mya!"

I shake my head, embarrassed. Mercifully, James decides this is the perfect time to shut things down. We might be living in an apocalypse, but he's still going to hold Hope House to the standard it was established under. That means there's no alcohol allowed on the premises. Not in the dorm or even on the front lawn.

James fans the grill as he tells Julie to head home. "Dinner is over, Caesar. If you wanna party, take it back to the frat house."

A very crooked smile slithers across Julie's face. He winks as he says, "Will do, preacher man. Frat house is bigger anyway." He says something in Delilah's ear that makes her giggle. And then, like I'm not even there anymore, Julie walks away and takes the crowd, the blonde, and the bottle with him.

13

Caesar

The greatest enemy will hide in the last place you would ever look...
Those are the words of Julius Caesar. I have never understood
them better until now.

I stand in my room, staring out the window beyond the
rows of dorm houses that line the neighborhood, past the
soccer field in the distance. I'm looking toward the Academic
Campus, wondering what the heck happened yesterday.
Wondering *why* it happened.

It's been a week since the power went out. Two days since
the water was poisoned. How did we go from normal—
friendly—college students to barbaric enemies battling over
bottled tea and cans of beans?

I knew some of the kids in that café. I got sucker punched
by a guy I sat behind in Bio 101 freshmen year. We weren't
friends, but we'd never been unfriendly enough to warrant this.
I'd beaten him off of me with that stupid stick I found. I don't

even remember grabbing it. It was suddenly in my hands, and I was fighting like I'd lost my mind. And it seemed like the fighting didn't stop for hours.

A kid from our campus died in the cafeteria. We didn't realize it until we made it back and took a head count yesterday evening. That's when things changed for everyone. That's when realization set in. This is real. We're in danger—serious danger. And danger does not discriminate, it does not play favorites. We're all up for grabs now.

"North Campus is our enemy," Coach Noble had announced once word had gone around about the student death. Some guy named Phill—I've no idea who he was, but he suddenly felt like a brother, knowing he'd been on our side during that brawl.

Coach Noble had paused to stare at the grass; we'd met on the soccer field last night, angry, confused, scared, bitter. No one knew what to do, but Coach took charge and united us.

His words ignited a fire in our hearts. In a single sentence we went from dorm buddies to battle buddies—and we'd just identified our enemy. This didn't feel like college anymore. This didn't even feel like real life, but it was happening whether we were ready or not.

"Supplies are low," Coach Noble had continued with a pained look on his face. "People are desperate. We need to stick together from now on." Heads nodded around the large group. "We share the supplies we managed to secure. If anyone has more food or water, then speak up. Let's help each other out. There are students out there who are willing to fight for what we've got. We can't afford to be divided. So, we'll unite on this. Our campus is a brotherhood—a family—now. Understood?"

The answer was unanimous. "Yes, sir!"

Hope House took the supplies in, and James started up the grill immediately. In that moment, we truly felt like a brotherhood. I can't even stop myself from smiling as I think of it now. We all sat on the ground or the porch steps with plates in our hands, eating with our fingers like we were at some bonfire tribal meeting.

We enjoyed an awful soup made of spaghetti sauce with beans and spam stirred into the mix. It was salty and gave Bunny the runs, but at least it was something to eat. It felt like a victory meal. We'd gotten in over our heads for a moment, but in the end, we came out on top. We had the supplies. We had more food than the day before. And we had each other. The power was still out, and the food was awful, but nobody complained because we'd fought for that food. We'd earned that nasty meal. And we had the battle scars to prove it.

Some of us were afraid. Some of us were worried. But there were a chosen few like me who'd felt electrified by the fight. I had suddenly come alive in this chaos. If I could go back, I'd do it all again. And I'd celebrate harder at our victory.

When Memphis brought out his stash and passed around his bottle, I felt like a king. From the chaos of this meltdown, we built a brotherhood of order. From the ashes of the burning campus rose a kingdom. We can make a life here. We can survive.

There's noise over my shoulder. I turn from the window to find Delilah rolling over in bed. She's still half-asleep, her blonde hair falling over the edge of my mattress. It's long enough to sweep over the floor, the ends of her silky strands covered in dust. The pink ribbon she wore last night is only partially tied now, tangled in her thick waves. I remember

111

yanking it out when we stumbled into my room. We were both drunk and laughing and whispering crap I don't even remember. But her hair had looked so pretty, I'd wanted to wind my hand in it and grab a fistful. Delilah had yelled at me, but I'd silenced her with a kiss and the rest is history.

Yes, the power is out and madness has taken over, but that doesn't mean I can't enjoy one night with a pretty girl. It wasn't the greatest time of my life. But the ecstasy I felt last night was far better than the fear I'd endured before then.

I'm not going back to fear.

Delilah groans again. "Wake up," I say in a raspy morning voice.

Her blonde lashes flutter as she opens her eyes and blinks at me. I can tell she's hungover from the droopy look on her face, but she offers her best smile. "Caesar."

"Delilah."

"Last night was fun."

I smile at her. "We should do it again sometime."

She gives me a sultry look and cocks an eyebrow, shifting to make room in the bed. "I'm game if you are."

Right now? Sheesh...

I shake my head. "I should talk to Coach Noble. There are some things I want to take care of this morning."

Delilah shrugs one shoulder and then climbs from the bed. She's stark naked but doesn't seem bothered so I don't bother to look away as she gathers her clothes and gets dressed. Once she snaps her bra closed, she looks up at me and winks. "I guess I'll see you around then."

"Guess so."

I wait until the door closes behind her before I return to my window. From my stance in my room, I can see Hope

House students walking down the street with plates and trays in their hands. It's just after sunrise which means it's breakfast time. Just as that thought crosses my mind, I see Mya walking up the driveway and my smile stretches.

I know she had a rough time yesterday. I'm not stupid, I saw those guys drag her away. I know what they intended to do, and I'd tried my hardest to get there but I just couldn't.

I'm not even a little religious, but a small part of me knows that God saved Mya yesterday. I can't explain the relief that washed through me when I barged into that bathroom and found Adrian already there. If his obsession with my best friend could serve any good in this world, it was at that moment.

None of us has spoken of it since. Not that I wanted to have a heart to heart with Adrian about it, and I certainly didn't want any details from Mya. But it feels weird going on like it never happened.

I hear a knock at my door, and I know it's Mya before she lets herself inside. There's a smile on her face, but it's frosty and forced. I'm too distracted by the plate in her hand to ask any questions.

"Breakfast?" I raise an eyebrow.

"Spam and crackers."

"Sounds delicious."

"Enjoy," she tells me with absolutely no enthusiasm.

I take the plate and eat in an awkward silence while she stands there with her arms crossed. After a moment, she clears her throat. "I saw Delilah on my way up."

I almost choke on my spam. When I look up, Mya's staring at my messy bed. Delilah's stupid pink ribbon is right there on my blanket. She must have left it behind. Normally, I'd think

113

the gesture was cute. I'd even stuff it in my back pocket and carry it with me so I'd have an excuse to stop by her dorm later to return it. But right now, with Mya staring at it, I want to snatch it up and burn it.

"She spent the night," I say in a quiet voice.

Mya just nods.

This isn't the first time I've made this sort of confession to her. There were lots of girls in high school, and my freshman year of college was wild. Mya's been my best friend long enough to know every dirty detail about me. We used to have these sorts of talks almost every weekend after a *long* Friday night. But something is different this time. Something makes me feel incredibly guilty.

Mya peels her gaze from my bed and gives me a brittle smile. "Coach Noble is offering coffee downstairs," she says, abruptly changing the subject. "He's only serving eight cups to preserve water. First come first serve."

"I'll pass."

Mya produces a bottle of water. "This is better anyway."

She watches as I drink half the bottle. I pass it to her once I'm done, and she frowns. "Don't tell me you're too old to still share drinks with me?" I smirk.

Her smile is just as crooked as mine when she takes the bottle. "I mean, it's been years."

"Mya, we're in the middle of an apocalypse."

"You don't know that," she says quietly, and I realize I've said the wrong thing. "Things might only be bad for *us*. The city could be in better shape."

Or worse shape. Two people are dead and dozens more are injured in just a week without food and water. I can't imagine what's going on in our hometown. There's a lot more people, a lot more weapons, a lot more frustration. Our isolation is our enemy but it's also our friend right now. The more people, the more problems. But I don't say any of this for Mya's sake. I know she's thinking of her father as she stares over my shoulder out my dorm window. He's older than my foster mom and a little kooky. Anyone would be worried for their parents but something about Dr. Brown makes me worry more for him than my own folks. Or maybe I just hate seeing Mya so downtrodden.

"Listen," I say awkwardly, "maybe we can visit Adrian's idea of leaving campus again. I'll talk to Coach Noble about it."

Mya doesn't respond, she's still staring over my shoulder. The look on her face isn't worried anymore, she looks confused—almost afraid.

I turn around. "What are you staring at?"

Just as the question leaves my mouth, I notice a figure moving down the sidewalk across the street. At first, I think it's a walking bush. But that doesn't make sense—and when I squint and step closer to the window, I realize it's a person. He's crouched and his body is painted in dark colors, so he blends in with the hazy morning shade still peeling back to let in the sunlight.

"What on earth—"

More figures appear on the sidewalk, stepping out from behind parked cars, fire hydrants, and streetlights. They walk single file, crouched, and moving quickly. Then, when they reach one of the nearby houses, the guy in front throws up his hand and they all rush up the porch steps and into the house.

Screams go off immediately.

"We ..." I can barely believe the words as I say them,

"We're being ambushed."

My door flies open and Memphis stumbles inside, his face sweaty and his eyes wide. Unblinking. "Caesar, we gotta go. Something's happening outside."

More screams fill the streets as I rush out my bedroom door behind him. Mya is on my heels, moving so quickly, she nearly steps on the backs of my feet as we run down the stairs.

I can hear the rest of the house moving frantically through the rooms as we make it down to the main hall. With all the noise outside, it's impossible for anyone to still be asleep. There's a group of guys in the living room, staring out the large glass windows in horror. None of them went with us to the cafeteria yesterday, so I understand their shock. They look horrified as more screams fill the neighborhood, and when someone pounds on our front door, one guy takes off running upstairs. I guess he's going to hide.

Coach Noble rushes in before any other cowards can escape, he's holding a baseball bat and wearing a scowl. "Don't answer that door." He points his bat at the pounding.

Some nameless freshman goes pale as a rock flies through the living room window. Glass flies everywhere and two kids duck and scream—Coach Noble calmly turns to leave, and to my shock, Mya follows him before I do. She shoves by me and practically runs to follow him to the attached garage.

Noble's talking over his shoulder as he moves, rummaging through the box of tools he keeps for his busted truck. "There are people in the streets—"

"I saw from upstairs," I say. "Who are they?"

"Probably students from North Campus."

The kids who were holed up in the cafeteria yesterday.

"What do they want? Why are they attacking us?"

116

He snaps his head up from the toolbox to glare at me. I feel so stupid as he hisses, "We went to the café and stole half their supplies yesterday, Caesar. What do you think they want?" He practically shoves the baseball bat into my hands and then passes a monkey wrench to Mya and retrieves a hammer for himself. Then the three of us stand there for an awful moment as reality grips us.

"We've got to fight," Coach Noble says finally. As if we hadn't figured that out yet. "We don't have to fight to kill, but we do have to defend ourselves. Because they're not playing games. They need food and water and they're willing to do whatever it takes to get it. We've got to be willing to do whatever it takes to *keep* it. Got it?"

Mya and I both nod.

"Stay together and watch each other's backs."

We nod again and follow him out the side door. It's not as chaotic as the cafeteria but it's immediately clear that we're in the middle of a warzone now. Students are running up and down the street, some of them are bloody, others are just scared out of their minds.

Someone runs up the driveway to Kappa Pi and tries to barge through the front door. He's shoved back by a guy inside and I smile as Memphis steps out and slugs the guy hard. There are two more dudes racing up the driveway, shouting incoherently, but Memphis doesn't back down.

Without thinking, I take off toward the fight. The bat feels light in my hands as I swing with all my might, grunting as it cracks across the back of a guy who never saw me coming. He falls to the ground, and I leave him there to keep running. When I glance over my shoulder, panic shoots through me when I see him getting back up, but he's taken down again

117

when Mya runs over and whacks the back of his knee with her wrench. He falls hard and stays there this time, holding his leg in pain. I smile, proud of my best friend, but there's no time to compliment her.

Memphis is fighting for his life at this point, and more people have rallied to help but there are just as many North Campus students fighting too. Like yesterday, it's another uncontrollable brawl.

Before long, it feels like the entire Kappa Pi frat house is fighting on the front lawn, but everything stops when I hit a student hard enough that his arm bends in the wrong direction. His shriek is loud enough to pierce the heavens. For a second, everyone pauses just to stare, wondering what happened.

That's when I get a good look at him; this hungry kid who tried to hit me with a metal pipe. Only God knows where he got that thing from. It's still clutched tightly in his other hand, the one that isn't broken, but he doesn't try to swing at me again. He falls to his knees with tears streaming down both his cheeks.

"We just want our food back," he says miserably.

I'm being honest when I say this, "We don't have it. Not here."

Then it dawns on me. Hope House has all of the food. We stored it there because they've got the largest kitchen, and their basement is set up like a pantry. They were the perfect storage space, but now their house feels like a death trap. If these guys were willing to storm our front lawn just for a chance at getting their food back, I can't imagine what they're going to do when they find the stash in Hope House dorm.

I glance back at Mya, and the size of her eyes lets me know she's thinking the same thing. "I have to go," she whispers.

"Mya—"

But she turns away before I can stop her, sprinting down the street in the direction of her dorm. I don't even blink before I take off behind her.

14

Caesar

Mya is so much faster than she looks. The fact that I—captain
of the track team—have to pump myself to catch up to her is
a testimony to the panic coursing through her mind and body.
It makes me start to panic when her dorm comes into view.
Even from our distance, I can see a crowd of people around
the front of both houses. They're surrounded.

Oh God... That's probably the first prayer I've ever prayed,
and I mean every word. *God, if You really love Mya like she says
You do, protect her friends.* I can handle all the chaos. I can live
through the violence. A small part of me even believes Mya
can tough it out too, but she doesn't have a bone in her body
that can withhold the sorrows of losing someone close to you.
I know because she's already lost her mother.

When the diagnosis came in, everything about Mya
changed, but you'd never know unless you knew her. On the
surface, she was still smiling. Still laughing. But she was dead
inside. If it weren't for her father, I'm positive she would have

drifted away, but he'd needed her. Probably more than she'd needed him. They got through it together—*with God*, she would always say, reaching up to clutch the silver crucifix around her neck.

I doubt Mya has gotten very close to anyone in Hope House just yet, but that doesn't mean she's fine and dandy with her dorm friends getting brutally attacked for canned goods.

"Mya!" I shout as she sprints forward. We're not far from the crowd outside Hope House, but she doesn't show any signs of slowing down. In fact, she barrels right into the students who are all packed together on the front lawn. Curses and shouts ripple through the mass as tiny Mya shoves her way forward.

I stumble through the idle bodies right behind her, breaking through the crowd with a gasp before I trip into Mya. She's standing perfectly still now. *Everyone* in the crowd is standing still. We're a mix of kids from both campuses; the hungry, half-deranged students who fought us yesterday, and the frightened students of Hope House. No one is fighting like I thought they'd be. In fact, it looks like we missed the fight.

I crane my neck to peer around Mya, and everything clicks into place. We *did* miss the fight. But it didn't end because the North kids got what they wanted. It ended because something awful happened.

There, in the middle of the crowd, is a kid lying at the bottom of the steps to Hope House dorm. But he doesn't look right. His back is bent at an awkward angle and his head is turned a little too far to the side. But he isn't dead.

Despite the blood pooling from his ears and his nose, he's still alive ... blinking at us, wondering why we're just standing here staring at him instead of trying to help. Blood sprays into the air as he breathes heavily, breaths coming out in desperate, choppy pants.

"What … what happened?" Mya whispers.

"He fell from the roof," says a tall Black guy from the other side of the crowd.

Mya gasps. "James!" she says with relief in her voice.

I almost roll my eyes. Mya mentioned James before, but she hadn't said he was tall, dark, and handsome.

"What happened?" Mya repeats.

"They tried to break in. Came from every direction. Things got wild when the fighting spilled onto the front lawn. There were guys on the roof throwing rocks down at us, and …" James looks down at the student and tightens his jaw. "He just fell."

As if on cue, the kid on the ground spits up blood and wheezes in pain.

Mya jerks forward like she's going to do something, but then she stops herself. "W-What can we do?"

I think we're all wondering the same thing right now. His back is broken. His neck is twisted. It's a miracle he's even breathing—but he is. And he's in unbearable pain, groaning like a wounded animal, making these awful inhuman noises that I can't even describe. His body twitches like he's trying to get up, but each movement turns into a writhing convulsion as his muscles spasm and his body cringes.

He shrieks but it's muffled and wet, mouth filled with blood, eyes rolling to the back of his head. A girl with bright pink hair shoves through the crowd and drops to her knees beside him. She starts removing her jean jacket and uses the sleeve to gingerly wipe the blood from his nose.

Like a light's been switched inside of her, Mya jumps into

action too, kneeling beside the girl. "Tell me what to do, Jupiter," she says calmly.

Jupiter, the pink-haired girl, nods as she wipes the guy's nose once more. "There might be blood in his lungs. We need to shift him so he's lying fully on his side."

Mya hesitates. "Won't that hurt?"

"We don't have a choice. He'll drown in his own blood at this point."

A pink tongue flashes across Mya's lips as she nervously licks them. Then she rolls up her sleeves and cautiously reaches for the boy. The moment her hands make contact, he lets out another one of those awful shrieks and the crowd hisses in response.

I can hardly watch this. The guy's back is broken, turning him onto his side isn't going to save him. But Mya and her friend don't give up. The boy keeps screaming and the crowd keeps watching. It all feels so wrong. He's dying right in front of us and we're just standing here waiting for it to happen.

"You're making it worse!" someone screams from the crowd.

"Just leave him!" another voice shouts.

James speaks up, "Guys ... I don't think he's going to make it."

"We can't just let him die!" Jupiter insists.

James nods and hangs his head. It takes me a moment to realize he's praying. *What on earth is he praying for?* I wonder. *This guy is as good as dead.*

"Mya," I whisper, watching in horror as the kid wails once more. She's holding his shoulder while Jupiter adjusts his legs, and they try to get him into position.

"Mya..."

She ignores me, staying focused on the boy and his screaming, which only gets worse. It's high-pitched and piercing now, so loud that I want to cover my ears. But just before I snap, his voice is violently cut off as he flops onto his back and lapses into convulsions. He's having a full-on seizure now.

Jupiter covers her eyes and starts sobbing. Her hands are stained with blood. But Mya just sits there staring at the boy, tears welling in her eyes. She starts to shake her head.

"Someone help," she whimpers. "Please help…"

Her head whips up and her watery eyes lock with mine, begging me to do something. To fix this. But what can I do? I can't stop a seizure. I can't heal his broken bones.

"Julie," she whispers.

"Mya, I—"

I'm suddenly shoved to the side as a large figure brushes by. I know it's Adrian before I even get a good look at him, but that's not what stuns me. It's the bat in his hands. He snatched it from me when he walked by, stepping into the middle of the circle now.

Adrian looks down at the boy for half a second, then he raises the bat above his head and brings it down with a sickening *thump*. The seizing stops. The wailing stops. Even James stops praying. We're all just standing there in silence. The only noise we can hear is the sound of Adrian swinging the bat again.

Whoosh … *thump*. Whoosh … *thump*.

He raises the bat again but Mya crawls forward and screams, "That's enough!"

Adrian lowers the bat.

"You killed him!" Mya says.

124

He glances down at her, then he looks around at the blinking crowd. "I did what needed to be done."

He was suffering. I know that. I *get* that. But ...

I don't want to look at the kid, but my eyes betray me, and I drop my gaze to the ground. The sidewalk is stained with blood, spattered across the concrete, on the grass, even staining the tops of my sneakers. The guy's face isn't even there anymore. It's caved in. Broken. Shattered.

Because of Adrian.

I can't explain why, but the crowd suddenly begins to disperse. As Adrian turns and walks away, dragging that bloody bat behind him, the mass of bodies parts to let him through and then unanimously decides this isn't worth it anymore. One by one, the students back away and dip into the shadows on the sidewalk, climbing over fences and ducking through backyards to return to wherever they came from.

Mya sniffles. "He'd dead."

"I know." My voice sounds raspy.

"What do we do now?"

"I should go get Coach Noble."

"They got our supplies," James blurts.

I'd forgotten he was even there, but he steps forward and helps Jupiter to her feet as he keeps talking.

"I don't know how much they took, but they found the stash and tried to carry it off. That's when the fighting turned brutal."

"Mya," I say softly. She's still sitting on the ground beside the dead body. It's such a gruesome sight I don't even want to go near it, but I don't think she's going to move unless I physically lift her from the concrete.

"Mya," I say again. "Let's get out of here. We've got to

meet up with everyone else."

She blinks. "Will Adrian be there?"

Most likely. I don't even know what he was doing over here on this side of the neighborhood. But there's no way he's getting out of this. He killed a kid in front of dozens of witnesses. It wasn't cold-blooded murder, but it was wrong. It needs to be addressed.

"I'm sure he's at Kappa Pi house right now," I say.

Mya closes her eyes for a long moment before she pushes to her feet and looks me in the eye. "Let's go."

It takes us over an hour to get back to Kappa Pi. The walk isn't long, but there are still dozens of students from North Campus littering the streets, so we have to climb fences and run through backyards of other dorm houses to get there safely. Adrian took my baseball bat, so the only weapon we had was Mya's monkey wrench and she clutched it so tightly I thought she'd bend the metal.

By the time we make it to Kappa Pi, the sun is up and burning. In the morning light, I can see all the trash left behind from the fighting. Broken glass, random bricks thrown across the lawn, discarded weapons like sticks and poles. There's a guy lying on the lawn that I think is dead for a second, but as I get closer, I can see his chest rising and falling. I guess Kappa Pi managed to chase away the guys who attacked us, or they realized there weren't any supplies inside and left on their own. Either way, I'm glad the fighting is over.

I'm drenched in sweat now and dying of thirst, but I put my discomfort aside when I see Coach Noble on the front lawn. He's kneeling beside Bunny who looks like he's in pain.

I immediately break into a jog.

"What's going on?" I ask. Mya is right beside me, still clutching that wrench like she's ready to whack Noble if she needs to.

"I think I twisted my ankle." Bunny hiccups like a big baby.

I roll my eyes. "Be a man, Bun. We need you."

He nods and then grits his teeth when Coach reaches forward and peels his sock from his foot. It's swollen and already starting to bruise.

Mya kneels beside them both. "I can help."

"How?" Bunny asks.

"We'll have to wrap it and keep it elevated." She presses her lips together and then glances up with a cautious look on her face. "Would you mind if I prayed for you?"

"You want to pray right now?" Coach Noble interrupts, but Bunny nods.

"I'll take any help I can get."

Noble looks like he's going to complain again, so I cut him off before the words can leave his mouth. "Leave her. Who cares if she prays? If you don't like it, then step back so she can handle this alone."

Coach Noble raises a single raven eyebrow as he stands and crosses his arms. "Who are you talking to like that?"

"We don't have time to fight about this."

"Then don't—"

"It's fine," Mya interjects. She stands and wipes dirt off her knees before looking at both of us. "I'm done praying. Can we move him inside?"

Coach Noble and I both have to carry Bunny inside together, he groans and whimpers the entire time, especially when we gracelessly drop him onto the sofa in the living room

127

and he whacks his leg on the side of the coffee table.

"I'll grab him a water," Mya mumbles, but Noble stops her.

"No. We haven't counted our supplies. Let's preserve whatever is left for now."

Speaking of supplies...

"They got into Hope House. I was just there. They trashed the place and took a bunch of food and water. The dorm leaders will count everything and report their numbers in an hour or so."

Noble rubs the gruff on his chin, it sounds like bristles scraping together. "How bad did it look?"

"They killed someone," Mya speaks up.

"Who?" Bunny gasps.

"No one from our dorm," I answer.

"They killed one of their own?" Bunny asks.

I shake my head. "Adrian killed him."

The room falls silent. That's when I glance around and realize we have an audience. Memphis, Connor O'Reilly, and three other guys from the track team have moved into the living room, probably drawn by all the noise we'd made with Bunny. They stare at me with their eyes wide open, filled with worry and fear.

"Are you serious?" Memphis says incredulously. "Adrian killed someone?"

"It wasn't like that..." The sound of Adrian's voice yanks a gasp from Bunny, everyone else just turns dramatically to find him standing in the entrance to the room. He looks just as tired and sweaty as the rest of us, but there's a bloody cut on his forehead that I hadn't noticed before.

"What were you doing at Hope House?" I ask before anyone else can speak.

Adrian steps into the room, glaring at me. The only time he breaks his gaze is when he notices Mya standing to the side—he actually falters his steps and blinks at her like she truly caught him off guard.

I squint as they stare at each other. *Am I missing something?*

"What were you doing at Hope House?" I repeat, just to get his attention so him and Mya will stop gazing at each other like angry lovers.

"I was out for a run this morning—"

"In the middle of all this?" Coach Noble interrupts.

Adrian doesn't even look at him as he responds, "Running helps clear my head. So yes, I wanted to get out and try to find some semblance of peace in this chaos."

No one speaks for a moment. I wonder how stupid Coach Noble feels.

"On my run, I heard screaming and turned back right away. But I never made it to Kappa Pi because I saw the madness going on at Hope House. I stopped to help."

"And ended up killing someone," Memphis sounds like *he* wants to kill right now. His eyes are filled with anger and his words come out as a growl when he steps forward and says, "We're not animals, Adrian—"

"I know that," Adrian snaps.

"You killed him like an animal," I say.

He glares at me. "It wasn't like that."

"You used a bat."

"It wasn't like that!" he shouts, silencing everyone. We're all stunned by his outburst, but Memphis and Noble both jump into action when Adrian walks toward me. They jump between us and start shoving him back, like they think my life is in danger. That only makes Adrian angry. He shoves Noble so hard that he trips backwards into Memphis.

No one knows how to respond. We all just stand there blinking at each other until Adrian points his finger at me. "Why don't you tell the entire story, Julius?"

"That is the story."

"It was a mercy killing..." Mya's gentle voice is such a startling contrast to the hateful grunts that'd filled the room a moment ago. It gets everyone's attention in an instant—even Adrian turns around to look at her, suddenly calm.

I stare at Mya. *Is she actually defending him?* She's the one who got angry about the whole thing in the first place. And now she's jumping in like we're all the bad guys.

She avoids eye contact with me as she continues. "Adrian did kill someone. But it wasn't out of malice."

"How?" Bunny asks.

"He beat him with a bat," I say before Mya can jump in and make Adrian out to be some merciful hero. She's the one who was screaming at him earlier. Now that she's calmed down, she wants to twist the story like he's the good guy here. I don't know what the heck happened between them recently but it's clear they've got some sort of connection now and I don't like it.

"He bashed his skull in," I add, just because I can.

"The guy was already dying," Mya clarifies. "He fell off the roof of Hope House and broke his back and his neck. There was nothing anyone could do."

"You didn't try to *pray*?" Coach Noble mocks.

Mya respectfully ignores him. "What Adrian did wasn't right, but it wasn't wrong either. We couldn't let him suffer like that."

"Where's the body?" Memphis asks.

"Why?" Adrian only says one word, but it comes out so hard it sounds like a curse.

Memphis says, "We should bury him. Or something. I don't know. Someone's dead, man. That just ain't right."

"We didn't go back to bury Phil," Bunny says.

"Because Phil was left in the cafeteria. We didn't even know he was dead until hours later." Memphis shakes his head. "This can't be happening."

"It is happening." Adrian glares at all of us. "I did what needed to be done. That's what it will take to survive. When will you all get that through your heads? Or does North Campus need to come back and throw a few more bricks through our windows for us to get it?"

"Calm down," Coach Noble holds both his hands up defensively. "Despite everything that's happened, we need to get along."

Adrian scoffs. "Whatever."

"What if something happens to one of us? Are we gonna let Adrian murder us with a bat as soon as we're injured?" Memphis says loudly.

Bunny shifts uncomfortably on the couch.

"You know what?" Adrian's voice is low and gravelly, like he's about to explode, but instead of bursting into a screaming match, his words come out in a tone so calm it sends a shiver down my spine. "You don't have to worry about me doing anything. I'm leaving."

"Leaving?" Mya repeats, and before I can get angry at the sadness on her face, Adrian replies, "Yes. I've wanted to get out of here since day one. I'm done." He looks at Coach Noble. "You can't keep me here anymore."

"It's dangerous out there, Adrian. Probably worse than

here on campus."

"We're running out of food and water. And every time we face off with North Campus, someone ends up dead. I'll take my chances on the road." Adrian turns toward the door and the crowd parts to let him through, but he stops at the entrance to turn back. His gaze lands on Mya. "I'm leaving at noon."

Why is he telling her?

She checks her pocket watch. "That's in two hours."

He nods, and then his gaze finally breaks so he can glance at all of us. "If anyone wants to join me, you're welcome to come along. We'll be safer in numbers."

15

Mya

Adrian is leaving. I know it's what he wants but part of me feels guilty about how it's happening. Maybe it's because I stood by and let Julie paint him as a villain. Or maybe it's because we planned to leave together. He's not supposed to make this trip alone. But I am not going with him.

I want to see my father. I want to make sure he's safe and okay. But … I can't leave. Not yet. Not with things so messed up here.

I know that sounds like a pathetic excuse to leave my father hanging in limbo, but the truth is that I'm afraid. I'm afraid of leaving Julie after we've been separated for so long. I'm afraid of finding out the truth regarding my father. What if he isn't safe? What if he drank contaminated water and is lying dead at the kitchen table? What if looters broke into the house and he's splayed on the ground like that kid in front of Hope House?

Sometimes, it's easier to hope that he's alright than to know that he's dead.

I can't handle that truth. After losing my mother, the thought of letting go of my father terrifies me. I know that makes me weak, but I'm strong enough to admit that. I'm strong enough to own up to how pathetic I am. That's why I decide to do whatever I can to make up for this.

Once Adrian leaves, I mumble some excuse about helping James clean up Hope House, then I head back to my dorm. The place is trashed and he really could use some help—especially with cleaning up that guy's body—but I have no intentions of lending a hand right now. I've got two hours until Adrian starts his journey, I need to grab supplies and meet him before then.

With all the chaos going on, no one notices me slip into the basement of the boys' dorm at Hope House. I've got my backpack in my hands as I creep down the wooden stairs, ready to load it with whatever I think Adrian might need. I'm sure Kappa Pi will lend him something, but I can't be certain. He isn't leaving on great terms. After that argument in there, his frat brothers are likely to send him out with nothing but the clothes on his back. But I'm grabbing supplies for more than just the fact that he needs them. I'm taking this stuff because I need him.

Adrian lives in Phoenix, like Caesar. I moved from Phoenix to Wakedon during the summer between 10th and 11th grade. It's two hours from Phoenix, but that won't matter because you'll hit Wakedon before you get to Phoenix—no matter which direction you take. In fact, it's quicker to travel straight through Wakedon rather than going around.

My plan is to ask Adrian to check on my father. I know it's a cheap way out of my responsibilities as a daughter, but it's the best I can offer. Adrian is strong enough to make it to

Wakedon. The trip won't take him out of his way, and … I think we're close enough for him to do it if I ask.

I have more history with Adrian than you think. I knew he liked me back in high school. I knew he'd planned to ask me out at the pep rally. In front of everyone. It wasn't exactly a secret, but I didn't find out through the grapevine. I knew about Adrian's feelings because I'd felt the same.

I wasn't always at Bible study whenever Caesar went to one of his house parties. Sometimes I was out too. I had a social life; I just wasn't as wild as my best friend.

Adrian knew that. He liked that I preferred a quiet life, and he liked that I valued my faith above everything. What he didn't realize, however, was that I valued my faith above him too.

That was why I rejected him when he asked me out. I'd made a promise to God that I would never compromise my faith for a man who didn't believe the way I did.

Adrian isn't Christian. I don't know what he is. But he'd made it clear that he didn't believe in God when we hung out together. My thumping heart had been loud enough to drown out our differences, but everything came crashing back into perspective when he put me on the spot that day.

I had no choice but to say no. I couldn't date Adrian. My promise to God mattered more than the way he made me feel. And God's expectations mattered more. The Bible is clear on Christians dating within the faith. There is no excuse to step out of the church while dating. I've known all this my entire life, and when it mattered, I was strong enough to turn Adrian down. But now he's back. It's been years and I've suddenly realized those feelings haven't cooled down at all.

Every time I look at Adrian, I see the boy from high school. Ashen hair so blonde, it's crisply white, like angels wove strands of silk together and placed it upon his head. His jaw is square and though it's always clenched in an angry scowl, I've seen the smile it hides. In the shadow of his frown there is a dimple. An unmistakable threat to his wrath, evidence of the boy he left behind in high school. He's got an athlete's physique—long legs, a strong core, and arms that stretch the sleeves of his shirt. Yes, he's albino. And he's beautiful. Ethereal. Like looking at something that descended from Heaven … or crawled up from Hell. Sometimes it's hard to tell.

Adrian is taller, stronger, and colder than before. So cold he's like ice now. But when I'm near him, I don't feel that chill. In fact, all I want is to burn.

I have to shake my head to clear my thoughts once my backpack is loaded with supplies. It isn't much, but I think it might just be enough to get him to Wakedon. If he can make it there, he can loot or resupply and move on to Phoenix. I'm sure he's already thought all of this through, but I still run through the plans in my head as I head back to Kappa Pi Frat House with my stuffed backpack.

I rehearse what I'm going to say while I walk, meticulously arranging the words like I'm planning to deliver a speech. That's what this feels like. A desperate plea for help, not a conversation with an old friend.

Bunny is still on the sofa when I walk into the Kappa Pi house, he glances up at me and smiles. "Hiya, Mya." He laughs. "That rhymes."

Bunny is a sophomore, but sometimes it's hard to see him as a twenty-year-old man when he acts like a fifteen-year-old boy most of the time. And the fact that he's prettier than a Disney princess and only three inches taller than me makes it

136

impossible for me to interpret him as anything but a cute little kid.

"How are you feeling, Bun?" I ask kindly.

He wiggles his toes; his foot is still wrapped up tightly and resting on a pillow. "In pain, but it could be worse."

"Any idea where I can find Adrian?"

He pauses. "He's in his room, getting ready."

Ready to *leave*... But neither of us says that aloud.

I nod and head toward the stairs before I stop and glance back. "Uh... which room—"

"Fourth one on the left." Bunny's laughter chases me away, but I stop once I reach Adrian's room. The door is closed but I can hear the distinct sound of footsteps on the other side, like he's walking around in there.

I swallow my nerves and knock on the door. The shuffling around inside stops immediately.

"Go away." Adrian's voice is flat, almost bored.

"It's me," I squeak out.

A breath of silence fills the hall, then I hear Adrian move to the door and yank it open. He blinks at me in shock. "What are you doing here?"

"Can we talk?"

He stands there staring at me for so long, I'm positive he's going to close the door in my face. But just before I give up, he nods once and then pulls the door open just enough for me to duck under his arm and walk inside.

I'm immediately washed in a wave of shame as I glance around. My room has been torn apart. My blankets are kicked off onto the floor because I'm not sleeping beneath them in the heat. I've abandoned my textbooks in a corner of the room, and Jupiter and I have resorted to tossing our dirty clothes in

137

a pile by the window. All the clean stuff is sitting in my open suitcase in the middle of the floor.

Adrian's room is the exact opposite.

First of all, he doesn't have a roommate—so that might help keep things a little cleaner. But even for one person, the room is immaculate. Everything is in perfect order. His shoes are arranged by style and color, there's a hamper full of dirty clothes by the bathroom but as I walk by, I glance down and notice they're all folded neatly inside. Adrian's bed is made, even the pillows look fluffed and arranged by size then color. It's so nice, I don't want to crinkle his blankets by sitting on the bed, so I stand by his desk and feel even more embarrassed for myself.

Adrian's desk has a notebook sitting in the middle with a stack of three textbooks off to the side. There is a pencil, an ink pen, and a highlighter sitting in that order next to the notebook. He's also got a calculator and an unopened pack of index cards arranged on the desk like he's going to take a photo and post it for a back-to-school ad. That's how good it looks in here.

I wonder when he's had the time to clean up and keep things so neat and tidy with everything that's going on. I almost ask, but when I glance up at him, he's already staring at me and all I can do is blush in response.

"It's so clean in here," I say with a stupid giggle.

Adrian nods. "I don't like mess. I clean my room each day."

"Even with everything going on?"

He nods again. "I like to keep things in order when I can. It helps."

Helps to what?

138

I don't question it. After that short conversation, Adrian's cleanliness feels more personal. Like there's a deeper meaning behind it, but I don't have the right to pry into his personal life. So I take a breath and blurt out the real reason I came here.

"I need to ask you for a favor." I take off my backpack and hold it up.

Adrian stares at it. "Go on."

"You're leaving in an hour—"

"Are you coming with me?" he cuts me off.

My throat feels dry as I swallow and answer, "N-No. That's what I came to talk about."

I can't explain the expression that passes over his face. An odd mix of disappointment, anger, and ... relief?

I blink once. "You didn't want me to go, did you?"

He lets go of a long breath. "I want you safe, Mya. Even if that means leaving you behind."

"You still care. After all these years."

He steps closer, almost too close—just like in the backyard last night. But unlike last night, there's a fat backpack between us so he can't get in my personal space. That doesn't stop him from reaching up and running his thumb along my jawline. I almost shudder at his gentle touch. This moment is so quiet. So simple.

"Why wouldn't I care?" Adrian murmurs.

I can't speak.

"Nothing about me has changed. Remember that." He finally steps away, and I take a huge breath. My grip on the backpack is so tight, my hands are shaking.

For some reason, my brain has gone blank and numb. The only thing I can think to say is, "Okay."

That seems enough for Adrian; he simply nods and then

glances down at the bag in my trembling hands. "Supplies?"

I thrust it at him. "It's the least I can do."

"Thank you, Mya."

"I had a favor to ask too."

He quirks a white eyebrow.

"To get to Phoenix, you have to go through Wakedon." I pause, hoping he can somehow put the pieces together by himself, but he just tilts his head to the side and waits. I lick my lips. "I live in Wakedon. With my dad."

Now he gets it. I can tell the moment everything clicks when his shoulders drop a little and he breaks eye contact to glance down at the floor.

"I get it."

"Adrian, please—"

"I'll do it, Mya. I want to see my family; I know you want to see yours too."

I exhale in relief. "I wrote down my address, it's on a slip of paper I put in the bag. Don't lose it."

"I won't."

We stand there.

That's one thing about Adrian that truly hasn't changed—he's never been a man of many words. Everything he says is deliberate, not a single syllable wasted. At least I know he means what he says.

"When you find him," I pause, unsure what to say next. I hadn't thought about what would happen after that. Should he grab my dad and drag him back up to Cross North? Does he even plan on coming back?

"What will you do once you find your folks?" I ask suddenly.

Adrian presses his lips together. "I was going to stay with

them. But now that I've got to check on your father—"

"I'm sorry," I blurt.

He shakes his head. "Don't be. This gives me a reason to see you again."

Sheesh, he's really laying it on heavy right now.

"Don't bring my father with you," I say. "Find a safe place and come back for me."

Adrian smiles—it's a small one, just one half of his mouth turning up a little—but it's enough to flash that hidden dimple. My heart skips a beat. How long has it been since I've seen Adrian smile? It almost looks foreign on him. I suddenly wish I could freeze time and stare at him forever, pressing rewind on the timeline of this life just to watch his smile form inch by inch. Just to watch the flicker of joy beam to life inside him over and over again.

As quickly as the smile appears, it's gone the next second.

"I'll come back for you," he says in a low voice.

Without thinking, I reach up and unclasp the chain hanging around my neck. It's a string of silver links holding a cross pendant; Julie gave it to me, along with the thorny crown ring on my finger. I take that off too and set it on the chain, so it hangs with the pendant. The crown and the cross.

I hold up the necklace to Adrian. I don't know why I'm giving it to him. It isn't a good luck charm. I don't believe in luck; I believe in God's will and His favor. Maybe I'm praying it's His will for Adrian to make it back. But I know my desire is deeper than that. And so does Adrian as he stares at the necklace, his gaze lingering on the dangling cross.

"You said nothing about you has changed," I whisper. "This is the part I want to change. Somehow."

He reaches for the necklace. "I don't believe in God, Mya."

141

"Yes, you do," I tell him. I remember the arguments we used to have over this, how he'd stopped believing when his stepfather picked up a bottle and his mother picked up a string of men to help pay the bills. Things got worse when his stepdad started hitting him, that's when he lost his faith. I don't exactly blame him. It's hard to have hope with all those scars on his back. But a small part of me has never been convinced of Adrian's beliefs or lack thereof.

I don't believe he's truly an atheist. I never will.

"You do believe in God," I say, my voice firmer now. "You're just angry at Him."

Adrian glances away, but I don't miss the way his grip tightens on the necklace. After a moment, he looks back at me and clears his throat.

"Help me put it on?" His voice is raspy, like he's holding back tears.

I nod and he turns around, passing me the silver chain. My hands shake as I work the tiny clasp, but I manage to get it over his head and hooked just fine. When I'm finished, Adrian turns and looks down at me. I keep my eyes on the two pendants around his neck, but he cups my chin and lifts, so I'll look him in the eye.

"I'm coming back," he whispers.

I nod.

"Pray for me."

"Of course."

He holds my gaze, then his eyes flick down to my lips. For a second, I'm sure he's going to kiss me—he even dips his head, and I shock myself by rising on my tiptoes, but he stops short. His lips hover over mine, so close that when he speaks, I feel the whiskers of his blonde facial hair brushing against my skin.

I yearn to capture each of his words with a kiss, stealing his promise so it stays between us instead of disappearing in the air. Drifting into this violent, darkened world. But I stay rooted in place, heart beating wildly, my throat stuffed with emotions, so packed I can hardly breathe.

"It's been years," he murmurs, words a gentle kiss. If love could tickle me, I'd feel it in that moment, each word a precious spark of emotion igniting something alive and hungry deep inside. "I still feel everything," Adrian confesses. "I'll feel it in a hundred years. I'll feel it for eternity, Mya. So trust me when I say I'm coming back."

"Okay," I whisper.

He reaches up to clutch the necklace. "This part of me hasn't changed. But it can. Somehow."

"Okay," I say again. I feel dumb repeating myself, but I have no other words in my brain right now. As Adrian pulls away and runs a hand through his hair, I realize I've said all I need to.

He gives me a sad smile and then nods. "I've got to go now."

I say it one last time… "Okay."

16

Caesar

It's time to lay down some rules on campus. The fight at the café woke up a small portion of us who witnessed it firsthand, but that assault on the entire dorm wing rang the alarm for everyone in the vicinity.

The world is doomed, we cannot hide from it any longer. Coach Noble finally realized this and let Adrian and a few others leave campus in search of help and family. They plan to make it all the way to Phoenix, locate their families, restock their supplies, and then truck it back to Cross North and deliver a report.

If the city is alright, we'll all make our way down there. But if it's in shambles, then we'll have some difficult decisions to make. Not everyone has family in Phoenix, we can't all pack a bag full of supplies and walk a few days along the highway to find our parents in their homes. Some students are from across the country, some are even foreign exchange studying abroad.

That means, for a few of us, this campus is the safest place to be. No matter what report comes back, we have no choice but to hunker down and do our best to survive until the power turns on again. That could be in hours or days. Or it could be weeks. The darkest parts of my mind whisper a nightmare of shadows—that the power isn't ever coming back.

I don't believe that. I can't believe that, because once I do, I'll lose all hope and motivation to keep going.

I keep myself busy by throwing all my energy into building up our campus. We cannot be taken off guard like that again. That kid who died might not have been from our campus, but his death was gruesome enough to leave us all spooked.

I wasn't there when Hope House cleaned up his body, but I was there when we finally took stock of everything that was left. Our supplies were dangerously low, our morale had hit rock bottom. The only thing I could think to do was set up a schedule and a system.

First, we assigned guards to watch the gates leading into the campus neighborhood. There are only two, so it's relatively easy to manage with a group of students on rotation.

Second, we split up the supplies. We'd initially believed it was a good idea to let Hope House store everything since their dorms had a built-in pantry ready for this sort of stuff. But that blew up in our faces when we got attacked. If our supplies had been spread out, we wouldn't have lost so much. So now each dorm has taken a set of supplies to store, and we've decided to ration servings per day.

The sorority keeps the water, Hot House has dried food, Green House keeps canned goods, Hope House has all the medical supplies, and Kappa Pi has a mix of supplies stashed in our basement. It took all day to separate things evenly, but we finally managed.

145

Now, we've got a security team in place to keep watch 24/7 and we have an organized pantry in each dorm. Despite Adrian's departure, we've managed to keep our heads up. Some people are still anxious, wondering when he'll return and what he'll have to report once he does get back. But so far, we're doing fine. We're holding out.

It's just after breakfast now, I can see the sleepy rays of sunlight spilling through the kitchen window. Like a drunkard, the light stumbles across the tiled floor and leaves patches of yolky morning light here and there. With the light comes an awful wet heat, like the sun just burped on us. I hate how sweaty it feels, but I welcome this dewy warmth because I know in a few hours the afternoon heat will feel like tongues of fire scraping down my back.

Beside me, Bunny sighs and wipes his forehead with the back of his hand. "I can't imagine how Adrian's walking in this heat right now."

"If he's smart, he took the backroads and cut through the foliage off the highway," Memphis says around a mouthful of canned ravioli. "There's more shade in the shrubbery."

"Adrian said he didn't want to take back roads."

"Well, he isn't travelling alone, so it isn't really up to him." Memphis uses his fingers to dig the last ravioli from the can.

"Who else went with him?" Bunny asks, but it's Coach Noble who answers.

"Connor O'Reilly—along with two other frat brothers. There's also a host of students from the other dorms."

Without meaning to, I glance at Memphis. He's got a guilty look on his face as he pushes his empty can of ravioli away. No one speaks for a long moment. We haven't forgotten how much of a fuss Memphis made when Coach Noble wouldn't let anyone leave. Then Adrian finally got permission to go but Memphis didn't volunteer to join the team.

I decide to change the subject but the second I open my mouth, the front door creaks. It didn't creak before but Noble took a hammer to the hinges the other night so now it screams every time someone opens it. I'm not complaining. It works as our personal alarm; no one is getting into this house without us knowing about it. Some of the other dorms have done the same thing—last night I heard Bunny's bedroom door creak when he opened it. He's a little more paranoid than the rest of us but at least he's taking precautions.

The doorway to the kitchen darkens and I glance up to find James from Hope House standing there. Everyone else is surprised too, Bunny frowns and Coach Noble stands to greet him with a confused look on his face.

"What's going on?" he says, immediately jumping to the worst possible conclusion. He makes an awkward motion, and I realize a second later that he's placed his hand on his hip—no—he's patting the hammer looped through the belt on his hip. I hadn't noticed it before, but I'm not surprised by it. We're all a little jumpy after that crazy attack.

James glances down at Noble's hammer and holds up a defensive hand. "There is a problem, but you won't need that." He pauses. "Hopefully, you won't need it."

Well, that doesn't sound scary.

James leads me and Coach Noble out of the frat house and down the road. At first, I think he's taking us back to Hope House, but he doesn't turn down the right street when we get to his corner. Instead, he keeps walking straight and my stomach starts to flip.

"What's going on?" I ask nervously.

147

James glances back at me. "There's a problem at the sorority."

"What kind of problem?" Noble asks.

"What's a *man of God* doing at the sorority house?" I blurt. I don't mean to mock him—okay, I *do* mean to mock him. I can't help it. I don't like James. And it bothers me that there's a nice guy living right next door to Mya who believes in God and prays with her and stuff. Meanwhile, I'm expecting Delilah to come over again tonight and I only feel *slightly* guilty about it.

Mya's my best friend, not my girlfriend. But still... I wouldn't complain if she showed a *little* interest. It'd be nice to know if she got a little jealous the way I get jealous over her.

James looks over his shoulder again while he walks, the look he gives me is sympathetic, like he just realized he's talking to a child. My ears burn with embarrassment when he says, "Omega Zeta Chi has all the water. I went there to request a few gallons for my dorm today. That's when I realized we had a problem."

"What sort of problem?" Noble asks.

James sighs as we walk up the driveway to the large white house. "They're not giving out water anymore."

I'm so shocked, I trip over my own feet and stumble into Noble. He gently stables me and looks at James. "What do you mean?"

James jerks his head at the double doors before us. "Ask and find out."

Noble bangs his fist on the door and steps back as we all wait. It takes exactly three seconds for someone to call out, "Who is it?"

The voice is feminine, and I recognize it right away.

"Delilah, let us in," I say angrily.

She pauses. "I'll have to check with the other girls first—"

I bang my fist on the door and my voice comes out as a growl. "Open this door or I'm kicking it down!"

James shifts uncomfortably but he doesn't complain when Delilah opens the door viewer and peeks out at us. I can see her big eyes blinking, filled with worry, but I don't have any sympathy for her. She should thank God the door viewer has a cast iron grid on it so I can't reach through and snatch her by the collar.

I can't believe the sorority girls aren't sharing their water. If James is telling the truth, then we're in trouble.

"Open the door," I say.

Delilah nods and shuts the door viewer, then she turns the lock, and the door slowly opens to reveal a sweaty blonde wearing yoga pants and my track jersey. Neither James nor Noble comments on her shirt—we all just pretend she stole a number 9 jersey with **Caesar** on the back.

Delilah flicks her hair over her shoulder and spears me with her glare. "I can't just let you guys in, okay? We have a protocol—"

"We all have a protocol," Noble says. "And we heard you've broken it recently."

She huffs. "Fine. I can take you to the other girls."

Delilah lets us into the house, and we follow her through the open foyer and down the hall. It's just as hot here as it is at the frat house, but this place is definitely cleaner. And more organized.

Kappa Pi has shirtless guys lying around everywhere, along with empty spam cans and piles of dirty clothes. Meanwhile, the sorority has transformed into bootcamp overnight. There's

149

a girl sitting at every window, watching for other students. They're all dressed in similar fashion; yoga pants and a t-shirt, with their hair pulled back into a ponytail. One girl even has black makeup smeared across her cheeks like war paint.

The whole scene makes me feel uncomfortable.

Delilah stops in front of a door that leads to a small office, there are two ladies inside, but I don't recognize either one, so I wait for Delilah to introduce us.

She walks around the desk to stand beside the lady sitting in the leather chair. "This is Jewels, our sorority mother."

I raise my eyebrows. Jewels looks like she could be my age, but she's got to be older if she's the sorority mother. Essentially, she holds the same position as Coach Noble at Kappa Pi. That makes her one of the only other adults I've seen here on campus. I wonder where she's been all this time. I didn't see her at any of the group meetings with the other dorms, and she certainly didn't come out to play when we had that brawl a few days ago.

Jewels looks up at us and takes us all in with a raise of a single eyebrow. She's got perfectly smooth brown skin and dark hair as short as mine. We've almost got the same haircut, except her hair has curled up in the heat so it looks more like a curly afro instead. There's no sweat on her forehead, despite the heat, and her clothes look clean. Almost fresh.

I'd bet Jewels hasn't left this house since the lights first went out. That isn't good. People only lock themselves away when they're truly afraid of what's outside. And people who are afraid do stupid things—like keep all the water for themselves.

"Hi, Jewels," I say politely. "We've come to talk about the water."

"Join the club," says the other lady in the room.

I look over at her for the first time. A tall woman with crazy red hair and forehead to spare. She's drenched in so much sweat I almost want her to take her shirt off and wring it out. A fat drop of sweat rolls down the side of her face as she wipes her hands on her damp pants and then extends one toward Noble who is standing right beside her.

"Mariam, from Green House."

"Are you the dorm parent?" Noble asks, shaking her hand.

"No. Our dorm parent was injured in the last fight." She leaves it at that and promptly returns her attention to Jewels and Delilah. "We've got a problem."

"We do," James echoes.

"Is this true?" Noble asks. "You're not handing out water anymore?"

Jewels gives us a slow blink. "It isn't entirely true. We will give water to whoever swears loyalty to us."

I have to stop myself from rolling my eyes. "Are you serious? We're all on the same team here. We're not swearing loyalty to anyone. Where is this even coming from?"

Delilah rolls her eyes. "Ask Hot House."

"Not this again," grumbles Mariam.

"Hot House has all the dry supplies," Jewels explains. "They've got flour."

"Okay." I shrug.

"And they've been using that flour to bake bread in their wood-burning ovens."

"Bread made from flour and *our* water," Delilah says angrily. "They used our water but didn't share their bread with us. So we're not sharing water with anyone who isn't going to share their supplies."

151

"If you want water, swear loyalty," Jewels says with a nod, like that's final.

I take a step forward but Noble beats me there, except he's got his hand extended and he's offering a stiff smile. "Fine. Kappa Pi swears loyalty—"

"Hold on!" I grab him by the shoulder and yank him back before Jewels can touch him. "Are you serious, Coach?"

He shrugs me off. "They have all the water, Caesar. What other choice do we have?"

"They don't have *all* of it," I remind him. Kappa Pi has a small stash which includes a little of everything. We did that in case something crazy like this happened. But it won't be enough for the rest of the entire campus to share. Zeta Chi is seriously screwing us over right now and it's for a ridiculous reason. But Coach Noble is kind of right. Swearing loyalty to them won't really mean anything, especially if everyone swears. We'll be right back where we started. Everyone working together. Everyone allied again.

I sigh and clench my jaw before giving in. "Fine."

Noble nods and extends his hand again. "Kappa Pi swears loyalty."

"So does Green House," Mariam says, stepping forward.

We all look at James, but he doesn't move. "This isn't right." He shakes his head.

"James," I say.

"We shouldn't be divided like this."

"We won't be if everyone swears loyalty."

"*Everyone?* Where's Hot House, then?"

"Forget Hot House," Delilah snaps. "They can enjoy their bread alone."

"Exactly," James says angrily. "We cannot have division

like this. We won't survive."

"But there *is* division," Delilah says like he's stupid. "This is how we're dealing with it."

"We should deal with it by talking to Hot House. Not by forming alliances behind their back." James turns toward the door. "You're not going to make me choose a side."

I grab him by the shoulder—to be honest, I don't care if James dries up and dies of dehydration, but he can't make this sort of decision for everyone at Hope House. Mya is at Hope House. If he doesn't swear loyalty, she won't get any water.

"Think about this," I say earnestly. "How long do you think you'll last without water?"

"Have you forgotten that Hot House has all the dry foods? How long do you think we'll last without that?"

"Green House has all the canned food," Mariam speaks up, "we'll survive long enough."

"And how long will your injured dorm parent survive without medical supplies?" James challenges.

The room goes silent.

That's when I realize the truth. We're already divided. No matter what happens in this room, no matter who ends up shaking hands, the relationship we had before has been fractured. Beyond repair.

"You said we can't have division," I remind James.

He looks at me like he can't stand me. "We were divided before we even got here."

He's right. Even if we all shake hands, James will never trust Zeta Chi and Zeta Chi will never be willing to work with Hot House again. That leaves Kappa Pi and Green House to sort things out. Not to mention the ever-looming threat of North Campus.

At this point, I'll have to choose between having access to medical supplies, water, or canned goods. Maybe Hot House will be sympathetic and give us some bread if we ask nicely.

17

Adrian

The worst thing about Arizona isn't the heat. It's the dust. Awful little grains of dirt and sand and grit that get everywhere. It doesn't matter how secure your windows are, doesn't matter how many layers of clothes you've got on, once a breeze kicks up, you'll be covered in a ginger film of dirt.

When I was younger, the twins wanted to go out bike riding for their birthday. Mom and my stupid stepdad had promised to take them but, as usual, they got busy and couldn't make it. I ended up taking them out myself. We got caught in a little haboob—nothing serious, but it was strong enough to leave Dinara a little spooked. We sat in the cubby of a bus stop, waiting for the wind to die down. Dinara had huddled in my lap while Danya stood by himself, staring through the clear glass in awe. Everything around us had looked red, like we'd been sucked into the eye of a scarlet tornado.

Even though we'd taken shelter, our clothes were red when the dust settled. Even Dinara's fine blonde hair looked fiery. I remember her looking up at me with tears in her eyes when the storm was over. She wasn't afraid of the wind anymore, she was patting her hair, asking if she looked okay.

I couldn't stop myself from laughing at her. At how silly and displaced her concerns were. But she was just a kid, the most important thing in her entire world were her ice-blonde pigtails.

"Adri, is it bad?" she had sobbed, frantically trying to get the red dust out of her hair.

I'd reached out and tugged one of her pigtails. "It's cute, kiddo. You're still my princess."

She hadn't believed me at all.

"You're lying!" she'd sobbed, and her tears had left streaks down her dusty cheeks. "Why would you lie about this?"

To this day, I remember my response.

"I lied to make you feel better."

I'd lied to the twins before I left. I told them they would be okay. I told them I'd come back for them. As I walk through the hot dirt roads now, with nothing but heat and death hanging around me, I can't decide if I lied for a good enough reason.

Were my words enough? Did I make my siblings feel better? Did they feel safe against the panic of the city, knowing their big brother would come for them?

Or did I feed them false hope?

I said I was coming. And I am. But is it too late?

The scarlet expanse before me is nearly blinding in this overwhelming heat. I'm wearing long sleeves and an overstuffed backpack with my running sneakers. I'm used to long sleeves in this weather, but I'm not used to being out for hours upon hours. Still, I think it's better to keep my skin covered so I don't end up burned like Connor O'Reilly.

He's marching beside me with his own pack on his back and his t-shirt wrapped around his head to keep the dust off his face. He took his shirt off yesterday within the first hour of our trip. He's flaming red now, swollen from burned, peeling skin. I'd offer him one of my spare long sleeved shirts but at this point, I think it's too little too late.

The sound of Connor's heavy breathing grates my nerves as we walk in stony silence, but it isn't any more annoying than everyone else's panting. We're travelling in a group much larger than I would like. With everyone so tired, hot, and thirsty, we're gaining terrible ground. Our group is sluggish, even in the evening when the heat is more bearable. I'm positive we're going to run out of water before we make it halfway there, but I keep that nightmare to myself. The best I can do is guard my backpack and keep an eye on Connor. He's the only guy here I care about. Even though we aren't friends, I know he'll have my back if something pops off.

We've come to a silent agreement to stick together. It began when we first set off and I suggested walking along the roads while the others wanted to keep to the back roads. Connor took my side and when we had a vote, it was his tally that broke the tie. Since then, we've been marching side by side in exhausted silence.

The others around us are too tired to grumble and complain, but I can see the contempt in their eyes whenever they gaze at me. When we slow down for a break, I don't miss the glares and eyerolls. Even as we sit on the side of the highway and sip our water in silence, the air is stale, and the tension is palpable.

I lean against the guardrail and sigh. Connor groans beside me, gingerly settling in the dirt. He looks like a maraschino cherry, and he hisses when the swollen skin of his back touches the hot metal of the rail behind him.

"We should've packed sunscreen," I joke.

He glances sideways at me and his mouth slants. I guess it's a smile.

"Water?" I hold up my canteen.

He takes it and gulps twice then passes it back. "How close are we?"

"Sign up there says there's an exit leading to Marway," says a feminine voice.

I glance up and shield my eyes from the sun. Daniella Martinez from Zeta Chi stands with her hands on her hips just a few feet away. She's staring between me and Connor like she isn't sure who to address.

I clear my throat. "That's good. We're not as far behind as I thought."

"How much longer?" Daniella asks.

"Maybe another day."

"I don't have enough water to last another day."

"Neither do I." Chris Morgen stands beside Daniella, he's an angry sophomore from Green House. I don't know him or care about him, but he's been a thorn in my side since we left. Chris was the most vocal about staying off the highway, since he lost that battle, he's made it his goal to disagree with me about every little thing or constantly point out every problem we're facing as if I personally summoned it upon us.

It's my fault Daniella is almost out of water. It's my fault it's so freaking hot out here. It's my fault the power is out.

I'm *this* close to ripping my own hair out, but instead of losing my crap, I sigh and rise to my feet, nodding toward the cars right behind Daniella and Chris.

"There are two reasons I preferred taking the highways over the back roads," I explain. "The first is that the highway is technically a winding map, if we follow the signs, we'll know exactly how many miles until Phoenix, and which exit to take to get there."

Daniella nods but Chris just grunts and folds his arms.

"The second reason I preferred the highway is because of all the abandoned cars. Just like at Cross North, the cars here are fried. Batteries are dead and the engines are busted. I have no idea what happened when the lights went out, but it's clear it didn't just happen to our university." I pause to glance around. There are cars everywhere on the highway—some of them are partially destroyed, like they stopped working abruptly and left drivers in dangerous collisions. Others are parked in the emergency stop zones, like they had enough time to pull over before everything melted into chaos.

"Search the cars around you," I tell Daniella. "Some of them are bound to have supplies."

I'm not stupid enough to believe we'll find everything we need out here. But it's worth a shot. The blackouts started rolling through town every weekend months before school started, most people were prepared for it. I'm sure there's a car or two with a pack of water stashed in the trunk or a few canned goods rolling around in the backseats. If the passengers didn't take the supplies with them when they left—and the cars haven't been picked clean by looters—we should be able to find something. Anything.

Daniella looks like she understands what I'm getting at. She chews her lip as she scans the crooked rows of cars, then she nods and turns away. Chris glares at me for a few moments before he begrudgingly pivots and stomps toward the nearest vehicle.

"Tell the others!" I call after them.

It takes us another hour to start packing up because everyone gets excited about looting the abandoned cars. To my shock—and relief—Daniella manages to find three water bottles and a pack of jerky. She offers a few strips to me, and I start to turn them down but the look on her face is so desperate, I can't refuse her.

"Thanks for telling us about the cars. Staying on the highway was a good idea," she says, walking beside me. She's so close I have to glance down and adjust my footing so I don't step on her.

"Sorry Chris has been so rude to you," she says, stuffing a piece of jerky into her mouth. "It's just so hot and we're all worried, you know?"

"Yeah."

"I mean, I don't even know what to expect when we make it to the city. I haven't even thought about it. I'm just focusing on surviving."

"Yeah."

"But I hope my family is safe. Don't you?" She looks sideways at me, and I have to take a slow breath to keep from screaming at her.

I do not feel like talking about my family with this girl. I get that she wants to be friends since I helped her find some water when she needed it, but it's too hot and I'm too tired for this chitchat. I just want to find my brother and sister and get back to campus so I can take Mya away from that madness.

I stop walking and glance around the highway. Daniella has stopped with me—she's still going on about her family, something about her *abuela* being so old now. I have no idea what that means so I grunt out a noncommittal response and shield my eyes so I can see past the glare of the afternoon sun.

All the light is being reflected off the tops of the abandoned cars so it's difficult to see, but I don't need great eyesight to *hear*.

Somewhere beneath Daniella's idle chatter ... I hear something. Not voices but sounds—something like a whistle.

"Shut up, Daniella," I say quickly.

Her mouth audibly snaps shut, and she blinks at me. "What the heck, Adrian? Why are you being so rude?"

"Did you hear that?"

I turn around, somewhat surprised to see Connor standing off to the side. He's staring in the same direction I thought I heard the whistling come from.

"I heard it," he says slowly.

"Heard what?" Daniella stares between us. "I didn't hear any—"

A gunshot cuts her off, followed by the *tink* of a metal bullet hitting the hood of a car. Daniella screams and drops to the ground. So does everyone else. Connor is screaming for everyone to take cover while I crouch between two vehicles and run toward Daniella. She's shrieking and trying to crawl away, but when she sees me coming, she immediately throws herself at me. Her arms latch around my neck and she sobs into my chest.

I pry her hands away to hold her at arm's length. "Are you hurt?" I say quickly.

She shakes her head. "What's happening?"

"I don't know. Someone fired at us."

I don't really need to ask who or why. That much is obvious. We're walking up the middle of an open highway like

161

moving targets. It was only a matter of time before someone spotted us and decided to take their chances. I had hoped we could make it a little closer to the city before bumping into anyone, but I should have known nothing would work out the way I wanted.

I take my chances and peek around the red car I'm hiding behind. As soon as my head pops out, I see the glint of a scope and duck back just in time. The taillight on the car explodes in my face as a bullet crashes through it. I'm spitting yellow plastic out of my mouth while Daniella screams and drags me further into cover.

"Someone's shooting at us!" she shrieks, as if that isn't obvious.

"They've got us pinned," Connor says angrily.

"What do we do?" I can hear the panic in Daniella's voice; it should fill me with masculine adrenaline so I can get us out of here alive but all it does is make me panic too.

Whoever is out there wants to kill us, and they've got the means to do it. They don't even know who we are, they saw us and started shooting. They don't even have a reason, except that we've got packs on our backs, and they probably don't.

This isn't another skirmish on campus for cans of spam and beans. These people are willing to shoot us down and keep moving.

"We should surrender," Connor says.

I shake my head, but before I can speak, another gunshot goes off and a high-pitched scream yanks my attention away.

Ahead of us, some of the students have panicked and started running through the cars. Shots pop off around us and they begin dropping like flies, screaming as they fall to the spray of bullets.

"Let's go," I say, almost to myself. When Connor doesn't move, I slap him on his sunburned shoulder and shout, "Let's go! We have to run!"

"They'll shoot us if we move!" Daniella says.

I turn and grab her by the strap of her bag, jerking her to her feet. "They'll shoot us if we stay."

The three of us sprint through the rows of cars, shoving past the other escaping students with no grace or mercy. These guys are not my friends. I don't owe them anything. So I don't try to save anyone. I don't try to look out for anyone. I just run until my legs start to feel numb. Connor easily keeps up—he's not the best sprinter on the track team, but he's good enough when he needs to be. Daniella has trouble matching our pace but each time a gunshot pops off, she screams and picks up speed.

She's about two cars behind us when she shouts my name. "Adrian! Adrian!"

I glance over my shoulder, but I don't get to see what she wants because Connor stumbles into me and we both crash into the bed of a pickup truck. I grunt and shove him away, but the way he cries out makes me pause.

Connor trips to the side and leans against the truck, his face mottled in pain. That's when I see it, the blood staining his sweatpants. He's been shot in the leg.

"Connor…" I blink at him.

"I'll be fine."

Another shot fires off, and we both duck behind the truck. I can't stop myself from staring at Connor's bloody leg. This is bad. He can't run with his leg messed up. He'll barely be able to walk. But I can't leave him behind. He isn't a nameless student like the others we abandoned on the highway.

Connor's my teammate. My Kappa Pi brother.

"Get up!" shouts a voice over my shoulder. I don't even register that it belongs to someone I don't know. I just start moving mechanically, like I'm on autopilot.

There's a gun shoved into my face, and a man screaming for me to take off my backpack. My entire body feels numb. I can't even make out the words being shouted at me. All I can think of is Connor's leg and how much it sucks that we've been caught. And now I'm going to die because we couldn't run fast enough. I'm on the track team, and I couldn't run fast enough.

Silver flashes, and then I'm knocked sideways. It takes me a minute to realize I've been hit on the head with the butt of a gun. I feel another stab of pain, and I stumble sideways. Another flash of silver—I get my hands up in time to block the blow, but it never comes.

Someone is screaming. It's Connor. He's thrown himself at the guy with the gun. They start to tussle, rolling on the ground. The gun flies out of the attacker's hand and I immediately snap from my stupor.

All the sound comes rushing back with a pop, and I feel like I've just surfaced from underwater. Adrenaline storms through my body; I'm not moving mechanically anymore, now I'm acting on instinct.

The attacker shoves Connor aside and dives for his gun but I charge over and kick it away. We both watch in shock as it flies through the guardrail and tumbles over the edge of the highway.

Then I'm tackled from behind. There's a second guy. He's bigger than the first, and he's armed with a crowbar. He takes a swing and I manage to step back and counter with a punch that whips his head to the side. I step forward to hit him again, but he screams and trips sideways as Daniella attacks him.

She's got a knife.

I have no idea where it came from, but it's in her hands and she's using it like she knows what she's doing—stabbing him in his neck as she screams like she's lost her mind. She pulls the knife out and the man drops to his knees, but Daniella isn't done. He takes three more stabs before she steps back, panting.

"You got him," I say softly. "It's okay, Dani."

She jerks her head to the side, and I glance over to find Connor on the ground. The gunman is gone—running back down the highway in the other direction. Guess he doesn't want to fight without his gun or his buddy. But there's no time to think about him.

I run and slide to my knees beside Connor. He groans as I roll him over. There are bruises on his face and his leg is still bleeding, but other than that, he looks fine.

"You good?" I say stupidly.

He groans again. "Did they take anything?"

"No." I glance up at Daniella and she shakes her head. "I've still got all my stuff."

"What about the others?" Connor asks.

The others are long gone. Half of our group is sprawled along the highway. Dead. The other half took off running. If I squint, I can still see some running ahead in the distance. But they're so far away, I doubt we'll catch up with Connor's leg busted like this.

"You can't walk on that leg," I say.

Daniella wipes her knife off on her jeans. "We can help him. I've got some bandages and alcohol to clean the wound."

"I won't slow us down," Connor says pathetically. We all

know that isn't true. But no one argues with him.

Daniella helps me get Connor to his feet and we walk to the nearest highway exit. On the ramp, there's another pickup truck pulled off to the side. We open the bed and set Connor in it. He grunts and tries to hold back his cries, but I can tell he's in a lot of pain. Who wouldn't be? The guy took a bullet to the leg.

"I think it went straight through," Daniella says. She's in the bed of the truck with Connor who's lying pants-less against the hot metal. He stares up at the sun as she uses her hunting knife to cut strips of fabric from the shirt he'd tied around his head earlier. Before we got shot at.

"That's a good thing," Dani says. "It means we just have to clean the wound and stop the bleeding."

"Easier said than done," Connor grumbles.

Daniella says something in Spanish and then clicks her tongue. "I've got alcohol. I can clean it and tie up your leg for now. But I don't think we should walk for the rest of the day."

We can't afford to sit still for that long. But I'm afraid of what'll happen to Connor if we don't rest. We got attacked by random thugs. We lost our group. We might be stuck out here for much longer than expected with Connor's injury. This isn't going the way I planned at all. But I can't let this stop me.

I nod at Daniella. "Clean him up and then we'll take it easy until the evening. Maybe we can try walking for a few hours when it's cooler out."

Dani gives me a stiff smile. "Alright."

18

Caesar

We managed to talk Omega Zeta Chi into a reasonable arrangement. They'll freely share water with anyone who swears loyalty to them, but for those who don't, they'll have to offer something to trade for hydration. It isn't ideal, but it's something.

I can feel the tension rising, and it's all thanks to the sorority. Everyone else has doubled down on their efforts to preserve their supplies too. Green House is only trading with Omega Zeta, offering canned goods for water. They've decided they don't need medical supplies from Hope House and anything we have to offer isn't worth their time. Meanwhile, Hope House has surrendered bandages and alcohol wipes for a few 8-ounce bottles of water, but Hot House hasn't done any trading at all. They've been baking bread and minding their business. I don't know how they've managed to survive this long without restocking their water supply, but they haven't even left their dorm since Zeta Chi started gatekeeping the water.

The smell of freshly baked bread fills the streets every day, and every day tensions rise a little higher. Nerves are wrung a little tighter. The battle with North Campus was bloody and brutal, but a civil war is on the horizon now, and it threatens to shatter us.

To keep ourselves hydrated, Kappa Pi has decided to go looting in the Academic buildings. We could easily trade with Omega Zeta Chi, but we want to explore every possible avenue before giving in to their demands.

Coach Noble thinks there might be a small stash of water in the sports center where the other coaches kept snacks and things in their offices. He hadn't thought to check there before because classes hadn't even started, so he'd only gone to his office three times before the power went out. In fact, before we made the trip over to the academic campus, he made it clear he isn't even sure if there *is* a stash here, but with our dwindling water supply, I decided it was worth a shot regardless.

We took a small group of volunteers, eight total, and then we split into four pairs when we finally made it there. One pair has been charged with keeping watch, in case more hostile students from North Campus show up. Meanwhile, the other three pairs have split up to search the sports center for food, water, and other useful supplies.

Mya and I have been walking around for about fifteen minutes. We've checked two offices and found a box of protein bars in the desk drawer of Coach Panell, she's the head coach of the women's volleyball team. Never met the woman, but that's what the tag on her door said.

Mya and I split a bar as we make our way to the men's sports area. I stuff my half down in three seconds flat, but Mya is still enjoying hers at a pace so slow it feels like torture. It takes more concentration than I think is possible to not stand there and drool as she eats dark chocolate and oats and dried fruit and everything else I normally hate. Right now, I'm starving, so I'd eat anything. Even dark chocolate—which tastes like toxic poison to me.

"Gosh, you've always eaten slow," I say with a smirk. "Even though we're starving, that still hasn't changed."

Mya laughs and offers me the rest of her bar. "You can have the rest."

"You're not hungry?"

She shakes her head. "I actually had a decent breakfast. And I hate dark chocolate."

We both snort together as I open the door to the track and field section of offices. Coach Noble already warned us that his personal office would be empty, but he said we might be able to find supplies in the other two offices. Coach Lambert and Coach Jackson. Both of them are old men with grey hair and sour breath; Lambert is always complaining, and Jackson is always, *always*, munching on a bag of sunflower seeds. So, at the very least, we might be able to find a packet or two of those. Except sunflower seeds are salty, so we'll definitely need water to compensate for that.

I take Lambert's office while Mya splits and heads into Jackson's office. As expected, Lambert's place is empty, but I do find a first aid kit in the file cabinet, so I stuff that into my backpack and join Mya.

She's going through his desk when I walk inside and toss the foil wrapper to the protein bar into the trash bin.

Mya looks up with a grin. "Nice to know some of us still have manners."

I chuckle. "Just because we've spiraled into chaos doesn't mean I've forgotten how to use a trash bin."

"Did you enjoy the bar?"

I shrug. "I was hungry. So yeah, I guess." I tilt my head to the side as I remember suddenly, "Did you ever eat your Daisy Bar?" I'd given it to her when we'd looted the café, right before those crazy North Campus kids stormed in and chased us all away.

Mya stiffens, but I'm not sure if it's because of my question or because she just found a box with six bags of sunflower seeds still wrapped inside. She sets the box on the desk and avoids my gaze.

"We'll definitely need to find water," she mumbles, walking around the desk to search the mini fridge in the corner.

I squint at her. "Something wrong?"

"No."

"Mya—"

She pulls out a six-pack of orange Gatorade and exclaims, "Bingo!"

"Put the Gatorade down," I say, turning around and folding my arms over my chest.

She frowns but does as she's told.

"What's going on?"

Mya sighs. "I didn't eat the Daisy Bar you gave me."

"Why not? Was it old?"

She shakes her head and I feel myself getting agitated. There's clearly something wrong but Mya won't spit it out. I can't even begin to imagine what sort of problem could arise from a Daisy Bar but the way she won't look at me makes me feel like she's about to break my heart.

"Just spit it out," I say angrily. "Whatever it is, I don't care.

You're making me anxious."

Mya finally looks me in the eye. "I gave the bar to Adrian. As a goodbye gift."

If I weren't already dehydrated, my mouth would've gone dry at that moment. I blink at Mya in stupefied confusion. It takes an extra moment for her words to sink in. My only reaction is a slow blink.

"I gave you that bar," I say in a voice so quiet, I'm surprised Mya can even make out the words.

She presses her lips together tightly before she nods. "Yeah. I know."

"It's your favorite."

"I know."

"I found it for you."

"I know, Julie."

"Then why?"

She fiddles with the Gatorade in her hand. "Because Adrian was leaving—"

"So what? Why did you even care that he was leaving? He's not your best friend—*I* am." I pat my chest like I've just delivered a great speech. I'm aware of how childish this sounds. I'm aware that this isn't really that big of a deal, but I can't stop myself from overreacting. Because it *is* a big deal to me.

Mya and I have been together since we were children. I've done everything I can to take care of her since the lights went out. Even getting her that nasty bar. And her thanks was to hand it off to someone she knows doesn't even like me.

I bunch my shoulders, trying to smother the anger before it reaches my brain and makes me do something I'll regret. "Adrian hates me, and you gave him the gift I gave you. When did this even happen?"

"The day he left," she answers. "I went to his dorm."

"You were in his *room?*" I step closer to her, and she scooches away. She's so tiny compared to me—compared to anyone, really—but I feel like a giant as I loom over her, glaring. "You went to his room to give him a chocolate bar," I say flatly.

"It was a goodbye gift."

"I doubt that was the only gift he got."

She drops the Gatorade to shove me back a step. I'm caught off guard by her strength, eyes bulging as I steady my footing.

Mya's brows are pinched together, and her jaw is locked. I can tell just from looking that she's pissed off, but I don't care.

"Adrian started a fight with me over *you,*" I hiss, "and the first chance you get, you run to his room and throw yourself at him."

"I gave him a *chocolate bar—*"

"Yeah, right."

"I'm not like you," she snaps. "I don't give my body to everyone who smiles at me."

Her comment stings, but I smother the insult with anger. "Right. You're just a judgmental little Christian girl—" I drop my gaze to where her cross pendant normally hangs around her neck, but it's not there. The realization makes me freeze mid-thought.

Mya's neck is bare. Her necklace is gone. I've never seen her without it. Not since I bought it for her—my gaze snaps to her hands, clasped in front of herself. It takes me a fraction of a second to find the finger she used to keep her thorny crown ring on... That's missing too.

"What the heck, Mya," I whisper. "What the heck..."

172

She looks away, biting her lip. "I'm sorry. I wanted him to have it—"

"*Him?*"

I know who she's talking about, there's no doubt in my mind.

"You gave him the chocolate," my voice is a dangerous growl, "fine. That's just a candy bar. But the necklace *I* bought you? The ring *I* gave you?" I take another step, backing her into the wall. "What's wrong with you?" I hiss.

"You're too close." Mya reaches up to push me back, but I grab her hands and pin them above her head. She's pressed against the wall, breathing heavily, shifting on her tiptoes because I've stretched her arms as high as they'll go. She winces like she's in pain, but I don't care.

My grip on her arms tightens. "You little traitor," I whisper. "You went behind my back—"

"And you did it in front of my face!" she shouts.

I lean back, blinking in surprise.

"I went to Adrian behind your back. But you've had whatever girl you've wanted right in front of me for years, and I've never said a word." She pins me with her angry gaze. "I've had to watch you with so many girls. Girls I knew. Girls I had class with. Girls who were my *friends*—but that never mattered to you. You've always gotten whatever you've wanted, Julie. And the first time I take something I want; you treat me like this." She tugs on her hands, locked in my grip. "You don't own me."

I can't think. The only words I heard through all of that are the ones I wish I could erase from my memory.

The first time I take something I want...

Does she *want* Adrian?

173

The question must be written on my face because Mya glances away and says softly, "I like him. I've always liked him. But I never said anything because I knew you didn't like him."

So Adrian was right. All this time, he was right. I am the reason Mya didn't want to date him. I am the reason she rejected him. She did it to keep me happy. Did it to maintain our friendship.

That can't be true.

She *can't* like Adrian. I hate Adrian. And he hates me. And all these years … it was supposed to be me and Mya. We were supposed to end up together. Isn't that how it always goes? I don't care about the other girls. I don't care about Delilah. The others have never mattered to me—they were just placeholders. Girls who kept me busy while I waited for the day I'd finally come to my senses. Waited to grow up and notice Mya. But all this time, she's only been waiting for him.

That isn't fair.

She doesn't get to like someone else.

"Take it back," I whisper, staring down at her in disbelief.

She shakes her head. "Julie, I can't take back what I feel."

"Yes, you can," I say earnestly. "Take it back, Mya."

"Or what?" she asks, then she lifts her chin—and I can't stop myself from kissing her.

At first, she fights me, yanking her hands to get them away, but I hold tight and keep her pinned there. She gasps for breath, and I deepen the kiss, sliding my tongue over hers with a groan—that's when she bites me.

I jerk back and wipe my mouth, staring at the blood on my fingers. "You bit me," I say. When I glance up, I see the brown blur of her hand—she's going to slap me, but I catch her wrist and yank her into my chest. When I kiss her again, she doesn't fight me.

It's a bloody exchange, my mouth burns from when she bit me moments earlier, but the joy I feel numbs the pain until I shiver and pull away.

Mya buries her face in my chest. I feel her shudder against me, and I realize she's crying. "I'm sorry," I whisper.

"Why would you kiss me?" Her voice is muffled against my dirty shirt.

"Because I'm a selfish monster." It's an honest answer. I have no other reason. No other excuse. I kissed her because I wanted to. Because I've *always* wanted to. And I stupidly believed that Mya would always be there waiting for the moment I was *ready* to kiss her. But in my absence, she'd moved on. While I was busy entertaining myself, she was busy putting her life together.

A small part of me wonders if this happened in my absence, or if her feelings had always belonged to someone else. If she'd ever felt the same as me.

"Was there ever a chance?" I ask in a raspy voice. God, I feel tears knocking at the back of my aching throat. This is so pathetic. So stupid. I've never cried over a girl before. I can't even remember the last time I cried period.

Mya looks up at me and her lips part just enough for her to speak, but the words never come. They're interrupted by loud cackling and footsteps walking through the halls outside the office.

We immediately pull away from each other like we've been caught doing something inappropriate. Mya starts packing up the sunflower seeds and Gatorade bottles and I stand there like an idiot, wiping blood from my cut lip.

When she's finished, she turns to me and inhales deeply.

"We should get going."

Someone pokes their head into the office, it's a kid from Hope House. "Hey, we found some of that electrolyte water in the locker room. And ... is it safe to drink the pool water?"

I roll my eyes. "Take the electrolytes out front, I'll go see about the pool."

Mya rushes out before I can say anything else, but I don't feel bad. Maybe it's better this way.

19

Adrian

We're moving too slow. We took a long rest after we managed to escape those trolls, but it's done nothing for Connor's leg. He's limping slower now than he was when he was first shot. Daniella did the best she could with what we had, but I think Connor needs real help. A doctor's help. Something we don't have.

This nightmare only increases my anxiety. If things are this bad out here, what will the city be like? What about my little brother and sister?

I promised I'd be there for them, but I stayed on campus with my friends. I stayed with Mya. And if she had asked, in that room, after giving me her necklace and saying how much she cared about me, I would have stayed even longer. I would have stayed for her.

That thought makes me burn with shame. That I would easily abandon my family for a woman. But it's the truth. I've always had strong feelings for Mya, and I can't really explain why. She's just one of those girls. A magnet. And once I got too close, I was helpless against her pull.

Without thinking, I reach up and touch the necklace she gave me. Her goodbye gift. It's a cross-shaped pendant and a ring fashioned as a thorny crown. Something about Jesus and His crown on the cross, when He was crucified. I don't believe in God, but I do believe that Mya believes. She's convinced God is real and her love for Him compelled her to give this to me.

No matter what I think of religion, I cannot deny how much this gift means. I cannot deny the proof of her emotion in this small gesture. God means a lot to her, so for her to share this piece of Him with me… well, it gives me the determination I need to keep going. Because I made a promise to my siblings that I would leave for them, but I made a promise to Mya that I would return for her.

Connor stumbles because I've stopped supporting him. He shifts slightly to the side, and I let go of the necklace to stable him again.

He waves a hand as he grunts. "I … I can't—I need to stop."

Daniella is on his other side; she heaves a sigh as she gingerly leans him against an abandoned car. We made it off the highway and decided to travel on the back roads the other day. It's just the three of us now. The rest of the students from campus were shot down or escaped and never looked back. I don't know if that's better or worse.

"This isn't good," Daniella says, looking right at me. She's been doing that lately, talking like Connor isn't right there. It creeps me out. It makes me feel like he's already dead in her eyes.

"What isn't good?" I ask, trying to force her to acknowledge him.

She crosses her arms. "He's moving too slow. And our supplies dwindle every day."

She's right. At this point, we'll run out of food and water before we make it to the city. This is the same problem we faced before, except there isn't much around for us to loot now. The back roads are mostly empty and feel just as dangerous as the highway. Even now, we're sitting out in the open, leaning against a car on the side of the road.

There is nothing in either direction. Trees line the sidewalks. Death waits ahead and behind.

I turn and peer into the passenger window of the abandoned car, as if a case of water will magically appear on the backseat. There is nothing inside, but I try the door anyway. It's locked.

Daniella pulls out her fancy hunting knife and gets to work making little scratches on the driver's window. She found that knife in the back of a Jeep Wrangler left on the highway—go figure. She also found a few bottles of water and some camping snacks. But that stuff is nearly gone now. Together, we have three bottles of water, a pack of trail mix, and a jar of hot peppers in olive oil. The peppers came from the café, I've had them since we battled the North Campus students, and I am not looking forward to eating them. Right now, it seems like I might be munching on them in a few hours.

Daniella steps back and kicks the driver's window. The scratches she made splinter into cracks and then the window shatters with a second kick. She reaches inside the car and unlocks the door. As she begins her search for food, I turn to Connor.

He looks awful. There's a bandage tied around his thigh, where he was shot. But it's soaked through with blood and part of it has turned black. His jeans are crusted with blood, there's so much, they actually look heavy. I can't believe he's still standing, let alone walking for miles in the hot sun. He still isn't wearing a shirt, but that's the least of his worries.

Daniella said the bullet went straight through. That's a good thing. But it doesn't mean he's out of the woods yet. He could get an infection. He could agitate the wound enough that it never fully heals. Worst of all, the injury is slowing us all down.

If we push Connor too hard, he will get worse and die. But if we don't hurry up, we will all die. Whether its starvation or more crazy people, something will eventually find us and kill us.

"How are you?" I ask Connor.

He looks up at me through weak, papery-lidded eyes. "I'm hanging in there."

Daniella climbs out of the car and holds up a can of Red Bull and a smashed Snickers bar. "Ain't much, but it's better than nothing."

She ain't lying.

Together, we help Connor into the backseat of the car so he can lay down away from the sun. Then we get into the front seats and split the bar and the energy drink. No one speaks. We just sit there licking chocolate and caramel off our dirty fingers and passing a hot can of caffeine around.

"How much further?" Dani asks, disrupting the silence.

"Probably another two days."

"You said that two days ago."

"I know."

Dani sighs. "We're moving too slow."

We have this conversation every few hours. It's starting to grate on my nerves.

"I don't know what you want me to do. We're moving as fast as we can."

"It isn't fast enough."

"You think I don't know that?"

"I'm sorry," Connor cuts in. He lifts his head and groans in the backseat, then he lets out an awful cough and repeats his apology in a hoarse voice. "I'm sorry. It's my fault."

"It's no one's fault," I grunt. Connor isn't as tall as me but he's big enough, and he's heavy, built like a runner with lean muscles and long legs. He's a lot to carry around all day, even though he's doing his best to walk on his own. It isn't enough. None of this is enough. We will die out here on this road. Daniella knows it. Connor knows it. I know it too, but I refuse to accept it. Except there is nothing I can do about any of this. I am running out of encouraging things to say to keep Connor motivated. We are running out of places to loot. I'm running out of energy. Food. Hope.

We are slowly dying.

If there is a God, I think to myself, *now would be a great time for a miracle.*

I toss the empty can of Red Bull out the open door. "We should sleep here tonight."

"It's only late afternoon, we can still walk for another hour or two," Dani says.

"And what if we don't hit town? It's better to sleep indoors than on the ground."

Daniella just nods. It won't be comfortable to sit upright in the seats, but it's better than stretching out on dirty concrete.

Besides, Connor has already passed out behind us, and I don't want to move him, so neither of us tries very hard to think of reasons to leave this car.

Except now we're stuck here staring out the windows in silence and I suddenly feel nervous. Like I should say something.

"Why don't you run ahead and see if there's anything to loot?" I suggest. She's been so worried about Connor slowing us down and our supplies dwindling, if she walked ahead for an hour or so, she might find a house or another car. Then she could loot it and come back.

I thought that was a good idea until Daniella snapped her head toward me. We make eye contact, and that's when I see it. The flicker of doubt in her eyes, tangled with fear. But it isn't a fear of being attacked or even a fear of running out of supplies. Daniella doesn't trust me. She's afraid if she walks away, I'll take Connor and the last of our water, and leave her behind.

So even though we're starving and barely holding off dehydration, Daniella shakes her head and faces forward. "I think it's best we stick together," she mumbles.

"Do you really think I'll leave you?" I blurt without thinking.

Dani doesn't look at me as she says, "They did. They were our friends, and they left us behind."

"We were being shot at. That's different."

"They could've come back. They were our *friends*."

None of them were my friends—Connor is barely my friend—but that doesn't mean Dani wasn't close to any of them. From the look of her welling eyes and quivering chin, I'm guessing she was close to them. This sucks. I'm stranded with a guy who's been shot and a girl with abandonment issues—ironically, that same girl wants me to leave Connor behind.

"Chris was my boyfriend," Dani mutters, wiping a fat tear from her cheek.

Chris? Does she mean Chris Morgen? That prickly sophomore who clearly hated me?

"He was my boyfriend and he left me on that highway." Daniella looks up at me with tears spilling down her face. "So why wouldn't you leave me?"

"If I haven't left Connor, who is clearly slowing us down, then you can trust that I won't leave you. I promise."

She looks at me like I've just promised to give her the world. "Thank you," she says, leaning toward me.

At first, I think she's going to give me a hug. She has her hand extended, going over my shoulders, but instead of sharing a quick embrace, she wraps her hands around my neck and pulls me to her lips.

I let her kiss me because I don't really have a reason not to. I've got to travel with this woman, that'll be easier to do if she doesn't hate me for rejecting her. So I let her kiss me. I let her pull me close and pretend I'm Chris Morgen. I know that's what she's doing in her head. I know she's using me to get over the pain of her boyfriend leaving her behind. For the moment, I don't mind. She's not a bad kisser. But when she scoots over and climbs into my lap, I pull away.

"We can't do this," I say.

She sniffles, still crying. Her tears wet my own cheeks.

"Yes, we can," she says.

"You have a boyfriend."

"I *had* a boyfriend—"

183

"And I'm not his replacement."

She stiffens in my arms and glances away. "Please let me have this." Her voice is a whisper. "Just this once."

I should tell her no. I should tell her she's crazy and shove her off my lap. But instead, I shock myself by murmuring, "Just this once."

Then she's kissing me again and tugging at my sweaty shirt, and she doesn't care about the scars that line my chest and back. She just wants comfort for this night. This quick fleeting moment. And I realize, as I toss away her clothing, that I want the same thing. I want some sense of comfort after being so worried for so long. So stressed. So angry. So frustrated. This isn't going to bring me any peace, but it will distract me for a moment. I suppose that's good enough.

So we stay there in the front of the car with the door open and the Arizona heat melting us, and we do this awkward dance of grunts and gasps. All while Connor sleeps soundly in the backseat.

When I peel my lids back, I see a sliver of sunlight crawling over the horizon. "Oh crap," I whisper, rubbing my eyes. "I slept through the night."

"That's not surprising," Connor says behind me.

I shift to look at him, taking in his furrowed brow and clenched jaw. He looks like he wants to punch me. I'm thankful for his injured leg all of a sudden.

"After all that action last night, I would've slept good too."

I feel my cheeks burn. "So, you were awake."

"You guys woke me up. And I had to listen until you finished."

I swallow then wince. My throat is dry.

"But even if I didn't hear anything—" Connor looks me up and down exaggeratedly and I suddenly want to curl up and die.

My pants are still down, piled up around my knees, proof of just how cheap I am. I feel awful. I feel pathetic. And also a little confused.

Daniella isn't in the car.

I shove open my door and step out to tug my sweatpants back up, then I tie the drawstring and blink around. The morning light is slow, but enough of it has spilled across the road for me to see that no one is out here but me and Connor.

I duck to look into the backseat. "Where's Daniella?"

Connor chuckles. "She left. Last night."

My heart stops. The shock I feel is so sudden and cutting, I grip my chest as it begins to ache.

"She left?"

That can't be true. She was so afraid of me leaving her behind. Why would she just up and leave in the middle of the night?

With a gasp, I lean into the front seat and search for my bag, but Connor's words stop me immediately.

"She took it. And her bag too."

"No," I whisper.

"Yes," Connor says, and I can't ignore the sound of triumph in his voice. Even though Daniella has run off with our food and water, he sounds happy. Smug. Like he's *this* close to saying, *I told you so.* Even though he's never voiced any concerns about Daniella before.

I shift in the front seat to glare at him over my shoulder. "How do you know she left?"

"I saw her. About an hour after you finished, she packed up and left."

"And you just let her?"

He motions to his leg. "What was I supposed to do?"

"You could have screamed to wake me up."

"She had a knife—she threatened me."

"You could have screamed after she started walking away."

"Or you could have kept your pecker in your pants and not fallen into a sex coma!"

I blanch. "She—She was afraid of being alone."

Laughter cuts me off. "You really believed that? Daniella played you for a fool and took off with our supplies."

I sink into the front seat, trying hard not to fall into despair. This is all my fault. We're going to starve to death because I believed a crying girl over my own gut instinct.

Connor shifts and holds up another backpack. "It's not all bad," he says, and the edge in his voice is almost gone. "When I got shot, we switched backpacks because yours was lighter."

My eyes widen as Connor empties the bag. "Daniella took my bag, thinking it was yours. That means we've still got a few supplies left."

Slowly, he pulls out a single bottle of water and a Daisy Bar.

I could burst into tears—for more reasons than one. First, I was an idiot and this whole thing is my fault. Second, we might still have a chance, and it's all because of Mya and her chocolate bar. Or maybe it's because of Mya and the God she prays to. I have no idea who to give thanks to, but if there *is* a God, I don't want to take my chances of stealing His credit, so I take a shallow breath and whisper a prayer for the first time in years, "Thank you, Jesus," then I grab the water and chocolate and stuff them back into the bag. "Get up, Connor," I say. "We're leaving."

"Are you serious?"

"Do you want to stay here and die?"

He shakes his head. "I'm still hurt. There's no way we'll make it."

He just might be right, but I'm not ready to accept that yet. I am literally living on a prayer and a Daisy Bar but that's been enough so far, there's no reason to believe it won't be enough for just a little longer.

20

Caesar

It's been a week since we searched the sports center of the academic campus. Kappa Pi is officially out of water. Memphis still has two bottles of vodka stashed in his room, but unless we want to drink Lizard Lemonade for the next few days, we've got to make a deal with Zeta Chi.

Bunny's been feeling good enough to limp around the house. I put him in charge of finding things to trade with. He took a couple freshmen brothers to help sort out supplies we didn't think were vital and came up with a few things. So now I'm standing outside Zeta Chi with Coach Noble holding a box of goods. There are two protein bars, a family size bag of Doritos, a package of dried fruit, and two sticks of lip balm inside. It isn't much—I know—but it's all we could spare.

This morning, Noble opened two cans of string beans we had left over from the café and passed them around. That was our breakfast. There are still a couple cans of beef stew in the basement, and three packs of sunflower seeds, but none of that will matter if we don't have water to wash it down.

We're so desperate, we drank the water from the canned string beans once we finished eating them. It was as awful as it sounds.

"You ready for this?" Noble asks.

The sound of his voice makes me glance over at him. He looks as nervous as I feel, which isn't good at all. I can't be the calm one between us. I'm still reeling from that fight with Mya. I'm reeling because I'm hungry. Because I'm thirsty. Because I'm exhausted and smelly and irritated. Everything around me is falling apart, I need Coach Noble to keep it together.

But I can tell the threads have already begun to unravel for him. He has been the point of authority for us boys since this whole thing started. He's done the best he could for as long as he could, and in some ways it still hasn't been enough.

We're still hungry. We're still stranded here waiting for help that may never come. And we've gotten into fights while we've waited—fights that left some of us really hurt, and some of us dead. None of that has been Coach's fault, but still; I know him. I know he's blamed himself on some level.

So instead of telling him the truth, that I feel like I'm losing my mind as fast as we're losing supplies, I swallow my screams of frustration and plaster on a fake smile. "I'm ready," I say, and then we walk up the driveway to the sorority house and knock on the door.

Delilah answers. This time, she doesn't give us any lip, she just opens the door and steps aside. I try to make eye contact with her, but she avoids my gaze with a quick pivot, speaking over her shoulder, "This way. Let's go."

We follow her down the hall back to the small office we used before, and like before, Jewels is sitting behind her desk.

There are square-framed glasses perched on the tip of her round nose, and she's reading what looks like a hand-written note. There is a tall glass of crystal-clear water sitting on a coaster beside her; it's probably warm but that doesn't stop me from staring longingly at it.

When we take our place before Jewels's desk, she sets the note down and looks over the rim of her spectacles. "I've been expecting contact," she says.

"And why is that?" Noble asks.

"Because I know you've been using Delilah for water. And now that I've intervened to preserve her dignity, you've run out of your supply." She smiles. "So here you are."

The room falls silent while Coach Noble blinks back and forth between me and Delilah, trying to figure out what the heck Jewels is talking about. I keep my vision forward like I don't see him at all, but Delilah stares at the floor, telling him everything he needs to know.

We had a fling and it benefited us both. Delilah spent the night in my room and sometimes she left water before slipping out of bed and returning to her sorority house. But a few days ago, she climbed out of bed and said she wasn't coming back. Apparently, she did it to *preserve her dignity*.

I wasn't hurt because she wasn't my girlfriend, and we had no real connection to each other. But I was surprised. And I was worried. Because without those hookups, I had no other way to get water for myself or the rest of Kappa Pi.

From the way Coach Noble stares at us, I know he had no idea this was going on right above him. But now he does know, and he's pissed about it.

Jewels's grin stretches even wider when Noble's head swivels back to her. "Your student was using my girl to obtain

190

water." She clicks her tongue. "How degrading."

I want to correct her. I want to tell her my relationship with Delilah had nothing to do with water, but I know Noble will never believe me. It isn't entirely wrong either. I didn't use Delilah—I genuinely enjoyed the time we spent together—but I can't deny that some nights weren't about us. Some nights weren't about anything but my next glass of water.

The only thing about this that makes me step forward in anger is how badly Jewels has twisted this around. I didn't use Delilah. If anything, she used me. And when she was done, she cut things off. Ended our relationship and our arrangement altogether. And now here we are.

Before I can say any of this, however, Noble clears his throat and says, "I don't know anything about what you're alluding to. All I know is that we've come to trade for water. Can you help us out or not?"

Jewels leans back in her chair and reaches for her water. She takes a long pull before smacking her lips and lifting the glass like she's making a toast. "I suppose I can help."

Noble sets the box on the edge of the desk and Delilah steps forward to rummage through. Once she's finished sorting the supplies, she leans down to whisper her findings into Jewels's ear.

Jewels looks up at us and presses her lips together. "Is this all you brought to trade with?"

"Everyone is running low on supplies—"

"You're going to need more than that," Jewels cuts Noble off.

"You can't even spare a single bottle?"

"No," she says flatly. "If you want water, you'll need more than this junk. A few more cans of food. Some granola bars. I know someone has spam somewhere."

I narrow my gaze. Something isn't right here.

"How much will all of that get us?" I ask.

Jewels and Delilah both stare at me.

"Excuse me?" Jewels says.

"If we bring you five cans of food, a box of granola bars, and three cans of spam—how much water could we get?"

Both of the ladies exchange glances, and that's when I realize the truth.

"It won't get us anything," I say quietly.

Noble whips his head to the side to blink at me like I've just spoken a foreign language. "What?" he breathes.

"All of that food will get us nothing. Because you don't have any water left to trade, do you?"

Jewels steeples her fingers on the desk. "You're smarter than you look."

"And you're more cunning than you look." I glance at Delilah. "You didn't cut things off to preserve your dignity, Jewels told you to stop coming over because she realized you were giving us water. Water she couldn't afford to hand out anymore. And since you don't have water, you also don't have much food because no one is going to give you spam for free."

I almost laugh as I fold my arms and wait for a reply. The trading system was initiated by Zeta Chi, and now it's the very thing tearing them apart. They thought they could trap everyone by holding the water hostage. If we wanted to avoid dehydration, we would have to give them food in exchange for a drink. But the opposite is also true, with no water to trade, the sorority will starve to death.

Jewels clears her throat and removes her glasses. She stares at the fancy glass of water on her coaster, probably regretting

192

the big gulp she took earlier. I'm willing to bet that's the last of their water right there. And they were willing to use it as a show of power instead of being honest and admitting they need us as much as we need them.

"You're right," Jewels says quietly. "We are nearly out of water. Down to our last few gallons." She looks up at us. "So, what are we going to do now?"

"*We?*" I question. "Now you want to work with us?"

"We can talk to Green House," Coach Noble says civilly, but Jewels shakes her head.

"They are not speaking to us anymore."

"What? Why not?" Noble snaps. "Did you try to screw them over too?"

Hot House left the sorority alone first, then Hope House threw in the towel, now Green House isn't speaking to Zeta Chi. Maybe working with them is a bad idea... But Coach Noble doesn't seem worried. Instead, he reaches up to stroke his short black beard as he waits for Jewels to explain what happened.

"We didn't do anything to Green House. They simply stopped showing up to trade with us. But I had a girl inside—"

I raise one eyebrow, wondering if this sorority girl had a relationship with someone in Green House the same way Delilah had a relationship with me.

"She told me there was something strange going on in Green House," Jewels continues. "She said they had water. From a well."

My eyes widen and I can't stop myself from looking at Coach Noble. A question leaps from my mouth before I can stop it. "Is that true? Is that possible?"

193

Noble continues stroking his beard. "I don't know. It could be like the grandfather clock in Kappa Pi—a geographical relic."

"I've never heard of a well on campus," I say.

"There was a well on campus when the university was first built," Noble explains. "In fact, Green House dorm was constructed around the well because of their garden. They were supposed to use it as a natural source of water for the greenhouse in their backyard."

"So, it's true then," I say breathily. "They have water."

Noble shakes his head. "They have a *well*. But I heard it dried up about twenty years ago. So there's no guarantee they have water."

"They have something," Jewels says. "Because they haven't been trading with us for water, yet they're alive and kicking."

"So is Hot House," I mutter.

"Do you think they've teamed up and left us out?" Noble asks, and Jewels nods.

"That's exactly what we believe. Which means our next move is to team up and raid their dorms."

"Wait—what?" I snap. This was not the course of action I thought she would suggest. "You want us to attack them?"

"We have no choice." She shrugs. Of course she shrugs. Jewels wasn't there when we went to the café and that kid Phil died. She wasn't there when North Campus returned for vengeance and one of their own students died. She's been holed up in this house—in this office—while the world has crumbled around her. Talking about fighting is much different from actually going out there and getting your head smashed in.

"I don't want to fight," I say into the silence.

194

Jewels takes a sip of that warm water. "We don't have a choice."

"Why can't we just talk to them and work something out?"

"We are out of food and water, Caesar. It is past talking time. Do you understand that?"

"What if we don't want to team up and fight?" I say coolly. When I see her jaw clench, I know I've issued the right threat. "Zeta Chi doesn't have the numbers to attack Green House," I explain confidently. "Not if they're teamed up with Hot House. That'll be two versus one."

They need us for this.

Jewels unscrews her jaw. "If you do not help us with this, we will gladly raid Hope House instead. That will be one versus one, and I'm positive we can beat the Bible thumpers."

Sadly ... she is right. Hope House is a Christian dorm; they won't fight back. Not very hard at least. If Zeta Chi moves in on them, they'll probably take over easily. So why haven't they?

Because Hope House has nothing to offer. They've got all the medical supplies, but no one needs bandages and alcohol when they're dying of thirst. Zeta Chi knows this, which is why they want to make a deal with us instead. And use Hope House as bait to force our hand. If we don't work with them, they'll crush an innocent dorm just because they can.

Worst of all, they know I won't let that happen. *Delilah* knows I won't let that happen—because of Mya.

I glare at her across the room, and hatred takes root somewhere deep inside. *How dare she?*

Delilah has the decency to drop her gaze and stare at the floor. Good. I've never hit a woman before, but I'm seriously close to breaking that peace record right now.

Coach Noble breaks the stony silence as he clears his

throat. "Let us talk to the rest of the guys first, alright?"

Jewels gives that cunning smile again and nods to Delilah. She stoops behind the desk and comes up with a half-gallon of water. We'll have to take small sips, but it's enough for the day at least.

"Take this as a token of good faith. And leave the box of food as a token of your good faith."

"Sure," Noble grumbles, taking the jug. "We'll get back to you soon."

"Very soon, I hope. We don't have much time to decide."

I almost spit in her face. The decision has already been made. I can tell as Noble turns and walks out without another word. I can tell from the way he won't look at me during our walk home.

We're going to team up with Zeta Chi. We're going to attack Green House and Hot House. We're doing it because we need supplies, and they've got them. The same reason North Campus attacked us. The only good part of this is that Hope House will be safe. Mya will be safe. Even though she hates my guts right now, I have to hold on to that small bit of peace because it's all I've got to live for.

21

Caesar

Delilah and a few girls arrive at Kappa Pi's door the next morning. Memphis shakes me awake at sunrise and I stumble out of the house to find a dozen angry blondes ready for war. By that time, the rest of Kappa Pi is awake, along with a few neighbors, so it's impossible to keep things quiet.

"What's going on?" Memphis asks. He folds his long arms across his chest and gives me a hard look. Bunny stands behind him, blinking back and forth between us. The other guys have joined the crowd too; everyone is waiting for an answer that I don't want to give.

I never told the rest of the house about Zeta Chi's deal. Never told them about the well, or about Green House and Hot House teaming up against the rest of the dorms.

Coach Noble takes the lead, giving me a very disappointed look before he takes a short breath and says, "Yesterday, we learned some concerning news from Zeta Chi."

"Concerning how?" Memphis says loudly. He speaks for

the rest of the guys who have gathered on the front lawn, looking very hostile and angry. Memphis always kind of looks angry, but it's a different look entirely when it's aimed at you.

Delilah steps forward and answers before Coach Noble can even speak. "There's a well on Green House's property. And we want your help to raid their house and take their supplies. Along with whatever Hot House has stashed away."

Memphis blinks. Murmurs ripple through the crowd of Kappa Pi brothers.

"They have a well," he finally says. "When were you going to tell us?"

I wasn't going to tell them. I'd never be ready to tell my brothers we had to go to war based on speculation. But I know now, from the way Memphis is looking at me, I've made the wrong decision.

"Green House has a well—they have *water*—and you didn't tell anyone?" Memphis steps off the porch. He's just a few feet away from me, it'll only take two more steps to close the distance between us, but Memphis doesn't come any closer and I don't back up an inch. We're fighting a silent battle right now. Trying to see who will make the first move; if Memphis will continue his challenge or if I'll back up and yield to his threat.

I stay exactly where I am.

"We don't know for certain that Green House has a well," I correct Memphis.

His voice comes out as a growl. "But you weren't even willing to take a chance and find out? You were going to sit in your room and let us dry out and starve without ever knowing."

"Do you know what it means to *raid* them?" I nearly shout. "Don't you remember what it was like when North Campus showed up? We cannot reduce ourselves to that!"

Memphis looks me up and down. He looks so pissed, when he opens his mouth, I'm not sure if he's going to speak or spit at me.

He says, "We cannot sit here and do nothing, Caesar," then he looks past me, over my shoulder at Delilah. "How many guys do you need for this raid?"

She smiles. "How ever many we can get."

"Anyone who actually wants to survive, follow me," Memphis announces, glaring at me. His hot gaze never leaves me as my brothers and teammates walk out of the house and stand on the lawn with the Zeta Chi girls.

"We're going to raid Green House, and we're coming back with supplies," Memphis tells me. "You don't have to join us. But if you stay here, you should spend the time packing."

"What are you saying?" I snap.

"I'm saying anyone who doesn't help doesn't get to call themselves a Kappa Brother."

I take a step forward. "I am still the captain of the track team—"

"What team!" he yells in my face. "Look around you, Caesar, the campus is destroyed. There is no track team."

"Then there isn't a fraternity either," I say. "Which means you don't get to make the decision to put me out."

"You wouldn't get put out if you joined us."

I turn around to look at the rest of my brothers who have joined the sorority girls. Some of them won't even look at me. They're not on my side. All because I withheld a rumor from them.

We could arrive at Green House and find nothing there. We could show up and get pummeled by Hot House. We're acting without thinking. But it's too late to reason with them now. I've lost any trust they might have had in me before.

But this isn't fair. It isn't fair that Memphis can step up and take over like this. These guys are my friends—my brothers—and they've never had a problem following my lead before. Then again, they've never been this hungry before. Never been this desperate.

So I don't say anything as Memphis joins the sorority girls and the rest of my brothers. I don't even react when he jostles my shoulder with his own. I just stumble to the side and stand there in misery.

Coach Noble startles me out of my daze when he touches my shoulder. "Come on, kid. We've got to go."

I whirl around and shove him away. "You just stood there!"

His eyes narrow. "Yes, I stood there while your brothers learned the truth. The truth you decided to keep from them."

I shake my head. "It wasn't like that."

"Caesar, I understand why you don't want to fight. But this is bigger than you," Noble says. "Think about Hope House."

I am thinking of Hope House. I thought maybe we could warn them about Zeta Chi's plans. Maybe we could team up with them and help defend their territory instead of raiding Green House. But that won't get us any more supplies. We need food and water and the other houses have it. We don't have a choice but to do this. I just wish it could be different.

"You made a good decision," Noble says beside me. "But it wasn't the right decision."

"They all left me," I say softly. "They left me to follow Memphis."

"They left to get food."

I turn to look at Noble.

"Memphis isn't a good leader," he says. "The boys will figure that out soon enough and come back to you."

"I can't wait for that to happen. They want me gone, Coach."

"Then go." He jerks his head in the direction of Green House. "It's not too late to catch up. Remind them that they elected *you* as their captain. And prove to them you're worthy of the title."

His words ignite a fire inside me. "Okay," I say, turning to leave—but Noble grabs my arm and presses something into my hand. I stare down at it. It's a pocketknife.

"You want me to use this?"

"I trust you with it," he says with a nod.

"You should keep it." I frown. "Aren't you coming?"

"Someone should stay and guard the house. If you stay, the guys will think you abandoned them." Noble pats me on the back. "Now go. And come back with some food. Please."

I give him a two-fingered salute and take off running.

It doesn't take much for me to make it to Green House. I'm captain of the track team for a reason, and as I run, I feel the adrenaline pouring into every part of my body. This is the same crazy high I felt the first night we celebrated our victory at the café. We'd been scared out of our minds, but we'd also been thrilled and happy. We'd made it back with supplies. Against all odds.

I haven't even broken a sweat when I jog up the driveway to Green House, but my legs almost buckle beneath me.

The house is pure chaos.

People are fighting everywhere. There are three guys beating up someone from Green House on the front lawn while two Kappa Pi brothers carry a crate full of boxes of cereal from the garage.

A girl is dragged out of the garage by her blonde ponytail. It's a Zeta Chi sister and the one with his hand tangled in her pretty hair is from Hot House. I can tell from his sizeable gut and the stained apron around his waist—almost everyone from Hot House is overweight or walks around dressed like a professional chef for some reason. I guess it's the same reason Kappa Pi wears their jerseys everywhere or Zeta Chi sports box blonde ponytails. Even the Black girls dye their curls during the semester.

The sorority girl is sobbing, but she doesn't go down easy. When the Hot House chef throws her onto the lawn, she launches at him with her fake nails bared like claws. He screams when she scratches him in the face, then he regains himself and cracks her across the jaw without a second thought. I flinch when she drops like a sack of rocks. I know this is war, but still... He hit her like she was a serious threat. Like he was fighting *me*.

Now, he *is* fighting me.

I don't know when I moved, but I'm suddenly across the lawn, my knife glinting in the morning sunlight. I hear it sing as the sharpened blade slices through the air, but the Hot House guy sees me in enough time to step back and dodge. Except he steps back and trips over the unconscious body of the sorority girl he just knocked out.

I watch him fall backwards; like a turtle on its shell, he flails and shifts to roll over, but I step on his belly to stop him.

"Get off me!" he shouts, fat fingers prying at my sneaker.

I raise my foot and kick him. Hard.

He sputters, "P-Please!"

"Did you listen when she said please?" I scream, jabbing my knife at the unconscious girl.

"She ran into the garage with a hammer!" he says. "I was just defending myself!"

I pause. She didn't have a hammer when I walked up. She was being dragged away by her hair. But she *could* have had a hammer when she arrived. She could have attacked first. Because that's what we came for.

So it doesn't matter that she's a girl and he's a guy. It doesn't matter who attacked whom first. All that matters is that a Zeta Chi is down, and I'm supposed to do something about it.

The knife feels heavy in my hand. I could use it. I could slide the blade across his fat throat, and no one would stop me. Zeta Chi would praise me for it. But Coach Noble's words ring in my ear.

I trust you with it.

We're here for supplies, not bodies. So instead of stabbing this ball of pus, I raise my foot again and bring it down on his face. The first stomp breaks his nose, the second knocks him out.

Without a word, I turn and run into the house, still clutching my pocketknife.

I'm met with screams and cries for help, but I ignore everything as I scan the mass of bodies for my brothers and sorority sisters.

I recognize a freshman from the track team in the foyer. He's fighting two guys at once and losing pretty badly. I don't hesitate to run over and help. The first guy never sees me coming, so it only takes one good whack with the hilt of my knife, and he crumples, clutching the back of his head.

The other guy's eyes grow to melons when he realizes this fight just took a turn. It's two versus one now, and I've got a weapon. He doesn't even bother taking his chances, he turns and sprints away, shoving his way toward the back of the house.

I follow him.

I have to leap over two bodies and a broken chair to catch the guy, but when I do get him, I tackle him to the ground. We've made it out to the backyard, just outside the door, so we land on the hard bricks of the patio. The impact rattles my teeth and knocks the pocketknife from my hand. I scramble to get it, shoving the big guy off of me, but as soon as I stand, I freeze in place.

Memphis and two Kappa Pi brothers are standing in the yard. There are at least a dozen students on their knees in the grass behind them, sorority girls stand guard. One of them is Delilah. Her face lights up when she spots me.

"Look who made it!" she says loudly.

Memphis turns and our eyes lock. I don't think anything between us will ever be the same again, but I know he isn't angry anymore when he nods and walks over to offer me his hand. I take it and stand, wiping dirt from my knees. Meanwhile, Delilah and two sisters grab the guy I'd been chasing. He groans as they roll him over and use rope to tie his hands behind his back.

"What's going on?" I ask Memphis.

He walks me to the center of the yard and points. "You were right and wrong."

I gasp. There is a well in Green House's backyard. But it

doesn't hold any water. Coach Noble was right, it looks like it's been dried up for a while, and then filled with rocks and sand. That was probably done to keep students from getting drunk and jumping into it at parties.

Except the well isn't entirely filled with rocks. The debris stops about ten feet from the top, and all that empty space is filled with food and water now. Cases of water bottles, cans of soup, even coal and lighter fluid for the grill so we can cook outdoors.

Memphis sucks his teeth beside me. "They had a stash all this time. Hidden from everyone else."

"They must have been one of the few dorms who got their cache on time before classes started. Unlike most houses."

"I just don't understand why they even bothered trading with Zeta Chi in the first place."

That's right. They swore loyalty before we did, but they had a stash all along. And they'd made some sort of deal with Hot House behind everyone's backs too.

"They did it because they're hungry," I say. "Like the rest of us."

Memphis looks at me. "Would you have done the same thing?"

"Maybe," I say. Maybe if Mya weren't here and needed food and water too. Maybe if I hadn't already been on the receiving end of a lie with Green House, I might have done it. But I've felt the sting of hunger. I've felt the painful bite of dehydration. I don't think I could wish that upon anyone. Not even the guys tied up and on their knees.

"Let them go," I say to Memphis.

He looks at me like I'm crazy. "Are you kidding me? They played us for fools."

"So, what are you going to do with them? Take them out front and give them fifty lashes? Should we string them up from the streetlights on the sidewalk?" I shake my head. "We got the food and water. Let's just go."

"If we let them go, they'll come for us. Just like North Campus did."

He's right, but I don't think he understands what our only option is then.

"What are you saying?" I ask.

Memphis doesn't hesitate. "You know what I'm saying. If we don't want them to come after us, then we have to—"

"We won't come for you!" someone shouts.

Memphis and I both turn toward the students tied up in the grass. Before I can figure out who spoke, Delilah walks over and punches a guy in the mouth so hard that he falls over and spits out blood.

"Please!" he shouts.

Delilah grabs him by his red hair. "You don't know when to shut up," she says, raising her fist.

"Wait!" I say quickly.

Delilah pauses.

When I walk over and get a better look, I recognize the guy. He's a big Irish man with stereotypical red hair and an accent so strong it's almost tough to make out his words. Plus, his mouth is all bloody now, so it's even harder to understand him when he says, "We won't retaliate if you just leave us enough to make it through the next few days. We'll figure out a way to survive. But please don't kill us."

"Why should we believe a word he says?" Delilah snaps at me.

"Because he's their dorm parent," I reply. I recognize him

from the meeting all the dorms had on the soccer field when the blackout first began. That feels like ages ago now, but it's not so long ago that I'd forget a flaming Irishman like this guy.

"Mr. Murphy," I say, kneeling beside him. I use my pocketknife to cut away the ropes tied around his hands. He sighs and sits up, wipes some of the blood from his mouth.

"Julius Caesar," he says.

I nod. "You recognize me?"

"You might not remember, but I was one of the men who carried you back to your room after that big albino fella knocked you out in the street."

I don't remember that. My black eye only faded about a week ago from that incident. But I don't remember seeing Mr. Murphy at the party. And why would he be there anyway?

He chuckles like he just read my mind. "I came to collect two freshmen girls from my dorm who snuck out without permission. While I was searching for them, I witnessed the fight and the blackout. I would've stuck around to chat but seeing as the power was out, I had to hurry back here."

"Interesting," I say.

"I helped you out," Mr. Murphy reminds me. His voice is pleading. "Will you return the favor?"

"I'm not going to let them kill you," I say confidently, then I rise and turn to face my brothers and sorority sisters. "Take only what we need. Leave the rest."

"Are you kidding me?" Delilah snaps.

Memphis starts cussing, but I ignore him. I might have lost the trust of my brothers before, but as I glance around at the rest of the Kappa Pi guys here, I know I've gained some of it back. They might have been willing to walk away for food, but they're not willing to go along with blatant murder.

Coach Noble was right. Hunger and thirst give birth to betrayal.

Just for emphasis, I brandish my pocketknife, pretending I'll actually use it if I must. "Take what we need. We're not animals, Memphis," I say firmly.

I can see a muscle in his jaw spasming, but he jerks his head at the guys around us. "Grab some food and water and meet out front."

I turn to Delilah. "Tell your sisters to do the same."

She doesn't even reply. She just storms off toward the well and starts yanking supplies out. I watch to make sure she isn't being greedy before I return my attention to Mr. Murphy.

"We showed you mercy," I say to him, looking him right in the eye. "Remember this, and don't let Hot House forget it either.'

He nods. "I'll relay the message."

22

Adrian

Sweat rolls down my face as I drag Connor along, he's doing the best he can, but it's not enough. Not anymore.

"Come on!" I yell. I tuck my arm around his waist and grip the waistband of his pants in a shaking fist, then I practically lift him off the ground and we run like that for the next block, both of us grunting and ignoring our pain.

We are being chased.

By a miracle, we've made it to Wakedon. It took us two days and Connor literally passed out along the way, but we split that Daisy Bar, sipped the water, and marched on. When we saw the **Welcome to Wakedon!** sign on the road, we both cried like babies, especially because the sign was one of those cheesy tourist signs that had a big map on it and a red X marked **You Are Here!** so, I was able to find Mya's address and make a mental map of where we needed to go.

She doesn't live far from the outskirts of the city. Just a few blocks and we'd finally be able to rest.

Connor and I hugged each other as we cried and celebrated. Then we huddled together so I could help him limp along. We were just two blocks from Mya's house when we saw them. Men in military uniforms. But not from the US Army.

I'm not the most patriotic guy in the country, but I know enough about our own military to recognize a uniform from any branch. Those guys weren't from our country, but they had military grade weapons and if that wasn't a dead giveaway, then their accents definitely were.

When we first spotted the group of soldiers, we immediately ducked into an alley and waited for them to pass. They walked down the middle of the street, looking into cars and occasionally going into houses. They were casually chatting, laughing, walking like this was a normal afternoon.

Connor had tugged on my sleeve, he was slumped against the wall, more focused on controlling his choppy breathing than seeing what was going on, so he didn't have a view like me. "What's happening?" he'd whispered.

I turned to face him, staring at his dewy face as I whispered back, "Soldiers. I think they might be hostile."

"Are you sure?"

"They're not American."

He frowned, and it seemed like a herculean effort just to do so. "Being foreign doesn't make you evil."

I should know. My mother is Russian, born in Rybinsk—an old city northeast of Moscow. She moved here when she was two, so she remembers basically nothing of her homeland, and she's never been back. She doesn't even have an accent and she's never mentioned much about her past. But that's not the point. My mother isn't evil, and I doubt the soldiers walking down the street were evil, but there's a difference between evil and hostile.

"What are foreign soldiers doing here?" I'd asked Connor.

He had sighed in response. "Why do soldiers go anywhere, Adrian?"

But that wasn't possible. It couldn't be possible. The United States of America could not be invaded. I couldn't fathom it.

"We're the home of the brave," I had stupidly whispered, like engraving something on a penny makes it so.

Fun fact: **Home of the brave** isn't engraved on our pennies. It says something in Latin—which Julius could quote—and it says **Liberty**, then, **In God We Trust**. But this invasion destroyed our liberty, and I don't believe in God.

So here we are.

I took another quick look around the corner. "Maybe they were called here to help," I said. It could happen. The US went to other countries during emergencies all the time. Maybe someone lent us a hand. Obviously, the blackout didn't stop at Cross North. But maybe it didn't stop at Wakedon either, or Phoenix—or all of Arizona. Maybe the entire country went dark. And these guys came to help us put ourselves back together.

Or maybe I was wrong. Maybe the country went dark, and these soldiers showed up to take advantage of that.

As I watched the soldiers walk down the road, I tried to catch snippets of their conversation. I knew it was pointless since they weren't even speaking English, but I had hoped to listen in anyway. I hoped that maybe they sounded like nice guys here to help. Then I could step out and ask for a hand. I could get Connor to a doctor, and we could get some food and they could tell us what the heck is going on. But as I watched, my hopes of getting help sank into oblivion.

There were two soldiers walking in the street while three others checked the houses and one held up the rear. As the soldiers neared us, their voices picked up and echoed off the cars and brick homes around us. But all conversation ceased when a woman's scream pierced the air. Even I froze, every hair on my body rising, every muscle tensing.

A soldier walked out of one of the houses, dragging a woman by her hair and holding a young child in his other hand. She screamed and sobbed as he marched down the porch steps while the kid kicked and punched at him. The other soldiers turned and started speaking in their native tongue, though I couldn't understand what they were saying, it was easy to tell they weren't happy.

Everyone was shouting. The soldiers, the woman, the kid.

Eventually, the soldier who'd dragged them out shoved both the woman and the child to the ground. They fell hard and quickly scrambled to hug each other as they cowered before the group of men. My heart hammered in my chest.

"What's happening?" Connor whispered beside me, he strained to get a better look, but I whipped my arm out and held him against the brick wall.

"Don't move," I whispered urgently. If we didn't want them to see us before, we certainly didn't want that now.

"What's happening?" Connor insisted.

"They found a woman and a kid in one of the houses."

"And?"

The first soldier removed the rifle that was strapped to his back and pointed it at the kid.

I closed my eyes as the shot went off.

"And they're shooting them," I said quietly. My ears were ringing from the sound of the gunshot, but I heard Connor clearly when he said, "No they aren't."

I whirled around to look again, easing closer to the edge of the alley. Connor was right. Sort of. They'd only fired one shot, leaving the kid lifelessly sprawled on the concrete. Meanwhile, the mother was still alive, screaming and hissing curses at the man who'd shot her child.

He aimed his rifle at her too, but he never fired. The other soldiers were talking loudly, nodding at each other. Coming to some sort of agreement. Once they were all on one accord, the soldier swung his rifle around to his back and grabbed the woman by her hair again.

She screamed, but it didn't matter. He waved to the other soldiers, and they all walked over to hold her arms and legs while he unzipped his pants.

I pressed myself against the wall again, breathing heavily. I couldn't watch. I couldn't move. But I also couldn't just *stand there.*

I looked at Connor. His eyes were squeezed shut, his nostrils flared. He didn't like this any more than I did. But what could we do? There were at least six of them and they were all armed—and definitely dangerous. They'd killed a kid!

The woman kept screaming, but her voice was abruptly cut off after a few moments.

Connor cursed.

"They must have knocked her out," I whispered.

"Does that make a difference?" he'd said hotly.

No, it didn't.

Angrily, I grabbed Connor and threw his arm over my shoulder to support him. "Let's get out of here."

"That's it?"

"There's nothing else we can do."

"They'll see us if we leave."

I peeked around the corner. "We'll stay low and move quickly. We should be fine."

23

Adrian

We weren't fine. In fact, a soldier spotted us as soon as we stepped out of the alley together. The good thing is, one of them had his pants down and two others were dragging that kid's body over to the sidewalk, so that left only three to chase after us.

Now, we've been running for two blocks straight. Connor is injured, but those soldiers are weighed down with gear. So the race is pretty even. I have Mya's address memorized, and I spent a while studying that map on the welcome sign. I know where I'm going. That's why I take a quick turn down a tight alley that makes Connor nervous.

He shouts something about a dead end, but I don't respond. There's no time to talk right now, I'm working for both of us at this point because his injured leg is nearly useless. He's moving at a jogger's pace, and we need to go at a full-on sprint. But as we near the end of the alley and squeeze through a broken gate, I realize we've done more than enough.

We hobble across the backyard of a small house and then

run right up to the sliding patio doors. I kick it hard, grunting with the effort, and it cracks. Then I kick it again and it shatters. I can hear the foreign soldiers behind me, tripping out of the tight alleyway, but I keep going.

I drag Connor through the house, and he helps by knocking over chairs and furniture to slow down our pursuers. Once we get to the front door, I fling it open, and we practically throw ourselves down the porch steps. Our destination isn't far, but we can't let those soldiers see where we go—they'll just follow us inside. So we limp around the side of the house across the street, ignoring the sound of thundering footsteps. A gunshot rings through the air, and I try not to panic.

How close are they?

I won't make it around to the back entrance. But this house has a side door. I kick it in without even thinking and practically throw Connor down on the floor. Then I turn around and very slowly close the door, trying not to make a sound.

I hold my breath as I lean against it, listening. The soldiers are in the alley. I can hear them talking. I can hear the anger in their voices.

"They'll find us," Connor says.

"Not if you be quiet," I whisper.

"They'll check," he says. "Just like they checked those other houses." Connor gulps. "And they'll drag us out and shoot us. Or worse. A guy as pretty as you—"

I curse at him. "Just shut up!"

A bullet flies through the door. I feel the air split around me as it zips by my face. Sunlight punches through the bullet hole, sending a beam of light through the dirty living room.

The silence that storms in is so loud I want to scream.

Instead, Connor and I blink at each other, so quiet and still, the foreign talking outside almost sounds like they're shouting through a megaphone.

Move, I mouth the word to Connor, and he lets me help him up. We tiptoe through the house together as the soldiers kick the door in. The house is dark and messy—the sort of mess that isn't from clutter but instead from chaos. Like someone deliberately knocked things over, the same way you would throw things around while searching for something.

Searching for survivors.

I drag Connor toward a door, I have no idea what waits on the other side, but I fling it open and pull him inside anyway. It's a small bathroom, barely large enough for both of us. We have to practically hug just to fit, but I quietly close the door anyway, and then I stare at the dirty mirror above the sink, taking in my awful reflection.

My cheeks are hollowed, which isn't surprising considering how much weight I've lost from nearly starving to death. My grey eyes are wide open and filled with panic, but my mouth is set in a hard line, hidden somewhere in the white fuzz of my short albino beard. I haven't had a good meal, shower, or shave since the power went out. I look like a madman, but I don't dwell on my appearance for long. Almost immediately, my attention is stolen by the flash of silver that winks against my chest.

I glance down to find Mya's necklace; a thorny crown and a cross-shaped pendant.

She'd given me this necklace the day I hit the road, asking me to promise that I would dig deeper. That I would find that part of myself where hope used to dwell. Where belief died and hatred was born.

I don't hate God. I hate His creation. I hate the evil that He allows to run rampant in this world. I hate the injustice. I hate my parents. I hate the people who shot Connor and the people chasing us now. Those soldiers who killed a child and raped a woman in the middle of a street. I hate that He sees all this and does nothing about it.

It makes me want *to hate You*, I pray inside, *but I can't.* I can't because of that thorny crown hanging around my neck. I can't because I know that crown is a sign of judgment—judgment that was placed on Jesus's head instead of the world. Judgment that He didn't deserve. But He suffered judgment anyway so we could live and be redeemed.

That's what Mya would say. I know because she's said it to me so many times during our arguments over her faith. And during each discussion, I'd get exasperated and blurt the same thing in anger.

If He was judged for all of our sins, then why is the world so screwed up now?

Mya would laugh, the sound sweet and patient. *He who watches over Israel never slumbers nor sleeps.*

I know that scripture. **Psalms 121:4.** And even a sinner like me knows what it means. God doesn't only watch over Israel. He is the watcher of all creation, and He is not unaware of the injustice in our world. He knows and He has a plan to rectify it. To judge it. To end it.

Be patient, Adrian, Mya would always tell me. *Just because it seems like God is absent, doesn't mean He truly is. God is longsuffering. That means He's giving your enemies time to repent. Time to acknowledge their wrongdoing and beg forgiveness. He might be quiet, but He is watching.*

As I hear footsteps moving through the house, I close my eyes and think of Mya. I think of the way *she* sees God, and I try to imagine someone—some perfect being—who loves the world so much that He gives even His enemies time to repent and change.

God, Mya's God... Please... If You're real like Mya thinks, if You're loving like she says You are, if You're truly watching, then please help us.

I can hear the soldiers moving through the house. They're getting closer with each step.

My heart is pounding so hard, I'm positive it's going to climb up my throat and leap from my mouth. There is someone standing at the door. I hear it when he grabs the doorknob. I hear the slow squeak of the metal as he begins to turn it.

And then I hear the crackle of a radio, and a foreign language fills the air. The doorknob halts, and the soldier takes a step back. He speaks into his radio, and then waits for a reply. Then he sighs and walks away.

I don't believe it.

Shock is the only feeling I can register, and it leaves me standing there in silence for a few moments. *Thank You*, I say inside, knowing exactly Who just saved us.

Connor and I stand there until we're sure the soldiers are gone, and then we leave the bathroom and limp out of the house. The street is empty, as if none of the madness earlier had ever happened. Together, we slowly make our way two doors down to Mya's address, and when we walk inside, Connor nearly passes out.

I help him onto the living room sofa, then I take a look around the house. The place isn't torn apart like the last house.

There are books on the shelves, trinkets on the table, even family pictures of Mya, her father, and her mother before she passed. I stare at them as I make my way through the little hall, watching Mya grow up. Julius is in a lot of pictures too.

I don't even feel angry when I see him. I feel slightly jealous that he's known Mya for so long. And I feel jealous that he's an orphan who was abandoned by his parents, but somehow, he managed to find two families to love him like he's their own. While I can't even find joy in the one family I've been given.

Julius looks just as happy as Mya in these photos. Her kooky father has his arm over his shoulders like he's the son he never had. An Asian woman stands in some of the high school pictures, I think that's Julius's foster mother. I've seen her at track meets before. She looks so proud. She looks like she loves him twice as much as Dr. Brown and Mrs. Brown do.

Mya looks like she loves him too. As far back as the pictures go, Julius is there by her side. He's there at birthday parties, he's there at family events, he's there at school dances. They wear braces together, show off scars together, and Julius even wears black in a few photos just like Mya. I still think it's weird that she's a Christian who dresses goth, but I can't deny how fashionable they look in their matching outfits in this picture. They're standing in what looks like a museum, in front of a large painting. Julius has his arm around Mya's shoulders, he's smiling down at her, but she's focused on giving the peace sign to the camera. She doesn't see the way he's looking at her. She doesn't see the way he's smiling at her. And for the first time since I've met both of them, I see what everyone else has missed.

Julius is in love with Mya. He always has been. In every

picture of them together, Julius is gazing at her the same way. His eyes are intense, his focus entirely captivated by Mya. I feel like a fool for never seeing it before, but I don't beat myself up over it. I doubt Julius has realized it himself.

How could he? He's always been popular. Always had a line of girls vying for his attention. He's probably as clueless about his feelings as everyone else has been. But I wonder if Mya ever noticed. And I wonder if it was wise to leave her there alone with him. Because I promised to come back for Mya, but she never promised to wait for me.

I grit my teeth and turn away from the photos. At this point, I'm not sure if I want to tear them from the walls or sit down and stare at them all day. I decide its best to get away from there, so I march down the hall and refocus on searching the house.

The door at the end of the hall is unlocked so I don't hesitate to step inside. Then I freeze. It's Mya's room. Shockingly white with grey carpeting and grim black posters of crosses, that thorny crown she loves, and the covers of Christian metal albums hang on the walls. She has a beanbag in the corner next to a chest that looks like it literally belongs to a pirate. Beside that is a small bookshelf stuffed with nothing but collector's editions of fairytales in foreign languages I know she can't read or understand. Unlit candles sit on a desk with a very retro cassette player and a stack of tapes marked with handwritten labels.

I want to look around. I want to snoop through every little piece of her that she's left for me to find. But instead, I step back and close the door. Mya gave me her address so I could find her father, not so I could rifle through her panty drawer. That isn't what I was going to do, but still. Like, you know what

221

I'm saying. Right?

Before I leave her room, I glance back at her dresser. But I don't touch it.

Anyway, I stomp back down the hall and check the only other bedroom in the house. It obviously belongs to her father with its dull brown carpeting and plain drapes. He's got an empty desk in the corner and there's a laundry basket in the middle of the floor with clothes neatly folded inside. I change my shirt before I leave, and grab a clean tee for Connor, then I make my way back to the living room where I find him struggling to sit up.

"You find any food?" he asks.

I pause. I hadn't even checked for food.

"I'll be back," I grumble, moving toward the kitchen.

This part of the house has been trashed. Unlike the bedrooms and living room, it seems like someone came through here a long time ago. The cabinets are left open and bare, the fridge door is actually hanging off its hinges. I sigh and check the freezer, not surprised to find nothing but melted ice cream inside.

I turn around and walk back into the living room. Defeated.

"Nothing," I say. "It looks looted. I don't know if it was travelers like us or soldiers, but whoever came through took everything."

"Did you search the basement?" he asks.

I frown. I hadn't seen a basement door, but Connor points to the storage closet across the room.

"That's not a basement," I say slowly.

He shakes his head. "This neighborhood is old. Houses built in this area during the 1920s had their basement entrances hidden inside their closets."

"What the heck?"

"It was during the prohibition. People would store liquor in the basement or throw illegal parties down there, but they'd get raided by the cops. So newer homes were built with the basement entrance hidden in the closet, like a secret passageway. If the house got raided, the cops couldn't search the basement because they couldn't even find it."

I almost laugh. Everyone has heard of the madness that happened during the prohibition, but I would never guess anyone went that far just to have a bottle of beer. Then again, I've never drank before, so I'm not sure what lengths people were willing to go to for a drink.

I find alcohol revolting. Anything that causes you to lose control of yourself is repulsive. But I'm the type of person who likes organization. Cleanliness. Discipline. Growing up in a household totally devoid of those things makes you obsess over it later.

I walk over to the closet and tug the door open. There are coats hanging inside, umbrellas poking out of a decorative holder. I shove past all of those things to find a door waiting at the other end, just like Connor said there would be.

"How'd you know?" I call over my shoulder.

Connor laughs. "I'm a history major."

Well, that makes sense. And it's awfully convenient for me. Without Connor, I never would've known to look here.

I yank the door open and walk down the flight of stairs, it's hard to see because it's so dim and there aren't any lights except what can reach here from the staircase. But it's enough for me to squint and make out all the metal racks full of canned goods and bottles of water. There's even a medical bed with supplies in the corner. The sight makes my stomach twist.

Mya's father was a little nuts, I'm not surprised he built his own fallout shelter in his basement. But the medical bed isn't because he's crazy. It's there because Mya's mother was sick. She must have spent her last few months here. It's possible Dr. Brown started building the shelter when she was alive and hoarded medical supplies under the assumption that she would still be here and would need it.

My heart breaks a little, but my sadness is washed away by the violent growl of my stomach. There's food here. There's water. There's a chance for us now.

I smile. *Jesus…* it's the third time I've prayed in a single day. This is honestly a record. *You didn't just save us for the moment, You've given us a way to survive.*

24

Adrian

For two days, we stuff ourselves with beef stew and crackers. There's a camp burner on one of the racks, it runs on butane gas so even though it's safe for indoors, we can't use it any longer than necessary because there aren't any windows in the basement to allow venting. I find a pot from the rack and heat two family-size cans of stew until it just starts to simmer, then I sit with Connor, and we shovel salty beef chunks and cubed potatoes into our mouths with an entire pack of crackers to share between us. Between yesterday and today, we've already guzzled a gallon of water each.

This morning, we split a can of pears in sugary syrup. I lick my fingers while Connor stirs the powdered eggs into something edible. He's pretty good at it, and I don't mind eggs for breakfast. It beats another can of beef stew.

"Get the pan ready," he tells me, stirring hard.

I light the burner and set the pan on the flame, enjoying the sizzle when Connor leans over and pours the mixture onto

225

the hot metal. He winces as he leans back against the pillows of the medical bed.

"How are you feeling?" I ask.

We cleaned his leg up pretty good yesterday. We cleaned up *everything* pretty good, actually. The shelter down here has a bathroom, the plumbing doesn't work but there are waste basins for us to fill with water and sponge ourselves clean, then we use them to collect our own waste and dump it at the end of the day.

Yesterday, I cleaned myself up at the basin and even gave myself a fairly good shave with one of the razors I found in Dr. Brown's supplies. While Connor took his turn, I emptied my basin upstairs and then sorted through Dr. Brown's clothes. He's nowhere near as tall as I am, but I didn't mind wearing his sweatpants because they were clean. The hem is halfway up my shin, but the length fits Connor perfectly fine. The waistline is huge on both of us; we use the drawstrings to keep them from falling down.

But new clothes don't make a difference for Connor's injury. Even though we cleaned his wound and applied fresh bandages, he's still in a lot of pain. I think it might be infected. We've got the meds to treat it, but there's a lot of black skin around the bullet hole. Dead skin.

Yesterday I suggested cutting away the skin and then burning the wound to seal it shut. Connor adamantly disagreed with that idea. He thinks the antibiotics we found in the medical supplies will flush out the infection—in theory, that's how it works. But his wound is surrounded by dead skin. Antibiotics can't *flush out* dead skin. It's got to be cut away.

Even after I explained that to him, Connor wouldn't let me near his leg. I had no choice but to respect his wishes. I'm not going to hold him down and take a knife to him, but I don't know how long he expects me to wait for him to get better. I've still got to find my family.

Connor lets out a long sigh. "My leg hurts pretty bad."

I keep my eyes on the goopy eggs as I reply, "It's not healing."

"I walked on a bullet wound. Give it time. It'll get better soon."

"We have to cut away—"

"You're not a doctor," Connor cuts me off.

I snap my head up to glare at him. "Don't be an idiot, Connor. You can see the dead skin as easily as I can. You don't have to be a doctor to know this isn't good."

He doesn't speak.

"Let me cut it away."

"Do you know how much pain that will cause?"

"You're already in pain!"

My shouting silences the room. I quickly glance up at the ceiling, listening for footsteps. We haven't heard any activity since we got away from those soldiers, but they were sweeping the area before that encounter. There's no way to tell if they already checked this neighborhood and aren't coming back, or if they'll start making rounds again soon.

That brings me to my next issue.

"How will you travel, Connor? Whether I cut away the skin or not. We've got a lot of ground to cover from here to Phoenix."

I shut off the burner and divide the eggs onto two plates, then I pass Connor a plate and sit on the edge of the bed as I wait for him to answer.

"I was thinking," Connor says slowly. "Maybe I could stay

here while you go to Phoenix."

"All alone?"

He makes a face. "I was shot in the leg, not the brain. I can still take care of myself."

Sure, he can move around the room and make food for himself. He can clean his rotting leg and even take the waste basin upstairs to empty out if he needs to. But that's not the part that worries me.

"What if those soldiers come back?" I ask. "They shot that kid; they won't hesitate to hurt you if they find you."

"I won't go outside. I won't even go upstairs if I don't need to."

"A lot could happen while I'm gone."

"I'll be fine until you get back." He scratches his chin. "You are coming back, right?"

"Yes. That's always been my plan."

"The others took off. Daniella too."

I wince at the thought of Daniella. The others ran off when we were getting shot at, but Daniella left after we hooked up in that abandoned car. It was a cheap move, on both sides, but the thought of it makes me angry because she made me look like a fool. I'm not so stupid to believe there were any real feelings between us. At the time, I thought she'd had a boyfriend, and I'm still working things out with Mya. So it was a one-time thing. Two people burying their pain in pleasure.

I can still feel her breath on my neck. I can feel the prickling sensation of sweat beading on my forehead, hear the throaty grunt that'd slipped from my mouth as I'd peaked. Daniella is a pretty girl. And she knew what she was doing. But I've slept with a lot of pretty girls, and none of them crawled out of my bed and stole from me the next day.

"Daniella was a lying whore," I hiss in anger.

Connor blinks at me, shocked by my vulgarity. I almost apologize, but I'm not sorry.

"We all left campus for different reasons," I say. "Everyone had family in different places, so we were bound to split up eventually."

"But you're going all the way back to campus. To give a report."

And to find Mya, but I don't say that. I just nod. "The others are waiting. They'll want to know what the city looks like and make a decision on whether it's better to stay or leave."

Connor snorts. "If Wakedon is any clue, the whole country is doomed."

I nod because I don't know what else to say. Connor is right, but I want him to be wrong. What will I do if I get to Phoenix and it's no different from this place? What will I do if I can't find my brother and sister?

I shake my head and try to focus. "You sure you want to stay here? What about your family? Didn't you leave campus to see them?"

He laughs, though it's mirthless and dry. "I left because I thought I had a better chance at surviving in the unknown than sticking around campus, waiting for North Campus to come back and take us all out."

I can't blame him for that one. Even if I didn't have my siblings to look after, I would have left the university. There was nothing there for me. For anyone. They're all just waiting to die.

"Out here hasn't been any easier," Connor says, pulling my attention back to him. "At least I hadn't gotten shot back at school."

I laugh, shoveling the last of my eggs into my mouth.

"I've only got a drunken father back home anyway. Nothing worth going back for."

"No siblings?"

He's quiet for a moment. "I have two older brothers. But they don't live at home anymore. One of them is married, has a kid and a wife. The other," he chuckles, "he's a marine."

"A soldier," I say.

"You think he's out there fighting those guys we saw earlier?"

"He's got to be." When I glance up at Connor, his eyes are glued to me, and I realize how much he needs to hear this. He might not care much for his father, but he still loves his brothers. He still hopes they're safe, somehow.

I don't know how much my opinion means to Connor, but every word I say is the truth. I'm not just trying to make him feel better when I reply, "I'm positive the military is fighting back. Think about it, those soldiers we saw earlier, they had a radio—and it worked."

We'd both heard it when we hid inside that bathroom. Just before the soldier opened the door and discovered us, we heard a radio crackle, and someone spoke on the other end. I know it was a miracle. I know it was a result of the desperate prayer I sent up, but I don't say any of that to Connor. It isn't because I'm unsure of his religious beliefs, I keep those details to myself because *I'm* still unsure of my own beliefs. I've barely begun to understand and accept what happened back in that bathroom.

I shake my head to clear my thoughts. "At Cross North, the generators were dead. Even the cars were fried. And the ones we saw on the highways were dead too."

Mya's father built some janky generator himself; it sits in the far corner of the basement now. But that doesn't work either. Nothing works anymore.

"But those soldiers had radios," Connor says.

I nod. "I think there's a chance that maybe the grid isn't down for everyone everywhere."

"How do you know? I mean, those soldiers were foreign. Maybe the rest of the world isn't dark, but Arizona sure is."

"Think about it, Connor," I insist, "we haven't seen any civilians out here except those guys on the highway and the woman those soldiers found. Where do you think everyone went?"

"Maybe those guys killed them all."

I shake my head. "This place isn't a warzone. The houses are torn apart, but they haven't been blown to smithereens or sprayed down with bullets. And those soldiers didn't expect anyone to still be here."

"Why not?"

"Because ... I think the town was evacuated. Meaning, there must be some places with power or at least with supplies and medical equipment. Some place where the military is set up and able to help people."

Connor rubs his chin contemplatively.

"Maybe word spread that foreign forces arrived on US soil. Maybe the National Guard was deployed right after the blackout and the town had to go to a fallout shelter," I say.

"Why didn't they come evacuate the university?"

"Maybe those soldiers pushed in before they could get there. Or maybe they simply couldn't make it because the highways are blocked. You saw all the abandoned cars. It'd be impossible to get a tank or supply truck through the main roads."

Connor looks around at the racks of food and supplies. "Even so, why on earth would Mya's father leave all this for a cramped shelter?"

"He might not have had a choice in leaving."

"You think the army would've forced him to go?"

"If they're positive there's an imminent threat to the city, then yes. The military would've forced everyone to leave during the evacuation."

"Sheesh, whatever happened to our rights as citizens?"

I bunch my shoulders. "What rights will you be able to exercise if you're dead? They would only force you to go if they truly believed staying would put you in danger. It's the same reason they force elderly people to take their meds in nursing homes. You can't just let someone die, Connor." I clench my jaw.

Connor holds my gaze, but his anger fizzles out the next moment. "Anyway," he says, "I guess this town was evacuated. And maybe there's a chance other places have power or at least shelter. But I don't have any family to visit. So let me stay here, Adrian. I'll only slow you down."

"You can only stay on one condition," I say slowly, and from the look on his face, I think he knows what that condition will be. He doesn't even flinch when I issue my demand.

"You've got to let me cut the dead skin away."

Connor's cheeks puff as he sighs heavily.

"I'm not gonna say it won't hurt," I tell him. "But it's got to be done. Or else you'll lose the whole leg."

He whimpers and his voice comes out in a warble. "I know. I just … give me a second, okay?"

I get up and turn on the burner, then I grab the medical kit

232

from the shelf near Connor's bed. Mercifully, there are razors, scalpels, and other tools here we can use, so I won't have to saw at his skin with a hunting knife.

In silence, I hold a razor over the open flame until it turns red. Then I dip it into a cup of alcohol to sterilize it. Connor has removed his pants and his bandages by the time I walk over to the bed.

Neither of us speaks.

He swallows. "You, uh, you think there's any liquor on those shelves? I could use a drink."

I almost laugh because that was the third thing I checked for, right after food and water. As expected, there isn't any alcohol in this Christian household. Not the kind you drink, at least.

Connor knows from the look on my face what the answer is before I even say it, but I tell him anyway. "I didn't find any booze. You'll have to tough it out."

He stuffs gauze into his mouth and then nods.

"First, I'll pour alcohol over it. Then I'll start cutting. It's going to hurt," I say calmly, "but no matter how bad it gets, you've got to stay still. And you've got to stay quiet." I look him in his panicked eyes. "Okay?"

He nods again, and then I grab the alcohol and brace myself.

The first cut makes him tense up. The second makes him scream behind the gauze stuffed into his mouth. The third makes him wet his underwear. The white sheets of the hospital bed are stained red and yellow now. After that, he throws his head back and passes out.

I keep cutting.

25

Mya

The Arizona sun roasts me as I stand in line on the soccer field. Ever since Kappa Pi and Omega Zeta Chi returned from their brutal attack on Green House, they've begun setting up a table and a wagon of supplies on the soccer field where they pass out goods to anyone willing to trade or beg. They only surrender one wagon per day, so it's first come first serve.

This is my third day here, and I still haven't gotten any food. The lines are long, the sun is high, and the food is low. I could say a lot about the morality in raiding Green House, but here I am, waiting for my portion of loot. As weird as it sounds, their ruthlessness has been a blessing to the entire campus.

Green House had a jackpot of supplies they'd been keeping to themselves, or secretly trading with Hot House. Now, we all have food. But for how long?

Even this will run out soon. Honestly, it hasn't even been enough so far. We're all tired and hungry, standing in the heat like this only makes it worse. But Memphis says he doesn't want everyone gathered at the fraternity. He's paranoid we'll riot and raid his house just like they did to Green House.

It would only be fair. Who says Kappa Pi and Zeta Chi get to be in charge now?

They stand behind their picnic table with their wagon of stolen goods and wait for us to beg or bargain with them. The Zeta Chi girls are hydrated and healthy-looking with pretty hair and sharp smiles. The Kappa Pi brothers look intimidating, standing tall in their matching track jerseys as they loom over the other students.

The guy in charge is a huge Black guy called Memphis. I recognize him from the mansion, as well as Bunny who stands beside him. Memphis handles most of the negotiations while Bunny just grabs the supplies from the wagon. The Zeta Chi girls charm the line of disgruntled students or merely stand there and look pretty.

Delilah is here. She's got her blonde hair in a ponytail and a smile on her face as she plays with the pink ribbon keeping her locks tied back. I wonder if it's the same ribbon she'd given to Julius. The smile she's wearing is the same one she'd given to him. But right now, it's aimed at Memphis who grins back while he leans toward her and says something in her ear. She laughs hard at his words, her dainty hand resting on his bicep in a very familiar fashion. He doesn't seem to mind.

I can't stop myself from scanning the crowd of frat boys in search of Caesar, but I don't find him. I haven't seen him since he kissed me. I don't know what's going on. It seems like Memphis is in charge now, and Bunny and Delilah don't seem to mind at all.

Jupiter sighs beside me. Her pink hair is plastered to her forehead, she's got a fourth of an inch of dark new growth

235

showing now. Evidence of how long we've been living on campus. At least three weeks. Maybe going on four. I used to think the Bible summer camp I attended every year was long because I hated leaving my phone behind and the thought of bathing in a lake for two weeks was awful. But I'd rather cool off in a lake than skip a bath altogether—wearing the same pair of panties for days at a time, flipping them inside out when the seat gets too grimy.

This is awful.

There is a layer of dirt covering everyone now. It is unavoidable and indiscriminate.

Guys walk around with pit stains, eternal morning breath, and unkempt beards which grow in patches or oily hair that leaves stains on their pillows. It isn't any better for us ladies. We're all sticky with sweat, our clothes are smelly, and three days ago Jupiter started her period. She measured her Advil down to the last pill and then clutched the empty bottle, staring at me with big, worried eyes.

"What will I do once I run out?"

I had no idea. But we'd have a month to figure it out.

I'd shrugged. "I'll pray for you." It was all I had to offer, and it was all she'd needed. She ended up only using half the pills she measured out for herself.

Even without a period, there's a host of other things we're trying to figure out in this world that's been thrust back into the Dark Ages. Like, how do you get something out of your teeth without any floss or toothpicks? How will you blow your nose or wipe your butt without any tissue?

I have a patch of hair under both my arms that's so embarrassing I've resorted to plucking but the process is slow and painful. I could shave without water, but that would leave me with a set of razor bumps that would become a rash and then morph into a problem I don't need.

Not to mention the hair on my head. I'm Black so my hair doesn't get oily when I skip wash day, instead it gets dry and brittle. At this point, my hair feels like a bird's nest on my head instead of the cottony soft afro I used to wear. Jupiter helped me braid it up last night, so I've got about fifty mini braids dangling past my shoulders now. I brush one behind my ear as I glance at Jupe, she's sweating harder than I am, wiping at the beads gathered on her forehead and then rubbing her eyes which have dark circles underneath.

"Do you think we'll make it to the front today?" she asks, squinting at the long line ahead.

I've got a loaded first aid kit and a box of crackers in my hands. Kassandra went to the campus chapel to pray three days ago and while she was there, she thought to check the ministry office. Bingo. The chapel had a stash of grape juice and crackers for their communion services—like nearly every Christian church does.

Instead of tearing into the food, Kassandra spent three hours praying over it, asking God for His permission to eat it. If you aren't Christian, then you wouldn't understand, but I'll try to explain it anyway. The crackers represent the Body of Christ when He was beaten and crucified, the grape juice (sometimes we use wine) represents His Blood which was shed for us so we could be redeemed and forgiven.

Taking communion isn't a tradition or a symbolic act. Once the bread and wine has been prayed over and consecrated, it is no longer food to snack on. It *is* the Body and Blood of Christ Jesus. So, for Kassandra to eat it as a meal could be considered blasphemous.

But God is merciful.

Just as He pardoned King David when he ate the consecrated bread at Nob, Kassandra prayed and asked for His favor with us so we could eat the bread and drink the juice of our communion without mocking Him or taking it in vain.

When she returned to Hope House with a backpack full of juice and crackers, the dorms rejoiced. But now we're running low on that too, so Jupiter and I are hoping we can trade some medical supplies and crackers for jerky or dried fruit—or anything really.

"We haven't gotten anything the last two days," I say to Jupiter.

The line moves forward but her scowl remains as she continues squinting ahead. "That's because Memphis is a jerk. He doesn't like us."

She might be right about that. Memphis treats everyone like they're a nuisance. I can hear him yelling at a student even from my distance in line. I get the feeling he doesn't want to share the supplies he stole from Green House, but Kappa Pi made such a show of everything when they returned, they had to share.

They paraded their loot through the street. So we all knew about the food and water they'd collected. And we'd all wanted some. Now, all that bragging and parading has bitten them in the butt and Memphis feels it worse than anyone. I can tell from the way he frowns and barks at everyone (except Delilah) that sharing was not his idea, and this certainly isn't his favorite part of the day. I still haven't decided if I blame him yet. Would I want to pass out my own food and water after I fought tooth and nail for it?

I don't know. Would you?

"I wish your friend was here," Jupiter says, regaining my attention.

I blink at her which makes her smile for some reason.

"You know? The hot guy with dark hair?"

My cheeks burn. She's talking about Julie.

"Oh yeah—"

"*Julius Caesar*," Jupiter breathes. "What a name."

"It's not that big a deal," I mutter. "Considering the last guy got stabbed in the back and all that."

Jupe sighs dreamily. "I have no idea how you've resisted him for so long."

"*Resisted* him?"

"He's had the hots for you since you arrived on campus. It's so obvious."

"I must have missed all the signs," I grumble, and I'm being serious. Caesar has always been a ladies' man, but until he pinned me against the wall and shoved his tongue down my throat, he'd never behaved like a frat boy with *me*. I can still feel his hands on my body, his palms hot and needy as they ran up and down my frame. I had fought him at first—but only *at first*. Because there was a small part of me that'd melted at his touch, a voice in my head that'd whispered, *yes*, when he'd pulled me close, *finally*, as he'd held me, and *don't stop*, as he'd kissed me.

It was the part of me that felt jealous of girls like Delilah. The part that'd yearned for Julius, even while I was with Adrian. But I can't entertain that part of me. I can't pretend a relationship with Caesar would be any healthier than a relationship with Adrian. Besides, there are other things I should be focused on right now instead of my romantic interests, but Jupiter won't let the topic go.

She gives me a sideways smile and says, "You think Caesar would let us skip the line if he were here?"

"It's hard to say."

"Well, let's ask him." Jupiter nods toward the front and I follow her gaze to find Julius strolling past all the exhausted students, past the flirty sorority girls who all beam at him, and past his own fraternity brothers. He saunters through the crowd like he owns the place and walks right up to Memphis—nods to Bunny—and then leans down to peck Delilah on the cheek. She blushes like a virgin. Which is funny.

Funny or not, I can't stop my stomach from folding inside out at the sight of their interaction. Even Jupiter murmurs, "Sheesh," and glances over at me. I have to pretend to be distracted by a bumblebee buzzing past because I'd rather look at anything other than Delilah and Julius.

I'm not hurt. Julius isn't my boyfriend. And even though he kissed me, we never made any commitments to each other. Plus, things are still complicated with Adrian. And I promised to stay away from guys who stay away from God.

It's not happening, I remind myself, even though I feel a familiar flurry of butterflies when I glance up and realize Julius has found me in the crowd. His eyes are hot just like they were in that sports office, like pools of desire threatening to drown me—even from here.

I swallow and pry my gaze away.

"He's waving us over." Jupiter nudges me.

You've got to be kidding me.

To my misery, she isn't kidding at all. I force myself to look ahead and, sure enough, Caesar is waving at us, beckoning for us to come over. We march through the crowd, ignoring the complaints of the other students, and stand right in front of the table.

"Well, hello there," Delilah purrs, latching her arm around one of Caesar's. He doesn't shift away, but I do notice the way Memphis casts a sideways glance at them. No surprise there. Delilah had placed that same dainty hand on his sweaty bicep before Julius showed up with his grin and his dimples and his bangs hanging in his eyes. He brushes them aside and leans over the table, if it were possible, I would have stopped myself from leaning toward him, but my body moves on its own, swaying in his direction like a fish on a line. I'm practically useless against his pull, my mind flopping for oxygen, eyes wide open, blinking. And all the while, Julius just keeps on reeling, keeps on turning the dial until we're close enough that he could kiss me again.

He pecks my forehead, shocking me enough that I snort like an idiot and lean back, rubbing my forehead. He grins, and the sultry spell that'd been cast over us is suddenly broken. This handsome boy before me goes back to being my goofy best friend and we laugh together at how silly he's being in front of everyone.

"Why on earth are you waiting in line?" he asks.

"Because we don't play favorites," Memphis grunts.

"Where have you been?" I ask Julius. Both of us ignore Memphis who is sharing a scowl with Delilah right now.

"Coach Noble and I guard the rest of the stash while these guys do the dirty work."

I nod.

"Man, it's hot out here," Julie complains, fanning himself.

I chuckle. "Welcome to the Field of Death."

"Field of Death?" He quirks a raven brow.

"That's what they've nicknamed the soccer field." It seems

241

fitting, not only is it hotter than an oven out here, but the soccer field has become a place of life or death. You show up, wait in line, and you either walk away with food or you don't. Life or death. Survival or starvation.

Jupiter interjects, "Can we make a trade?"

"What've you got?" Caesar asks.

Before I can present my goods, a whistle rings through the crowd and everyone turns to find a group of students approaching. They're all wearing aprons, so we immediately know they're from Hot House, this is both a shock and a relief.

First of all, no one has seen students from Hot House dorm in a long time. They've been voluntarily locked away, baking bread to keep themselves alive, and trading with Green House and their secret stash when necessary. But since Green House's stash was raided by Kappa Pi, they've been forced to emerge. And they've brought some of their tasty bread to trade.

My mouth waters at the smell. Freshly baked bread... how long has it been?

"You've got to be kidding me," Memphis mutters.

Even Julius is staring. Bunny actually runs around the side of the table to get a better look. The Hot House kids walk right up to him and set their basket of fresh goods on the white plastic table. There are five of them, and they look relatively healthy—all things considered. They've had hot bread to eat and whatever Green House had been providing for them. It was a wonder Kappa Pi didn't raid Hot House, but then, what would we do with wheat and flour? That was the culinary dorm, almost everyone there specialized in some sort of food-related study. And their dorm came equipped with an industry grade kitchen.

Julius couldn't bake a loaf of bread any more than I could

use a wood-burning stove—if I even managed to get it lit. No point in taking supplies you couldn't use on equipment you didn't have. So Green House fell instead.

Now, those bakers and chefs have showed up with goods to trade and I know without even glancing at Memphis and Bunny that this bread will replace every pack of jerky left in the wagon. Maybe I can trade a pack of crackers for a few loaves? I doubt it, but I keep my hopes up anyway.

A Hot House girl steps from her group and walks up to the table. She speaks to everyone, unsure who exactly is in charge, but I notice the way Memphis angles himself forward so her gaze naturally drifts to him.

"We heard about what happened to Green House," the girl says. "So we brought this gift as a peace offering."

"A peace offering?" Memphis repeats.

"You raided our allies. We have every right to retaliate, but instead we come in peace."

Retaliate? Five different alarm bells ring in my head. I could have sworn we were all allies a week ago. I could have sworn our 'enemies' came from North Campus, and only because they attacked us first. But as I look at this Hot House student with her hair pulled back and her face painted with stripes on her cheeks like a warrior's, I realize how wrong I am.

The other dorms have made alliances, connections, and relationships without us—they've done it right in front of us. And we're just now noticing.

Kappa Pi and Omega Zeta Chi.

Hot House and Green House.

Which means Hope House has been left out to dry.

I look up at Julius without even meaning to. I thought he was my ally. I thought I could trust him. And maybe I can, but

243

as I notice the way Memphis discusses a trade with Delilah, I realize that perhaps Julius cannot trust *them*.

"What do you want for the bread?" Memphis asks the Hot House girl.

She smiles, it's like a split in her pretty face, cutting open to reveal sharp little teeth. She is thin and lanky, in a way that reminds me of a broken Barbie Doll. But her smile is cunning, if not confident.

"We want peace. Promise you will not attack us, and we promise not to retaliate for what you did to Green House."

Memphis gives a slow nod, his eyes locked on the basket of bread, just like everyone else's.

The girl notices. Her smile stretches.

"As a token of good faith, we wouldn't mind taking the supplies you've got left today."

A groan rumbles through the very long line behind me, that's when Julius steps forward and speaks up for the first time.

"No deal," he says plainly.

Memphis snaps his head toward him. "Are you serious?"

"There are other people waiting here. They've *been* waiting here. We can't just let Hot House take all the supplies."

Memphis's nostrils flare, he looks like a bulldog. "That's not your call to make."

"It isn't?" Julius challenges.

"Caesar," Bunny says pleadingly, "that's a lot of bread."

It is. Dozens of loaves in a bunch of different sizes. Up close, it looks like there might even be different *kinds* of bread too. White bread, cornbread, wheat bread. I think I see a spotted loaf—dried blueberries? Or maybe raisin nut bread?

Julius doesn't budge. "These people have been waiting for

food and water. It isn't fair—"

"It's not fair to let all your girlfriends skip!" Memphis practically shouts. I feel my cheeks start to burn, it gets worse when he points at Delilah and then at me. "You can't give special treatment to every girl you bang."

Bang???

I know it's obvious there's something between me and Julius—there's something between Julius and *every* girl on campus—but we're *best friends!* We're not *sleeping* together! I can't believe Memphis would ever jump to that conclusion.

Then again… Jupiter's words play in my head, drowning out my pounding heart. *He's had the hots for you since you arrived on campus. It's so obvious.* Is it obvious to Memphis too? Can Delilah tell? *I* couldn't even tell. But Julius did kiss me, and he called me to the front of the line as soon as he saw me. And he also kissed Delilah and slept with Delilah. And I've heard there are other sorority girls he's been with too.

I guess I'm not that special. But I'm special enough to have Memphis waving his finger in my face like I'm somehow responsible for Julius turning Hot House away. He's still yelling now, barking about how hungry they are and how much they need this bread. That's strange. They stole so much food from Green House, yet they're hungry.

Julius shakes his head. "We have a deal if you leave the bread. But we're not making any promises of peace by giving you our loot," he says firmly. "If you want peace, those are the terms."

"You don't want us as your enemies," she warns.

One corner of his mouth turns up. "Green House was our enemy once."

It's a threat that doesn't need any explanation. The Hot

House girl glares at Julius but doesn't offer a comeback. She knows as well as anyone else, Julius isn't changing his mind. And even though Memphis and Bunny are grumbling beside him, they don't make any moves to stand against his decision. The only thing the Hot House girl can do is pack her bread and go.

Everyone watches in silence, wondering the same thing.

Did Julius make the right decision? And who will pay if he didn't?

26

Caesar

The guys are stony toward me for the rest of the day. I don't blame them for their attitudes, but I wish they wouldn't blame me for mine. It wasn't right to accept Hot House's deal. Maybe on the surface it was right. Maybe in hindsight. But I just... I had this feeling. I didn't trust them. And I didn't want to give the rest of our food and water to them.

Students from Hot House and the dorm apartments had been waiting for hours for their turn to trade. Judging from all that bread, Hot House obviously has supplies in their dorm. They're only coming out to form a new alliance because we ruined their last one.

They need us. They need our cooperation. They need what we have—what we took from Green House. They didn't come for peace; they came to take back the supplies we took from their buddies. And they thought the only thing they had to do was offer us some of their bread and we'd snatch it up without a second thought.

There's a reason for everything. There's a motive behind every deal.

In the Bible, Judas was known as a traitor because he turned his back on Jesus and set in motion many of the events leading up to His crucifixion. In Hebrew, the name Judas means *praise*. That's funny because Judas only praised Jesus with his mouth. His heart was far from Him. He was deceitful until the very end.

Do you know the Latin word for deceit?

It's *decipis*.

Although Judas was a traitor, his actions were no surprise to Jesus. He is the Son of God; He'd been sent to earth to be sacrificed for our sins. So, He knew His crucifixion was coming from the very beginning. But I am not Jesus. I am not all-knowing. I cannot pinpoint the betrayal that awaits me, but I know something is off. Something about this whole bread deal feels deceitful.

Hot House could have sought peace with us at any time, but they chose to close their doors and start their ovens. Now that their secret stash has been discovered, and taken, they want to make a deal and form an alliance.

I'm not having it.

It's obvious I'm the only one who feels this way. Bunny doesn't speak to me for the rest of the day. Delilah takes her girls and heads home before the trading is even done for the day. Memphis acts like I don't exist.

I'm not even angry about Memphis, I prefer things this way. He's openly hostile toward me, and if it weren't for my relationship with Coach Noble, I'm positive he would have wrestled leadership of Kappa Pi away from me by now.

It was his idea to leave me at the mansion to guard the

supplies while he works the trade table every day. It was his idea that Coach Noble stay back to make sure everything is in order too. I could have pointed out how convenient it was that everyone who opposed him was left out of the trade table, but the truth is that I didn't want to be there.

Memphis is one thing, but watching Bunny and Delilah kiss up to him is another thing entirely. The rest of the track team has fallen in line with their groveling. They're all afraid of him. They're all unsure of what will happen next, so they're picking sides, following the person they think will come out on top if any more chaos runs through campus.

Their choices have not been wise.

I was their leader because they respected me, but Memphis is slowly taking over because they fear him.

I can hear him in the kitchen now, barking out orders to Bunny and the others. Coach Noble must be in the garage taking count of our supplies like he does every few hours. We're all a little paranoid these days. We have officially searched every inch of this university for food. I think this is truly all that's left.

Our only hope is for Adrian to return with supplies or help. Worst case scenario, he doesn't return at all. But I doubt that's going to happen. I hate to admit it, but Adrian is a tough guy. He isn't going to let anything stop him, not when he's working toward something he cares about.

I've seen him train harder than the rest of the team. I've watched him run faster. Push himself further. And I've seen the way he's refused to give up on something as simple as a secret crush. He's still chasing after Mya. I know he is. And I know he's coming back for her.

I figured it out when she told me she'd given her necklace

to him. At the time, I had no idea what to make of that, but now it's obvious. There are feelings growing in places there shouldn't be. I know it's selfish to feel angry about Adrian and his connection to Mya, but I do.

Memphis's yelling pulls me from my thoughts. I blink up at the ceiling, lying naked in bed. It's too hot for clothes. It's too hot for anything. But if I don't get up and go downstairs, Memphis will continue to pry away every ounce of control I once had over this house.

Someone knocks on my door. "Yeah," I call, lazily stretching across my bed like a cat. I feel my back pop and it draws a groan from my lips. I should roll over and put on my clothes, but I'm positive whoever just knocked is one of my brothers or some sorority girl. All of whom have seen me naked at some point. So, I lie there and continue staring at the ceiling when the door opens to reveal Delilah.

She takes one look at me and smirks, then leans against the frame. I watch her eyes narrow as they dance down my body. She lifts her chest, so her cleavage is easier to see. When I show no reaction to her little show, she meets my gaze with a snap.

"We're having a meeting downstairs," she says.

"I hear it isn't going so well."

"Memphis is always yelling." She can't stop herself from dropping her gaze again, checking to see if anything's changed.

It hasn't.

Does she think I'm fifteen years old? It'll take more than that to get a rise out of me—and I mean that in the most literal way possible.

Since neither of us are enjoying this, I roll over and grab my clothes from the floor. It's at that exact moment that Mya pokes her head into my bedroom with a smile on her face. She startles me and Delilah who yelps and hops to the side so Mya ends up with a clear view of my bare butt falling out of bed as I scramble for my pants, my shirt—*anything* to cover myself with.

"Um…" The smile has vanished from Mya's face. She's blinking between me and Delilah, trying to put together the very odd pieces of this puzzle.

I clear my throat and stand, realizing, to my misery, that the only piece of clothing I was able to grab in that moment was a single *sock*.

It is not enough to cover me. Aha.

But I hold it against my crotch anyway and pretend this is all totally normal.

"Morning," I say, waving my free hand.

Mya… Sweet, precious Mya. She keeps her eyes focused on my face, but she licks her lips before she speaks, and I feel every drop of blood within me rush downward.

Please don't, I beg my body, but it's too late.

Apparently, I *am* fifteen years old.

I have no choice but to turn around, scoop up my jeans, and gracelessly cram my legs into my pants while both girls stare in shock behind me. The embarrassment, and the pain of jamming a rod (aha) into my jeans without notice, washes away the lust. I'm good to turn back around after I zip up my jeans. But when I do face the ladies, I want to crawl under my bed and die.

Delilah is smiling, two steps from outright laughing in my face. But Mya is staring at the floor, her eyebrows drawn together, her lips pressed into a thin line. I don't think she's angry that she saw me naked, I think she's angry that she saw me naked in my bedroom with Delilah.

I want to tell her that nothing happened. And nothing was going to happen. But I can tell from the look on her face that anything I say right now will go in one ear and out the other.

I grab my t-shirt from the floor. "What did you need, Mya?"

She clears her throat. "There's a crowd at the soccer field."

"What?"

"We've been waiting for you guys to come set up the table and wagon—"

"Why hasn't Memphis left yet?" I ask Delilah.

"That's what I came to get you for." She shrugs like this is no big deal. "He says he doesn't want to trade anymore. The others aren't sure what to do."

I groan and tug on my shirt, then I step into my sneakers and start toward the door.

I'm only wearing one sock. I couldn't find the other one.

The soccer field is in chaos. It appears Memphis and the others left while I was flailing around naked on my floor. He's yelling at the crowd of students who have come to trade, telling them there isn't enough to go around anymore.

That isn't true. Coach Noble takes stock of our supplies every day—every few hours. We have enough to continue trading for at least five more days. After that, I have no idea how we'll survive. But we'll make it somehow. We've got to.

Mya and Delilah walk on either side of me as I approach the crowd, some of the kids move out of the way once they recognize me, but others get angry and start shouting.

"There he is!" one guy yells. "We could've had bread yesterday!"

Bread? Are they angry because I told Hot House to scram? Memphis finds me in the crowd and beckons me forward.

"What's going on?" I ask. I have to lean forward and shout into his ear because the crowd has resorted to yelling at us now. Most of them are complaining about a lack of supplies, the rest are mad about bread.

They could have gone to Hot House on their own and made their own deals with them. But somehow this is all *my* fault.

"They want food," Memphis explains bluntly.

"Why haven't you set up the table today?"

He shrugs. "I think we're giving away too much food."

"We're not giving it away. We're *trading* it."

The trades aren't always great. Most of the time, we get things we don't really want, like sticks of gum and bags of tea— but no water to make it with. One guy tried to trade two blunts for a case of water, but he didn't realize he was negotiating with college athletes. Being a Christian university, the Cross North board is really strict about their drug tests. They might turn a blind eye to the underage drinking that happens at frat parties on campus, but we get dragged into Coach Noble's office once a month to piss in a cup and hope everything turns out okay.

I've never smoked marijuana before. My track scholarship is the only way I can afford college, and track is the only way I know how to afford a living once I graduate. I'm a sports management major. The best outcome is that I go pro after college or end up coaching some dumb kids and telling their parents they'll go pro.

Basically, I can't afford to lose everything to a blunt. And neither can any of my brothers. I'm pretty positive none of us smoke—marijuana or otherwise. It's bad for our lungs. So the pothead was turned away, along with a guy who wanted to trade a pack of mints for a pack of jerky. We'd given away enough that day, we couldn't afford any more poor trades. But regardless of all that, we should have enough to negotiate for today.

"Memphis, what's really going on?" I say hotly. "You're causing a scene."

"I'm keeping Kappa Pi and Zeta Chi afloat. If you wanted goods to trade, you should've taken Hot House's deal yesterday. Maybe we'd have some bread to give away."

I knew it.

"So is this your petty way of getting back at me?" I ask.

Memphis can't stop himself from smirking as he crosses his arms. "I'm just doing what I think is best for the fraternity and sorority."

"You're pathetic."

He nods toward the crowd. "That's not what they think." Then he steps forward and raises his hands above his head, trying to quiet everyone down. "I'm sorry we don't have anything to trade!" he shouts over their grumbling. "We might have had bread today. But as you know, Caesar turned down a deal that would have been a benefit to us all."

The grumbles rippling through the crowd slowly shift into hissing. I feel it the moment they decide I am their enemy. I feel it when the tables turn and I'm suddenly standing on the Field of Death, not the soccer field from weeks ago.

A wise man once said, *it is not these well-fed long-haired men that I fear, but the pale and the hungry-looking.*

I don't know the circumstances behind that statement. I don't know the set of men Julius Caesar faced when he made that declaration. But I know who I'm looking at now. And they make me feel the exact same way.

I'm not afraid of Memphis who enjoyed a can of chicken soup and two bottles of water from our stash this morning. I'm not afraid of Bunny who looks just as well-fed as the rest of our brothers. I am afraid of the crowd hissing around me. These hungry, half-starved men and women. People who would kill me for a cup of water. People who thanked me for organizing the trading in the fields three days ago but blame me for their hunger now.

I swallow, trying to find something to say. Trying to find a way to salvage the situation, but before I can even form a coherent thought, a whistle rings through the crowd, silencing everyone.

We all stare into the distance as the same group from before walks through. They've got even more bread than last time, and they're all wearing smiles. They know I haven't got a choice except to join forces with them.

I have no idea what to say or do. So, without even thinking about it, I turn around and reach for Mya's hand. She takes it and squeezes it, and I immediately know that all the awkward, unspoken things between us no longer matter. Not right now. Not in this moment. There's a lot we've both got to say to each other, but when it matters most, it's our silence that binds us.

I suddenly wish I could sweep Mya off her feet and just walk away from this madness. I wish we could pack a bag and leave campus together. Just the two of us. But I know she would never leave, not until Adrian returns, and I know she'd never let me run away without facing this problem. So I let go of her hand and step forward.

Memphis steps forward too. "You came back," he says breathily.

The girl in front nods, though her eyes shift past Memphis and land on me. Her name is Amanda, she's a junior like me, and she's a biology major. We hooked up three times last semester. She was my tutor when I started falling behind in Health Science 300. I passed with an A- when we finished.

"We thought about what you said, Caesar," she says loudly enough for everyone to hear. "We've decided to accept your deal."

My eyes buck.

They came to accept my deal? Not the other way around. It doesn't make sense. The crowd already hates me. It's clear Memphis is subtly fighting me for control over the fraternity. It would have been so easy for Hot House to swoop in, offer their bread to everyone, and snatch my leadership away. It might even place them at the top of this pyramid of survival we've built here on campus.

This doesn't make sense.

I get the same feeling I had yesterday, and I shake my head. "I'm sorry," I say slowly. "But we don't want your bread."

The crowd boos. Memphis actually turns around and shoves me. "I am not letting you turn them away twice!" he shouts in my face.

"We shouldn't take the bread," I snap.

"Why not?"

"Because... Because..." I look out at the crowd. I look at Memphis and his scowl. At Bunny and his confusion. Even Delilah looks like she has no clue what to think of me.

How am I supposed to explain that I have a *feeling*?

Mya touches my shoulder. I know without even looking at her that she understands. Is it because of her faith? Isn't that what all crazy Christians claim? That they get a *feeling* inside when God speaks to them?

I won't even begin to entertain that. I'm not doubting God or the fact that He speaks to His children—I'm doubting that He's speaking to *me*.

I just rolled out of bed naked, and exposed myself to a girl I know takes her faith seriously. I'm the epitome of immodesty and I know it. I don't deserve to hear anything but judgment from God.

I shake away those thoughts and square my shoulders. No matter where this feeling is coming from, I'm not taking that bread. "We can have a deal," I say, "we'll honor the peace between us. But we're not eating that bread."

I stumble to the side as Memphis bumps me hard with his shoulder. He walks right past me and stands in front of Amanda. "Give *us* the bread then," he demands, and she gladly obliges.

Memphis takes the bread and starts throwing it into the crowd. They scream and begin pushing forward, arms extended, trying to catch the free loaves.

"There's enough for everyone!" he shouts, like he's their savior. There's a huge smile on his face, there's a spark of joy in his eye. He's eating this up. He's loving this. And so is the crowd—right until someone lets out a bloodcurdling scream.

27

Caesar

The scream is high-pitched, almost piercing. Like a reedy cry for help that we all know will not come. It spills from the lips of a small guy I have never seen before. The crowd does not hush when he shrieks because more screams ripple through the field immediately after his. The joyful pushing for bread quickly becomes frantic shoving as people try to get away from the bread.

One student drops to her knees right in front of me and spits out a mouthful of blood. She reaches up and digs into her mouth and holds up a thin piece of metal that I recognize right away.

It's a razor.

"The bread is laced…" I whisper, eyes flitting through the crowd.

More screams fill the air, students double over in pain. Some of them begin to vomit, others pull needles, nails, and even rocks from their mouths. It's an awful sight but I cannot pull my eyes away. I cannot stop the screaming from filling my ears. I cannot stop seeing the blood on the hands, mouths, and fingers of the students in front of me.

This is truly the Field of Death.

Behind me, Mya grabs a handful of my t-shirt. I glance back to find her staring wide-eyed with tears in her eyes. Beside me, Memphis stands there with a loaf in his hand, but he doesn't try to throw it into the crowd like before. He isn't wearing that jolly savior smile anymore, and he isn't shouting that everything will be alright. His eyes are stretched wide, and his nostrils are flared. His large brown hand clutches that little loaf like he's holding a weapon.

I watch as Memphis lifts the bread and crumbles it in his palms. A solid rock appears through the dough, large as a baseball. He stares at it.

"They played us," I say behind him.

For some reason, that revelation makes Memphis angry. He whirls around and lifts the rock, spittle flying from his mouth as he spews, "You did this!"

I'm so caught off guard by the accusation, I don't react when he shoves me back a step. It isn't until Mya yelps as she trips behind me that I even realize I've been shoved.

"You did this!" Memphis shouts again, he moves like he's going to shove me once more, but Bunny steps between us.

"Stop it!" he shouts. "You're overreacting!"

"Overreacting?" Memphis glares down at Bunny, and for a second, I think he's going to hit him with that bread rock. Memphis is a big guy—not as tall as me, but certainly meatier. Built like a ram instead of the leaner horse-like runners on the team. Right now, he seems lethal. Especially with that rock in his hand.

259

For what it's worth, Bunny is unfazed. He might be 5'3 and cuter than Mya, but he isn't afraid of Memphis. This is the kid who spent a week on the couch because his ankle was sore. Now, he's standing up to one of the beefiest guys in the frat house—in my defense.

It would've made my heart swell if he'd done it earlier, instead of kissing Memphis's butt for days and avoiding me like I was the enemy. But he's here now. When it mattered, he chose the right side.

"There's no way you can blame Caesar for this," Bunny says to Memphis. He's so small he has to tilt his head back when he talks, which immediately takes away any grit he might have had before. He's just too cute to come off as a tough guy.

"I can blame whoever I want," Memphis replies. He takes another step, and a sophomore I don't even know joins Bunny in defending me.

A thick vein bulges on the side of Memphis's head, like an angry worm wriggling just beneath his skin. "You too, Trenton? You're siding with the guy who got us into this mess?"

"You're the one who accepted the bread," Trenton points out. "How could you blame this on Caesar?"

Memphis jabs a thick finger at me. "Don't you see? Hot House came in peace yesterday, but Caesar sent them away. This time, they came back for vengeance. It's his fault! He should have taken their deal when they first offered it!" Memphis is screaming so loud that others have turned to observe this little spat.

Most of the crowd is still screaming, still trying to pry razors and needles from their gums and teeth. But the rest— the ones who hadn't greedily stuffed their bread into their mouths the second they got it in their hands—they're watching us like hawks. Trying to find out who deserves their rage.

I can't let Memphis pin this on me.

I lick my lips and blink around at the bloody crowd, desperately searching for those Hot House kids. But I don't see them anywhere. They handed off the bread and skedaddled out of here. Their absence doesn't make me angry, it makes me confident. This solidifies what I've suspected all along. Their deal had never been in earnest. They've always wanted this. Always wanted to cripple us for hurting Green House, effectively crippling them by removing their secret little stash.

They couldn't fight us outright because they don't have the numbers or determination. But they could weaken us like this. They could divide us. And then they could move in.

I gasp, cutting off Memphis's wild accusations. "*They* did this!" I nearly shout. The realization hits me like a storm, I can barely get the words out. "They've hurt us on purpose, Mem, don't you see?"

"I see you making excuses for yourself," he says. "This is your fault, and you will answer for the blood you've shed today."

"Hot House is gone!" I shout, pointing frantically into the mass. "Why do you think they left?"

Memphis stands there looking stupid, so Bunny speaks up. "They planned this. They left the bread for us here so they could attack our house. Where we keep the rest of the supplies."

Trenton nods, even Delilah looks convinced, or at least she looks like she doesn't blame me. But Memphis isn't fooled. He's still holding that rock, squeezing it so hard I'm afraid it might crack in his hand. Or he might crack it over my head.

261

But instead of hitting me with it, Memphis drops the rock and full-on attacks me.

It's so sudden, all I can do is trip backwards as he tackles me. Bunny and Trenton both jump to intervene, so I don't fall to the ground. I've got enough footing to grit my teeth and shove back. Memphis stumbles but doesn't slow down. He starts swinging like he's mad. I get cracked across my jaw, Bunny takes a hit, even Trenton grunts as he's slugged in the gut.

It's shocking that it takes three of us to fight one guy, but Memphis is *big*, okay? And he caught us off guard. It's also worth mentioning that Bunny is as small as Mya and Trenton sucks at fighting.

I retrieve Noble's pocketknife from my jeans and flick the blade out. I have no intentions of using this, but I figure just the sight of it will scare Memphis off.

It doesn't.

Memphis shoves Trenton aside and he falls into the sorority girls nearby. Bunny doesn't even try to attack, when he shifts his footing, I know he's turning to run away from this madness—but Memphis doesn't. Memphis doesn't know that Bunny is a coward who only followed his orders because he was afraid. He doesn't know he wants no part in this. In Mem's mind, everyone is his enemy right now, so it never occurs to him that when Bunny moves, he isn't attacking.

That's why he hits him so hard that Bunny falls and doesn't get back up.

I have no thoughts in my head except to lunge forward. I don't even remember moving, but I know I must have because I'm suddenly on top of Memphis. My hand hurts as I punch him because I've made a fist around the pocketknife. It would be so easy to use this thing and take out the guy who started all this drama in the first place. But I'm not like Memphis, I'm not going to kill him just because we disagree on things.

I punch him hard in the jaw and fire burns through my hand, running past my wrist to my elbow. It's so painful, I pause long enough for someone to grab me from behind.

I'm suddenly dragged backwards away from Mem. "Get off!" I scream, thrashing, throwing my body around.

The voice behind me is full of fear. "No more fighting!"

Trenton. He's hardly bigger than Bunny, so I know it won't take much to throw him off. It *shouldn't* take much, but the kid has a hold on me, and Memphis is getting up, and the crowd is still screaming, and Bunny still isn't moving. *Why don't they care about Bunny or the razors or Memphis who is staggering away?*

He started this. This is his fault!

A cry tears from my lips. It's raw and animalistic, echoes of the overwhelming rage I've tamped down every single day since we raided Green House. Anger at Memphis for his grab for power, anger at my brothers for cowardly following him, anger at Coach Noble for letting all this happen, and anger at myself for never taking a stand until now.

I watch through blurry, pissed off tears as Memphis stumbles away. He cannot get away with what he's done. The decision is set in stone. I've got to stop him.

So I twist my body and use my height to my advantage, wrenching free of Trenton's hold. He stumbles back but quickly regains himself and latches onto my arm just as I turn to chase after Mem. The feel of his hand clamping down on my bicep makes me so angry that I turn and shove him off me. But I've still got Noble's knife in my hand, and I'm no longer making a fist, trying to be the nice guy here. Right now, I'm angry, and I just want Trenton to leave me alone. So I don't think when I shove him away. I just move.

When he staggers back, and clutches his chest, I realize what I've done. Trenton stumbles backwards and falls to his knees. A splotch of red blooms under the hand clutching at his chest, right over his heart. He looks at me and tilts his head to the side in confusion, like he's just now realized he's been stabbed.

We both glance down at the knife in my hand, slick with his blood. And then Trenton topples over in the grass and doesn't get back up.

Delilah and the other sorority girls are still nearby, some of them are kneeling beside Bunny, but now all of them are looking at Trenton. Staring at the crimson pool leaking from his chest. Mya drops to her knees beside Trenton. I hadn't even known she was still here. My entire mind had been consumed with anger. All I could think of was Memphis, but now…

I turn around, searching the crowd, shocked to see that Memphis hasn't left. He's a few feet away, but he isn't interested in fighting me anymore or running off. His eyes are focused on Trenton lying motionless on the ground.

"You—You killed him," Memphis says.

Never mind the fact that Bunny is lying on the ground too. All anyone sees is Trenton because he's covered in blood, just like my blade. Bunny isn't moving, but even from where I stand, I can tell his chest is rising and falling. He's unconscious but alive.

Trenton isn't. Trenton's eyes are wide open, and his mouth is parted like he's surprised how this whole thing turned out. Like he can't believe he's dead. No one can. But there he is, and there's all his blood. And here I am, standing over his body.

"I didn't mean to..." I whisper. Truly, I didn't. But I don't think that matters right now. Nothing matters except the blood staining the grass. It seeps into the soil and cries out for justice, its voice louder than the razor-sharp wails that still fill the air around us.

I knew things would be bad if I tried to keep fighting. I knew things would be bad for challenging Memphis like this. But I never expected anything to happen this way. A wise man once said, *No one is so brave that he is not disturbed by something unexpected.*

Do you know whose quote that is? By now, you should be used to me quoting Julius Caesar. By now, you should have learned that I'm nothing like him.

I used to think I was brave. Used to believe that even I would not be disturbed by the unexpected. But I was wrong. It's not entirely my fault. I mean, who could call themselves brave after watching their own friends die? Who could be brave when faced with starvation and death?

None of us are brave.

I dare to lift my eyes and look into the faces around me, each one wearing a different expression, bearing a different emotion. Shock, fear, worry, sadness. It's clear some of them can see that this is nothing more than a freak accident, but it's also blaringly clear that some of them blame me.

This isn't my fault.

I lift my chin as I remind myself that this was an accident. I've learned that acting guilty makes people think you're guilty, so I don't sulk or grovel. I stand in the middle of the Field of Death, one hand holding a knife, the other dangling at my side. Limp. Unusable. I think my thumb is dislocated. My knife is coated in blood, it's thick and visceral, coagulating already. There's so much blood out here, and that's what scares me. It scares me to think that just a few weeks ago the Field of Death was just my university's soccer field. That I had run this field with the track team and had laid in the grass on my break after orientation.

It scares me to think that weeks ago my friends were just guys I went to frat parties with, now they're staring at me like they want to kill me. Some of them *do* want to kill me. Not because I've done something wrong. Not because I've betrayed them.

It's because I made the decision to share our supplies with the other dorms. Supplies we needed. Supplies that are the difference between life and death.

At the beginning of the semester, these bloody, half-starved men and women before me were my best friends. Now, they could slit my throat in my sleep for a glass of water. That's what happens when chaos breaks out. When terror rules over peace, and hunger is the driving force in all your decisions.

To think this simple college romance started out so peacefully. So sweet and intriguing. And then, in an instant, everything changed. It happened so fast, a flicker of light and it was all over. *A power outage*—that's what we kept saying as we emptied our fridges and opened canned goods. *The grid is down, it'll be back.* That's what we told ourselves when the water stopped running. *Someone will send help; they won't leave an entire college campus to starve and die.*

But they did.

It took four weeks for Cross North University to go from an excited, thrilling campus to a battleground. I won't wait another week. I don't think I'll *live* another week. That becomes clear when Memphis steps forward and raises his voice, "Grab him!" he shouts.

The command is such a shock that at first, no one moves. Delilah and Mya blink at each other and then at me. No one knows what to do.

"He just killed Trenton! You all saw it!" Memphis shouts. And when everyone remains frozen in place yet again, he grunts and walks toward me.

For reasons I cannot explain, I tuck my knife into the makeshift sheath at my hip, sighing loudly as I dry my bloody hand on my pants. There is a dead man at my feet. His head is tilted back, eyes wide and unblinking, mouth open in a silent scream.

I didn't kill him on purpose. But I wish I had. I wish I weren't such a coward. I wish I could make the decisions my friends need me to make. The decisions that will keep us alive, fed, healthy. But I'm not that guy. The problem is, I realized that about myself a long time ago. My friends? They still haven't gotten the memo.

All except Memphis. He grabs me roughly by the arm and shoves me into the blood-soaked grass, grumbling the whole time. "He killed someone. We can't let him get away with this."

"What are you going to do?" Delilah asks.

"It was an accident!" Mya shouts. She runs over and tries to shove Memphis off of me. To her credit, the little spitfire is stronger than she looks. Memphis falls sideways and curses as his grip on my arm loosens. I shift to get a look around and my hope fizzles away. No one but Mya is on my side. The rest of the crowd blames me.

I can see it in the way they stare at me, gazes flicking between me and the corpse on the ground. They're waiting, trying to see if I'll declare war or tuck my tail and run. I could fight Memphis. I could remind them that Hot House is the true enemy here, but what is the point?

This campus has dissolved into madness, and it couldn't be clearer right this moment. I know you see it too. You've seen it from the beginning, haven't you? And now you know how we got to this point. Now you know this would be the perfect reason to run. The razors from Hot House, their cunning betrayal and impending attack on Kappa Pi is the excuse we need to get out of here and find our own way. But we're divided on that point.

I'll bet half of us still believe that help is coming. The other half knows the truth. That we're on our own. That we will die if we stay here. Or we will drive ourselves mad and tear the campus apart. Just like we're doing now.

Memphis shoves Mya away and holds me down in the grass. I don't try to fight him. I simply lie there and listen as he rallies what's left of the campus.

"Hot House tricked us, and they're probably on their way to Kappa Pi right this moment. But we cannot let them have their way!" he shouts, like a raging bull. He's talking to a bunch of hungry underclassmen and sorority girls, but they eat up his little speech like true soldiers heading out for war.

"We must work together to protect what's left of ours!" Memphis shouts.

The crowd shouts with him, all except Mya. She was thrown to the ground by Memphis when he shoved her away. She's lying there blinking at him in fear and deep confusion. We're both on the same page. We're both wondering how we were so easily and quickly consumed by this madness. We both know there's no way out now.

Memphis yanks me to my feet. "I'll deal with him. The rest of you prepare yourselves for an assault on Hot House!"

The way the crowd cheers makes my skin crawl. I've never seen so many people so pointlessly hungry for blood. But when you're half-starved and thirsty, what else is there to hunger for?

28

Adrian

There were soldiers crawling through Wakedon. I hadn't realized just how overrun the small town was until I left Mya's house for Phoenix. I had to duck through alleys, hide around corners, and tiptoe through the city. But once I crossed onto the interstate again, I was home free.

In comparison, Phoenix is a ghost town.

I haven't seen a single soldier since I arrived. Not any looters or random people who want to kill me either. But that's a good thing. It gives me hope that maybe Phoenix was evacuated just like Wakedon—maybe they were evacuated first, since it's a bigger city. I don't know what to think of the lack of enemy soldiers. They could have combed through Phoenix first and made their way out to Wakedon, or they could've started with the smaller cities and are making their way here now. Either way, I've got to hurry.

Despite the emptiness of the city, I don't take my chances by travelling out of cover. It only took me a day to get here, so

I know I'll still make good time even if I move more carefully. I didn't want to leave Connor behind, but he was right, he would have slowed me down. Any other person would've taken 2 days or more to make it to Phoenix, but I'm a senior runner on the track team. There's a reason I should have been chosen for captain. Even carrying a backpack stuffed with supplies, it takes me just a few hours of jogging to make it to Phoenix. The only reason I stopped was because travelling alone at night didn't seem like a good idea. So I ran until the sun kissed the horizon, then I slept in the back of an abandoned car and started again at sunrise.

I've read there were runners in ancient eras, they're even mentioned in the Bible as men who ran on foot to deliver messengers for their king, general, or whoever had hired them.

It might sound dumb to send a man on foot rather than giving him a horse. But you have to understand that horses need to rest too. They need to drink water and graze and some horses are stubborn. They'll slow to a trot when they're tired, no matter how important your message is.

Humans, on the other hand, can be beaten into submission. The Apostle Paul said as much about himself—*I punish my body and bring it into submission.* I remember Mya reading that passage from I Corinthians years ago. Funny that it would come to mind now of all times. It's even funnier that Paul was talking about self-discipline as one who preaches the Gospel. Because I'm not preaching, but I know what it means to discipline yourself. To beat yourself into submission because you recognize the goal is greater than your pain. I never thought I'd have much in common with a preacher, but I suppose we're all working for something, so we all understand the need to deny oneself at least a little.

That sounds animalistic. That sounds the opposite of what you would expect from a person than a horse, but it's true. Humans can ignore pain; they have the comprehensive ability to prioritize their important message over their aching muscles. And the fear of what will happen if they don't make it in time can give them the strength to push beyond their exhaustion.

Some of the fastest runners could cover over 100 miles in a single day. You don't get to be that practiced without experiencing a little pain. Apparently, you don't get to be a preacher either without any pain. At least Paul didn't. According to Mya, he spent most of his ministry in chains. Wrote half the New Testament in a dank prison cell with metal cuffs chafing his wrists. Yet, he spoke proudly of his beaten body. He wore his scars like personal little prizes. And in the end, he finished his race. My race won't be over until I get back to Cross North but making it to Phoenix is not an achievement to be overlooked.

I run past the old Ma and Pop shops of my neighborhood; I sprint by the bakery I used to stop at on my way home from work. Every building looks different now. Empty. Dark. Hopeless. Somehow, the broken little house I call my home looks exactly the same.

The stone steps are still cracked and lopsided, the door is splintered, and the knocker hangs ajar. I have never fooled myself into thinking this home was worth anything more than the awful people who owned it, but it was my home. Now it feels like a shell. Like I'm walking into a museum display home of some other unhappy family who used to live here.

The front door is unlocked which isn't surprising. We stopped locking the doors when I was a kid; we were too poor to worry about anyone stealing anything from us, and my stepfather had kicked the door in so many times the lock didn't always line up for us to engage it anyway. Being able to walk right inside now doesn't faze me for a second. Besides, Mya's house wasn't locked either.

Dr. Brown is a paranoid man, there's no way he voluntarily left his front door unlocked. There's no way he voluntarily *left*. So even though I know it's normal for my door to be open, I still get the feeling that whatever happened in Wakedon also happened here in Phoenix. But that's a good thing.

As I walk through my dirty home and realize it's entirely empty, I don't allow myself to worry or panic. If Wakedon was evacuated, then Phoenix must have been evacuated too. I have to believe that. If I don't, the alternative would drive me insane.

The living room is dark and empty. It's so messy in here, I can't tell if it's from the rushed evacuation or just normal living conditions. My family has been dysfunctional for so long, I have a hard time imagining what my home would look like if it'd ever been clean. Every memory I have is covered in dirt, dust, and old food. There's also plenty of blood in my memories, probably more than the dirt.

There's an old wooden coffee table in the middle of the living room, it used to hold a pretty glass vase, but my stepdad, Ryan, threw me onto the table during a fight and I landed on it. It shattered, cutting deep into my skin—that's how I got all the scars on my back. Took my mother all night to peel the glass from my flesh; she didn't like going to the hospital because nurses ask questions. So I had to sleep lying on my stomach for the next three weeks.

I was only eleven at the time. Too young to actually hurt Ryan when I'd attacked him, but not too young for him to toss me around like a ragdoll. He'd been hitting my mother, like he always did. I guess I thought that maybe he'd stop if I tried to jump in, but Ryan didn't care that I was a kid any more than he cared that my mother was a woman or his wife or that she was pregnant with his kid. She lost the baby in that fight, but she stayed with Ryan anyway. So I stopped trying to stand up for her.

I kept my head down and focused on school. And when I got to high school, I focused on track. That was when everything changed. My mother had the twins when I turned fourteen; I thought bringing Ryan's kids into this world would soften him toward her, but he didn't care. And she'd started fighting back, so I tried not to let the violence bother me. But it did. Even worse, it bothered my siblings.

The last time I got into a fight with Ryan was the day I came home and found Danya and Dinara huddled together in my bed, hugging my pillows. They were only two years old, but you don't have to be very old to understand it's wrong for your parents to fight the way ours do. When I walked into my room, they both burst into tears and begged me to do something.

I was sixteen years old, and the memories of my last fight with Ryan still made the scars on my back ache. But I wasn't a kid anymore. The moment I hit puberty, I grew like a beanstalk. I was six feet tall at fourteen, and by the time I hit sixteen, I'd added another three inches and sixty more pounds. I ran two miles before school and another one afterward for track training. I was in good shape. Far better than Ryan.

So when my siblings looked at me with tears in their eyes and begged me to make the screaming stop, I immediately turned around and headed for the door. Except by then, the screaming *had* stopped. The hallway was silent except for a slow sound I could only describe as **heavy**. Like someone was dragging a sack down the hallway.

I slowly opened my bedroom door and my heart nearly stopped.

My stepfather was dragging my mother down the hall by her hair. She was naked, limp, and bleeding from a busted nose.

To this day, I have no idea what he'd planned to do with her, but I didn't stop to ask any questions. Honestly, I don't really know *what* I did next. There's a gap in my memory that starts with me charging out of my bedroom and ends with me running into the emergency room with my mother cradled in my arms.

I didn't even notice my own injuries until I collapsed in the waiting room. Apparently, the fight between me and Ryan got so bad that he pulled a knife. That's how I got the scars on my chest.

After that, an investigation was launched, and my life changed for two years. Two of the very best years of my life.

CPS forced my mother to take out a restraining order against Ryan on my behalf. That was the only way she was allowed to keep custody of all three of us. Since I was a minor and Ryan was not my biological father, he was forced to move out of the house. Social workers did welfare checks every other week for the next six months, and Ryan was only allowed to visit the twins with supervision on the weekends.

My mother had to go to counseling with Ryan, couples therapy, I think. And she had to get herself cleaned up and get a real job. For the first time since my real father died, I felt like I had a home. My mother cooked us dinner, especially when she knew the CPS agents were coming by. She worked nine to five, and the money was enough that she stopped letting men into the house at night for extra pay on the side. We had food in our refrigerator and the twins had shoes on their feet.

I was happy.

And then I turned eighteen.

The day after my eighteenth birthday, I walked through the splintered front door and found Ryan lying on the sofa. He was entirely naked with a bottle of beer in one hand and the television remote in the other. He had his dirty foot propped up on the coffee table, he wiggled his toes hello when I walked inside and froze.

"Your mother is in your room," he'd said in his raspy drunkard voice. He peeled his blue eyes from the TV and blinked at me. Then, just as quickly, his gaze returned to his cable program like he was bored. "She wants to talk," he said.

I stomped down the hallway with full determination to ask my mother what the heck was going on, but as soon as I opened my door, she snatched me inside by my shirt collar and slapped me in the face. The hit didn't hurt as much as it shocked me. I stumbled backwards, and she shoved me hard enough that my body slammed the door shut.

My mother stood on her tiptoes to get into my face. When she spoke, I could smell Ryan's beer on her breath. "Listen here, Ryan is back and he ain't goin' away again. You got that?"

"That's not possible," I'd said.

She slapped me again.

This time, tears burned my eyes. I wasn't hurt. I was pissed off. Because I'd never hit my mother before, but if she slapped me again, I was certainly going to. I'd seen Ryan punch her in the face more times than I care to remember. She's a sturdy woman. I doubt I would've hurt her.

To her benefit, she didn't hit me again, she just pointed her finger in my face. "Your restraining order expired yesterday," she explained.

On my birthday. Then I understood. I was eighteen, a legal adult. The courts had done their job in protecting an innocent minor from a predator. But if I wanted anything done to Ryan, I'd have to handle that myself from now on.

I could have taken out another restraining order, but at eighteen, I wasn't sure what the courts would decide. It wouldn't have been farfetched for them to insist *I* should move out this time. Ryan is the father of the twins; it could be argued that the household needed him more than me. I wouldn't have put it past my mother to do so.

"If you don't want to be around him," my mother said sternly, "then move out."

"I can't move out." I was still in high school, working weekends at the grocery store three blocks up the street. I couldn't afford to live on my own. I still can't. My scholarship is great, but I've got to pay for textbooks and food and soap and everything else I'll need for the semester. But track takes up all my free time, there's no room in my schedule for a job on campus. So I work my butt off through the summer, picking up doubles and working weekends, so I can pinch off my savings during the semester. That's the best I can do for myself right now. I'm twenty-two years old and my greatest hope is a mile high dream to go pro when I graduate. Or else I'll be pulling doubles at the Karty Mart up the street for the next few years.

My mother really didn't care if I could afford my own place or not. She stuck her finger in my face and hissed, "Ryan. Ain't. Goin'. Nowhere. You got that?"

What could I have done?

I nodded. "Yeah. Whatever."

"You might like him if you actually tried to get along with him for once."

"Uh-huh."

She'd rolled her eyes and shoved me out the way so she could leave. "This is how it is. Get used to it, *predatel'*."

I had blinked in shock as she'd walked away. My mother was Russian to her core, from her delicate features to her feathery blonde hair. But she had never spoken Russian to me before. I didn't even know she *knew* Russian. The fact that she'd chosen that moment to use her mother tongue was not lost on me.

When I typed that word into Google translate and learned that it meant *traitor*, I realized she would never forgive me for taking her to the hospital that day. And she would never choose me over Ryan.

So the twins became my world. I lived to see them smile and I worked hard so that I could somehow provide a better future for them. I don't want my own place anymore; I want an apartment for the three of us. They are the reason I've returned, so it's their room I check first as I walk through my childhood home, even though I know they're not here.

Their scattered toys and threadbare blankets make my chest ache. On the dresser is a torn teddy bear, scattered gum wrappers, and a shoebox. I recognize the box as Dinara's hope chest. She started keeping things in it when she was five, I told her to make a hope chest to collect things that were important to her. Really, I just wanted her to start hiding her special stuff from Ryan because he liked to destroy things when he was drunk, and it was hard to constantly replace their toys on a part-time job.

I open the shoebox and smile at the contents. An

278

unopened pack of Oreos, a note sealed shut with a glittery sticker, a pair of my socks—I have no idea how she got those—and a lock of her blonde hair. She had to shave her head when she was six because she fell asleep with gum in her mouth, and it got tangled in her locks. She cried when our mother took the kitchen shears to her head, so I told her to keep a lock to remember how pretty her hair used to be and know that it would be pretty again.

I take the lock of hair out of the box and close my hand around it. I don't know where my family is, but I have to believe they're alive and okay. So far, this place isn't any different from Wakedon. So there's hope.

When I check the safe in my parents' bedroom, my hope rises just a little more. The gun is still in Ryan's safe. That means they must have been evacuated. If the gun was missing, I would've assumed they packed up and tried to make it on their own out there. They would need a weapon travelling alone. I know because I've been out there, and I've been shot at. But the gun is still there. So, they must have left with little to no time to pack. The only reason I could think they would have to leave like that is a mass and sudden evacuation.

Evacuations lead to shelters. All I've got to do to find my family is find out where the National Guard set up shelter points and public havens. That shouldn't be hard. But it will be time-consuming. And I don't have much time.

I promised Mya I would come back for her. I promised Coach Noble I'd come back and tell the campus what I found out here. Connor O'Reilly is still waiting for me back in Wakedon. I can't just run off to find my siblings. It wouldn't be right. All I can do is hope they're safe in a shelter, waiting for me. Until then, I've got to get back to Cross North and then I'll come back for them.

It'll be a long trip, but I've survived it once. I'm positive I can do it again. I don't have a choice.

"I'm coming," I say, clutching the gun in one hand and Dinara's hair in the other.

29

Mya

God, you have to help me. My prayer is fervent and desperate. I'm on my knees in my bedroom, trying hard to ignore the smell of dirty clothes and fear that fills this entire house. Three days ago, Memphis dragged Julius away like a criminal. I haven't seen him since.

I've heard whispers that Julie has been locked in his bedroom without any food or water. No one knows what to do with him because he killed someone, but it was an *accident*. If you ask me, I'd say we should be a lot more focused on Memphis and what he's doing rather than Julius who's never intentionally hurt anyone in his life.

According to Kassandra and James, Kappa Pi and Omega Zeta Chi are locked in a full-on war with Hot House. James told me the rest of the fraternity blames Julius for Hot House's betrayal and has been keeping him locked up in his room as punishment.

It was Memphis who'd wanted to take out Green House

for good, but Julius had stopped him. It was Memphis who'd wanted to accept Hot House's terms for peace, but Julius had refused. Because of that, Hot House fed us laced bread and the campus has dissolved into war. And somehow in the midst of all this, Memphis has managed to convince the fraternity that Julius isn't just responsible for it all, he's telling his brothers that Julius *planned* it. That he wanted to join Green House once the dust settled, so their only option is to take out both enemy dorms and then deal with Julius later.

That's the craziest thing I've ever heard. It's like the entire campus has lost its mind. Everyone has gone feral—kill or be killed, as if we have suddenly been reduced to barbarians.

Miraculously, Hope House has been left out of the drama. Kassandra and James have kept us updated since Kappa Pi brothers have come by every day to recruit members to their war. At first, everyone in Hope House refused to join them. We wanted no part in this drama, and there was no way I would ever help the people keeping my best friend hostage right now. But then Zeta Chi girls went to the Hope House boys' dorm two nights ago. They didn't leave until the next morning, and when they did go, ten of our guys went with them.

The girls' dorm wasn't so easily swayed. The fraternity did stop by, but after seeing the boys give in the night before, Kassandra answered the door with a baseball bat and sent the frat boys running with their tails tucked. This morning, James apologized for what happened at the boys' dorm, but we assured him we weren't angry. He's the dorm leader, but he can't control the guys over there. I could say he shouldn't have let the scantily clad girls into their dorm in the first place. I could ask if he received a lap dance too, but I keep all those thoughts to myself.

282

Last night, we had a group prayer for guidance. We couldn't afford to lose any more of our brothers, and the girls in our dorm were getting scared. Jupiter worried that Kappa Pi would come back again, but they'd have their own baseball bats this time. I didn't blame her for her worries. The war has gotten out of hand. We can hear the screaming even from our rooms, and this morning, we saw smoke rising from Hot House. None of us believes it's from their wood burning stoves.

It's foolish to convince ourselves that Kappa Pi and Zeta Chi will simply sit by and let us keep our hands clean. They've already asked for soldiers once; I doubt they will *ask* again. If they come by, I firmly believe they won't take no for an answer.

That's why I've decided to leave before that happens.

"God," I whisper, hands clasped together on the bed, "please give me Your favor. I know I don't deserve it, but I don't see a way out of this without You. Keep me alive and keep my friends safe. In Jesus' Name I pray, amen."

I have no right to ask for God's help when I've hardly spoken to Him these recent weeks. Since the power went out, I've been avoiding God. I don't know what to pray. I don't know how to pray about everything going on. The power, the lack of supplies, the war—not to mention my confusing feelings. For two different guys.

I'd promised Adrian I would wait for him, but while he was gone, I'd kept myself distracted with Julius. He'd kissed me, and I hadn't exactly stopped him. I had enjoyed it. And until now, I hadn't felt very guilty about it. Adrian and I had a complicated past, and a complicated present, but he isn't my boyfriend. We've made no commitments to each other. But even I know that's a cheap excuse.

If Adrian had walked in on that emotional moment, I

would have lost him. A week ago, when he first left, the thought of losing Adrian would have frightened me. But now I'm not so sure. Now, I have no idea what I want. But I know I shouldn't want either one of them. I made a promise to God, and even in an apocalyptic meltdown, I intend to keep that promise.

"One last thing," I pray aloud, "please remove these feelings, Lord. I know it's never Your will for me to be unequally yoked, so please protect me, God. Protect me from myself because I'm not strong enough to resist these emotions or temptations. In Jesus' Name…" my voice trails off as someone knocks on my door.

I stand, feeling my knees pop, and turn around. "Come in."

Jupiter pokes her head inside. "Sorry, I heard you whispering. Did I interrupt?"

"I was just finished, actually."

She smiles, though it doesn't reach her eyes. It's just a polite gesture because there's nothing else to do.

I clear my throat.

"Well," Jupe says, pulling the door open further, "I came to get you because Kassandra has called a meeting downstairs."

"Right. Okay."

I'm not looking forward to this meeting because Kassandra and I haven't gotten along these last few days. She did her part in protecting us from getting seduced by the Kappa Pi boys, but she's made it more than clear that she believes we're in this mess because of Julius. She's never liked him, and she definitely doesn't like the fact that we're best friends.

With all this drama going on, even James has pulled away a little. He hardly speaks to me when he's around, and he's made more than one sly comment about Julius. When I insisted

Julie was innocent and hadn't killed that kid on purpose, he replied by saying he wasn't there so he wouldn't jump to any sort of conclusion. Kassandra had asked what I was doing with Julius at sunrise in the first place.

I hadn't replied. It was clear no one would believe I was simply visiting my friend. No one would understand that it's possible to be a single woman alone with a single man and not end up rolling around in the bed.

This is all so ironic because the last time Julie and I were alone before then, we *did* end up in a very curious position. So maybe Kassandra's quirked eyebrow wasn't entirely unjustified. But still ... what right did she or James have to assume that Julie had killed someone *on purpose*? Kissing me does not make him a murderer.

And anyway, the final straw between Kassandra and me happened yesterday during our meager dinner of more crackers and grape juice. I had announced my desire to leave campus. To somehow find Julie and get out of here. But both Kassandra and James shot me down. They insisted that leaving was not a wise idea, even though we're starving and thirsty and the campus is literally burning down around us.

I am not excited about this meeting now, but I'm not going to miss it. I don't need my dorm parents' permission to leave. In case they hadn't noticed, the campus is no longer following the rules set by the university. Those went out the door the moment the power went out. Someone died back at the café, that was the day everything changed. And those changes became irreversible when we buried that kid whose skull was bashed in by Adrian.

With a sigh, I pull my loose braids into a ponytail that tickles the back of my neck as it sways while I walk around my room. I grab the cleanest shirt I can find, it's a white tee that says *Holy Nation* on the front in black letters. Then I slip on a pair of artfully torn tights and step into black jean shorts to wear over them. Jupe passes me my favorite pair of black platform Doc Martens, and then we make our way down the hall together.

Since almost half of the boys' dorm is gone now, we're able to fit everyone into our living room, though there's only standing room left. Neither Kassandra nor James acknowledges my presence when I enter and find a spot in the back corner. They simply exhale matching sighs and begin the meeting.

Kassandra starts with a prayer, then James takes over. "Kappa Pi has been here every day to ask for recruits in their war," he says, then he sets his hands on his hips and drops his head. James is a big guy, he isn't particularly tall, but he is heavy with thick muscles and a sturdy frame. He's built like a wrestler, though these last few weeks have certainly shaved a few pounds off him. When his shoulders sag, he looks like a shadow of the guy I remember flirting with me at freshmen orientation, in fact, I'm positive his t-shirt is a size too big now. All of us are swimming in our clothes at this point.

"We need to figure out what we're going to say when they get here this time," James says in a shaky voice.

I gasp as I realize what he truly means.

"You want us to join them," I blurt.

James snaps his head up and his eyes lock with mine, they're wide and filled with fear, but he shakes his head in denial. "No. No, I didn't say we would join them."

"You didn't say we wouldn't," I point out.

He clenches his jaw. "I said we need to figure out what to

say to them."

"Say *no*."

"Stop speaking out of line," Kassandra snaps.

I glare at her. "So you want to join them too."

"What I want is for us to survive this."

"We can survive by *leaving*."

"And how will we leave?" she asks in an icy tone.

"We'll walk out. They can't keep us here. We should've left a long time ago, honestly."

"Yeah, with your other boyfriend," James mumbles.

My heart turns brittle at his words. So that's what he thinks of me.

I refuse to dignify his petty statement with a response, instead, I push from the wall and march right out the living room and down the hall. I have no clue where I'm going, I just want to get away from those two—and from everyone else who apparently feels the way they do. No one spoke up for me or even acknowledged that what James said was rude and inappropriate.

No one except Jupiter.

I hear her jogging to catch up to me as I round the corner toward the staircase. She grabs my arms and holds me in place. "Wait, Mya, don't go."

"I'm not joining the crazy fighting and I don't want to talk to James. He was rude to me."

She nods and offers an apologetic smile. "I know. Don't let him get to you."

"You don't agree with him, do you?" I look into her face, not long ago, she was saying Julius had the hots for me. But now she can't look me in the eye.

"James is ridiculous. He's probably jealous because he likes

287

you."

I used to think he was cute. Now I can't stand him.

"Anyway," Jupiter tugs on my arm, "let's go back. You don't want to miss the meeting."

"Yes, I do. I meant what I said, Jupe, I'm not joining the fight. I'm leaving."

"But how?" She shakes her head. "We have no supplies— we're down to crackers and grape juice. We're eating *communion* to survive, Mya! Who knows how long we'll make it out there?"

I turn so I can tug my arm from her grasp and take her hand, give it a squeeze. "I don't know how long we'll make it out there. But we are guaranteed to starve or get killed in here."

She glances away. "Caesar killed someone."

My blood freezes. "It was an accident, Jupe. You know that."

She doesn't respond.

"Jupiter, you know it was an accident, right?"

"I wasn't there."

Dear Lord, she sounds like James now, but I quickly swallow the panicky anger I feel rising inside. Jupiter is my friend, my only other friend on campus besides Julius. She has to see things differently.

"But *I* was there," I say softly. "You believe *me*, right?"

"I mean… You're best friends with him."

"What's that supposed to mean?"

She finally meets my gaze, her eyes swim with tears. At least I know her betrayal isn't malicious. Her words hurt her as much as they hurt me.

"It means you might be blinded by your emotions."

"I'm not blinded, Jupiter. I've known Julius my entire life—he would never kill someone."

"Mya—"

I grip her hand hard enough that she gasps. "Come with me. *Please*. It's not safe here anymore. You must see that."

Jupiter tugs her hand away and steps toward the living room, her eyes are wide and filled with fear. She's looking at me like I've lost my mind, but my expression matches hers. This can't be happening. Everyone in this house has turned their backs on me. All because I'm friends with Julius.

"Jupiter..." I whisper, but she shakes her head.

"I'm sorry, Mya. But ... They said we should stick together. And you're the only one who wants to leave..."

She's still talking, going on about how dangerous it is on the road, but I'm not listening anymore. The only thing blaring in my head is the first part of her statement. *They said we should stick together.* That had been our plan when we first realized we were roommates. My hand still tingles with nostalgic joy as I think of the day I met Jupiter. When she took her wig off and revealed her bright pink hair. When we shook hands and realized we were made for each other. Like sisters.

Mya was the glitter to my gloom. A pink-haired rebel who lit up every room she walked into. I loved her because she was different. Like me. She was living proof that God looks at our hearts, not our wardrobe. She's faced the same sort of Christian bullying I have for my goth clothes. We stuck together because we understood the pain we'd both faced and the persecution which scarred our past. But we were happy to be roommates because we knew we didn't have to face such unfair judgment alone anymore.

It'd been hard wearing these clothes as a Christian. Secular goths only hung out with me until they realized the crosses I wore weren't for fashion. Christians didn't want to hang out with me period. I didn't look holy enough to them. I didn't meet the arbitrary, manmade dress code they'd created for themselves—which apparently didn't include the color black. So I was cast out. I was left alone with no one but Julius, my father, and God.

None of the Christians who mistreated me even understood what it meant to be goth. The Bible says, *My people perish from a lack of knowledge.* The average Christian doesn't even read their Bible daily, why would I expect them to know that gothic art, music, and fashion all originated in the Christian church? That the gothic sculptures which have survived throughout history today are depictions of Christ's crucifixion and the life of the disciples?

Gothic culture *is* dark and gloomy, but it was created by medieval Christians to remind Believers that the Light of Christ shines the brightest in the darkest moments of your life. Gothic Christian culture was meant to inspire hope.

The crucifixion was dark. The persecution early Christians faced was dark. Even the lost Visigoth tribes faced unspeakable horrors. They erected entire Christian kingdoms that were invaded and conquered by Muslim Arabs around Year 711 AD, wiping away most of their history—including the fact that they were God-fearing kingdoms, not a bunch of devil worshippers like so many blinded Christians believe today.

I have been persecuted by my own brethren for enjoying a culture that is Christian to its core. It's funny, the most high and mighty church folk love to tell me that Christians don't dress goth. Yet, I am dressed more 'Christian' than any Believer today. My fashion is inspired by an entire Christian movement.

No matter what people have to say about me, I've never let it bother me. I know the way I dress is different, so I expect to be treated differently. I've never cared to fit in. But as I look at Jupiter now with tears in her eyes and her head shaking back and forth, I realize the same is not true for her. She wants to fit in. And she finally does … because she has finally abandoned me.

Like everyone else, she has decided I'm not good enough. I don't meet their standard. I don't think the way they do. Jupiter doesn't either. She wants to leave too; I know she does. But she would rather die in a group than live alone.

So I watch her walk away and return to the living room, and I pray to God that He gives me the strength to forgive her for this betrayal. Because it hurts to be alone, but it's almost unbearable to be *abandoned*.

"I don't have time for this," I whisper, wiping bitter tears from my cheeks. I sniffle and turn around to go upstairs, but just as I pivot, I see someone out the windows on the side door.

I pause. It's Bunny, and he's crouched and running low, looking left and right like he's trying to be inconspicuous. As happy as I am to see him on his feet again after taking that hit on the Field of Death, I have to wonder what the heck is going on right now.

"What on earth…"

I move from the staircase to the side door and crack it open. Bunny jumps in surprise.

"What are you doing here?" I ask, then I frown and step outside. Anger rises within me. James had mentioned Kappa Pi would stop by soon to recruit more people to their stupid suicide mission. "We are not joining this war," I say firmly. "Just forget it. Go home, Bunny."

He shakes his head, his words spilling from his mouth in a desperate string. "Please—I'm not here to recruit anyone.

Kappa Pi doesn't even know I'm here, but they're coming. They need soldiers, Mya. Lots of them. The fighting is bad. Memphis has lost his mind." He gasps, trying to hold back his tears. "We need to get out of here—"

"What are you saying?" I cut him off.

"I want to get Caesar and leave campus. But I need help. I can't do it alone, and you're the only person I can think of who'll help." He steps back, staring at me, waiting for a response. "You'll help me save Caesar, right?"

I don't even hesitate. "Absolutely."

30

Caesar

Let justice roll on like a river... Do you know whose quote that is? You might expect me to give credit to my namesake, but not even a Roman emperor could string together such a statement. That, my friend, is one of the only scriptures I have ever memorized.

Maybe I was drawn to that verse because it seemed like something a Roman emperor would say, but when I heard it, I knew I wouldn't forget it. It's from Amos 5:24, by the way. A verse that plays through my mind as I lie on my bedroom floor sweating out my sins and regrets.

It was foolish of me to believe I ever had the loyalty of my friends. It was foolish to believe my friends could rely on *me* for as long as they did. I tried to be the leader they needed, but I failed to become the leader they *wanted*. And that is why I've been locked in my room for three days with no food or water.

Bunny visits when he can. He's repentant and filled with apologies, but he's also afraid of getting caught by Memphis and locked in his room too. He can't sneak me any food, but he's been able to slip me information.

Memphis has taken over the fraternity and is currently fighting an all-out war against Hot House. It's been brutal because everyone is desperate. We're all fighting for scraps now, even Hot House.

Green House doesn't even exist anymore. Bunny told me they left the day after I showed them mercy—packed up the supplies we left for them and scampered off campus during the night. Even their dorm leader left. A wise decision.

Half the girls from Omega Zeta Chi left two days ago, but they didn't abandon the university, they trekked across the campus and are currently holed up at the destroyed café with North Campus students. I don't know how large their stash of supplies is, but they've apparently got enough to take in stragglers, so the girls are gone for good. That's left Memphis in a pickle.

He's fighting with half his manpower for a nonexistent stash of supplies. There is no chest of gold waiting for him inside Hot House, and there isn't any treasure hidden here either. At this point, the fighting is futile and senselessly bloody.

"We're fighting just to say we've won," Bunny told me yesterday, nervously running a hand through his blonde hair. "Won what? I can't say. But all Memphis cares about is coming out on top."

That much is evident. If Bunny's telling the truth, then Memphis has gone as far as begging Hope House to join them in this war. When they told him no, he sent a string of Zeta Chi girls to their dorm and returned with guys who're willing to fight if it means they'll get laid for it. I doubt it's enough but who am I to say? I'm so weak, I can hardly lift my head as noise escalates outside my window.

There's no way to tell what's going on out there. Memphis has a guy outside my door all day. I don't know what he thinks I'm going to do. Maybe go crazy and stab someone else. But I don't have to be outside to understand just how much chaos has unfolded beyond the Kappa Pi mansion.

The screaming outside my window reaches a peak, I'm not sure if someone is getting killed or just screaming senselessly. A lot of that has been going on lately, like we're all slowly going mad. We *have* gone mad.

Bunny says Coach Noble is still guarding the garage stash, but it gets smaller every day, especially since the Zeta Chi girls left for North Campus. They took a few boxes of food and water with them, I guess as a peace offering with the wild students who'd once been our enemies. I'm honestly surprised Memphis hasn't packed up and decided to march on them. Maybe he remembers the fight at the café. Maybe he remembers how crazy those kids were. Maybe he knows a fight with them in the condition we're in is a death sentence.

Let justice roll on like a river...

There is no justice here. Or maybe I'm simply on the wrong side of it. Is this fair? To be locked away in this room as I slowly starve. Then again, I did kill a kid. But I'm sure I'm not the only one here who's done the unthinkable. I don't see anyone else locked away like this. According to Bunny, the only thing that will get you locked away is helping me out. Which is why he's been tiptoeing around the mansion, speaking to me whenever my guard leaves for food or a bathroom break.

I groan as someone shrieks outside, the high-pitched sound giving me a headache. My mouth is so dry it hurts to swallow, my tongue feels like a bloated slug withering in my throat. I think I have reached the point of no return. I am so starved I don't actually feel hungry, just empty. Void.

If this is justice, I wonder what will happen to Memphis for his sins. I'm not even sure what I believe where the Bible is concerned, but I know what Mya says, that God is fair and just. So I take solace in the knowledge that Memphis will not die in peace with a smile on his face. If I go out like this, then what he faces will be much worse. It's got to be.

"The world calls this *karma*," Mya told me once. "The idea that you get what you give. Your sins or your goodness comes back around eventually. But that isn't true. Karma doesn't exist, only God and His righteous judgment."

I used to think she was spouting religious nonsense, disregarding the way other people think and see the world just because it didn't align with her own beliefs. But I get it now. In my desperation, I understand what she was saying back then.

"Karma says good and bad are eventually balanced, but who is karma to decide what is good and what is bad? And if everyone got what they deserved, then there would be no point in Jesus dying on the Cross," Mya had said. "If we live by karma's standards, then, eventually, we'll all be punished for our sins. But the Bible says, once you accept Christ as your savior, you are forgiven for your sins once and for all."

I had pressed my lips together, resisting the urge to roll my eyes, but Mya had ignored me and kept going. Now, I'm glad she did.

"The Blood of Jesus washed away our sins at the Cross and made us whole again. So all the bad things karma says we deserve were placed on Him, making those who serve Him righteous—no matter what karma says." Mya had looked at me with the most serious expression I'd ever seen. "Karma says if you're bad, then bad things will happen to you. Unless you start doing a bunch of good things to make up for it. But God is the exact opposite of karma. We don't deserve grace and mercy, but He extends it to us anyway. Not because we did a bunch of good things to balance it out. He extends His grace and mercy to us because He loves us, and He promised to redeem those who claimed salvation through the Blood of His Son Jesus Christ. That's why I don't believe in karma. Because God says you are forgiven, but karma says you get what you deserve. That isn't righteous. That isn't justice. That isn't of God."

Screw karma...

I don't want to suffer. I don't want to be punished. Even though I've killed someone and let down my friends and allowed the dorm to whittle into madness. I want a second chance. I want to make it out of this alive.

Karma cannot give that to me. Karma says I should die here to balance the good and evil I've doled out in this world. *But God says...* I blink my blurry eyes, trying to understand all of this.

I don't deserve mercy or forgiveness—I know that, but isn't that the point of all this? Isn't that what it means to receive God's *grace*? That's what Mya would say.

"Please, God..." I whisper, and it takes all of my strength to do it. "I don't know what I believe, but I know what Mya believes. She's convinced You are good. She's convinced You are fair and just." I let out a shaky, weak sigh. "Please show Your goodness and Your fairness to me. I'll turn everything around. I'll get it together..."

I don't know what I expect to happen when I finish that

desperate prayer. I just lie there and stare at the ceiling, hoping for a miracle. But nothing happens. The screaming outside intensifies and eventually I smell smoke outside. Something is burning, but that's no surprise. I smelled smoke yesterday too.

I sniffle and roll onto my side. So much for all of that. Maybe God is fair, and He's decided it's fair to just let me die. If that's the case, then my fate is in my own hands.

With a grunt, I summon the little strength I have left and struggle to my feet. I'm so weak and hungry, this act alone makes me dizzy. I feel the floor sway beneath me, and I stumble sideways, arms flailing out to grab anything for support. I wind up falling into my bed, knee whacking against the metal beam of the frame.

I hiss as pain thunders up my thigh and down my shin. "I cannot die here … like this…" the words leave my mouth in a hoarse whisper. My throat burns and my body aches, but I limp to the door and heave a sigh of relief as I slump against it.

"Come on, Julius," I tell myself, trying to summon strength I know I don't have.

This is the part of the story they never tell you about. We all know Julius Caesar's death—his famous last words. But what about his last few breaths? The wide-eyed look in his eye as he realized everyone around him was a liar. The way sweat dappled his face and gathered between the folds of his wrinkled forehead as he gazed at his betrayers.

I am not that Julius Caesar. I have been blindsided by my closest friends, but that dagger hasn't cut me deep enough. I haven't died yet, and if I do, it won't be on the ground at the feet of my lying friends.

I pound my fist against the door and rasp, "Hey… who's out there?"

Sometimes my guard is a dweeby freshman, sometimes it's a kid from Hope House. Bunny says the guards are shuffled around so no one is there long enough to start feeling sorry for me.

I put weight on my injured knee and turn to jimmy the doorknob. It's unlocked, which isn't a surprise because it locks from the inside. The real shock is the empty hall that greets me when I poke my head out. There's no one in either direction of the hallway—even creepier, the hallway is dim and hazy. Since there's no electricity, the entire house has been dim, but this lighting is different. It's almost ... smokey.

Suddenly, I'm more than aware of the burnt smell in the air. I'm aware of the screaming outside, and even the sound of rushing footsteps running around the side of the house.

"What's going on?" I whisper to no one.

It doesn't matter what's happening, the house seems empty so I've got to take my chances and escape while I can.

I turn back to my room and limp around the small space; I grab my backpack and dump out the notebooks I've never used, swapping them with clothes and an extra pair of shoes. I've got a first aid kit in my bathroom that I dump into my bag and after I sit for ten seconds to catch my breath, I force myself to my feet and I get the heck out of dodge.

The hallway is even hazier than before. My eyes burn from the smoke, but I force myself to move. Adrenaline is the only thing keeping me going, but fear joins the fray when I hear footsteps on the first floor.

Someone is in the house, and they're running straight toward the stairs. I'm more than halfway down the hall—I can turn around and run back to my room, or I can see who's coming.

Before I can even weigh my options, a blonde head pops up over the railing and I sigh in relief as Bunny smiles at me—then my sigh becomes a sudden gasp when I see Mya running right behind him. She shouts my name and crushes me in a hug the moment she sees me.

"You're okay!" she says, holding my face in her hands, she's standing on her tiptoes and reaching all the way up since I'm so much taller than her. I duck my head and kiss her cheek.

"I'm okay," I say softly. Then I glance up at Bunny. "You came for me."

"Of course I did."

"And Mya too?"

"We're leaving," she says, pulling away. She grabs my hand and starts leading me down the stairs, talking the entire time. "Bunny came to ask for help. I packed what I could—it isn't much—but it's enough. It's got to be."

"We're leaving," I repeat dumbly.

Bunny nods before peeking around the corner into the kitchen. He gives Mya a hand signal and she takes me toward the back entrance of the house.

"We can't stay any longer, Julie. The campus is doomed."

"The campus is *burning*," I say with a cough.

Bunny looks over his shoulder with a goofy smirk. He nods at Mya. "You can thank her later. She set the garage on fire just to create a distraction."

That's what all the smoke was from, and the running I heard outside.

"The last of our supplies were stored in there," I say.

Bunny pushes open the back door and waves me out, we dart across the backyard in a single file line before stopping near the fence. When I look back, I see the angry flames

300

bursting into the air, licking at the sky. I don't even want to know how Mya started that fire, but it's not like we didn't have plenty of charcoal and lighter fluid from the grills we barely used. Everything was lying around in the garage, ripe for the taking. And now it's being burned, pretty much guaranteeing the death of everyone here.

"Those were the last of our supplies," I say again.

I can hear frantic shouting somewhere through the smoke, but we're in the backyard, behind the house and garage, so I can't see exactly what's going on. It's not hard to figure out … whoever is over there is fighting the fire. Fighting for everything we've got left.

I know Mya and Bunny wanted to get me out, but am I worth this much sacrifice?

I look down at my friends to see them watching the fire too, somber looks on their faces. Bunny takes a breath. "Let's go," he says, then he turns and guides us along the fence toward the backyard gate. Once we step through, we jog two blocks before I feel like I'm going to faint. I fall to my knees and Mya shrieks, dropping beside me.

"He's weak," she says to Bunny.

A handful of crackers and a small bottle of grape juice appears in Mya's hand. She shoves them at me. "Please eat."

I stuff the dry crackers in my mouth and gulp down the juice, it's cloyingly sweet for someone who hasn't eaten in three days, but it's enough to get me on my feet again. Instead of feeling the burning pain of food hitting my empty stomach, I feel strangely revitalized.

The campus neighborhood is unrecognizable. Houses are scorched, lawns are littered with trash and people. Some are sleeping in the grass; some aren't moving at all. This place

301

looks like a massive gravesite.

"Why didn't we leave earlier?" I wonder aloud.

"Because we thought help would come," Mya says. She helps me to my feet and nods at Bunny. "I think he's good enough to move now."

"Should we really leave now?" I ask.

"We have no choice," Bunny says. "Memphis is tearing the campus apart. Mya says Hope House is ready to fight too."

When I look at her in shock, she shrugs sheepishly. "It's why I left. I don't know what they're doing for certain, but both of my dorm parents seemed open to the idea of fighting when I walked out of their meeting today." She sighs. "It's time to go. There's nothing left here."

"Literally." Bunny nods at the burning garage behind us, but I don't look. I'm still not sure how I feel about them wasting the rest of our food. Sentencing the rest of this campus to death.

"You could've at least packed some supplies to take with us," I say.

Bunny gives me the strangest look, jerking his head back and squinting his pretty green eyes. It makes me feel stupid.

"We *did* pack some supplies away," he explains. "Coach Noble is waiting for us at the campus entrance. He got away first before we lit the flames."

"Coach Noble?" I raise one eyebrow. "He's in on this too?"

"I guess he's trying to make up for letting everything fall apart."

I nod slowly. It wasn't his fault alone. He was one of the only adults left here on campus, but he's not to blame for the madness that unfolded. We all are.

"You think you can stay on your feet for a few more blocks?" Bunny asks me. "All we've got to do is find Noble, and we can finally escape this chaos."

I reach for Mya's hand and answer without hesitation, "Absolutely."

31

Mya

Half the campus is blanketed in smoke. We move as quickly as we can, ducking through the backyards of dorms and climbing over fences. Most of the fighting is near Hot House or gathered at Kappa Pi's garage as more and more students realize the loot they've been fighting over is currently burning.

The fire was my idea. Saving supplies for ourselves was Bunny's. I knew the only way we could get everyone out of the house and focused on something other than fighting or guarding Julius was to attack something more important. Bunny asked Coach Noble to help us out, which I initially thought was a crazy idea. He's the dorm parent of Kappa Pi and he let Memphis imprison Julius and launch an unnecessary war with another house.

Maybe there's more to it than that. Maybe Coach Noble felt just as threatened as Bunny who had to sneak away from his own dorm and then burn it down just to escape. I don't know all the details, but I know I definitely have my reservations about Noble.

Bunny insists he's a good guy. He insists he'll be there waiting at the campus entrance when we arrive. I can only pray he's right.

My heart clenches in my chest as we pass through the backyard of Hope House. I should be happy; my dorm is the halfway mark. We're almost free. But instead of feeling relieved, I feel a deep sadness as we rush through the bushes and climb over the other fence. There's no electricity, so I don't expect any lights to be on. But Hope House seems eerily empty now.

There's no visible movement through the windows, not even in the living room. It dawns on me as we round the corner and hit the sidewalk, maybe they really did leave to join forces with Memphis. Or maybe they ran out when they saw all the smoke in the distance. There's certainly enough of it to cause concern.

Julius trips and slows down, but Bunny grabs his arm and drags him along. "We've got to keep going! We're almost there!" he insists.

"Let him rest," I say, puffing for breath. My lungs burn, and I'm not sure if it's because of the smoke or my exhaustion.

Bunny looks angry but he lets go of Julius and pulls out a half-empty bottle of Gatorade. After he takes a slow gulp, he passes it to me and wipes his mouth with the back of his hand. I sip twice and give the rest to Julius who tilts his head back with his eyes closed. His throat bobs with each swallow, I have to look away for fear of Bunny catching me ogle someone's throat.

Like every part of Julius, even his neck is nice to look at. It feels weird to fixate on such an odd part of the body, but he's one of those guys who's good looking from head to toe. Much different from Bunny who is cute but in a way that makes him look feminine and almost unreal. Adrian is the same. I'd call him beautiful before I use the word handsome. But Julius is different. He's boyish and charming and never fails to make you smile.

Even now, once he's done with the Gatorade, he winks at me and tosses the bottle away. Then he stretches and groans; I watch the action like a scene from a movie, my focus only disrupted when Julius squints into the distance and says, "Isn't that your friend?"

My eyes bulge as I snap my head in the direction of his gaze. Sure enough, Jupiter is running down the street, right toward us. She's waving her hands over her head, so instead of turning to leave, we wait for her to catch up.

"What's going on?" I ask quickly.

Bunny steps away, scanning the neighborhood, looking for enemies. I feel his anxiety overflowing onto me; we have no idea where Jupiter came from or if she was running away from pursuers.

She doubles over to breathe. "Kappa Pi is burning! Kassandra and James said we had to go help since they were housing the last of the supplies. When I didn't see you in your room, I got worried. But the guys at the fraternity said Caesar was missing too. So I ran back to try to find you."

I pat her on the shoulder. "I'm alright, Jupiter." Part of the heartbreak I felt earlier ebbs away now. Leaving doesn't feel so bittersweet now that I've got the chance to say goodbye. I don't care that Jupiter betrayed me earlier. She came back. She's here now. So I offer her one more chance to come along.

"Jupe, I'm leaving," I say, squeezing her shoulder.

She straightens and looks at me with a frown on her face. Jupiter is so pretty, creamy brown skin that stands out behind her neon pink hair. If I had to describe her to a stranger, I'd say she looks like a living fairy. Just as small as me with a little round nose and big almond-shaped eyes. It makes me angry that anyone would ever bully her for her hair and call themselves a Christian. But I hold no judgment against them. We're all just trying to survive and serve God the best way we know how.

"You're leaving?" Jupiter repeats slowly. She looks over at Bunny and then at Julius. "You set the fire, didn't you?"

"Jupiter—"

She shakes her head and steps away, so my hand drops from her shoulder. "We needed those supplies, Mya. You knew that, but you burned them anyway so long as it meant you could escape with Caesar."

"Jupiter, we had no choice."

The look she gives me feels hotter than the flames burning the supplies. "There's always a choice."

"Why do you want to stay so badly!" I exclaim. "There's nothing here!"

"It's not that I wanted to stay. It's that I didn't want to abandon everyone here." Tears form in her eyes. "This campus is crazy—it's dangerous and everyone here has lost their way. But that's no different from the world outside. You can't just leave because it's gotten hard to stay, Mya."

I understand what she's saying. I know where she's coming from. But ...

"We'll die if we stay," I whisper, watching her tears roll down her cheeks.

She shakes her head again. "You don't know that. God

307

could provide a way. He wouldn't just leave. Jesus wouldn't give up on this campus."

"He isn't," I say firmly. "You don't have to be in the storm to pray for it to end, Jupiter. That's the miracle power of prayer, it acts even from a distance. Otherwise, God wouldn't tell us to pray for each other around the world."

She seems to understand, sniffling back her tears now. I never knew she'd been struggling like this on the inside. I never knew just how compassionate she was—especially because she hadn't extended that compassion toward me when I left the dorm earlier. She'd stood back and let Hope House gang up on me.

I take a deep breath. "I'm leaving, Jupiter. You can stay and pray for God's provision here, or you can come with us and pray for His provision along the way."

Jupiter's shoulders sag and she presses the heels of her palms to her wet eyes. I feel for her, but we don't have time to stand here while she cries. Obviously, this decision is difficult, so I make it for her.

With a heavy heart, I grab Jupiter by the wrist and drag her down the street. "Lead the way," I grunt to Bunny. His eyes are wide, watching in shock as Jupiter trips behind me, but he doesn't protest my command.

We all turn and march down the street, turning corners and slowing our pace whenever Bunny gives the signal. Jupe whimpers behind me the whole time, but she doesn't pull away. In fact, after another block or two, she turns her hand in mine and interlocks her fingers with mine. That's when I know that everything will be okay. It sucks that we have to leave everyone behind. It was awful of me to burn the supplies—the only lifeline left here on campus—but I had no other choice.

We aren't just abandoning everyone, we're *escaping*. They had Julius locked in a room, starving. They'd begun pressuring my dorm to join the fight. More than one person has died on this campus. It isn't safe here anymore. I have no idea what will happen here once we leave, and I'm not ashamed to admit I sincerely don't care. I've got my two closest friends with me, and Bunny now too. We've got a plan to escape and supplies waiting for us at the campus entrance. All we need to do is make it there.

It doesn't take long before the entrance comes into view. This side of campus isn't downwind from the smoke, so it's easier to breathe here. Our vision is clearer too, so we all see Coach Noble waiting by the campus sign. We also see when he steps forward with a solemn look on his face.

Delilah steps up behind him, holding a baseball bat.

I gasp and stop moving, but Bunny and Julius both rush forward.

"Stay right there!" Delilah shouts, and both boys stop on a dime.

"Delilah, what are you doing?" Julius asks, but his eyes are focused on Noble. He looks terrible, his shirt is torn, and his hair is disheveled. There's a dark spot on the side of his head, making his dark locks stick to his temple. He winces when Delilah shoves him forward, jabbing him in the back with the tip of her bat.

"I'm taking back what was stolen from us," Delilah answers. She shoves Coach Noble again. "You can have him back. I just wanted to see who he was waiting on."

"I'm sorry," Noble mumbles as he falls forward. He lands on his knees and cries out in pain, catching himself with his palms. Bunny runs and kneels beside him, checking him for injuries.

"What did you do?" he shouts at Delilah, but it's obvious what she did. Her bat is as bloody as Noble's head.

"I saw the smoke and started to return to Kappa Pi, but I saw him running in the opposite direction and decided to follow him. He was carrying two packs, stuffed with supplies." Delilah spits on the ground. "It didn't take much to get the story out of him, but he wouldn't tell me who he planned to run off with. Wasn't hard to guess though."

"Delilah," Julius says, calmly approaching her, "we just want to leave, okay? Just give us the packs and we'll go quietly."

She makes a disgusted face, but the anger I see quickly shifts into sadness. "Caesar, I didn't do this to stop you. I did it to go with you."

We all blink at her.

"You would have left without me," she says, gripping the bat. "After everything we've been through together."

She's got to be kidding me. But Julius doesn't seem surprised by the conclusions she's drawn. It isn't like they didn't have some sort of connection. Perhaps it had been casual sex for Julie, but that obviously was not the case for her. I choose not to comment on the fact that she had quickly cuddled up to Memphis when it seemed convenient for her. Instead, I watch in silence as Julie inches ever closer, hands in the air like he's surrendering to her.

I can hear Bunny whispering to Coach Noble beside him, asking if he's okay. Noble responds with an appropriate grunt and from my peripheral, I see him clutch his ribs. I wonder if Delilah is truly strong enough to attack a fully grown man with a bat, or maybe Noble was caught off guard and didn't fight back because she's a young woman and a student he trusted.

"Put the bat down," Julius says slowly.

Delilah narrows her eyes. "You were going to leave me."

"I'm asking you to come with me now."

"What about her?" Her eyes narrow on me, and I audibly gulp. "You were leaving with her and not me."

This is madness…

"Julie, we don't have time," I say and, as if to emphasize my point, I hear a whistle pierce the air behind me.

We all turn to find a line of bodies dotting the edge of the parking lot. It doesn't take a genius to guess that it's Memphis. If Jupiter and Delilah both put the puzzle pieces together, I suppose it was only a matter of time before the others caught on to what'd truly happened. Now they've all showed up with the same goal in mind. Get the last of their supplies back and take vengeance on the ones who stole them.

Basically, we're all about to die out here.

"They found us," Delilah says breathlessly.

I can't tell if she sounds excited or worried, but I feel my heart begin to pound when Memphis screams, "JULIUS CAESAR!" and takes off running behind us. He's right in front of the pack, a metal pole in his hand, and his face marred by wild rage. There are two backpacks of supplies left, not nearly enough for the rest of the campus to survive on. But I get the feeling they're chasing us down for more than the food and water. Memphis wants blood—nothing else will satisfy him.

Julius turns and yanks the bat from Delilah's hands, it is so sudden we all yelp in surprise. He grabs Delilah by the back of her neck and shoves her toward us. "Get the bags and start running!" he orders, but Coach Noble doesn't listen. He forces himself to his feet and reaches for Julie's bat.

"Give it to me," he says in a raspy, tired voice.

311

Julie stares at him. The sound of pounding feet fills my ears. We have seconds before Memphis and his group overtake us. Delilah and Bunny have already put the backpacks on their shoulders. Jupiter takes off running first, clearing the row of abandoned cars in record time. I just stand there, watching as Julius realizes what Noble is saying.

"Give me the bat," he repeats, standing a little taller. "I'll hold them off while you guys get away."

"Coach..." Julie's voice cracks. "They'll kill you."

"Better me than all of you."

He starts to shake his head, but there's no time. We can't afford to argue over this or even sniffle through a teary goodbye. I force my legs to move and run over to my heartbroken best friend. To my surprise, he lets me take the bat from his hands and toss it to Coach Noble who nods at me with a somber look in his eye.

I nod back, then I grab Julie by the shoulders and turn him toward the parking lot exit. It's so easy to do it. He doesn't fight or resist me. He even runs at a decent pace as we make our escape. While we sprint away, I wonder if he didn't fight because he knew what needed to happen. Maybe he was just too weak to hand the bat over himself. Maybe he was too overwhelmed to run away alone.

If that's the case, then I'm glad I'm the one who helped him do it. I'm glad I was there to give him the strength he needed. Because the sound of Noble's screaming behind us is almost enough to take me to my knees. I can't imagine how Julie or Bunny manage to keep running. But that's easy to do when it's your only option.

32

Caesar

The cars on the highway are covered in dust, even though they've only been abandoned for a few weeks. Their presence tells a hopeless story.

For some reason, we'd convinced ourselves the outside world would be full of joy and water and food. For some reason, we thought we'd be better off on the road than on campus. In some ways, we were right. But in many ways, we were wrong.

The first day on the road is the hardest. We ran because we had to. We ran with the sound of Noble's shrieks giving us the adrenaline we needed to outrun the guys who pursued us. There were just a handful of them, and they eventually ran out of steam. It's hard to chase down someone determined to get away, especially with us being members of the track team. Despite the ladies being slower than us, they held their own and ran with everything they had.

I remember looking back after a little while, squinting into the distance to see our enemies standing on the tops of cars, weapons in their hands. Watching us.

We kept running after that. And I didn't look back. But it was hard to face forward too. Reality settled in when we took our first break. Jupiter broke down crying. Delilah shut down completely, not speaking to anyone. Bunny vomited.

"He's dead," he kept whispering, eyes wild and filled with shock and fear. "They killed him, Caesar. They killed Noble."

They did. And Delilah is at least partially responsible for that.

As the night settles and we trudge down the highway, I glare at the back of Delilah's blonde head. I will never forget what she did. I will never forgive her for it.

Someone touches my hand, and I flinch. I'm not surprised to find Mya standing beside me, a concerned look on her face. "We should call it a day," she says softly.

I glance behind us to see the sun drifting toward the horizon. It'll be dark in an hour or so.

"Good idea," I say.

When I look around, I realize the rest of our group is watching me. Waiting for an order. It gets tiring having so much responsibility placed on my shoulders. I've always blamed it on my name, but that doesn't seem to justify it anymore.

Why? I wonder. *Why do they keep looking at me?*

I'm the last person who should be given the reins. Look at what happened to Kappa Pi. Look at what happened to the entire campus. My own friends killed my coach.

I don't have time to lament the past, though it's screaming in the back of my head. Instead, I lead my friends to a cluster of cars which have been packed together to block one of the highway exits. I can't tell if this is the result of an accident or if someone deliberately moved the cars, but there's a pickup and two minivans beside each other, it's the perfect setup for us.

"Let's eat in the back of the pickup," I say, hopping inside. I pull down the tab inside the bed and the metal door falls flat with a rusty squeak, then I help Mya and Jupiter up while Delilah and Bunny climb up on their own. We spread out a blanket on the metal bed and then count all of our supplies as the sun begins to set.

We have two bottles of Gatorade and three bottles of water. There's an entire box of granola bars, a bag of unsalted peanuts, and a jar of jelly. It's not the most appetizing arrangement, but it's all we've got.

"Let's each take a granola bar," I say, searching through the variety box. "We'll split a bottle of Gatorade, and do the same in the morning."

"That's it?" Jupiter asks.

I nod and hold up the box. "Chocolate chip or peanut butter?"

She sighs. "Chocolate chip, please."

"We'll split into groups and take watch shifts," I explain, munching on my granola bar. "Bunny and I will take the first shift while you ladies rest in the minivans. Then we'll swap with two others. The last person will take a shift alone, but it'll be the shortest shift just before sunrise." I look down at everyone, wiping crumbs from my mouth. Some of the granola gets stuck in the little bit of scruff I've got growing on my jawline now. I haven't shaved in a while, but my facial hair grows in slow, so I don't look like a caveman just yet. Bunny says it's impossible for him to grow a beard, his face is bare as a child's right now. I'm kind of jealous. Beards make my face itch.

I scratch my chin as I look at the girls. "You guys will have to decide who'll take the last shift alone."

I expect that person to be Delilah. It's obvious she doesn't get along with Mya, but to my shock, Mya volunteers to take the last shift herself, forcing Delilah and Jupiter to work together. I can see the betrayal on Jupiter's face as she snaps her head toward Mya, silently demanding an explanation, but Mya keeps her vision locked on me.

"I volunteer," she says for the second time.

I nod. "Ok then. Red van or green van?" I glance at the abandoned vehicles beside us.

"I guess we'll sleep together in the red one," Jupiter says, sounding very heartbroken.

"That means you get the green until one of the others wakes you for your shift," I tell Mya.

She smiles. "Cool."

"Ladies," I look at Delilah and Jupiter, "Bunny or I will wake you for your shift. Try to fall asleep as quickly as possible. We all need to be well-rested tomorrow. We've got a lot of ground to cover."

"Where exactly are we going?" Delilah says. She actually raises her hand like a child. The sight of her behaving so demurely is almost laughable. She must be scared out of her mind or still in shock, knowing that she basically got Coach Noble murdered.

"We're going home," I say, glancing at the rest of the group. Bunny isn't from Arizona, so he's just along for the ride, but I know Mya's home is in Wakedon and I'm from Phoenix. I can't speak for Jupiter but from the smile that forms on her face, I'm guessing she lives somewhere nearby.

"We'll hit Wakedon first," I say, glancing at Mya. "Then

we'll move on to Phoenix, or wherever else you guys have family."

"I'm from Koshen," Jupiter says quickly. "It's a few hours from Phoenix."

"Then we'll hit that after we check Phoenix for our families."

"I'm from Wakedon too," Delilah whispers, then she reaches up and wipes tears from her eyes. "But I don't know if my family will be there when we arrive."

"We have to try," Mya says.

Bunny nods, but that doesn't encourage Delilah at all. She glares at all of us as she says, "Am I the only one who's looked around while we've walked? These cars are all dead. Everyone is gone. The city is probably worse than campus or abandoned altogether."

"That doesn't matter," Mya snaps, undoubtedly thinking of her father. "We've still got to try. What other option do we have?"

"Adrian was supposed to come back and give a report—"

My laughter cuts Delilah off, it's sharp and grating, like nothing at all is funny. "Adrian is gone. If you haven't realized that by now, then you're a fool."

"We don't know if he's gone," Mya says quietly. "He could be on his way to us right now."

"Ever hopeful." I don't mean for the words to come out as sharply as they do, but they sound like curses slipping from my lips. Mya jerks back at my harsh tone, then she reaches for the box of granola bars and starts packing them away.

"We should head to bed," she says, grabbing the water and Gatorade. Everything gets divided between the two backpacks, though Mya takes a blanket for herself before moving to the

317

green van. The rest of the group exits in silence until it's just Bunny and me left, sitting in the bed of the pickup together.

He sighs and scoots to the edge of the bed, swinging his legs over the metal door so they dangle in the air. I do the same, except my feet nearly touch the ground.

"How are you feeling?" I ask after a few minutes of silence.

"Tired."

"Anything else?"

Bunny gives me a sideways glance. "Should I feel something else?"

"Noble died," I say flatly. "And we were there. He died to save us, Bun. It's okay to feel something about that."

He shakes his head. "Preach to yourself, Caesar."

"I'm not preaching—"

"He died trying to help us," Bunny cuts me off. "But the person who attacked him first was Delilah, one of your many flings. And then Memphis finished him, yet another person obsessed with you."

"What Memphis did wasn't my fault."

"Maybe. Maybe not. But he did all of that madness because of you. Hot House laced their bread because of you. We attacked Green House, but you showed them mercy and they didn't even bother to help us out when we needed it. They packed up and left with the rest of the supplies *you* gave them."

"Bunny, you can't blame me for what other people—"

"Yes, I can!" he snaps.

This isn't fair. Bunny is the one who recruited Mya to help me escape. Now he's blaming me for everything that's happened. But I guess things are different now that Coach Noble is dead.

I stare at Bunny in silence, watching as tears slip down both of his cheeks. He looks like a little kid. I've always seen him as the younger brother I never had, though he's pretty enough to pass as my younger sister too.

I reach out and pat his shoulder, but he smacks my hand away. "You got him killed."

"I know," I say.

"You screwed Delilah, and she went nuts and killed him."

I don't think it's fair to put it that way, but I nod anyway. At this point, nothing I say will excuse what's happened. Bunny is determined to blame me for Coach Noble's death and everything else that's happened.

The sad part is that he's not entirely wrong.

I think about how different things would be if I'd never gotten involved with Delilah. She wouldn't have tracked Coach Noble down and hurt him. She wouldn't have insisted that we take her with us, slowing us down so that Memphis could catch up. And if Memphis hadn't caught up to us, Noble wouldn't have volunteered to stay back so we could get away.

I am responsible. There's a string of events in the way, there are decisions that were beyond my control. But everything links back to me. Back to my irresponsibility.

I swallow thickly, wiping sweat from the back of my neck. "I'm sorry," I mutter.

Somewhere in the distance, a cricket chirps. "Whatever," Bunny mumbles.

"Do you want to do this shift alone? I can pair up with Mya during the last shift."

He nods. "Yeah. I think that's best."

Without another word, I hop out of the pickup and walk to the green minivan. Mya's inside beneath her blanket, lying across the back seats. I watch her through the window for a moment, almost afraid to go in. I wonder if she hates me too. That can't be true, she burned down the garage to rescue me. Then again, so did Bunny. And he hates me now.

I take my chances and knock on the window. Mya stirs, sitting up and blinking at me. Once recognition sets in, she crawls over and opens the door.

"Is it my shift already?"

She sounds groggy enough to have fallen asleep but not for long. I laugh at her sincere confusion. "No, Bunny's taking first shift alone so I'm sleeping now." I duck down to peer into the van. "Let me in."

She does, scooting over and opening the blanket so I can lie beside her. It's a squeeze. We should lay the seats flat to give us more room, but I don't mind being close like this, bundled up beneath the blankets, holding Mya against my chest for fear of rolling onto the floor. But also holding her close because she's all I've got right now. She's always been all I've ever had.

"What's wrong?" she whispers into the dark.

Leave it to Mya to know exactly what I'm feeling.

"Bunny hates me. Says it's my fault Coach Noble died."

She lifts her head to peer at me. In the moonlight, her skin looks chocolatey and smooth. I reach up and touch her cheek without thinking. "Do you think it's my fault?"

"They didn't have to kill him. They had a choice."

"But Delilah—she attacked him with a bat. All because she thought I should've taken her with us. She got attached because…" my voice drifts off. I don't really want to talk about sleeping with another woman right now.

Mya sighs and lays her head on my chest again. "I don't blame you."

"Because you're too nice. And perfect."

She laughs. "I am so far from perfect."

"Okay, but you're innocent. You would never get mixed up with as many guys as I've been mixed up with girls."

"I've made mistakes," she says so quietly, I dip my head to listen better.

"Mistakes…" I repeat slowly.

She looks up at me again, chewing on her bottom lip. I try not to stare at her mouth when she does this. "I never told you what I felt for Adrian."

The sound of his name makes my jaw clench. "Right. You gave him my necklace."

"It was mine," she corrects.

I grunt in reply.

"We were close in high school."

"I don't remember that," I say.

"You weren't always around, Julie. You had parties and girlfriends. When I wasn't with you…"

She doesn't have to finish her sentence. I get it. And I don't want to hear the rest.

I look down at her, running my thumb along her cheek again. "But I'm here now," I say in a murmur.

She closes her eyes when I lean in but turns her head at the last second, so I end up kissing her cheek instead.

"Julius," she whispers.

"Just give me a chance," I say quickly. Desperately.

Before she can reply, I shift so I'm on top of her, pinning her to the seats. She doesn't fight me, just stares at me with sadness growing in her eyes.

"Do you feel anything at all?" I ask.

"I feel everything."

"Then give me a chance."

"What about Adrian?"

I lean down again, my nose brushing hers. "He isn't here."

She opens her mouth to speak, but I swallow the words with a kiss. It drowns out her worries and shoves away her reservations. Like a dam has broken, passion floods into the van and we drown in it.

Mya tilts her head back to gasp for breath, and I slip my hand beneath her shirt—it draws a gasp from her lips, but I steal a kiss to silence her.

"Wait," she turns her head to breathe, pressing a hand to my chest. "Julie … I'm not ready for this."

I'm panting, trying to catch my breath and think clearly. "O-Okay," I say, licking my lips. "We don't have to do anything you're not comfortable with."

"Promise," she says softly.

My promise is a kiss which she accepts fully. And she accepts another and another, until she feels my hand running along her leg, inching higher. I feel her pull away, ready to stop me again, but I speak before she can.

"Relax," I whisper against her neck, "I just want to make you feel good."

I feel her body tense beneath me, and that's when it hits me. The question storms into my head so violently, I actually jerk away from Mya, blinking down at her in surprise.

"Mya," I say softly, "are you a virgin?"

She looks everywhere but at me. No words leave her mouth, but the look on her face is answer enough, and the revelation goes straight to my groin.

"*Jesus*," I whisper.

Mentally, I have no idea how to react, but my body is doing all sorts of stuff against my wishes. I shouldn't even be surprised. She's been Christian all her life. But even so … I definitely fooled around with a couple girls from the youth group she used to drag me to. I figured the whole *wait until marriage* thing was something everyone said they would honor but didn't. Just like those weight loss resolutions for New Years. We all set the goal but end up failing miserably.

I never set that goal. I lost my virginity when I was fourteen and I've never regretted it. Then again, I've also never claimed to be Christian. And I've never valued sex the way Mya seems to. But that doesn't give me the right to take something like this from her.

"I'm sorry," I whisper, shifting off of her. I sit up and run a hand through my hair. "I didn't know."

Mya sits up and clutches the blanket to her chest like she's naked underneath. It makes her seem even less experienced and I suddenly hate myself.

"I didn't know," I say again.

"I never said I was," she whispers.

I stare at her, trying to read between the lines, understand what she isn't saying. But there's nothing there. Mya can make all the vague statements she wants, but I know her. I know the embarrassed look on her face. I know why her hand trembles as she brushes a little braid behind her ear. But I won't make her admit it aloud. Her virginity is none of my business. I just want her to know that I respect it. That's all.

"Mya, you don't have to lie about it," I say softly.

She looks up at me sheepishly. "Will it make you less interested?"

God no…

"Mya, I—"

"Caesar!"

It's Bunny's voice, high and filled with an emotion I can't place. Maybe fear? Excitement? I can't tell, but it doesn't matter. I jerk open the van door and rush out without a second thought. Jupiter and Delilah emerge from their vans too. Delilah blinks at me, then her eyes widen when Mya steps out the van behind me. She's clutching that blanket, and her clothes are a little disheveled.

I know how this must look. Both Delilah and Jupiter stare at me and Mya with odd expressions. I swallow and look away. Either Mya doesn't notice them staring at us, or she doesn't care. When I glance ahead in the direction of Bunny's extended arm, I realize both assumptions are true.

Mya doesn't care what her friends think of her because she's distracted by the familiar figure walking through the rows of cars in the distance. I know who it is before she says his name, and even though I'm not entirely happy to see him, I can't stop the crooked smirk that crawls across my face as Mya announces his arrival.

"It's Adrian. He came back."

33

Mya

Adrian is our ram in the bush. He showed up when we had nothing left. Our granola bars had been divided up; the water passed around to share. We were prepared to walk all the way to Wakedon with nothing but the clothes on our backs. But none of us knew what would happen next. None of us knew if we'd really make it.

That's why we're all excited to see a guy we weren't even friends with. Even Julius is happy, though he doesn't offer Adrian anything more than a tight-lipped smile. I don't give him much more than that either, but not because I secretly hate him. I feel weird about seeing Adrian because of everything that'd happened right before he showed up.

I can't describe how amazing it was to finally be with Julius in a way I'd never been before. We grew up as best friends, closer than brother and sister. But there had always been something else there, something we could have—and *should*

325

have—explored. Except we didn't.

We went our separate ways when it came to romance. Julie had his girls, and I had Adrian. Until I decided to take my faith seriously, to not be unequally yoked. But, somehow, I've been dragged back around that mountain by the hem of my lace panties.

While I snuggled up with Julius in the back of a car, Adrian had been rushing through the barren fields of Arizona alone. Trying to make it back to campus. Trying to get back to *me*.

I feel so cheap, like a sloppy one-night stand. Especially because it happened at night in the back of a car, like teenagers sneaking away from our parents. Whispering between kissing, groping, and grabbing at our clothes while we check the clock with one eye, hoping there's enough time for what we want to get done. And then Julius asked the worst question he could've uttered.

Are you a virgin?

I couldn't answer because I didn't know how he would feel about it. I wasn't sure if it was something that would come between us or bring us closer together. And then Adrian showed up and reminded me of just how divided my heart truly is.

I haven't been able to look either of them in the eye since Adrian arrived last night. It's the next morning now, we're all marching down the road with Adrian in the center as he retells the story of all that'd happened to him since he first left campus. It's an exciting tale that feels more like an apocalyptic thriller than a personal experience, but I can't get myself to concentrate.

I keep thinking of everything I did wrong last night. And then I think of how right it felt. And my heart breaks for the boy before me. Meanwhile, it seems like Julius is totally unaware of my inner battles.

He goes back to treating me like his best buddy. Slapping me on the back, offering hi-fives, and even sharing his can of beans with me like we're pals again. It's weird to think his hand was under my shirt last night. And now we're both pretending that never happened. For a moment, I convince myself it *didn't* happen. Maybe it was a vivid dream. Or maybe I'm overthinking things, and that's what scares me the most—the idea that I could ever be *just another girl* to Julius.

My only solace is that he hasn't gone back to flirting with Delilah. At least not openly. She's still quiet, staring off into space and walking silently beside Jupiter like reality hasn't sunk in yet. She got Coach Noble killed; I don't think her guilt will ever fade, and I don't feel sorry for her about it—mostly because I don't have time to think about Delilah.

I'm too distracted by Adrian's piercing gaze. The way he looks at me sends tingles through my skin into my heart and straight through my soul. I feel it in my toes which curl inside my boots. I feel it in my palms which go clammy with sweat. I feel it in my chest which tightens and restricts like I cannot even breathe with his eyes on my face.

Adrian glances over at me while he eats his breakfast, staring over the rim of his water bottle. He looks up while he packs his bags and catches me staring. I look away with my cheeks turning red—something that is not easy to accomplish as a Black girl. The worst of it happens now as he's talking about his heroic events in Wakedon, running from soldiers, his gaze flickers across the row of friends and lands right on me.

I gulp, and almost look down at my feet, but I manage to hold his gaze. This feels like a challenge. Like I'm confessing my guilt by looking away first, so I try my hardest to maintain eye contact, but then I trip over a rock and stumble forward.

Adrian pauses, watching with concern on his face, but Julius bursts out laughing and shakes my shoulder like his good old buddy. I feel my face heat with shame and push him away as I force my feet to move forward. I don't even bother looking at Adrian again for the next hour, not until I hear Bunny ask, "What happened to everyone else?"

Adrian stops walking, drawing everyone's attention.

I wait for him to tell us they went their separate ways. That everyone decided to find their families on their own. But instead, he heaves a sigh, and tells us a story of gunfire and betrayal. Connor was shot, some girl named Daniella took the rest of their supplies. They barely made it to my house alive.

When Adrian is finished, he looks up at us and drops his shoulders. They're broad and wide and muscular, even beneath his grey t-shirt. He still looks strong and healthy, despite being starved for the last two weeks. He's cleaner than the rest of us and his face is cleanly shaved. He makes me miss home.

"So, Connor's been shot," Julius says slowly. "And the rest of the group just ran off."

He says this in a way that almost sounds like an accusation. Adrian doesn't miss his tone. He narrows his sharp grey eyes at my best friend and takes a step toward him. "You have something else to say, Julius?"

Bunny immediately jumps to Julie's defense. "It's just a lot to take in, that's all."

"How do we know you didn't shoot Connor?" Julius says flatly. "Or the others."

Adrian looks like he wants to punch him, but his words come out calmly, and slowly. "Are you kidding me?"

"You do have a gun." Julius raises one of his raven eyebrows. The look on his face is an odd combination of serious and sarcastic. Even I find it hard not to roll my eyes when I see his expression, I have no idea how Adrian manages to stay so calm.

He works his jaw like he's unscrewing it before he replies, "I do have a gun." Then he pulls out the weapon he showed us yesterday, and everyone holds their breath.

Apparently, Adrian got the gun from a safe in his home. But now Julius is making everything sound so much more sinister. Like there's something Adrian isn't telling us.

"I have a gun," Adrian repeats. "But I didn't get it until *after* everything went down. Otherwise, I would have used it."

"Used it on who?" Julius folds his arms.

Adrian's response is a low growl. "Who do you think?"

"Caesar is just trying to—"

"*Shut up*, Bunny," Adrian snaps without even looking at him. "I was talking to your boyfriend, not you."

Bunny's face turns red. I'd find it hard to recover from that one too. It's enough to shut him up for now, he doesn't even look up from the ground—let alone interrupt again.

"What are you really saying, Julius?" Adrian challenges.

"I'm saying it's mighty weird that you claim the rest of the group was chased off by armed vagabonds while you somehow made it to a stash of supplies all by your lonesome. Connor was shot. And you have a gun."

"I didn't shoot him," Adrian says calmly.

"We don't know that," Julius says.

"You can ask him when we get to Mya's house."

"For all we know, Connor is dead," Julius says, looking around at the rest of us. I drop my gaze when he looks at me.

329

I want no part of whatever storm Julie is trying to stir right now.

"Connor isn't dead," Adrian insists. "If I wanted to kill my own classmates and steal all the supplies for myself, why would I bother coming back for you guys?"

"You came back for *Mya*." Julius rolls his eyes. "Let's not play stupid."

"If I had only come back for Mya, I wouldn't have brought enough supplies for the rest of you." Adrian motions to the two packs he'd hauled along the highway for miles. He'd even stopped and hid some packs in abandoned cars to mark as rest stops since he couldn't carry everything all the way to campus. But for some reason, this doesn't convince Julius of Adrian's innocence. He stands there with his eyes narrowed like he isn't buying any of this.

Adrian gets angry. "I care about Mya," he admits, which makes everyone stare at me. "But I know Mya cares about you. So I came back for everyone. Because she would be devastated if I didn't help out her friends too. You know her well enough to know what I'm saying is true, Julius."

He smirks and shifts so he's standing closer to me. Towering over me. Possessive. Dominant. "You're right. I do know Mya quite well."

That's when I see it. Realization. The way Adrian's gaze glides between us, taking in Julie's smug look and my embarrassed face, tells me that he knows. He knows something happened between me and Julie while he was gone, but he doesn't acknowledge it. He just blinks at us in silence, a muscle in his square jaw spasming.

"I believe him," I say, desperately trying to end this conversation. I feel Julie's eyes burning into the side of my face, so I lift my head and look him in the eye. "I believe Adrian's story."

I expect him to question me, to ask me if I'm just taking up for Adrian. I expect my best friend to feel betrayed and get angry. I *don't* expect him to turn and silently walk away from me.

Julius leaves me standing there in the awkward silence that follows, watching him march up the highway like a stranger. He doesn't look back. Doesn't even acknowledge the rest of the group. He just keeps moving, leaving us no choice but to catch up or be left behind.

Adrian sighs, staring at Julie's retreating figure. "We don't have long before we reach Wakedon. If we pick up the pace, we should make it by tomorrow." Then he turns and walks away too.

One by one, we all follow Adrian and Julius through the weaving cars abandoned along the highway. When it's time for us to exit, we stick together and march through the backroads, ignoring our sore feet and praying to God to keep our thirst and the blazing sun at bay. When we break for the evening, I'm too tired to care about the events of the day.

We're in the parking lot of an auto shop. Adrian retrieves the duffel bag he stashed here; he says it's the last one which means this will be our last stop before we make it to Wakedon. I should feel relieved, but I'm just tired. So I take my portion of canned spaghetti, half a bottle of water, and a granola bar, then I move to the back of the shop to find a quiet space to spread out my blanket for the night.

I've just set my things on the ground when I hear footsteps approaching. With a sigh, I turn to find Julius leaning against the metal rack of tools just a few feet away from me. He looks angry.

"What the heck was that out there?" he demands.

I'm too tired for this. "Julius, you were being crazy. Do you seriously think Adrian killed Connor and shot our friends?"

"It doesn't matter what I think," he snaps. "You're my best friend. You're supposed to have my back. Especially in front of *him*."

The way he says *him* makes me jerk back in surprise. The word comes out like an angry curse.

"Adrian isn't our enemy," I say calmly.

Julius lets out a mirthless chuckle. "He sure isn't yours."

"What's that supposed to mean?"

He shoves away from the beam and closes the gap between us in two large strides. He's right in front of me before I even realize it, and there's no time to step back. Julius grabs me by the wrist and yanks me toward him, his voice comes out as a hiss. "I mean, you gave him my necklace. And my Daisy Bar. You went to his dorm and begged him to come back for you. And after everything that happened between us last night, you took his side."

"It's not a matter of *sides*," I insist. "You weren't being fair."

He shoves me away from him. I stumble back a step and blink at him, holding my wrist.

"*You're* not being fair. You're playing us both."

The words are like a slap. Julius and Adrian have always been at odds, and I've always somehow existed at the edges of their fights. Now, I've been dragged into the middle of it. But instead of fighting *over* me, Julius is *fighting* me. I've never seen this side of him. I'm so shocked, I have no idea how to react, but he doesn't even give me time to. He keeps talking, insults

332

rolling off his tongue like a snake spitting venom.

"And then you gave me that little innocent act last night."
He makes a noise and his face wrinkles in anger. "I bet he bent
you over before he left."

He trips sideways, eyes wide and jaw slack. It takes us both
a moment to realize I've slapped him. The sting in my hand
feels good, but the sound of the smack echoing through the
empty auto shop sounds even better. It's loud enough to turn
heads; I glance around to find Delilah, Jupiter, and Adrian, all
watching us. Bunny is busy unpacking his bag, pretending he
didn't hear anything.

I'm not sure if they saw me slap Julius, or if they heard us
arguing before that, but everyone is looking now, and I don't
know what to do.

Julius touches his cheek, staring at me in confusion. "Over
him?" he says. "You hit me over him?"

My hand balls into a fist, if only to keep from hitting him
again. "I slapped you for myself."

Julius shakes his head and storms off, leaving me staring
behind him again with no words to say. I have no idea where
this anger came from, but it isn't hard for me to figure it out.
When I glance around the room again, watching my friends go
back to unpacking and getting ready for bed, my gaze lands on
Adrian. He's looking at Julius, and there's a very small smirk
on his face.

34

Caesar

I hate myself. What was I thinking?? The things I said to Mya were awful—there's no justification, just the ugly truth that I was jealous and angry because I saw the real reason Mya still hasn't given in to her emotions.

Adrian Nikols.

He has been a thorn in my side. It burns me that this is how he must have felt for years. Watching me prance around with Mya while he loathed my existence from the sidelines. Now the roles are somewhat reversed, and it's the worst experience of my life. What makes it insufferable is that this is entirely my fault.

While I was out partying, Mya was moving on. While I was cuddled up with other girls, Mya was falling for someone else. And even though I'm here now, it's still not enough. Even in Adrian's absence, my open affection toward her isn't enough.

They haven't spoken since Adrian returned, but I cannot

ignore the way they've been stealing glances at each other. It almost makes me nauseous. Mya can barely look him in the eye, meanwhile, Adrian can't keep his gaze from drifting her way. He's like a puppy searching for a lost toy; every time he looks at Mya, I half expect him to start barking.

As if their silent connection isn't annoying enough, I had to go and make things worse by picking a fight with both of them. I know it was ridiculous of me to accuse Adrian of any foul play. To be honest, I don't think he shot anyone. And I genuinely believe Connor is safe somewhere. But I can't stand the fact that Adrian showed up like a hero and swept everyone off their feet.

Weeks ago, these same people looked at me with stars in their eyes. I was their leader. I was the closest I've ever been to a king—a real Caesar. Then I got stabbed in the back by the same guys who'd sworn loyalty to me as their captain and their fraternity brother. They blamed me for their hunger, called me weak for not murdering a dorm full of people, and then called me a killer for *accidentally* stabbing someone. They locked me away. Starved me. Mocked me. And chased me down when I tried to escape.

All of that happened in the blink of an eye. One day, they loved me. The next, I was facing some sort of twisted sense of justice. And after getting away from it all, in walks Adrian Nikols and my friends are back to scowling at me.

Bunny blames me for Coach Noble's death. Delilah hates me because she knows I'm in love with Mya. Jupiter isn't a fan—for whatever reason. And Mya...

I groan as I roll over onto my side. Everyone else is asleep, their snores echoing through the dark auto shop. It's drafty in here, the sort of chill you get from a damp basement with no insulation. I'm not shivering, but I wish I had a blanket. I'm lying on top of an extra pair of sweatpants I packed from my dorm. That's it.

I shouldn't feel bad for myself. I deserve to sleep on this awful concrete floor. I deserve the anger I feel radiating from the far side of the room, where Mya is resting. I even deserved the backhand she gave me earlier. It didn't hurt as much as it shocked me. But I'm sure my words shocked us both. I don't even know why I said that. I just wanted to hurt her as much as she'd hurt me.

I know Mya hasn't fooled around with Adrian. I'd honestly wondered before, but from the way she got all shy and weird in the back of that van, all my doubts washed away. But now I'm confused. When she told me she was a virgin, I thought it was because she's a Christian and she's saving herself for God's ordained marriage. But from the way she keeps stealing glances at Adrian, the darker side of my brain can't help but wonder if she's really holding out for him instead.

I have half a mind to march back over there and ask her about all of this, but I know that'll only start another argument and push us further apart. We've gotten into fights before, but this one feels different. This one feels like we've crossed into uncharted territory. I have no idea where we stand now, or how I can fix this. I'm sure Mya feels the same.

At least we're in this together. We share our pain as much as our joy. Mya is my happiness and my biggest headache. It's always been this way between us. I don't think I love anyone as much as her, and not just because things have slowly grown romantic. It's because she's all I have.

I've never had a real family. Never had anyone love me just because. Except Mya. My foster mother comes dangerously

336

close, but there's an invisible wall between us that I've always been too afraid to tear down. I think she has too. She never adopted me, but she did everything she could to make me feel loved and cherished while growing up. With her being Korean and me being ridiculously Italian, there was no mistaking the fact that we aren't related. But I still knew she loved me as much as she could. She just couldn't love me enough.

Mya filled those gaps. The cracks left in my heart from my parents who abandoned me, and the crevices that splintered my mind from the foster mother who never adopted me. Mya was the glue who made all the pieces fit and stay together. And now I've pushed her beyond her limits.

I slowly exhale, rolling onto my back and staring at the ceiling. It's ink black in here, so dark I can barely tell if my eyes are opened or closed. I feel a tiny rock stab into my lower back, and I shift my weight a little to adjust. I don't think I'm going to get much sleep tonight. I don't think I'll get much sleep until I make things right with Mya.

Something brushes my arm and I turn my head, though I can't see anything. I feel a sudden warmth and realize a person is beside me now.

"Who's there?" I say softly, praying that it's Mya.

"It's me," a gentle voice replies.

I almost roll my eyes. It's Delilah.

She shifts closer to me and I'm suddenly able to map out her body in my mind. Her head is tucked against my shoulder, her brilliantly blonde hair woven into a heavy braid that rests across my chest. Her dainty fingers grip my bicep, her slender legs are bent at the knee, so her thigh rubs against mine. I can feel her breath on my arm as she exhales.

"Can't sleep?"

"No," I say softly.

"A lot on your mind."

She doesn't say that as a question, so I don't elaborate on it, I just answer plainly. "Yeah."

We lay in silence for a few minutes.

"What's keeping you up?" I whisper.

It takes her so long to answer, I figure she's fallen asleep, but then I hear her soft voice fill the air. Delilah has one of those sultry voices that sounds like she needs a cough drop, but in a good way. It's a feminine rasp I've come to enjoy, even now as she speaks, the sound of her voice makes me relax and feel a tiny bit better about my awful day.

"I'm afraid of the dark," she admits.

Interesting, especially since there's no power so there's no light unless you've got a solar powered flashlight. Weeks into this outage, I'm used to functioning by the sunlight. My body has slowly rewired itself to just *know* when it's sunrise and feel tired around sunset. I wish I could tap into that rewiring now, but I'm wide awake. So is Delilah.

"What about you?" she says in a whisper. "What's keeping you up?"

"I already told you. There's a lot on my mind."

She chuckles. It's sexy, I'll be honest.

"There's more to it than that," Delilah says. "I've admitted something to you, it's your turn now."

My chest inflates as I take a deep breath. Delilah is afraid of the dark, but what do I fear?

"Let's just say I'm afraid of being alone," I mutter.

She snuggles closer to me; her body is so warm it's almost uncomfortable. "Okay. Then let's stay like this tonight."

I know what she's doing, but I'm not going to fight her on

it. Delilah is everything that would normally hold my attention. But I've moved on from that sort of stuff—or at the very least, I'm consumed by the idea of dating Mya. Which means nothing can happen tonight with the woman beside me.

It's not like I don't remember the way she dumped me for Memphis when it was convenient for her. But I'll let that slide. She did what she had to to survive the chaos we faced. I don't exactly blame her.

"Is this okay?" she asks, and I know she means more than what she's saying, but I nod anyway.

"It's okay."

She snuggles even closer, and after a few moments, I feel her hand leave my arm. The tips of her fingers brush over my chest and dip lower, slipping into the front of my pants. I stifle a groan at her touch, squeezing my eyes shut tightly. It would be so easy to just lie there and enjoy this. I *want* to lay here and forget about the world. Bury my frustrations in ecstasy.

But this isn't right.

I grab Delilah's wrist. "We're not doing this, Lilah," I whisper.

She doesn't speak. For a moment, I think she didn't hear me. But then she retracts her hand and rolls onto her side so her back is facing me. "Goodnight, Caesar," she says softly.

I shift so we're back-to-back. "Goodnight, Delilah."

In the morning, I wake up in time to find Mya walking past. My vision is blurry and I'm slightly delirious because I probably fell asleep five minutes ago, but I'm conscious enough to make out the frown on her face as she glances down at me and then glances to the side.

I turn my head to find Delilah lying right beside me. I know how this looks, but nothing happened between us. *You* know nothing happened between us—but Mya doesn't.

I should scramble to my feet and chase after my best friend, but I doubt she will believe anything I say. I've just dug myself an even deeper hole, one that will take time and careful planning to get myself out of. So, as much as I want to run behind Mya and explain myself, I stay put and watch her walk away.

We're out here on the road, walking toward oblivion for all we know. I've got time to make amends. I've got enough hope to beg a God I'm not even sure I believe in to work things out for me. I can set aside my broken friendship to focus on survival. To focus on myself.

God ... It's an awful time to pray, with Delilah snoring softly beside me and Mya ahead chatting kindly with everyone else except me. But there's no one else here who will hear me out.

I don't even know what's real and what's not, I pray inside. *But if You are real, could You do me one more favor? Could You work things out with Mya?*

I sit there and wait for an answer. Nothing comes. Just like nothing came before when I was locked in my dorm. I don't know how this whole prayer thing works but apparently, I suck at it. Or maybe God just doesn't like talking to me.

Either way, I cannot force Mya to talk to me or to understand where all my frustrations come from. The best thing to do is let time sort things out. No matter how vicious our arguments get, we always find our way back to each other. She can't hate me forever. We're meant for each other. I believe that. I believe it more strongly than I believe in the God who refuses to answer me.

One of these things has to work out for me, and right now, faith isn't doing too hot. So I settle back down on the floor and watch Mya get ready for the day—grabbing a water bottle and a granola bar, even praying before she eats it. I wonder if she begged God for forgiveness last night, asked Him to wash away the filthy sins we committed in the back of that van. We didn't have sex, but I'm sure she went further than any unmarried Christian girl should. I was responsible for that. I initiated that. And if she hadn't spoken up, I would have taken things as far as I wanted.

No wonder God doesn't answer me. I'm so awful, I wouldn't answer either if I were a holy God looking down at a perverted sinner like me. I'm not worthy.

Maybe one day Mya will think I'm worthy of her time. And maybe one day she can convince God that I'm worthy of His time too. I think that's how it works. I hope that's how it works. For now, all I've got are my lost thoughts and a desperate prayer for a better day.

Please work things out between us, I beg God. Until He answers, I can think about surviving. I can focus on finding my foster mother. I can wish Mya the best, because even though she wants nothing to do with me, I still want the world for her.

35

Adrian

The rest of the walk is silent. I'm not shocked. I could see the twisted emotions distorting Mya's face the moment I walked up and found everyone on the highway. From the guilt on Mya's shoulders and the stench of lust wafting from Julius, I knew something had happened between them. And I wasn't surprised.

Julius Caesar is a handsome guy. There's a reason girls have always flocked to him. So I wasn't at all taken aback when I noticed the complicated storm brewing between the so-called best friends. I was only surprised it'd taken this long to reach its peak. Two attractive single people of the opposite sex cannot run around campus holding hands, whispering secrets, and calling each other *besties* before it turns into something else. They were basically begging each other for a one-night stand.

I don't know if it happened and made Julius angry because he wanted more. Or if they were cut short, and now Julius is angry because he doesn't think he'll get a second chance to pick up wherever they left off. Because I'm here now.

I should be angry that Mya fooled around behind my back. I should want to punch Julius and forget about her, but the truth is that I'm not upset. I promised Mya I'd come back. Not that I would be her boyfriend. And it's not as if I didn't hook up with Daniella while I was on the road.

She isn't my girlfriend. We don't owe each other anything. So I'm not angry that her eyes began to wander in my absence, because I'm confident they'll find their way back to me very soon.

Instead of flying into a rage, the only thing I feel is a sliver of satisfaction as I watch Julius stomp down the road with the rest of the group. *How does it feel to be rejected?* I wonder as I match his pace. *How does it feel to lose the one girl you want more than anything?*

I have felt that pain for years. And I thought I'd forgotten about it. I thought I'd moved on. Until I saw Mya again. Then I thought I'd have to fight again; I'd have to do everything in my power to capture her heart like I did in high school. But that wasn't the case this time.

Mya came to me. And she has drifted from that path since then, but I know she will come back. She already has—she proved that on the highway when she defended me against her precious best friend. Even after their cute little moment together, or whatever it was, Mya chose me. And Julius can't get over it.

That's what happens when you're a man-child who's never been told no. That's what happens when you think every woman on earth is willing to wait for your attention. He took Mya for granted, and he can't handle that devastating mistake.

I want to laugh at him, but I don't have it in me to be so

petty. Not when we've got to survive together. Julius has already accused me of being a murderer once, I'm not going to stretch the tension between us any further.

It's a relief when we make it to Wakedon and find Connor waiting for us, alive and somewhat healthy. His leg is doing much better; he can limp around the basement on his own, but he isn't going upstairs if he doesn't have to.

Bunny is happy to see Connor, the girls seem unimpressed since they barely know him. Julius grunts a greeting and stomps off to finish sulking in a corner. That's when I realize just how small this place is. It's a house that kept three people alive, stocked with enough supplies for just three people. And now I've just brought a party of five to join me and Connor.

We're a group of seven now, more than twice the number of people this place was built and stocked to sustain. The math makes me worry. But I don't voice my concerns. There's no point in getting everyone worked up when we've finally found some sense of peace. We have food, water, and a place to sleep. We feel safe from the soldiers down here. And we have the comfort of knowing each other. Bringing up the size of our group versus the number of supplies will only restart the cycle of worry, lies, and betrayal we all suffered at Cross North.

No one is ready for that.

Julius told me about Coach Noble. He told me about Memphis. He told me that he was held hostage in his own room. We cannot let this house crumble into that same madness. So I keep my mouth shut as the girls arrange a bathroom schedule and Bunny and Connor scribble down a travel plan for the future.

That's right… we're not staying here. This town is empty, and so is Phoenix. It's safe to assume the entire area has been evacuated. That means there's a chance our families are alive. Somewhere. We've got to make plans to track them down.

When I bring this up to the rest of the group over dinner, passing around steaming bowls of canned cream of chicken, they all look at me like I've lost my mind.

"We just got here," Bunny says, wiping a thick smear of soup from his chin. "Let's rest for a while."

"We'll rest until Connor is good enough to walk on his own again," I say. "But we can't stay here forever. I want to find my family."

"I do too," Mya agrees.

Of course she does.

Delilah surprises me by agreeing too. "I have family I want to check on—"

"Adrian said the town has been evacuated," Bunny cuts her off.

"So what?" Delilah says. "Should I just forget about finding my parents and siblings?"

"What do you want to do? Go search your empty house for them?"

"Believe it or not, my family loved me and could have left me clues to where they were going when they left."

The room falls silent. Delilah has a point.

"Either way," I chime in again, "we can't stay here forever because we'll eventually have to restock our supplies, go scavenging, or move on to a better place."

Bunny glares into his soup and doesn't respond. I know his family isn't from around here, so he has little hope of finding them anytime soon, but I can't believe he's being this much of a jerk about finding everyone else's families. I guess it's true, misery loves company.

"So, here's the plan," I say slowly, eyeing each member of our little group, "we wait until Connor is better before we set out. And once we do, we don't look back, alright?"

They all nod, albeit slowly.

"It's not safe out there, so once we hit the road, we've got to keep going. And we've got to stick together. First, we'll search Delilah's place for clues. Then we'll make our way to Phoenix and check on Julius's house."

Julius nods stiffly. I didn't check his home when I first entered the city because he hadn't asked me to. I'm positive his pride got in the way. I could have checked on my own, but I have no idea where he lives. So whatever.

"If we don't have any clues by then," I continue, "we'll check landmarks. Connor and I believe the National Guard evacuated the city. That means there could be popup shelters at public locations—hospitals, local churches, maybe even the armory."

"Why didn't you check those places already?" Bunny asks.

I give him a flat face. "Because I was busy trying to make it back to you guys as quickly as possible. Judging from the nightmarish stories you told me; I'd say it was a good thing I decided to head back."

Bunny doesn't respond because he knows I'm right. They were down to a few bottles of Gatorade and a box of granola bars with no map or clear direction on where to go. If I hadn't shown up when I did, they'd be starving or shot down by someone by now.

"One last thing," I say, "we've got to promise to get along. Right now, we're all we have. We cannot become the monsters we ran away from."

Julius and Delilah had a fling that obviously didn't last. I've noticed Bunny hasn't spoken to Julius unless he absolutely had to. Jupiter looks like she'd rather die than be here with everyone. And the drama between Julius and Mya is so loud it's giving me a headache even though their disagreement benefits me.

"Let's agree to put our differences aside and start fresh. Right here. Right now. Everyone." I look around the room, watching them all nod one by one.

Mya and Julius immediately lock eyes. I watch their silent conversation, knowing them both almost as intimately as they know each other. There's an intense moment unfolding right in front of everyone, and I'm the only one who notices. Unspoken apologies, silent pleas for forgiveness, and hushed promises to never hurt each other again.

Finally, both of them peel their brokenhearted gazes away from each other and look at me at the same time. I awkwardly clear my throat. I think I might have just mistakenly cleared the air for them. I might have just reignited a flame that'd nearly burned out all on its own.

"So, are we in this?" Julius asks.

I cannot unhear the confidence in his voice any more than I can unsee the smug look on his face. How quickly the tables have turned on me. I suddenly feel like an outsider fighting his way back into the mix all over again.

Whatever semblance of peace they've just established, I tell myself as Julius shifts to sit a little closer to Mya—she doesn't shift away from him—*this won't last. They will crumble again.*

Julius is smirking at me, waiting for an answer. When I still don't respond, he repeats his question, and the rest of our group looks at me too. It's a collective stare, six sets of blinking eyes, silently waiting like I have to respond. Like I owe him an answer just because he asked, even though I'm the one who initiated this entire conversation. The discussion has been wrested from my fingers; the mic passed to another.

And just like that, Julius Caesar is back in charge. Back on top. Where he's always been, for whatever freaking reason. Everyone always chooses Julius.

This won't last, I tell myself again. Then I let go of the calmest breath I've ever taken, probably the last calm one I'll enjoy for a while.

"Are we in this?" Julius repeats.

"Yeah," I say, "we're in this."

Because what the heck else am I supposed to say?

Continue the series...

Exodus
Coming 2024

More books by Valicity Elaine & TRC Publishing!

Christian Fantasy
The Scribe

Christian Post-Apocalyptic Fiction
The Barren Fields

The End of the World series

MAGOG saga

Christian Science Fiction
I AM MAN series

Christian Romance

The Living Water
Withered Rose Trilogy
Fractured Diamond
The Woof Pack Trilogy
Singlehood

Christian Children's Fiction

Too Young